Blue, Upstate

Blue, Upstate

John Painz

First paperback edition • August, 2021

Edited by Jayne Lewis
Book cover art by Michael Gaydos
Graphic design by Al Rotches
Fonts by junkohanhero

ISBN – 978-1-7373633-0-9 (paperback)
ISBN – 978-1-7373633-1-6 (ebook)

Published by Words From Here Productions, LLC
www.wordsfromhere.com

To Mom, Karen, and Julie:

Thank you for the constant support, love, and pushes.

This book is dedicated to my father, John William Painz.
After all, he would have helped me write this.

PART I

The Robbery, and Ancient History

CHAPTER ONE

John was sitting in a stolen car, thinking about the last time he'd sung to Caroline. Four years ago. "Let 'Em In" by Wings. She was near the end, lying there next to him in bed half asleep, which was a minor miracle, as he tried to get the pitch right. He'd been struggling miserably, but she didn't seem to care. The words were what soothed her, and so he figured he'd keep at it.

The only time I think of Caroline is when I'm in a car, he thought.

He'd never sung to anyone before her. What got him started was him sitting in someone's apartment at some party, before all this, before all this shit. Some guy on his feet, walking back and forth in a living room with six people captivated by his talking about Jeff Buckley. Specifically about his version of "Hallelujah," which the guy said was quintessential. Not just his take of the song, though. The guy said that Buckley's version was the best track ever recorded by a single artist.

John had gone home that night not knowing a thing of what the guy was talking about, but went out and bought the album the next day. Two days later, he could sing the track by heart. Then he sang it to her.

It would be years before someone would tell him that "Hallelujah" was originally a Leonard Cohen song, and he felt like an idiot.

Those were the days, he thought, *when one's main concern was being in the know.*

The engine was rumbling. The sound, the smell, the slight rocking back and forth shifted the cracked black leather seat on its springs.

None of it had anything to do with Caroline but, every time before a job, without fail, there she was. She'd had insomnia, mostly due to the worry, and the only thing that helped her sleep was him driving her around. He would end up taking three-, sometimes four-hour naps during the day because, for that year and a half, he rarely got a good night's sleep. And then she was gone.

For a long while after, he stuck to the routine because it was easier than trying to forget her.

John kept his eye on the street, the pedestrians. It was still three and a half weeks before Christmas, 2018, and the small town was unreasonably busy. He hated jobs like this. There were too many unknowns. So much could go wrong.

On top of it all, the memories, the people, the worry... the sunlight was bothering him. And the cold. It was one of those rare has-to-be-seen-to-be-believed days with a clear blue sky normally reserved for a Coney Island beach day. Views as far as the eye could see, except there was a wind chill of minus two degrees, and it looked like he was the only one who was bothered by it.

They were in Sherborn, New York. Somewhere between Binghamton and Syracuse. Population 3,647. Slightly larger than a one-horse town, with a grocery store and a barber and their own daily newspaper.

And a bank.

The sun was bouncing off an office window from across the street at just the right angle, perfectly hitting the windshield of his freshly painted 1972 Nova. He'd ripped the visors off about six months ago after a job gone wrong, and now his arm was at a crooked angle, with his hand just so, to cover his eyes from the blinding sun.

Even though it was too early to wear it, even with the heat blasting and the warmth from the engine, he had on a full ski mask. A prop for the job. His breath had started to fog up the windshield, so he'd opened the window an inch, hence the cold.

Across the intersection, a car very similar to his own—a matte black '69 Camaro with a driver wearing a black ski mask and sunglasses.

John shook his head and adjusted his hand again to the light, wondering why he hadn't brought *his* sunglasses. He watched as his partner Hal walked towards the back of the Camaro, looked around a bit. "Oh, hi everyone," John said to himself. "I'm just walking here, minding my own business, waiting to rob the..." John saw Hal fidget. "No, don't... you don't need to tie your—"

Hal bent down to tie his shoe.

"Jesus Christ..." John rolled his eyes. "You're a walking—he's a walking cliché."

Hal played with his shoe for what seemed like forever until he suddenly got onto his back and slid directly under the Camaro.

"This guy..." John said to himself and chuckled. *The balls, right?*

John did a check of the landscape and suddenly came face to face with a little girl who had her hands on his passenger-side window, peering in. He looked at her, his mouth open.

She looked at him, fearless.

Fucking kids.

"*What*?!" he yelled.

She kept looking at him.

From some far-off place, he couldn't tell where, a woman yelled, "Becky!"

Becky turned, caught in the act, and fell back on his freshly painted... Jesus fucking Christ. He'd just done it this morning...

"You get over here this instant!" John could hear it in her mother's voice. The menace. It was the second command in every mother's lexicon, only just after counting to three.

Becky obeyed her mother and ran off, a patch of black paint on her pink coat and one caked in her hair.

"Fuuuuck," John said and scoffed. He tried to picture what the outside of the car looked like. Worst case scenario, she took half the paint off the door.

What a bitch.

Nothing he could do about it now. He shook his head, looked to his left. A single beige SUV stood out, with a blonde mom type behind the wheel. Couldn't get a clear look at her face because of the sun. He wasn't sure how long she'd been there. The car was idling, she looked bored, and every once in a while peeked through her rear view.

Which was weird.

There was nothing behind her except the…

"Shit, lady," he said. "Bad timing for you and yours." Didn't matter. Witnesses were inevitable. He glanced at his phone. Three minutes. John hit dial and the line connected. "Cold out there?" he asked.

"Fuck you," Hal said, whispering, breathless.

"Which are you going for?"

"Whatever's closest." Gasping now.

"Well, what are your options?"

"If I'd lost some weight I could get to the power wire," Hal grunted, whispering. "Goddammit!"

"Don't go for the gas line."

"I'm going for the gas line."

"I just said—"

"Look, it's either that, or I try and remove the bolts from the fucking drive shaft, and have the car collapse on me."

Long pause.

"So, you're going to remove the bolts—"

"Fuck you," Hal said and chuckled.

"It's going to make a mess…"

"I feel like Mad Max under here, for chrissake—" John heard a spraying noise. "Pfftt! Fuck!" Hal got out from under the Camaro on his hands and knees, looked around and spat out some gas. John laughed.

4

Hal looked over, saw John laughing, gave him the finger, got up, tried to act as nonchalant as possible, then ran over to a truck that was parked a hundred yards behind, and got in. "You know we'd be shit out of luck if this kid had a car made in the last decade."

"Because you wouldn't fit—"

"Because I wouldn't fit, yes!"

John smiled, slid his hand down to the gear shift. "Two minutes."

"Yeah," Hal said. "I'm gonna start now."

"OK."

Hal looked at the underside of the Camaro, saw the puddle growing. He started up the truck—a sixteen-footer, white panels with ten wheels—that belched out diesel as he hit the starter. It lurched forward. He'd rented it the night before from a place in Bethlehem, Pennsylvania, but not before hitting the Indian casino and losing four hundred dollars on slot machines.

"Couldn't find a bigger truck?"

"For fuck sa... it's the only fucking truck they... man, not now!"

Once he got about twenty feet past the Camaro, Hal made a turn towards the sidewalk and forced a stall. John put the Nova into drive, kept his foot on the brake, and waited as the watch on his phone's display click, click, clicked.

Hal dug in and started stripping the gears. The truck bounced back and forth as he switched between the gas and the brake and the clutch. He started chuckling, wondering how his performance was going. People were stopping, gawking. "This is ridiculous," he said to the air.

"It's going to work." Ten seconds before 2 p.m. John threw the Nova into gear. As he did, the front door of the bank opened and a gangly figure stood there wearing a matching black ski mask, holding a shotgun and struggling with two duffle bags slung over his shoulders. He had a blonde mustache and wide blue eyes that John could see even from that distance.

No one paid any attention to him. They were all looking at the truck.

"Is he...? He's out on the fucking street?" Hal said.

"These kids today," John said and hit the gas. The tires caught on the salted pavement. He spun out, turned onto what was literally called Main Street, drifted into the curb outside the bank with a hard rubber thud and reached over, opening the passenger door. The robber threw the duffle bags and the shotgun into the back, sat down and slammed the door shut. John took off, wheels spinning for a full second until they caught. He cursed under his breath, regretting making the whole thing look and sound like a robbery. It was a rookie mistake.

Hal, meanwhile, had gotten the truck into reverse, waving here and there to the cars he'd been blocking, the people watching. He looked through the windshield to see the Camaro there, idling, waiting, the driver raging behind the wheel. Once Hal was finally out of the way, the Camaro took off and quickly sputtered to a stop some twenty odd feet from where he'd been parked.

Hal put the truck in gear and headed down Main Street in the opposite direction of his friend.

The puddle of gas was enormous.

John drove in silence down a two-lane forest corridor, snow covering both sides, a little sunlight breaking through. The guy next to him was hyperventilating, looking in the side-view mirror, turning his body around and looking out the back, just in case they were being followed.

The phone call out to Hal was still live.

Around the first wide bend John eased his foot off the gas. The robber, his breathing a bit more under control, ripped his ski mask off. The blonde mustache came with it. Underneath, an adrenaline-rushed fifteen-year-old kid too hyped up to realize what was different.

"What the fuck was that shit, Charlie? I was waiting for you! I was there, watching for the car... people were asking me if they could deposit their checks!"

John chuckled. "You saw the truck. I had to go around."

"What truck!? What the fuck are you talking about?"

"Forget it. How much did you grab?"

"I don't know. What does it matter? We had to refill the bags, Jesus Christ, and then they had just the two tellers, they gave me everything but the bundles."

"You took the singles?"

"Hell, I was about to take the quarters! It looks like enough, right?" He dragged one of the duffle bags between them, opened it, showed John. Lots of singles.

John didn't understand the question, but made a noise of agreement.

"I hope to Christ this works. I don't know what millions of..." the kid said and stopped. As he closed the bag he took a big sniff. "What's that smell?" He rolled down the window. "And what happened to your door? It's like aqua—" He wiped at the passenger door, brought his gloved hand to his nose and when he took it away, a smear of black paint was on his upper lip.

John hit the brakes. The kid hit the dash with his whole body, and the car fishtailed and spun to a stop. John put the car in park.

"Charlie, what the fuck?"

John stared straight ahead. "Get out."

"What...?"

John unclicked his seatbelt, turned, elbowed him in the face. The kid made a noise, brought his hands up, covering his mouth in more black paint. Blood bubbled out of his nostrils. His upper lip was gnashed a bit. "Charlie, goddammit!" John punched him in the stomach, reached past him, opened the passenger door and pushed him out.

The kid fell to the ground bleeding, confused.

John stared down at him. "I'm not Charlie. Charlie is either in jail or high-tailed it out of town. There can't be too many souped-up black Camaros in this shithole, so he won't be hard to identify."

The kid got up, tried to get back in the car. John closed the door on him. The kid made a grab for the money through the open window. "What the fuck is this?"

John held him off with a stiff arm. "It's called keeping your mouth shut, kid. This might be one of those rare moments in life you find out how much smarter other people are than you." He pushed him away from the car, put it into gear. "Oh, and thanks for the shotgun." He drove away.

The kid yelled, "It's empty, shithead!" He kicked the ground, threw his gloves off, and screamed at the world.

Carla watched it all unfold from her SUV. The Nova, the Camaro, the panel truck, the bank, the buffoonery.

Hal had said it would go like clockwork.

Hal said the plan was perfect.

Nothing she saw that afternoon would she define as "perfect." It seemed overly complicated, like a game, like out of a bad movie, working only because of luck. Because the good guys had to win.

She sighed, put her car into drive, and went home to make dinner for her family. It was lasagna night, and she hated making lasagna.

CHAPTER TWO

John took his mask off and traveled down the road until he came to the left his GPS told him to take. "By smarter, you meant me, right?" he heard in his ear.

"No, you're more the poster child of what people shouldn't become," John said and snickered. "A fifty-something—"

"Forty-something!"

"—balding, overweight criminal."

"Sounds more like a politician."

"I rest my case."

"Hey, this *was* my plan."

"Yeah, yeah," John said and leaned back.

"He took the singles, huh? Was it a stripper's bank?"

John smiled, even though he'd heard that joke before.

"You're smiling. I can tell," Hal said.

The wind was whipping into the car, making a reverberating noise John's ears couldn't stand. He reached over, carefully keeping his eyes on the road, closed the passenger-side window, then his own. He took a left onto a road with no painted divider and entered Edgerton, population 218. It was the sole street in town dedicated to a small grocery store, attached to a single gas station. Then, all of a sudden, he was in a new town.

Jesus.

"Sounded like he was pissed," Hal said.

John could hear the diesel engine through the phone. "I'm sure he's still pissed," he said, holding the steering wheel with the tips of his fingers.

He let his mind drift.

He hated Upstate. The constant quiet, the people, the barrenness of it. On the left was an old farm with a silo, like he'd seen a thousand times. On the right was just a vast emptiness, space for crops when it was warmer, maybe. Or for grazing.

John sighed. "These trips out of the city always drive me a little batshit. It all fucking looks the same."

"It's a living." Hal sounded like Hal always did after a job. Frustrated.

John made a noise, somewhere between disgust and acceptance.

"What did he say the take was?" Hal asked.

"Twenty, but I doubt the kid knows what he got. It's two big duffles, but singles mostly. He said something like, 'will it be enough?' or something. Had to repack it... you hear that part?"

"No."

"Strange. Oh, yeah, and it was a KID, Hal. Like a fifteen-year-old kid. What the shit is that all about?"

"I don't know. Peer pressure?"

"Peer...? Who the fuck are his peers, Butch Cassidy and the Sundance—"

"I robbed a bank when I was *six*teen."

"No you didn't."

Silence.

"No, I didn't. Anyway, who knows? Maybe it's drugs. Or some girl put him up to it. Or whatever these kids are into these days. How much do you think he actually grabbed?"

"Fuck, I don't know." John picked up the duffle and hefted it. "Small bank in the middle of nowhere, and if both bags are a similar take, I'd say closer to nine."

"Jesus, our cut's going to just cover expenses. Fuck."

"Hey, we're not in it for the money," John said, making a right. "No, wait. We are in it for the—"

"What time are you expected back?" Hal asked.

"I don't know. I have to dump the car. Probably have to get it washed first. There might be a bit of a problem with that."

"You mean washing a freshly painted car that helped in a major felony, and in the middle of the day? What possible problem could that give us?"

"Ok, two problems. There was a... well, a little girl who rubbed off some of the paint on the passenger side."

"How much?"

"Hell, I don't know, a jacket's worth." He had a mental image of the girl walking away, shook his head. "I swear, nothing's easy anymore."

"Well, take care of it. You flying back?"

"I don't think so. I think I'll find us a four-door for the future."

"Oooh, a Cutlass?"

"I'll see what's out there. See you tonight, regardless."

"Hasta luego," Hal said and clicked off. John took the earpiece out, put it on the seat next to him and rotated his neck. He drove in quiet until he reached I-88, turned on the radio and found an oldies station that didn't annoy him.

Hal wiped the truck down before returning it to the rental depot. He'd rented it under a fake name, used a fake license, wore a hat and sunglasses when he signed the paperwork and picked up the truck. He paid with cash.

He drove his 2005 Lexus past the casino on his way out of town, sighed, made a U-turn, parked in the free lot way in the back.

Gambling was the only thing that got his pulse up these days. Poker, blackjack, and craps were his favorites. He didn't have the time or the money for those this trip, so he stuck to slots. Again. He spent two hundred on a $5 machine with a max bet of $15, won back three of the four he'd originally lost. Paid for the buffet and got some prime rib, mashed potatoes, a salad and a beer. He ate and people-watched. He grabbed a piece of chocolate cake for dessert, some coffee, threw in another hundred on a $10 slot machine, lost it, tried his luck again. The same. He called it quits, went back to his car and punched in a scenic route back to New York on his phone.

He'd drawn the short straw this time.

The two had made a habit of alternating routes on their way back to the city, no matter where they were coming from. One would either fly home or take the main highway. The other took the back roads. Depending on how fast he drove, he thought he might beat John back to the garage, especially since he would have to dump the Nova, which was a damned shame.

Hal stopped at a gas station, got a sandwich, two bottles of water, a bag of salt and vinegar potato chips, two candy bars, and went to the bathroom on his way out. He'd purchased an audio book for the eight-hour round trip. *Blood on the Moon*, the first in the Lloyd Hopkins trilogy by James Ellroy. He was halfway through it.

He drove past a farm that had horses out. They were big ones, with steam shooting out their noses, steam drifting off their bodies. A hand was out walking them around, patting them, leading them.

The sun was starting to set. Hal stretched out to enjoy the ride and the book. His hands were steady. He rarely had post job anxiety these days. He'd seen too much, been through too much. And if he found it sneaking up on him, well... that's what the food was for.

An hour after kicking the kid out of the car, John was outside Big Dean's Auto Yard. He pulled in after being waved through by Dean's son Tony, who looked bored as hell. He drove up to a trailer that had seen better days. Bars on the windows, the trailer was a faded pink that blended into the background of a hundred wrecks. It served as the office.

John walked in, dumped the two duffle bags on an empty table. One of the bags had the empty shotgun shoved halfway in.

Dean was at his desk with a wet cigar sticking out of his mouth, coke-bottle glasses resting on his nose, minding his own business. He never left the office these days. He had his TV, his internet, his fridge, a stove, a hammock, an air conditioner, a portable heater, and his dog Bay, who was asleep in the last of a sun beam.

Tony was in the corner, picking at dead skin on his arm.

"Is it empty?" Dean said in his gravel voice.

Tony looked over at the shotgun.

"It's empty," John said, grabbing it. Tony reached behind him. Dean put a hand under his desk. John racked the slide a few times, ejected air, dropped it on the table.

Everyone relaxed.

John separated bills into piles. There *were* a fuck-ton of singles. He was close. It came out to just under ten thousand.

John grabbed two big stacks and placed them on the desk in front of Dean. "Sorry about the singles," he said. Dean grunted and jerked his thumb. Tony held the office door open for John, who left the bags and the shotgun. He got back into the Nova, drove it about a thousand feet, deep into the yard.

He found himself surrounded by layer upon layer of cars crushed flat, all in various stages of decay. He'd been there before. Many times. The place still felt like a lost city.

John parked, got out, looked at the passenger-side door where the little girl had been. It wasn't as bad as he thought, but the original turquoise was showing. "Aqua my ass," he said under his breath. It *was* something someone would notice—especially a mother.

He took a long last look at the Nova. It had nice pick-up, handling, and wouldn't crumple at the first sign of offensive driving. But it had to go. They'd used it one too many times. He opened the trunk and grabbed his backpack, putting it off to the side.

Tony showed up with a power washer unit and a long hose, didn't say a word. John took it and spent the next half hour getting rid of as much of the new black paint as he could.

By the time he was done his hands were shaking from the cold. Tony brought him a cup of coffee that was hot, that was about it. No milk, no sugar.

"There a body in there?" Tony asked.

John shook his head.

"Not that I care, but I gotta know which cars are going to start stinking once it gets warmer."

"No body," John said. Body disposal was always such a pain in the ass. It was worse than transporting guns, or drugs, or money. The fear was greater, and he would always get a peculiar feeling... otherworldly, as if he was responsible for ferrying their souls. It took a long time to divorce himself from the guilt of transporting a body, even though he wasn't responsible for their death.

Tony nodded and signaled for the magnet. It landed with a crunch, caving in the roof. The magnet's current came on with a low whirr, grabbed hold, and took the Nova up and over some piles and out of sight. John heard it get crushed as they made their way back to the office.

He sat in the corner, finished his coffee, and consolidated the two duffle bags. There was just under eight thousand left in there after paying Dean his two.

Their cut *would* be just expenses.

"You expecting someone to get you?" Dean asked. His voice sounded like whiskey and tobacco.

"No."

"I'll sell you a ride. Good price, too. You can take your pick."

John smiled. "No. Thanks. Cheaper to just steal something."

Dean smiled back. John couldn't tell what was teeth and what was rot.

He said his goodbyes, slung the duffle over his shoulder and walked the mile or so to the rest stop that connected I-88 to I-86. He grabbed a late lunch at a McDonald's, sat and watched the tourists as they looked at maps, tried to contain their kids, and were generally done with the road.

John went to the bathroom, washed his hands, grabbed a paper towel, dried them, then used it to wipe his face. He adjusted his clothing in the mirror, looked at his tired eyes and stood there a long moment. Longer than usual.

He was in his mid-forties and he was still playing fast and loose with other people's lives. And it showed.

Outside the rest stop he looked at the cars, the parked ones, the ones coming and going. He watched the people, too. There were some higher-end cars. An Audi, a BMW; there was one late model Corvette. Newer cars were always a pain.

John and Hal had a mandate. Nothing after 1996 if they could help it. Not unless they were in close proximity to the garage, or needed an exact duplicate for a job.

He passed a VW Bug, a couple of compacts... and finally settled on a late 80s Ciera that he prayed wouldn't crap out on him when he drove away.

He hated stealing cars from working-class people. Sometimes, it was all they had in the world. It was their lifeline to work, to family, to wherever. He used to hesitate, empathizing with the owner, even if it was just for a moment. Almost got caught a few times because of it, too. After a while he came to the conclusion that these people, more than most, understood that life wasn't fair.

Either that or they learned pretty quickly.

Carla drove home in a fugue. She hadn't wanted to watch the robbery, it was just that so many things had gone wrong over the past couple of days, and she needed to see it through.

Not that she could have helped if things had gone sideways.

"I promise. Things won't go sideways," Hal said on the phone.

Even though she'd known him for years, she hadn't spent enough time with Hal to know if he was telling the truth by his voice alone. But she said OK.

Hal said don't get involved. Hal said don't watch it happen. Don't fret over it. He'd take care of everything. "And don't tell John," he said.

"You mean 'John' who I haven't seen in sixteen years? Yeah. OK," she said, hung up, and ended up going anyway. It was one of those things where she knew she was partly responsible. Took the day off of work from the hospital and drove down to the bank a half an hour before 2 p.m.

She kept her eyes mostly on the rear-view mirror. Worried. Then more worried when John pulled up across from her. It took a lot of willpower to not look at him, or say something, or do something. Anything.

And then it was over, for better or worse.

She got home after it all, grabbed a bottle of white wine out of the fridge, poured herself a let's-forget-everything sized glass, and sat in the kitchen, reminding herself they did the right thing. *She* did the right thing.

Ten minutes passed. She'd refilled once already, pre-heated the oven, got the spaghetti sauce and the pre-made lasagna sheets out of the pantry. Got out the Pyrex dish, the ricotta, the already browned ground beef, mozzarella, and just stared at it all for a long while. Then, piece by piece, layer by layer, she started building dinner.

When the front door opened, she stopped breathing and started to sweat instantly. It was hard to tell how the next few minutes were going to play out... depending on who it was.

The door slammed shut. Still could be anyone—

Her son rushed passed her. His face was red. And black.

She went to say something as he ran up the stairs and slammed his bedroom door.

Carla put her hand up to her mouth and breathed a sigh of relief the likes she hadn't in a long time. Her son was home. Pissed, but alive.

She took a big swallow of wine, finished the lasagna, stuck it in the oven, and tried to get into the mindset of lying to her son.

CHAPTER THREE

John took out a pair of protective gloves, put them on, grabbed his slim jim from the backpack, did a quick circuit with his eyes, and popped the window. He smelled the stench of decades of cigarette smoke before he even sat down. He threw up in his mouth, did a mental coin flip on whether he wanted to bother with such a disgusting car.

He got in when he decided Hal would do the clean-up.

The front seat was covered in duct tape.

Ten seconds.

He broke the steering column with a Phillips head, brought out a wire cutter–splicer, cut the wires from the ignition cylinder, then separated the battery wire from the starter wire from the ignition wire.

Twenty-five seconds.

He stripped the wires and did a peek over the dash.

Nothing doing.

He grabbed the ignition wire and twisted it into the battery wire. The dash lit up.

Forty seconds.

"You're slowing down, pal," he said under his breath.

He touched the starter cable to the ignition and battery wires.

The car turned over.

He moved the starter wire away from the rest and revved the engine once. Twice. Not the worst he'd heard.

One minute.

He tilted his head up and looked at the people who were coming to and from the main rest stop building.

A couple who looked like they might be on the verge of stage three lung cancer made their way towards the car.

"Goddammit," John said, ready to tear ass. He started sweating. A mixture of adrenaline and the stench of cigarettes had his head swimming. He put one hand on the gearshift, one hand on the door, ready to either throw it into drive or bail. He didn't know which the best option was.

The couple were chatting and looking at the ground. Holding hands or steadying each other, he couldn't tell. They were taking their sweet fucking ti—

The two labored by, not giving the car or John a second thought.

He sighed, relieved, shut the door lightly and twisted the wheel hard until he heard the pins in the steering lock break. He put the car in reverse and pulled out of the spot. He perked up his hearing just in case he heard the worst words one could hear in a situation like this.

That's! My! Car!

He checked the gas gauge. The God of Car Thieves must have been looking out for him because the tank was full. He turned the heater on full blast and opened all four windows, making breathing just above bearable.

The ceiling was smoke and nicotine stained.

The seats had cigarette burns even through the duct tape.

The ashtray was full. He removed it from the holder and threw it out the window.

An hour later, he passed a sign that said New York City: 180 miles.

The engine was solid. The sky was still clear. Stars dotted the horizon to the east, along with a crescent moon.

As he drove, he passed a yellow cab station wagon from a no-name company. The driver had the look of all taxi drivers. Resigned.

He drove past, thankful those days were over.

Unemployed in 1995, John started driving a cab for a living. He was 22. He got his hack license on a whim. Bored, restless, knowing that his landlord didn't care where his rent came from, as long as it was on time. He found a Pakistani man, Abbas Kashani, who'd bought his first medallion in 1980, and rented one of his five cabs out to John for $100 a shift. Abbas was 52, had four grandchildren, had his cars going all day and night, and took a liking to John almost immediately.

John, who stood six foot three, weighed two hundred and ten pounds, fit in the 1990 Caprice reasonably well, and quickly succumbed to the routine of driving a cab.

"Don't go to the outer boroughs if you can avoid them," Abbas had warned. "You'll bleed gas money!"

John traveled wherever fares pointed him to. At $100 a day, he didn't have much choice.

He was quiet with the customers, and didn't listen to music when fares were in the car. It didn't take him long to figure out the quickest routes to most destinations, and he learned to drive offensively.

Bicyclists were a pain in the ass, as were tourists and city dwellers who owned cars but didn't know how to drive them. But pedestrians were the worst. Crossing when he had the light, jaywalkers darting out between cars, and their general attitude towards cab drivers when they weren't needed made for some severely open hostility.

John had a shitty one-bedroom apartment in a fourth-floor walk-up in Bensonhurst. Rent was cash, included heat, hot water and electric. The walls were generic beige, the appliances were from the 80s, and he kept the windows open in the winter due to the four white-hot radiators in the apartment. He had one air conditioner. It was in the living room, where he would sleep most of the summer. He was a block away from the F train, a 24-hour fruit stand, and the kind of grocery store you don't buy meat from.

He was single for the most part. Had a girl here and there who called when they were lonely, but never picked up when he was.

Most times when he told people he drove a cab, they asked what was wrong with him.

On May 23, 1996, John was sitting on a bench in Madison Park, his cab parked with less than an hour left on the street meter. He was eating a ham sandwich with Swiss cheese, tomato and mustard. It had been his father's favorite sandwich and, after many years of being the only kind offered (his father always ordered two. He felt that giving the guy at the deli the least amount of work was the least *he* could do), it became a favorite of John's, too.

He'd had a good relationship with his father. Derek Moore had married young after coming back from Vietnam. He'd had a shitty childhood and made up for it by spoiling his kid whenever he could. Movies, toys, fast food, ice cream, candy. He died from lung and brain cancer when John was nineteen. It was a sore subject for John. He felt he'd been cheated out of some great future wisdom from his father.

He'd been working for Abbas about a year by this point. Abbas, who said John had a fun and carefree lifestyle. "Wonderful for someone in his twenties, but, you must have a plan, young man," he said during one of the frequent Sundays he'd invited John over for dinner with the family. "Working for someone your whole life isn't a career. It's servitude."

Abbas's wife, Nasreen, nodded. She'd never worked a day in her life.

The food was decent. The conversation was the pits. But he loved them all the same.

After his sandwich, John bought a cup of coffee off a street vendor, walked to his cab, settled in and turned the roof light on. He was about to put it into gear when the back door opened and a man in a three-piece suit, carrying a briefcase, slid in, closed the door, made a motion of his hand and said, "Drive."

It wasn't the first time he'd experienced that type of passenger.

The first few times it had happened, he'd turned around in questionable frustration and told his fares, *That's not how this works at all.*

The last time had been in the middle of a domestic dispute. The husband had tried to pull his wife out of the car before John had a chance to take off. He ended that particular shift with a low-grade concussion, nine stitches on the side of his head, and a future court date that would end up getting tossed. The guy just pleaded out.

These days, John just did what he was told.

He went north, figuring that was as good a direction as any since he was pointed that way. He took Madison up into the 30s, took a right and rode 38th Street straight down to 1st Avenue. He was heading to his favorite part of the city, the drive past the UN building.

"Queens," the man in the back said. He was staring out the window, looking over the East River. John could see he had clear grey eyes, heavy bags under them, and dark, thick hair with eyebrows to match.

"Yes, sir," John said, and drove up to the Queensboro Bridge. Traffic was light, and he found himself on Queens Boulevard quickly, heading towards Sunnyside. Still not sure of the direction he was supposed to be going, John had to brake suddenly when he noticed a truck up ahead, stalled. They had the light; traffic was moving in the other direction.

He couldn't get around.

John looked into his rear view mirror at the man who was still staring wistfully out the window. He didn't seem to have noticed the trouble. John sighed. As he went to put the car in park he saw an SUV barreling down the street in his lane behind him.

A moment passed as he watched, waited for it to slow down. It didn't.

John hit the gas and spun towards the sidewalk to avoid it. He wasn't fast enough, and the cab's rear end got smashed. His seatbelt tightened and gripped him as his arms tried to brace for impact against the steering wheel. His passenger wasn't as lucky. John heard him smash his face against the partition. The man made a wet and hurt noise and then nothing. The cab hit the sidewalk and smashed into a post office box, which went flying.

In the seconds that followed, John tried to keep his wits about him, realizing, knowing the hit was deliberate. Quick pieces came together. He'd seen both the SUV and the truck in the city. He hadn't paid any attention to—

A figure jumped out of the stalled truck and ran to his left towards the SUV. He looked in the rear-view mirror but couldn't see out the back window. He turned to his right and saw blood smeared against the partition, then looked in the back. His passenger's face was a mess. John turned his head left, looked through the driver-side window and quickly ducked as he saw three men point assault rifles at the cab. They fired.

The car was getting perforated.

John hit the gas, heard a wrenching that didn't sound normal at all, poked his head up and watched in horror as the car made a slow turn towards the three men, all on its own. He heard the wheels spinning, saw smoke billowing around the cab, but they were barely moving.

Bullets tore through the driver-side window and went out the other side. They tore through the driver-side door. One skinned his arm. Another grazed his ass. The heat and pain was unlike anything he'd ever felt.

He screamed, terrified. His heart was hammering like it had never done before. He yanked the wheel, trying to make something happen.

Something heavy dislodged and fell to the ground as the car continued to get shot to hell. He couldn't tell if it was something from his cab or the SUV. The car still wouldn't budge forward. He coaxed the wheel left, hit reverse, forced the cab back into the street and noticed that the gunfire had stopped. John looked out his window to see the three men reloading.

He put the car in drive and hit the gas as the closest guy slapped a magazine into place. John wasn't going fast enough to do much damage, but the guy hit the hood hard as he made his way down the block.

Behind them, the two remaining guys got into their SUV.

After about a block, the man on the hood pointed his rifle at John, who hit the brakes and sent the guy tumbling onto the street. John hit the gas again, pointed the hood emblem at the guy's head.

John ran over his chest. Twice.

He watched in the rear-view as the SUV stopped in front of their fallen companion. He hit the gas. The cab limped a few blocks before John bent over to the passenger side, threw up, steadied himself and turned down 36th Street. The cab was almost completely hobbled. He could hear, or imagined that he could hear, the whining reverb the engine was making, echoing off of the buildings. He also thought he heard sirens. He wasn't sure of any of it. His ears were ringing and he could hear blood rushing through his body.

He drove another two blocks, made a right, tried to act as inconspicuous and casual as possible, and pulled into a parking garage. He grabbed a ticket from the machine, thankful there was no attendant, and found what he hoped was a secluded spot.

He shut the car down and realized he wasn't breathing right. He was skipping an intake here and there, as if he'd forgotten how. He tried to use the brown paper bag his lunch had come in to calm his hyperventilating. As he tried breathing into it, he comically noticed the bullet holes torn through.

It was then that he remembered his fare.

Lying prone, full of holes, a single eye looking at the ceiling, the man was clearly dead. Next to him was a briefcase, broken open, also full of holes.

Inside, some paperwork, a gun, and a punctured cellophane bag containing white powder, elegantly mixing with his blood.

John slid the partition open and as he fit his body through, he felt the wound on his arm. His ass was throbbing. Cursing, he reached over to his customer and checked for a pulse. He knew it was futile, but his mind was still reeling.

"Shit," he said, and brought his hand down from the meat of the man's throat to his inside coat pocket. He found a long leather billfold wallet with a bullet hole in it. Grabbing it awkwardly as he tried to shimmy back to the front of the cab, he slid his finger into the hole, to make sure he had a firm enough grip. When he sat down in the front seat, he saw what he'd done. Looking around to see if anyone was watching, he twirled the billfold around his finger. Once. Twice. He laughed out loud when he saw what he was doing. He put his free hand over his mouth to stifle it.

He began to feel manic. *So this is shock*, he thought. *OK.*

He'd never been shot at before.

He'd never been shot.

Hadn't seen a dead body before.

Never run over someone with his car before.

A lot of firsts.

He knew it was self-defense. He understood the situation and figured he'd have no problem with it in the morning, or in the future.

But he never wanted to do it again.

John quit twirling and opened the wallet. Inside were more than a dozen hundred-dollar bills, credit cards fanning their way down both sides, a picture of a woman with three kids, and a license.

A closer look at the license gave him an address.

In Queens.

CHAPTER FOUR

H al paused the book on tape. He had two fingers on the wheel, cruising at around 40m.p.h. on a backwoods road, marveling at the white landscape. Snow as far as the eye could see, over hill and dale.

Hill and dale? What the shit...?

He grabbed half the sandwich (turkey, American cheese, and yellow mustard for chrissake), stomached through it, and guzzled an entire bottle of water in an attempt to get the taste out of his mouth.

He was old. Older, anyway. Fifty was knocking. He *was* overweight, balding, had high cholesterol, wore glasses to read since forever, and creaked when he stood up. Regardless, the day had gone well. Surprisingly well. And still...

His mind was in a strange place. A combination of in-over-his-head and a sereneness that came naturally with a gorgeous landscape. It was quiet and peaceful, snow-covered and clear, and even the busiest mind would have taken a moment to appreciate it all.

He ate some chips, licked his fingers clean and sighed, remembering the first time he committed a felony.

It was 1989. The first time Hal had driven a getaway car, and his cousin Ben was robbing a five-and-dime outside of Miller Grove, Texas. It hadn't been a getaway car when they started the trip. It hadn't been a getaway car when they'd woken up earlier that morning.

They'd been driving cross-country on some crusade to save Ben's sister from an abusive boyfriend. Binging alcohol and speed as they drove, two-thirds of the way there they'd run out of money and everything else. Ben decided robbing the place was a good idea because they were out of cigarettes, too, and let's just kill two birds with one stone. You know?

Hal said just steal the cigarettes. Ben said he'd think about it. Hal said, you only have a knife. Ben said look at the place, and got out of the car.

They were driving a Chevette Hal had borrowed from a friend in Brooklyn. It had zero pick-up, with one wheel sitting on a donut that was half bald. Both of them were working on no sleep, so it didn't come as a surprise to Hal when someone in the middle of fucking Texas shot Ben, propelling him through the front glass window of the store.

Ben's chest was shredded by rock salt. His arm was bleeding profusely and he ran towards the car as Hal reached over, opened the passenger door, and drove them out of town.

Hal had never seen someone shot before, rock salt or not. He stressed out as he watched Ben try and breathe, scared his lungs had gotten punctured or collapsed or something.

They were stopped twenty minutes later. A cordon of eight cop cars covering both sides of the highway. A dozen deputies more than ready to blow them and their car to kingdom come.

Ben got twenty years for armed robbery. Hal got fifteen for being the getaway driver and fleeing the scene. It was his first offense, but white boys from out of town didn't rate much higher than Blacks or Mexicans in East Texas.

The Chevette was impounded. Hal's friends didn't think it was worth the trip to retrieve it. They dined out on the story for years after. It ended up in the hands of a deputy's sixteen-year-old daughter as a starter car.

Hal did ten years, got out on good behavior, and left the state.

He never visited Ben, and he hadn't been back to Texas since.

CHAPTER FIVE

C arla finished off the bottle of wine and found a replacement. Something from California that had a fancy label, probably left over from a party. It wasn't her usual brand. She opened it, poured a taste, tried it, and filled the glass. It would be fifteen minutes before she had to uncover the lasagna, then another half an hour in the oven.

She wondered if her husband Alex was going to come home. Ever.

She heard music coming from upstairs. Her son, Jesse, drowning out his anger with whatever shit he listened to. One day it was metal, another day it was rap, another day it was some pop bubblegum bullshit that no one in their right mind would consider "music." She harkened back to her own musical tastes at fifteen—R.E.M., The Smiths, The Cure, Van Halen, Guns N' Roses. Actual fucking music.

"Damn right," she said to herself and took another sip.

Slow down, she thought.

Why? It's not like your son hasn't seen you drunk before. You'll be sharing a drink with him before long. Or smoking pot. Something. The kid just committed a major felony, so relax.

And she did. She took another drink, let out a big sigh, and remembered the first time she got drunk with her mother.

Carla sat behind bars for the first time in her life at the District 3 police station in Tampa. She was sixteen.

She knew her mother, Connie, was waiting for her in the lobby. She knew because Officer Tomlin had told her. "You're lucky you didn't pull this shit on a Friday. You'd be off to Hillsborough for the weekend."

Carla nodded. He was the second officer to say such a thing. Like they were doing her a big favor.

She sat alone in the cell, a slow night in Tampa for a Tuesday. It was June 12, 1991. Eight days before her seventeenth birthday.

She was worried about her mother.

Connie was waiting in the lobby, just like she'd done three times before when she had to bail out her long-time boyfriend Eddy.

Connie was waiting in the lobby instead of going to the hospital.

What started it was what always started it. Eddy was seven beers into a twelve pack of Meister Brau. Carla's friends, who would know, said it was about the shittiest beer on the market. But cheap. Carla's "boyfriend" Dylan said it was almost as bad as Coors or Bud. "Miller's where it's at, babe," he'd say. Dylan was eighteen and a junior. They still hadn't done it yet. Carla's mother said hold out for someone with an IQ higher than her grandfather's age. "You're worth more than that," she'd said on more than one occasion.

Eddy knocked over a half-full beer and cursed and yelled for his dinner.

Carla was in the middle of Social Studies homework and had to put on headphones just so she could concentrate.

Connie was trying to cook a fatty piece of steak she got at the Ocean View Supermarket, a family-owned shithole that she hated going to. The people who worked there were mean and smelled a little, but she couldn't ignore their prices. Especially since she was the only one working.

She got the steak home and found out they put the nice looking side up and the shit side down. No time to return it, she was trying to cook it anyway, hoping Eddy wouldn't notice (because he was drunk), or wouldn't care (because he was drunk).

The fat was making a lot of noise and a lot of smoke, and it was taking forever to cook through.

She had baked potatoes in the oven and she'd dumped frozen green beans into a pot with some water. She was fretting over the steak when Eddy came in and grabbed her by the shoulders.

She tensed up. She hadn't heard him.

"Jesus, what?" he said.

The smell of that beer—

"Nothing, you just scared me," she said.

"No, you pulled away like you're—"

"No—"

"Like you're disgusted by me or something."

"Eddy, you scared me is all."

"You think I'm scary?"

Yes.

"No, honey. You startled me. I didn't hear you. OK?"

He didn't look convinced. "The fuck is taking so long with dinner?"

She looked at the steak. Thankful it was nice side up. "I'm just frying it up; it'll be done any minute."

"Looks like shit," he said. "The fuck is it so smoky in here?" He grabbed the grilling fork she was using.

"No, Eddy, listen—"

He turned the steak over. "What the fuck is this shit?"

"Eddy—"

"What is this shit? Who the fuck... who would eat that shit? What the FUCK is that shit?"

It was the FUCK that Carla heard. She had been lying on her stomach, reading, headphones *still* on. She dropped her head into the book in both frustration and exhaustion.

"This is what you were going to feed me? Are you fucking kidding? This isn't... you wouldn't feed a fucking *dog* this shit, Connie. What the fuck are you doing with this SHIT!"

Carla heard the SHIT through the headphones, too. She took them off.

Most times it was yelling. Eighty percent of the time. And then it was over and he'd sit in the living room with his legs over the armrest of the recliner Connie found on sale three years prior. He'd worn out both arms, worn out the seat. Connie bought a throw for it so it wouldn't get more damaged. He hated the throw, sat on it anyway.

The other twenty percent of the time, Carla would have to go into the living room to referee. Silently. To be a presence, just in case he thought a few slaps or punches would make his points for him.

She got up to go to the living room, just to be safe. As she crossed the threshold of her bedroom door she heard her mother scream. Carla ran down the hallway, turned the corner and saw Eddy pressing the steak up against the side of her mother's face.

It looked like an ordinary steak.

It didn't register with Carla that anything was wrong with it. That he was just pissed off because of whatever, not because of the steak. But when he took the steak away and dropped it on the ground, the white of it...

That color would stay with her for the rest of her life. It looked exactly like what she imagined was lurking directly under her skin.

Carla had seen enough and heard enough and listened to enough of her mother's excuses about Eddy to know that she was too weak to leave him. She had friends in similar situations and they'd compare notes about the state of their parents. The depression. The fear of being alone. The instinctual need for subjugation.

Carla remembered hearing that word subjugation for the first time and thought, no word had ever applied to a human being more than her mother.

But she understood. Amongst a circle of her closest friends, boys and girls, all of those parents... could that many people be wrong about what they needed from others?

"You should just kill him," Dylan said. They'd been making out and she stopped because of his breath. He was a smoker and, as cute as he was, sometimes... Jesus.

"I can't kill him."

"Please. They don't do shit to juvie girls. I'd do it, but I've got priors, girl. Plus... eighteen. Tried as an adult. You'd think they'd take that I was still in high school under consideration, but my dad's lawyer said nope."

Carla walked over to the stove as her mom was screaming. Eddy had frozen up, knowing what he'd done, and was trying to reconcile it all when Carla hit him over the head with the frying pan. Hard.

Grease went flying and burned her hand and face. She didn't care.

He toppled to the ground, grabbing the back of his head hard, and then his consciousness left him and his arms kind of flopped down to his sides.

Connie was still crying, gripping the side of her face, which was red. That's all Carla could see. Her mother's red face.

Carla stood over Eddy and brought the pan down again. This time onto his shoulder. Then his arm, which she heard break. A scream came out of him as he came to, and he tried to move a bit. Carla brought it down one more time on the back of his head, and he stopped moving.

She dropped the pan, held out her hand to her mother, who took it. She got her into a chair in the living room, out of the sight of him, went to the freezer, grabbed a pack of frozen peas and handed it to her. Her mother looked at it strangely. Carla moved her mother's hand over to the burned side of her face and Connie nodded, sobbing. She made a noise, that sucking in breath sound, when the frozen peas touched her face,

Carla walked over to the phone and called 911.

"911, what's your emergency?"

"I need two ambulances and the police. 1487 Peach Street."

"Can you tell me the nature of the incident?"

"Domestic violence."

"OK. Can you tell me who's hurt and how?"

"My mom got a hot steak to the face, and her boyfriend got hit numerous times with a frying pan."

"OK. By your mother?"

"By me. Hurry up. She's in pain, and I think he's dying."

Eddy didn't die. He had a major concussion, some neurological symptoms, and was in the hospital for eight days. When he got out, a friend drove him to Connie's house, where his belongings were in boxes out on the front lawn. They'd been picked over thoroughly by the entire neighborhood. He grabbed what was left and lived on couches for three years. Every once in a while he thought about calling Connie, to ask for forgiveness.

He tried. Once.

Carla picked up. In the silence he left hanging there she said, "Eddy, if this is you... if you ever show your face here again, I'll finish the job," and hung up.

In the end, Eddy shot himself under the chin in a bank near Land O' Lakes, when he found out his account was overdrawn for the fourteenth time that year.

When the police arrested Carla that night, she told her mother to go to the hospital. Connie said absolutely not.

Carla said, "Call Dylan."

Dylan got his father's lawyer to make a few calls and got Carla released into her mother's custody, with a promise to appear for questioning the next day.

Connie went to the hospital that night with second-degree burns on the left side of her face.

A nurse wanted to treat Carla for the grease burns on her hands and forehead. She told her to fuck off.

They both left the hospital the following morning, went to the station with the lawyer, Burt Manor.

"I can't afford this," Connie said to Burt. Half her face was bandaged up. She was on painkillers and steroids for the inflammation.

"Don't worry about it, this won't take long."

Connie's face, Eddy's priors, and him being well known amongst both city and state police... the Assistant D.A., who got the case dropped on his desk, declined to press charges.

Connie and Carla went home and cried about it.

Connie begged for forgiveness.

Carla felt the only thing she could do was give it. Her mom pulled out a two-thirds finished bottle of vodka, two glasses and some ice. She poured one four-finger, one two.

"I don't know what I'm going to do," Connie said.

"With what?"

"With my life."

"What life? You mean the one where you pay for everything and stress about a useless sack of shit all day? That life?"

Connie laughed and cried at the same time and downed her drink. "Yeah, that life."

Carla grabbed her glass, sniffed it, downed it and faked a cough so her mom didn't think less of her. She'd been drinking for years. "I think you can do better, Mom. I know you can. We both can."

They finished the bottle and watched shitty TV the rest of the night. Ordered a pizza and ate way too much of it. Both of them fell asleep on the couch.

The next day, Carla let Dylan take her virginity.

CHAPTER SIX

John left the cab at the parking garage and ate dinner at an Arby's. He tried to quiet his brain and come up with a story that would keep him out of jail. He couldn't. There wasn't a story on God's green earth that would explain what he just went through.

So he ate his roast beef sandwich and fries and drank his Coke. It was almost like his taste buds had reset. Everything was delicious.

His ass was hurting. So was his arm. He decided not to go to the hospital. He wasn't sure if they'd know the wounds came from gunshots. If they *could* tell that, he'd be in even more trouble. Before he'd ordered dinner, he cleaned up in the Arby's bathroom. His arm was the real bleeder. Thankfully, no one came in.

He finished his food, got up with a wince, went to a pay phone, dumped in a couple of quarters, called Abbas and told him he was going to keep the cab for another shift. "Good for you. Work builds character. Don't pick up any weirdos, and bring it back with a full tank."

John hung up. Now he was in to Abbas for $200, and the cab was a wreck.

He did a circuit around the parking garage. Nothing stirring.

He bought a cup of coffee at a diner, used their bathroom, rechecked his ass in the mirror (there was a red streak across the entire left cheek, and some meat was missing), and went back to the garage.

There was a leak of antifreeze going from the car to the street. He ignored it.

It wasn't until midnight that he took the chance and drove the cab to the address on the license. Forest Hills. He took side streets in an attempt to keep a low profile. It took forever. Anything over 25mph, the taxi made a whining sound he'd never heard from a car before.

He pulled up to a stop light next to another taxi. The driver looked over at him, looked at the car, back at him. John nodded, waved. The guy nodded back, drove off when the light turned green.

John smiled. He was never going to leave this city.

He finally pulled over across from a massive brick home. Two levels, gated driveway, security cameras, floodlights. A fortress that looked brand new.

He parked outside of the place and waited. And waited. By 2 a.m. he began to doze off. He slapped himself in the face a few times and readjusted his seat. The smell of puke from earlier was doing a number on his stomach.

Another hour in, a black limo pulled up to the front of the house. John noticed that the man who walked out of the gate to greet them was tall, solidly built, and classically Italian. The hair, skin color, bone structure, gait, the outfit. The attitude.

Two even larger Italians got out of the limo—the driver and one from the front passenger side, who walked up to the guard and started talking.

The driver stared at John's cab.

"Oh, shit..." John said, and sank down, his eyes peeking out over the driver-side window, which was just shards.

He watched as the driver said something over his shoulder. Then everyone was looking at the cab.

The driver went to the back of the limo, opened the trunk and came out with a shotgun so large John assumed it was for elephants. Or giants. He began sweating through his clothes. After everything he'd been through, all of the excitement, he hadn't realized his night could get worse.

The three men walked over, the shotgun pointed at the cab.

John slowly, deliberately raised his hands.

One of his hands had the wallet. One of his fingers was in the bullet hole. He'd been twirling it out of boredom.

The guy racked the shotgun and John felt his soul trying to escape. "Jesus Christ, easy, take it easy! Are you with Vincent?"

That stopped them. They all shared a look before the guard said, "Who's Vincent?"

"I don't know. You tell me," John said, not understanding the situation at all.

"If you mean Vincenzo D'Escopio, you're in more trouble than you thought."

John opened his mouth to talk, closed it, opened the wallet with his free hand and looked at the license again.

"Vincent... the Scorpion?" There it was. Clear as day. "Holy shit," John said, and looked behind him.

The two limo guys peered into the back seat. One of them said, "Oh. Oh no." The other said, "Fuck!" They were so tall John couldn't tell who said what. "What happened?"

"I, umm, I... with, you know, and shots... guns and—" John tried to talk. Then he tried to pantomime the scene. Pew, pew, pews and everything. "And then I threw up and—"

It only made things worse.

"Put him in the limo. I'll get the Scorpion," one of them said.

Hands dragged John out of the cab. He put his own up reflexively as he got pulled towards the back of the Lincoln, turned to see the remaining man open the back door of the cab, grab the briefcase and put it on the hood. He lifted the Scorpion out carefully and slung him over his shoulder. He kicked the cab door closed, grabbed the briefcase, and walked towards them.

One of the guys opened the limo, motioned for John to get in.

John looked up at the guy. "You've got to be fucking kid—" He pushed John in.

John sat down hard with his back to the driver's seat, on what could only be described as the plushest leather he'd ever felt. And warm. Across from him, a short half-balding man with horn-rimmed glasses and a pencil-thin mustache. He, too, was dressed in a three-piece suit.

John went to talk when the man carrying the Scorpion sat him down next to him, the limp body leaning against his shoulder. John tried to shrug him off once, twice. It wasn't working. The Scorpion was leaking blood out of his mouth onto his arm.

Doors opened up front and the two enormous men got back into the limo. The entire vehicle moved, shifted, settled.

Cigar smoke mixed with some kind of alcohol finally hit John's nose. He took a better look at his surroundings. The interior was dark wood and leather, well used, but in great condition.

The man in front of him was looking at the Scorpion with a combination of amusement and condescension. "You get shot?"

"Uhh, no. No sir."

"Not once?"

"Well, not through. Just... there's a—" he showed the man his arm. "And... well..."

"Well what?"

"My ass."

He looked at John, half smiling. "You got shot in your ass?"

"Not in... just... you know. Around. Or... on? I don't know. Could have been worse." John looked at the cab. It was a miracle he wasn't dead.

"You go to the hospital?"

"No."

"Why not?"

John looked him in the eyes. "Too many questions."

"Uh huh." The man clucked with his tongue. "Let me ask you a question. Always wanted to know. The partitions in taxi cabs—are they bulletproof?"

"Some more than others," John said. He'd heard enough graveyard shift horror stories to know. Abbas was always concerned about his drivers, but he also knew if someone wanted to rob them, bulletproof partition or no, they'd figure out a way.

"But not the windows," the man said and sighed.

"Or the doors. You know…" John said, trying to be helpful.

The man looked at him and shook his head, turned to the Scorpion. "You were so stupid. Mom always said you were stupid." He looked at John. "You know what his problem was?"

"Uhh… hard to say—"

"He thought he was invincible. You can't reason with people who think that way about themselves. And this is what happens. You leave yourself wide open." He hit a button. The partition dividing the back from the driver went down. "What's left in the case?"

The driver said, "I'd say a half a pound. Some of that's got blood in it, though. More in the taxi on the floor."

"Have Milo tow that piece of shit out of here, tell him to bring it up to Dean. Then get Max to test the sample."

"Yes, Gino."

"If Max's happy, tell him to wait before he makes the deal. We have to find out who was responsible; see if those motherfuckers set Vincent up."

"I ran over a guy," John said, trying to up his worth.

"Where? What did he look like?"

"Fortieth Street. In Queens. White guy—"

Gino arched an eyebrow. "A white guy? Not Asian?"

"Not Asian. Thirties. Brown hair… all three of them were white, in fact. They were in a black SUV. And a truck. Couldn't have gotten very far."

"*You* did." Gino looked at the driver through the rear view window. "See if Hong contracted with any… Caucasians."

38

The partition went up again.

"You're a business man?" Gino asked.

"I guess so. Not like I owned it." John looked at the cab, remembered Abbas. "Shit…" he said under his breath.

"But you're smart."

"Well, I'm alive. I guess you could consider that smart. I think it was just luck. I mean, look at it…" John nodded towards the cab. "Any one of those bullets could have been for me, not…" he patted the Scorpion's leg. "Not Vinnie here." Gino arched an eyebrow, again. "Vincent. Mister, uh… the Scorp… not… here…"

Gino smiled. "It's true, but I think it's something else. You didn't take his money, or the drugs… you didn't report it to the police."

"Hey, I didn't come here to bargain or for a reward or nothing. I came to give you back, well… what's left of your brother. If I were in the mob and into drugs and guns and killing—" John swallowed hard "—people, I'd want someone to bring my brother back to me. I'm not looking for anything."

"Nothing?"

"Nope."

"Don't want someone to check those wounds for you?"

"I'll live."

Gino nodded. "So, no favors?"

"No. No favors." John looked at the cab again. "OK, maybe one favor… uh, see, that's not my cab. I rent it. I don't know if insurance handles mob hits… can't see that falling under an act of God. Might be a grey area and the guy who owns it…"

"We'll get you a new cab."

"You will?"

"It's the least I can do."

John sighed again, looked at Vincent, said, "You hear that?" He patted Vincent's leg again, looked at Gino. "Great. That's great. Thank you."

"You're welcome." He leaned back and took a long probing look at John. Like he was reading him from the inside. After some thought he made a satisfied nod, like he'd come to the right conclusion. "You like this?"

"What?"

"Being a cab driver?"

"I... I mean, I did. It was OK, you know. Not sure I'll just jump in again. Might take some time off. Think about doing something else."

"Like what?"

"I don't know, something less dangerous, like being a bike messenger." John giggled, nervously.

Gino was not laughing.

John stopped giggling. "Uhh, yeah, not sure. I haven't given it much thought."

Gino looked at the cab. Looked at John. He thought before speaking. "Maybe I'll regret this, I don't know... but how about you come work for me?"

It took John a second to realize what the guy had said. After everything that had happened, all his mind could come up with to reply with was, "Fucking what?"

CHAPTER SEVEN

In July of 2000, Hal was twenty-nine years old. He was a felon with an anxiety problem. He'd been home for six months. Home being Brooklyn. He couch-surfed for a while with some old high school friends who weren't still living with their parents. Most situations didn't last long.

He couldn't hold down a regular job, let alone get in the door at a corporate or white collar or whatever you want to call it. Under-the-table jobs were either paying shit or asking for kickbacks due to his record. The two times he took an under-the-table gig, the guys he worked for treated him like utter garbage. One of them slapped him in the face after he talked back. It took all of his will power not to break his hand. Or his nose. Or maybe his jaw. Or all three of them.

Hal was broke and had no support system in the tri-state area. His mother was gone. With his cousin still in prison, what relatives he had left turned him away. His Aunt Judy, that's his cousin Ben's mother, blamed him for what had happened, saying her son was "a good boy and wouldn't do nothin' like that. Not ever."

He tried to explain that it was Ben's idea and she stopped taking his calls.

Hal had been on a friend of a friend's couch for two weeks before the guy's girlfriend said enough was enough. The last three nights, he'd slept on the subway. He spent the day wandering the city, trying to figure out his next move. He had eighteen dollars, no apartment, no friends to take him in on a more permanent basis.

Earlier that morning, and for the first time in his life, he begged for money. At first, there was a deep self-loathing. It made him sick to his stomach, but he was able to quash it quick enough. He looked at what he was doing as survival. A shit form of survival, but survival none-the-less.

He found a corner just south of the main branch of the New York Public Library. Every hundredth person or so gave him some change. He got looks, he was ignored. One woman told him to find Jesus.

"I will, ma'am, just as soon as I've had something to eat."

He had a hard time figuring out if eye contact helped or hurt. At some point he found a piece of cardboard and wrote out a sign.

Homeless, hungry. Please help with anything you can.

He had a used (not by him) large wax paper cup in front of him and quickly removed what few bills he got. After a while, his ass started killing him. Whether it was the heat or the concrete, he wasn't sure.

He tried the subway next.

The percentages were a bit better, it was air-conditioned, and his ass was thankful. His knees not so much.

Someone gave him half a sandwich. Someone else gave him a Sprite.

People bad-mouthed him on two separate occasions in loud voices and in full view of the other passengers. He felt tears in his eyes as the train made its way to the next station. He knew there were some people that, when it came to begging, it was their job. Like JOB, job. People who excelled at the art of preying on the sympathies of others. He figured some of the commuters were thinking that exact same thing as he went from subway car to subway car. That he didn't really need the money. Or the food. That he was just a scammer. That he was just lazy.

The thing that really stayed with him whenever he took a break was thinking about the other people who were doing it for real. There simply had to be some out there. People who had nothing, and no one. Hal was at what he thought was rock bottom and figured, in a city this big, he couldn't possibly be the only one.

The other thing Hal knew was this type of life wasn't sustainable. Even though he was young, he'd burn out. He'd turn to drugs or crime and end up in prison or dead. Murdered or by suicide. The plan for the foreseeable future was work the trains for the summer, find a shelter in the winter. Like a homeless snowbird.

That night, he tried to get comfortable on an empty A train as it headed through Brooklyn on its way to Manhattan. Comfort was relative. The A/C was down, which was awful, but the windows were providing a reasonable breeze. He had a sweatshirt as a pillow. He had a bag of chips and a bottle of water someone had given him.

I may or may not make it to breakfast, he thought, and tried to close his eyes. His stomach was already grumbling. He had money to buy something, but he didn't want to eat too early. That would just mean an early lunch.

A woman got on the train at the next stop. She was Black, long straight hair, jeans, T-shirt, a purse, and flat tops.

Pretty. And exhausted.

She looked in one direction, looked in the other, saw him, and sat down towards the opposite end.

He mentally shrugged. He could see himself through her eyes and understood. His clothes weren't in great shape. He had a week's worth of growth on his face, his hair was dirty, and he was pretty sure he smelled of sweat and B.O.

He rested his head up against the train car wall and tried to sleep. The rocking motion was soothing after a while. The noise, not so much.

The next station, the doors opened, closed, no new passengers. He adjusted the hood from his sweater to cover his eyes from the forever fluorescents and dozed off.

By the time they hit Hoyt-Schermerhorn, they were still the only two on the train. It was three in the morning, and this was his second circuit back and forth from the Rockaways up to Inwood. His plan was to travel way uptown again, swing back around, get out at West 4th, try and get some breakfast. Find a diner or a street vendor for a bacon, egg and cheese sandwich, and a cup of coffee.

He hoped he wouldn't need to take a piss beforehand. Balancing between cars with one hand was an art form.

At Jay Street, three young guys got on the train. Drunk, high, just happy to be alive, it was hard to tell. It was a mixed group. Two Black guys, one Hispanic. They were medium build, nothing to speak of, but young. In their prime.

Hal had peeked out from his hood when they got into the car, alerted by the noise they were making. Loud this late, this early in the morning. He figured they'd leave him alone. They did.

But they started in on her straight away.

Hal remembered when he was younger, taking the train home late. There was always one woman on the train in a car full of men, and he imagined they were all thinking the same thing. *Here's the last chance for pussy tonight. All I have to do is catch her eye.* Like a moving bar full of desperate people. She didn't even have to be particularly good-looking. Just a warm body until the morning.

This was different.

"Where you goin' girl?" one of the guy's asked.

Hal sighed. He wasn't in the best shape. He hadn't lifted weights or boxed in months. His back hurt and his knees were fucked. He wondered if there was some arthritis somewhere. Everywhere, maybe. Not to mention, he was sore from walking all day, and because he was trying to sleep on the fucking subway.

He could feel his palms getting sweaty in anticipation of having to step in. He knew all about what happened late at night on the trains to men and women. The news creamed for those stories. He'd heard a particularly telling quote from a drunk one night, ranting about the trend of the city's doom and gloom newspaper articles. "If it bleeds, it leads."

He peered over.

Like jackals circling a wounded animal.

Fuck.

He shook his head. He wasn't just outnumbered. He was a mess.

"You want to come with us? Going to a party downtown. You should come. Marquez, right? She should come."

The Hispanic guy said, "Hell yeah, Shawn, she should *come*," and giggled.

Downtown. OK. That's two, three stops, tops.

"No thanks," she said, and tried to busy herself with looking at her nails. Her hands were shaking.

"It's a party. Who doesn't like parties?" the last guy asked. He giggled, too.

A bunch of gigglers.

They'd basically surrounded her at this point. Shawn sat down next to her, got close on her left. Marquez was standing in front of her. The third guy was on her far side, a foot on the seat next to her.

Just kick Marquez in the balls, Hal thought. *Just do it.*

She didn't.

"What's your name?"

"Leave me alone."

"That's a fucking weird name." More giggles. "I'm Darryl, baby. What's your name? I'm just asking for your name… shit."

Hal glanced over. She was nervous, but caught his eye. It made the others look over.

Shawn decided Hal wasn't a threat, turned back to her. "What you into? Coke? I've got it, baby. You want some weed? We can blaze here, get you in the mood."

Hal grabbed his right leg, pulled it in and stretched it. Then the left. Just in case. They both popped. There was a particularly bad gristly feeling in his right knee.

"Please leave me alone."

"We're just talking, jeez, what the fuck—"

"I don't want to talk to you," she said, doing her best to make sure her voice didn't break.

"You don't have to, what we want to do."

45

More giggles.

Hal rotated his neck, heard a pop, another, and then went into a coughing fit. He'd swallowed wrong.

"The fuck—" Daryll said, looking at him. Hal raised his hands over his head to try and clear it. It was something his mother had taught him. It did the trick.

"The fuck is he doing?"

"Praying," Marquez said. It got a laugh.

"Sorry," Hal said. "Sorry." He stood up and stumbled over. "Just wanted to apologize. Baby? Look, I know we're fighting, just, come on over, OK?"

"Baby?" Shawn asked. "Fuck you, *baby*."

"Yeah, honey, baby. You know. Come on." Hal put his hand out.

Daryll slapped it away. "Fuck, I can smell you from here. There's no way this bitch is with you. Get the fuck out of here before I pop a cap in your ass."

Sigh. It was the mid-90s.

Hal looked at the guy. His arms had that ropey muscle you just hate to see before a fight.

Then he looked over at his friends. They had the same.

There was no way to control the situation.

The train pulled into the first station in Manhattan, Fulton Street. An old man got on, looked at the passengers who were all looking at him. He quickly got off and went to another car. The doors closed.

"Fellas, let's take it easy," Hal said. It was funny. He was anxious, but he wasn't scared. More and more, he was adjusting to rock bottom. "Sweetheart—"

"Sweetheart," Shawn said under his breath, shaking his head. "Bull*shit*."

"Come on, come with me." Hal held his hand out again. This time the woman went to take it, and that's when things fell apart.

Shawn grabbed her by the arms. Daryll stood up and got in Hal's face. And right then, at that moment, she kicked Marquez in the balls. He fell on the ground.

Hal had little room to maneuver. Anything he did, Daryll would fall back into the woman and the other guy, Shawn. So, he did the only thing he could think of.

He opened himself up to get hit.

Daryll drew back to punch him in the face. Hal moved forward a bit to lessen his momentum, a move he'd learned in the ring as a teenager. And in prison.

It did the trick. Daryll's arm was at an awkward angle when it hit Hal in the left cheek. It hurt, but there was barely any follow through. The momentum of the punch, the movement of the train, made both men stumble back a bit. Satisfied with the distance between them and the woman, Hal got himself into a boxing stance. He hadn't been a very good fighter, but he'd learned a thing or two.

"Oh yeah?" Daryll said, and went to take off his jacket.

Hal pounced.

Daryll saw him move and his eyes went wide, one hand stuck in the sleeve of his jacket. He raised his right for a quick jab, hoping to fend Hal off. Hal pushed it aside with his left, dropped his body and drove up, his right fist coming at a steep angle, squarely under Daryll's jaw. It connected.

The sound was disturbing.

A piece of tongue came flying out, hit the ceiling, and landed on the ground.

Daryll screamed. Like *scream* screamed. He clamped his hand over his mouth as blood poured out. Hal cocked his right elbow and threw it like a punch, smashed the side of Daryll's face. He felt bones crack, watched as the guy crumpled to the subway floor, unconscious.

Marquez was on the ground, a puddle of vomit next to him. He was wiping his mouth and cupping his balls when Hal stomped on his ankle hard, snapping it.

He screamed, too.

The final guy, Shawn, had a fistful of the woman's hair and was walking them both backwards. He pulled out a switchblade.

"Fuck off!" Shawn said, and took another step back. She was crying at this point, silently sobbing.

"Let her go, and you can go," Hal said.

"Stop!" he screamed as they kept moving backwards. They were running out of room.

Hal half chuckled. "Where do you think you're going?"

"I said fucking stop!" Shawn's back hit the end of the car at the connecting door. He used his knife hand to grab the handle, but it wouldn't budge. "Goddammit, fucking bitch!" Shawn pulled her hair tighter, put his knife to her neck. "Step closer, I'll fucking cut her fucking throat!"

"OK, OK," Hal said. He put his hands up. *Just relax*, he thought as the train started to slow down. *He's not going anywhere.*

Hal watched as they moved through the Chambers Street station, and saw something he'd never thought he'd see at 3:20 in the morning.

Two transit officers shuffling about, waiting to board.

And they saw him.

He looked back at the guy to see if he'd noticed them. He hadn't. He was busy holding the only leverage he had.

"Why don't you just let her go? You let her go, and you can go home and forget any of this happened," Hal said, stalling.

"Just shut up!"

The doors opened.

"I'm just saying, it didn't go your way tonight, why not just—"

"FREEZE!"

Simultaneously, the three of them, Hal, Shawn, the woman, they stopped breathing. "Freeze" was a world stopper.

Hal already had his hands up, but he couldn't see behind him, and decided not to make any sudden moves. He knew they had their guns out, and they were maybe probably pointed at his back.

Maybe.

48

He stepped to the side just so, just slightly so the officers could see what he may or may not have been blocking. A woman with a knife to her throat.

"Get down on the ground!"

He got to his knees. Hal figured that, regardless of whether he was the good guy here, they didn't know it. So he did what they said and laid down on the floor of the subway. It was disgusting. Just ahead of him lay the piece of tongue.

"Ugh," he said.

"Fuck you!" Shawn said.

The woman had that half-relieved, half-fucked look—that the situation could go either way. All of a sudden, the floor of the car was wet. Hal looked up. Her pants were soaked. A line of urine spread until it flowed under Hal's body. "You gotta be fucking kidding," he said to the floor.

"Put your hands behind your back!"

Hal did it.

"Cuff him. I've got this piece of shit."

One of the officers handcuffed Hal with a knee in his back. The guy's name tag said McDonnell.

"Motherfucker—" Marquez said and went to get up. McDonnell spun and hit Marquez in the face with the butt of his gun. "We weren't doin' nothin'!" he screamed as he cradled his broken nose. McDonnell turned him around, threw him to the ground, and cuffed him.

The other cop had his gun trained on Daryll. "Let her go."

"Fuck you!"

"Let her go or I'm going to shoot you in the face."

"Fuck you!"

"Just do it already, Tim," the other cop said. "Try not to hit her."

"What?" she screamed.

"LET HER GO!" Tim screamed. His hands were steady.

"Kill the bith!" Daryll tried to say. He'd come to after the screaming started. His face was a mess and his mouth was leaking. He tried to stand, and fell back down, dizzy.

McDonnell came over, pointed his gun at Daryll. They'd run out of cuffs. "Try and stand up again. It'll be the easiest paperwork I'll ever fill out."

Shawn hid his face behind the woman's head. She started crying for real. Loud, with full body sobs.

From behind them, a third transit officer opened the far connecting door in the car, slowly. His gun was drawn and was pointed at the back of Shawn's head.

"OK, OK," Tim said. "Just take it easy, I'm gonna lower this and we can talk." Tim didn't lower his weapon.

"Damn straight!" Shawn said when, all of a sudden, the cop behind him tapped on the glass behind his head.

He turned to look and saw a gun pointed at his head.

"Fuck," he said and swallowed. He looked at the cop behind him, turned and looked at Tim in front of him, who was smiling and shrugged.

Resigned, Shawn dropped the knife, let go of the woman, and put his hands up.

She went for the nearest seat and started shaking from crying, from the adrenalin. The cop from the other car opened the door and took his cuffs out while Tim kept his gun on Shawn.

"You said it was going to be a slow night," the third cop said.

"What are you talking about? This is slow. Night's already half over," Tim said.

The commotion kept the train in the station another half an hour. Hal tried to talk his way out of the cuffs, but the officers kept telling him to shut the fuck up. The woman was half coherent, half babbling.

An officer, brass, in a starched white shirt showed up, talked to the three officers, then to the woman. They all looked at Hal, who smiled and side waved with his hands cuffed behind his back.

An hour later they were at 1st Precinct on Walker Street. Hal had the cuffs removed and was given a Coke and some peanut butter crackers from the machine. He told his side of the story to a Detective Bridges, who was bored, pissed he missed the action, and wanted to go home.

Hal was told he was free to go, with an understanding he would be called upon as a witness at a future court date. He said no problem.

The detective asked where he could get in touch. Hal said he wasn't sure, all things considered. Bridges nodded, wiped his face with his hands, dug through his desk and gave Hal the number of a pastor at a local shelter, said he'd facilitate a meeting. Bridges said something about the D.A. and an interview. "I know how things go, OK? But stick with the shelter for a week. Just a week so I can find you, and we'll go from there."

Hal said OK.

He left with half the Coke gone and the crackers finished. He sat in Tribeca Park until the sun came up. He barely moved. Everything looked brighter. Everything looked clean. Blue sky peeked through the trees and he felt that if he died at that moment... it wouldn't be the worst thing in the world.

Then he found a food cart.

Hal got a large cup of coffee with milk, a cinnamon raisin bagel with a square slice of cold, hard cream cheese, and a plain roll. He went back to the park, ate most of the bagel, drank his coffee, and fed some pigeons. It was the best food he'd had in a long time.

He found out later that the woman, Latisha Bowman, twenty-six, had just gotten off a double shift from Kings County Hospital and couldn't afford a cab home. She'd relayed the situation to *her* pastor, who got in touch with a free local paper. When they interviewed her, she said enough to make Hal not only a hero, but a poster child for the city's genuinely unwashed.

Hal was tracked down at the shelter three days later by a hungry reporter named Sally Hampton, who was six years out of college and still circling the bottom rung of the journalism ladder. She bought him lunch and they talked for an hour, a portable recorder between them.

They followed it up with coffee, talked for another hour.

The recorder ran out of tape. She changed it.

They took a walk near Washington Square Park and kept talking. Most of the questions she asked had little or nothing to do with the business on the subway. Every once in a while she'd circle around to it. But what she really wanted to know was how Hal became homeless.

The recorder ran out of batteries. They stopped at a bodega and bought some double AAs. She changed the tape out, again, just in case.

They had dinner and drinks at a Chinese food place on Houston.

She paid for it all.

The night ended with them back at her place in the East Village, having sex in her shower.

It was the first time Hal had been with a woman since he was a teenager. When they were done, she found a leftover men's razor from an ex, handed him some shaving cream, winked, and left the bathroom.

He'd spend the next twenty minutes on the floor of the tub, crying, and not feeling worthy of anything.

CHAPTER EIGHT

Nursing school. It's what her guidance counselor suggested. Her grades weren't shit, but they weren't stellar. "Honey, the problem is, you don't really want to do *anything*," Ms. Grey said to her. "Not that you don't want to do ANYthing, that's not what I mean. But when I ask you what your interests are..."

Blank look from Carla.

"This is what I'm talking about," Ms. Grey said and sighed. "You know what I tell the boys around here? The ones who don't have any direction, except for drugs or maybe prison? Find a trade. Something that will always be in demand. Mechanic, plumber, something with a union and benefits and a pension. Air conditioning repair, for God's sake. I mean, look where we live!" She studied Carla for a moment. "You know, I'd suggest becoming a teacher, but—"

Carla scoffed.

"Yeah. It's not for everyone. More of a position of calling, if I'm being honest. And masochism. Nursing school is a good career path. You're smart, Carla, but you're not driven enough to just go on your own without any skills. You need some structure in your life, and I'm afraid you won't find what you're looking for in a regular college. You'd have fun, I'm sure of it. But you won't find your place in the world there."

She handed her a pamphlet on nursing degrees.

"Two years? That's it?" Carla asked.

"Two years for the basics. You'd get your associates and you'll find work. But from what I've learned, hospitals want nurses who went through the full four years."

"So, four years of student loans. Great."

"Shit, Carla. These days? That's everyone."

Carla sort of loved Ms. Grey.

Graduation came and went. Connie took her out to dinner to celebrate at a pasta place where they feed you a pound of pasta, however you want it.

They had leftovers for two days.

Carla spent the summer of 1993 working at a grocery store and stayed out of trouble.

Her first year at Keiser University was stressful. Humanities classes, basic anatomy and physiology, and nutrition.

She still lived at home. Her mom, who was a career receptionist, was still struggling with men. Not as bad as before, but boy did she have a knack.

Her finances weren't terrible. They were ten years away from paying off the house. On top of school and part-time work at the grocery store, Carla was taking care of the family's books. Every month, they were able to put a little bit away.

Carla met Greg Halloway at a fraternity party three months in. He was a junior at the University of Southern Florida and member of Alpha Epsilon, his father's alma mater. Greg was from Philadelphia and was going for his finance degree to follow in his father's footsteps. Mr. Halloway helped run the fourth largest investment firm in Philly.

They had fun for two years. Greg graduated by the skin of his teeth. She called it love. Greg would say it, but it seemed more procedural than real. She didn't mind all that much. He was a vast improvement over the Dylans of the world.

After graduation, Greg moved back to Philly. He sent emails asking her to come visit. Begging her. She couldn't afford it. She didn't ask him to pay, and he didn't offer.

By July, he was begging her to *move* up to Philly. "Transfer your credits. It's easy. There's a great nursing school here and then we can see each other all the time."

Hardly, she thought. If her second year of nursing school, which had kicked her ass, was any indication... third year was going to be a flat-out nightmare.

She reconciled the fact that she was happier with him than without, and what with the begging and all, she was certain he was going to grow into the relationship. It's not like Philadelphia didn't have women, especially women in the stratosphere Greg lived in. Clearly she meant something to him.

She gave it some real thought.

Her mother was doing great by this time. She was dating a guy who repaired air conditioners for a living. Seriously. Larry. Big guy, big belly, big laugh, didn't drink. "He's got the biggest cock I've ever seen," her mother said one night. Carla just nodded and let her talk. It had been a long time since she'd seen her mother happy.

When Carla broke the news to her mother that she was going to Philly to follow a boy, her mom uncharacteristically said, "The heart wants what it wants," and shrugged, as if she had always been full of sage wisdom.

That August, Carla got accepted to the University of Pennsylvania School of Nursing, found an apartment to rent, transferred her credits and, two weeks before classes, made her way up to Philly via Amtrak.

She had four bags with her. Everything she owned.

Getting to the station was easy. Getting on the train was harder. A conductor said he'd try and find help. She never saw him again. She got onto the train piece by piece. She got the bags on the shelves above the seats and collapsed into one, thankful for both the air conditioning and the empty space next to her.

She'd never been on a train before. The countryside blew by her window. So much of it looked the same.

After eight hours, she was dying of boredom.

By the time she got to Philadelphia station, she'd sworn off trains for good. Remembering that Philly had its own mass transit train system, she appended her ultimatum to cross-country trains only.

Carla got her bags out of the train car and lugged them, one by one, to the front of the station. She'd move two, drop them, grab two, move them further, drop them, and so on. It took twenty minutes. No one bothered to help.

She got to the northeast corner of North 30th and Market, where Greg said he'd pick her up.

She waited two hours before hailing a cab. The driver took pity on her and helped take her bags to the front door of her apartment building.

The place she found was a really cute studio with vaulted ceilings, heat, hot water and utilities included, and a view of Drexel Park. She carried the bags up three flights of stairs, one at a time. Opened the apartment door with the keys that had been mailed to her, dropped her bags, closed the door, went back down the three flights, found a pay phone and called Greg.

It was August 24, 1995.

"Hello?" a man asked.

"Can I speak with Greg please?" She tried to keep the anger out of her voice.

"Who's calling?"

"Carla Allen. His girlfriend."

"Carla Allen... his girlfriend?" Away from the phone she heard "Who is it?" from a woman. "Some girl saying she's Greg's girlfriend?"

Carla got the drift almost immediately.

"Give me the phone," the woman said. "Hello?"

"Yes."

"Who is this?"

"Seriously?"

"Pardon me?"

"I'm the woman who's been fucking your son (gasp!) for the past two years while he's been at USF. Go Bulls. I'm assuming that he's never told you about me."

Silence.

"Yeah. That's what I thought."

"Young lady, I—"

"Is he out with another woman?"

Silence.

Carla closed her eyes, used her free hand, her fingers to pinch the bridge of her nose. "Just cut the shit and tell me what's going on."

Deep breath. "Greg is with his fiancée Jacqueline. They've known each other since they were five, and have been together these past five years."

"No shit."

"No sh... no. No."

"She rich?"

"Excuse me?"

"Yeah, she's rich. I could tell he was from that kind of family. A socialite. And her father's a friend of your husband's, or some country club bullshit like that. It's like a movie. A bad one."

Long silence. "I'm terribly sorry to be the bearer of such news. Greg is..." The woman let it hang. She sounded exhausted.

"Thank you." Carla sighed and looked up at the sky. It was just about twilight time. She hadn't slept in almost twenty-four hours. "I'll leave it up to you to tell..."

"Jacqueline."

"Right. Jacqueline. Pretty name. Well, you can put her out of her misery, or you can saddle her with him for another seven years. She'll be miserable, and if she ever finds out you knew about your son not being able to keep his dick in his pants... well, she'll hate you forever. But it's up to you. Goodnight."

Carla hung up. She held on to the receiver for too long, her lower lip quivering. "Are you fucking kidding me," she said out loud. "Are you *fucking*..." she looked around her. She saw a fast food place, a fancy restaurant, some shops, and a dive bar across the street.

She walked across the street, opened the door to the bar, grabbed a stool and waited for the bartender to come over.

"Whiskey, neat."

"I.D.?" the guy asked.

She sighed. "Mister, I'm a twenty-one-year-old woman who just uprooted her life for some douchebag who I just found out has a fiancée. In my heart, I'm a ninety-year-old woman who's experienced more pain and suffering than Mother Theresa, and all I want to do is murder the world. So please, for the love of God and the sake of humanity, just pour me a motherfucking drink."

The guy went to talk, decided against it, grabbed a shot glass.

"No, no. A real pour. Make it a double."

He grabbed an old fashioned glass, poured it and placed it in front of her.

"Ten bucks," he said.

Carla got out a twenty, slapped it on the table. The bartender went to grab it. "Let's keep it open, shall we?"

The guy smiled, nodded, walked away.

Carla just sat there, trying not to shake. Breathing was almost impossible.

"Trouble in paradise?" she heard some guy say.

She turned, slowly, agonizingly slowly, as if she misheard. Because no one would be fucking stupid enough to—

It was a blonde guy. Smiling. Not like an asshole, but like he was commiserating. Cute, maybe. Like an everyman, but with confidence, and not for no reason.

She turned away from him. "You think this place is fucking paradise?"

The bartender said, "Hey..."

She shrugged.

The guy said, "Well, it must have looked like it, back in the day. All white men and wigs..." he laughed. "Right? Sounds like heaven."

"Yeah, to a white supremacist."

"Oh, you're quick. And funny."

"Listen—"

"Alex."

"Alex. Listen, I get you're putting forth some effort here but I'm not in the mood."

He nodded. "Well, how about I keep my mouth shut—"

"Perfect."

"—hah, and you drink some of that and we'll see what kind of mood we can get you in. How about that?"

She grabbed the drink, downed it. "Sure. But there's a strong possibility I might just cut your throat."

Alex smiled, motioned to the bartender. "I'll take my chances."

The bartender gave Alex a fresh beer, refilled Carla's glass.

"What are you in for?" he asked.

"What?"

"School. What are you in for?"

"How do you know I go to school?"

"So you *do* go to school. For what?"

She shook her head. "You're not going away, are you?"

"I mean, I could lie to you and say yes and then just sit here… but that would just be awkward for both—"

"Nursing."

"Nursing?"

"Yeah. At UPenn."

"Huh."

"Huh?"

"Well, yeah, I mean… it's not what I expected. Not that I expected anything, but if I was given ten guesses, that wouldn't have been one of them."

"What would you have guessed?"

"Well, you drink like a lawyer. Or a banker. Or a teacher…"

"Too stressful."

"Yeah, all *you* have to worry about is killing people. Or *not* killing—"

"I'm not all that worried."

"That's good." He looked at his beer, looked back at her. "Because you're good at it?"

"Malpractice insurance."

"Oh. Yeah. Sure." Alex looked around the bar. It was more than half empty. "So, what happened?"

"Don't."

"Don't what?"

"You were... benign there for a moment."

"Benign? Like a cancer?"

"Harmless."

"Oh. That's a medical term, right?"

"And now you're getting personal, and all I really want to do is tell you to fuck off."

"OK, but—"

She stared straight through him. "I'm not what you're looking for. You're not what I'm looking for, more to the point."

"OK."

"Not now, not tonight, not a week from now. Not any time soon. You understand what I'm saying?" she asked.

"Perfectly."

"Good."

"Great."

Long silence.

"Honest, I was just asking about your troubles," he said.

"What are you, writing a book?"

"Well, I—"

"Leave that page out."

Alex nodded, turned away from her and sat at the bar staring at his beer.

They were quiet for a few minutes.

She sighed. "I moved across the country to be with a guy—"

"Who has a fiancée. I heard."

"You heard?"

"You told the bartender."

"Right. That's right. So what the fuck are you asking me what happened for?"

He shrugged. "I was just wondering if there was more."

"Does it sound like there has to be more?"

"No. I suppose it doesn't." He stretched, looked around, looked her up and down and nodded. "Well, OK. So I'm not what you're looking for… or, you're not what I'm… something. So, fine. OK. I mean, I guess we'll just be friends."

"What?"

"Friends. We'll be friends."

"I don't need friends."

"You *don't* need friends? You just moved to a strange city and the one person you know here just fucked you over. Sounds like you need a friend."

"You want to be my 'friend' or my friend?"

"What's the difference?"

"Well, one has quotes around it…"

"Oh, you mean '*friends*' friends…"

"Yeah."

"Yeah, no. I get it. No."

She nodded, sipped her drink. The first glass had already gone to her head. This was just the kind of situation she hated. She pushed the vulnerable side of her brain out, grabbed on to her anger and held it. Fuck this guy. *Friends.*

"I'm sorry," he said.

"For what? Being annoying?"

"For what happened."

She looked at him a long moment. Bullshit sincerity. Had to be. "Thanks."

"The guy's a fucking asshole."

"Most guys are."

He nodded. "That's probably true. *I'm* not."

"Uh huh." Silence, again. Fine, she thought. "So what about you?"

"Who?"

"You."

"Me?"

"No, the guy behind you. Yeah, you. Tell me something about you."

"Like what?"

"Like what are you in for?"

"Ohhh... yeah. I was wondering when we were going to get to that. Accounting. At Temple."

"Accounting?"

"Yeah."

"Fun."

"No, it's not. It's shit. I hate it. But you can make a fuck-ton of money and the world will always need accountants. At least that's what my guidance counselor told me."

He stared at his beer.

She felt something click.

It wasn't love or attraction or anything, kismet or whatever you'd call it. Her previous introductions to guys had always been more primal. Or pathetic. This was more personal.

She watched him smile and complain about classes. She watched him order another round of drinks. He asked a barrage of questions. She was too exhausted to fight. She answered them.

And he listened.

They sat in the bar for another hour before she decided she needed something to eat. He said he'd take her. She said no thanks. She needed to be alone.

He looked at her a long moment and nodded. "I've got a pretty clear understanding of the Allen family history. I got why you came up here. I got that you're actually twenty and not twenty-one, but it'll be our little secret."

"Thank you."

"And I hope we hang out again."

"You do, huh?"

"Yeah."

"Why's that?"

"Well... because you don't know shit about me, lady."

She laughed. "Touché. Yeah. OK. Give me your number."

"Why don't you give me your number?"

"Because I just moved here and I don't have one."

He looked at her closely. "That might actually be true. It *sounds* like bullshit..."

"Whatever."

"But I'll take your word for it." Alex wrote his number down on a receipt in his pocket, handed it to her.

"Yeah, well, OK. Thanks for the company, Alex."

"Thanks for talking to me, Carla."

He held out his hand. She looked at it a moment, took it, shook it, and walked out of the bar.

She found a 7-11, bought two hot dogs, a coke, some chips, a bottle of water and a brownie.

She got back into her apartment, ate the hotdogs, ate the chips, ate the brownie... in that order.

She unpacked some pajamas and her toothbrush and toothpaste. She went to the bathroom, brushed her teeth, changed, fell onto the unmade bed, and immediately started crying when she realized she hadn't told her mother what happened.

CHAPTER NINE

Present day. An hour outside of New York City, John stopped for coffee and a Danish at a diner that looked straight out of *Happy Days* or *American Graffiti*. Or *Diner*.

It's a wonder so many of these places still exist, he thought, and waited for his coffee to cool down a bit. He'd already eaten half of his cheese Danish, and he was considering ordering another.

He flexed his right hand. It popped two or three times. He figured one day it would lead to severe arthritis. If he lived that long.

Hal and I are falling apart, he thought, and that nagging question he hated asking himself drifted back.

Just how long can we keep this up?

The sedan was in the back. He'd given it a wipe down, just in case he had to walk away, and left the windows open to try and air it out. The diner was practically empty on the cold, late afternoon. He half expected there to be a police officer or two, but it was just locals. The waitresses were gossiping, the bus boys were chatting in Spanish, and the cooks were waiting for something to do. Behind the register, an old lady was doing a crossword puzzle or Sudoku or whatever.

He spent a lot of time in diners like this over the years. Gino D'Escopio, the brother of the Scorpion, took him under his wing shortly after they met that night in the limo. Gino loved meeting at the diner on Astoria Boulevard and 31st Street, The Neptune. He loved the look of it, the baked-in smell, the revolving door of twenty-something waitresses, and some of the food.

Gino started him off slow at first. Small jobs. Mostly it was drop-offs and pick-ups here and there throughout the city. Whether it was money or drugs or what, John didn't ask and didn't care. He created an internal working scenario that made the job morally and ethically ambiguous. For a very long time, he was fine with lying to himself.

His thinking was: who was he hurting? *Him*, personally?

Facilitating? Well... that was overthinking things.

He'd never had any interest in the drug business, let alone in being any kind of criminal, even a clandestine one. But the money was impossible to deny. And, he had to admit... it was fun.

It ended up being reasonably safe work, since he was picking up for Gino. The people he interacted with knew who he worked for, which was enough to get him in and out without trouble. Some would inevitably front here and there, acting like they'd been disrespected out of thin air. John didn't engage. It was safer to say, "I guess we have a problem, then," and go to leave. Then the hemming and hawing would start, maybe some anger, maybe a gun placed on a table. A whole lot of talk, too. Usually, they came to their senses. Gino didn't work with stupid people... for the most part. And certainly not for very long.

Knowing the city like the back of his hand, taking back streets, scenic routes, what Gino always frustratingly referred to as *the fucking long way*, John managed to stay out of trouble while on the road, too.

Maybe it was paranoia. Maybe he was smarter than he thought. One of the things he started paying attention to was whether anyone was following him. The problem was, as soon as he started paying attention, he'd find himself panicked when a car or a van or a truck followed him for more than a few blocks. It took a while to let that initial feeling go. To be patient. He would pay closer attention to the cars he was concerned about, and would work the streets in random patterns until satisfied.

He hadn't been hassled by rival families, or stolen from. Locations he visited hadn't been raided. Gino hadn't mentioned any problems with him from anyone.

Still, he stayed vigilant.

After a while, he started making real money. Not fistfuls, but he was left with a chunk of change at the end of each month, after bills and rent and food and his cable bill.

The day after the Scorpion was assassinated John went to Abbas's home. He tried to explain to him that he'd gotten into an accident and that the car was totaled.

Abbas said he wanted to see the cab. "For the insurance. Are you OK? You look OK. You're walking OK. What kind of accident? Whose fault was it? Is your back OK? Where is the cab now? Why didn't the police contact me?"

John tried to make up some excuses.

Abbas wasn't stupid.

Neither was his wife.

John got him out of the house and walked him down the block and told him what had happened. He left the names out. Abbas became increasingly agitated. John said they'd have a new cab in the morning, same medallion, and he'd have the car free and clear.

"No."

"Abbas—"

"No. I don't deal with such people."

"They don't want anything from you—"

"No! I know all about these people, they'll come back—"

"They won't."

"How do you know that? How can you know that?"

"I can't say."

"See? These people cannot be trusted!"

"Abbas—"

"No!"

John grabbed him by the arm. "Listen to me. They were going to kill me, those men. They were going to fucking kill me. Now, I can't give you all the details, and believe me, you don't want them, but what I did... trust me, I'm these people's best fucking friend right now and a cab is nothing. It's nothing, Abbas. It's fucking nothing compared to my life. Right? Isn't that right?"

"Of course, John, but—"

"Take the cab. I swear on my mother, you'll never hear from them again. This is how I am getting rewarded. It's *their* debt. Not yours, not mine. Not ever. I swear to God. Take it. *Sell it* if you want to, but just take it."

John shook Abbas's hand and then hugged him.

Abbas took delivery of the cab the next day, a brand new Crown Victoria, decked out: A/C, stereo, CD player, V8. It put his other cars to shame. It stayed in Abbas's garage overnight so he could sleep on it.

In the morning, he put it up for sale.

Three months later, John got a license to carry, his paperwork fast-tracked through back channels. He bought a 9mm and learned how to use it. One of the things he figured was, as much as he wanted to bring some dignity to crime, he was way in the minority.

He'd been driving a loaner since he started working for Gino, a boring four-door with a working radio, heat, air conditioning—the usual. It did the job and was inconspicuous. On his days off he'd drive out of the city here and there, usually for a long weekend.

The scenery was nice. The car was the pits.

And then one day, out of the corner of his eye, he saw Blue. He braked hard. Didn't really know why. Almost caused an accident. He reversed and saw her alone, surrounded by weeds in an abandoned car lot in Jersey, after making a drop. He got out and went to the fence for a closer look.

A 1970 Dodge Charger with a manual transmission that had, at one time, been a dark metallic blue. Black top. It was rusty and sun faded and an echo of its former self. The interior looked like it had been nested in by spiders and bugs, squirrels and other creatures that had sought refuge over the years, but even in the condition he'd found it in, it had the meanest front grill John had ever seen. Like, a sliver of something from another dimension had broken through... and it was angry.

It looked like she hadn't been moved in years. Weeds grown up around the wheels, no tire tracks. He did as close to a 360 on it as he could. No *For Sale* sign.

He got home and couldn't get her out of his mind. He'd never been a car fetishist. He'd never thought of them as more than tools. A thing to get from here to there. But there was something... he couldn't put a finger on it. It was almost a romantic feeling. Or a longing. Which was ridiculous.

Right?

He dressed all in black, grabbed work gloves, bolt cutters, and a small flashlight he could put into his mouth. He brought the gun, too.

He borrowed a flatbed tow truck from an auto repair shop Gino owned, and went back the next night.

There's something about stealing something one believes is rightfully theirs. All of the anxiety, all of the fear... it turns into purpose. John drove up and stopped across the street, waited. It was three a.m. and the place was a ghost town. No cars, no pedestrians. No sound at all.

The quietest night he could remember—ever.

He drove the truck over, got out and shut the driver-side door gently. A street lamp provided enough light and, once he felt secure, he grabbed the bolt cutters and snapped the lock off the gate. There were six cars inside the lot. Half looked like they were in use, the rest were junkers, including the Charger. John reversed the truck into the lot and brought it as close to the trunk as he could get.

He dropped the flatbed by the back of the Charger. He grabbed the tow chain from the back of the truck and brought it under her, found two secure latch points on the undercarriage. He walked over to the Charger's driver side and opened the door.

He took a look around the neighborhood. Nothing doing.

John sat down and saw that the keys were in the ignition. "Jesus Christ," he said. No sense turning it on. He put the car into neutral and unlocked the parking brake.

He got out, closed the door, jogged over to the truck and hit the hydraulics that pulled the Charger onto the flatbed.

He prayed that the undercarriage would hold. It did.

He secured the front of the car to the bed, jumped up, put the parking brake back on, and went to leave.

Standing outside the gate was a man. Medium build. Late fifties. Holding a baseball bat.

"Hi," he said.

John swallowed. "Hi."

"You stealing my lady?" He patted the bat in his hand twice.

John said the only thing that came to mind. "Yeah."

"Just like that?"

"Well… shit. Yeah. Sorry."

"You're sorry?"

"Well, I gotta be honest, sir. She looked like she was going to waste here; I didn't think anyone cared about her."

"Well, I do. Not that it's doing her much good." He walked over. Worn looking. Hard eyes, but reasonable. "Two thousand."

John arched an eyebrow. He'd done the heavy lifting already. He had the 9mm. He had almost a foot on the guy.

John had never owned a car before. He looked at her and smiled. "Deal. I'll bring it by tomorrow."

"You expect me to believe you're going to come by and—"

"Mister, I don't lie. Here's…" he dug into his wallet… "Eight hundred. I'll be back with the rest. Tomorrow."

The guy counted it. He turned his head, looked back at John. "And you owe me a new lock."

"You got it."

John towed the Charger back to the auto shop in Queens, locked it in an empty stall, went home, slept for eleven hours. He woke up, ate breakfast, drove back to Jersey and gave the man the twelve hundred and a new lock. They shook hands and parted ways.

He spent the next two years fixing Blue up. All of his spare money went into her.

Gino called it the Money Pit Car. He thought that was hysterical.

John combed the internet for parts. eBay ended up being a major boon for the rear-view and side mirrors, a new dashboard, an original gear shift. He drove all the way to North Carolina to buy an original passenger seat and a left taillight.

One by one, the pieces came together.

In late July of 2000, John was driving through Gravesend, on Lake Street, after a pick-up. He'd finally gotten Blue in driving condition and was taking her out for a spin. She still needed a ton of work. The driver seat was a springy mess, the paint job was still faded. Rust was eating out the front driver-side wheel well and under the trunk.

But he was happy. The sound of that car made him happier than—

A red Corvette ZR-1 that had seen better days abruptly screeched to a stop in front of him.

John hit the brakes just in time. He was about to lower his window and yell at the guy when a black Jeep slammed into the back of his car at an angle, sending John against the steering wheel, hard. He felt a rib break, maybe two, and the wind got knocked out of him. He couldn't breathe, and he was seeing bright spots at the corners of his vision. There was a strong feeling of déjà vu.

From the Corvette, a guy got out with an assault rifle. It was the kind he'd seen in a thousand movies, but couldn't put a name to it. The guy was white, red hair, mustache, Irish looking. He walked up to the driver-side window, reared back with the rifle and smashed it.

Just smashed it. An original.

The 9mm was under his seat. Not totally out of reach, but—

John groaned in pain, in frustration as the rifle barrel was pushed against his cheek.

70

OK, OK, assault rifle trumps semi-automatic. Jeez.

Later on at home, he would remember strange details about the day. One of the Vette's taillights was broken, replaced by layer after layer of red tape. He'd stopped next to an almost cherry 1953 Chrysler Imperial—black, beautifully polished, and somewhere deep down, John figured the owner was a World War II vet. Or maybe Korea. Heat radiated off of the car in waves.

Four of the houses on the right side of the street had perfectly formed hedges. One was a mess.

There were eight electric lines stretched across the street.

The barrel was cool against his skin.

It was the first time John had been threatened close up. He fought through the pain in his chest, got some of his wind back. His eyesight cleared.

He understood the situation and reacted accordingly. By pissing his pants.

Through the rear view mirror, he saw a guy get out of the Jeep with his own assault rifle and watch the street.

"Open the trunk," the guy at his cheek said. Definitely Irish.

"I can't," John said.

"The fuck you mean you can't? Hit the button for the trunk!"

John shifted his gaze to the Irishman. "Hit the button? It's a fucking 1970 Dodge Charger, not a minivan."

The guy looked at the car. "So get out and unlock the fucking trunk!" He pulled the gun back.

John remembered wanting to say to him: *You know, you already have a gun in my face, do you really need to yell at me?* But he kept it to himself.

It was daytime, and they were in a very Hasidic area of Brooklyn. The houses lining the streets were all two stories, with small yards and porches out front... and people were starting to get curious. John didn't know the type of men these were, whether they'd panic easy or not, so he got out slowly, painfully, grabbed the keys out of the ignition and made his way to the back of the car where he saw the damage.

"GodDAMMIT!" he yelled when he saw the back of his baby. Forgetting where he was for a second—the situation, the guns—he felt a pang of anger, of depression, said, "Can you believe it..." to no one in particular, and shook his head. While not a total wreck, there was a sizable dent in the trunk.

"What?" Irish asked.

He looked over and, sure enough, the left taillight was crushed. "Oh, man, do you know how long it took me to find that—"

"Open the TRUNK!" the Irishman yelled and pushed John towards it.

John went to the trunk and attempted to open it. The lock was bent and the key wouldn't fit. "Won't open."

"What?"

"It. Won't. Open." He showed the Irishman, trying to put the key in.

"Bullshit."

"Come on, man. Are you fucking blind? Watch!" He tried again.

The guy from the Jeep looked at the Irishman. "Come on, dude! Let's get the fuck out of here!"

Irish pushed John out of the way. "OK, stand back."

"Stand ba—?"

The Irishman opened fire.

The reverb from the gunfire was so loud, so close, that John heard screaming from some of the stay-at-home moms. More than a dozen rounds perforated the back of her. John gritted his teeth as he started counting holes.

And the trunk still wasn't open.

Nineteen. Twenty. Twenty-one.

Twenty-one. Jesus.

Where the fuck am I going to find a new trunk lid?

Irish went over to the trunk, bashed it once, twice, three times with the butt of his rifle. It finally opened.

John shook his head, said, "Fuck, man, like you couldn't have tried that in the first—"

"Shut UP!" Irish yelled. "If he moves, shoot him," he said to his partner. John put his hands up, resigned.

A third car showed up behind the Jeep and started honking.

In the trunk were two briefcases. Both with bullet holes. John wasn't sure what was in the cases, but they weren't leaking. Not this time.

Irish slung the rifle over his shoulder, reached in, grabbed the cases and tore ass towards the Vette. His partner turned around and saw an old Jewish man in the third car, honking and gesturing to the three of them, as if seeing a hold-up with assault rifles in broad daylight was a daily occurrence.

"Come on!" Irish said to his partner.

He looked at the Jeep. "But what about the—"

"LEAVE IT!" Irish screamed, and got into the Corvette's driver seat. His partner ran for the passenger side, climbed in and the car streaked off. John noticed, at the last second, that there was no license plate in the back.

He relaxed against Blue, wiped sweat off of his face. His heart was pounding. He checked his pulse at his neck but couldn't remember how to gauge it.

The old Jewish guy was still honking his horn.

John laughed.

Old ladies, middle-aged women, young mothers, children—they all watched. They'd have something to talk about for weeks.

John looked up at the sky, thankful for the dark jeans that hid his piss stain.

73

CHAPTER TEN

"Well, I'd say that the city is full of heroes. Cops, firefighters. Ordinary people you don't hear about because they're doing, you know, they're helping people every day with things that they need, not necessarily stopping crime or whatever."

It was Hal's eighth interview in two days. He was getting tongue-tied.

"I was just in the right place at the right time," he said humbly, sheepishly. Sally's advice whenever he was about to make an appearance was be approachable.

"And thank God you were!" the host of *Morning in America* said. Nancy Altman, mid-forties, very attractive, blonde, fit, wearing a smart business outfit. She'd been in the business for twenty years. Jake Thompson was next to her. Chiseled jaw, full-bodied head of hair, tan, thirty maybe. Too handsome. He had the air of being a kept man. Professionally or not, it was hard to tell.

Hal knew the feeling.

"Our guest today has been Hal Shipley, hero of the A train, of Manhattan, and of New York City. Thank you so much for joining us."

"Yes, thank you," Jake said. He'd barely gotten a word in in the entire interview.

"Thank you, Jake. Nancy."

"And we'll be back, after this."

"And we're out!" someone said.

Hal unhooked the microphone from his lapel. He shook hands with the hosts, gave the man a knowing nod and wink, and left the stage.

Sally was waiting in the wings. Her article, *The Tragic Life of a Hero*, had been picked up nationally. There was early talk of a Pulitzer.

Practically overnight, Hal had gotten a call from the chief of police, the mayor, the governor, four New York congressmen and women, and two state senators.

Someone told him it was an election year.

"That was fantastic," Sally said, straightening his lapel and tie.

"Isn't it a bit late for doing that?" he asked.

"We're going out in public," she said. "It's never too late. We have to work on your posture."

"Come on."

"It's important. For the photos."

"No one gives a shit about my posture; they're all looking at my gigantic stomach, anyway."

"I'm not worried about your stomach. I'm worried about your chins."

He sighed. She had an answer for everything. And she was right. Every time.

They had lunch at Le Cirque. Hal had no idea what a Le Cirque was, but the place was packed and had a dress code. At lunch.

He'd been with Sally pretty much constantly since their first night together. She was grooming him—her words—to take advantage of the story for as long as humanly possible. "The end goal here is a job. A well-paid job. Preferably in public service, medium to high profile. Not that you should run for office."

"I don't want to run for office."

"Like I said," she gestured, and looked at her food. "But it's important that you keep this momentum going. You don't want to run for office *now*, but..." She dragged her fork around and ate what clung to it.

"Listen, I don't... I'm not sure I want the momentum to keep going." He didn't mind telling his story over and over again, but it seemed to be getting to the point that people knew all the bullet points before he even opened his mouth. He was having an impossible time coming at the story from a fresh perspective, and he didn't want to be that guy who lived off of something forever.

"Sweetheart, this... this is once-in-a-lifetime opportunity land. People *wish* they could fake the kind of thing you just fell into. In fact, *they try* and fake it, and it ends up fucking them spectacularly in the end. Your story is one hundred percent genuine. It's the kind of deal where you write your own ticket."

"To do what?"

"*Not be poor*," she said, like it was the most obvious answer in the world.

He couldn't argue with that.

He looked around the place. He was in a social sphere he'd never experienced before. The people looked untouchable.

The food was very good, but the conversation turned into a headache and they left shortly after finishing their meals.

She had him go to a meet-and-greet with some people down at City Hall. He shook some hands, paid attention to his posture, had some photos taken, answered some questions.

Every once in a while someone would ask, "Where are you living now?" It was inevitable. The entire city knew he was homeless. His only answer was to say, "With Sally. She's been very generous."

It was another facet of the situation that bothered him. And while he was happy with the home and the sex and the general care she took of him, he was concerned where it was leading. She'd bought him clothes, fed him, but he also felt like she was using him. Her career, after the story, was soaring upwards, rocket speed. She'd gotten some job offers at bigger papers, gotten an agent. They were waiting to see if there would be a salary bidding war.

He felt, under the circumstances, that it was understandable. Reasonable even, their give and take. But he also felt trapped... and, more and more, Hal just wanted to be left alone.

By the time they got home that night, he had to say no. No more conversations about tomorrow, no more conversations about future meetings and how he should act. No more scheduling. "Please."

"Fine," she said, but in a way that meant anything but.

"Honey, I'm just tired."

"I said fine, so it's fine. It's not like I'm trying to help or anything." And then there was the silence. It hung there and dragged for an eternity. Then it evolved from silence to waiting for an apology.

He had a feeling she wasn't going to wait long.

He didn't think he had it in him. The past two weeks of constant attention, of networking and photos and interviews and handshaking. He didn't understand the type of person who craved this kind of life. Who sought it out. Who prayed for it.

But he wasn't stupid.

Hal mentally acquiesced, and sighed, spread his hands out, looking for forgiveness. "I'm sorry. I hope you know I appreciate all you're doing."

"I don't."

Oh boy. He dropped his arms. "OK, well, I do. OK? I'm tired. Beyond tired. I just need to stop right now and sleep and then we can go over all this tomorrow." His eyelids were drooping.

"But it's important."

"I understand. But sweetheart, I won't remember it, because my fucking brain is mush."

"Don't use that language."

"What language?"

"Fucking."

"But—"

"Don't use it. It's a bad habit, especially in front of other people. Just don't."

He sighed. "OK. OK, I get it. You're right. OK."

He held his arms out to her again. She begrudgingly entered them. Whether out of caring or self-preservation, he couldn't tell. Not that it mattered at this point.

They went to sleep.

Him, out like a light.

Her, thinking of the future.

The next day, Hal decided it was time for him to move on when he found out she'd gotten him another three interviews. He wasn't part of the decision-making process anymore. Not that he ever had been...

The first interview was a live daytime talk show where he was seated at a table, surrounded by women of all different ethnicities, who praised his intervening. Latisha Bowman was also seated at the table next to him. It was the first time he'd seen her since being invited to her church a week after the attack. He'd spoken briefly to the congregation. Near the end of the service, the pastor presented him with a check for three thousand dollars. Donations from church members. He felt nauseous accepting the check and when he got home that night tore it up. Sally found the pieces and asked him about it. Hal said, "I'm not going to accept money for doing the right thing."

She jumped him right then and there.

Latisha talked about her experience in frightening detail. Sally's article covered most of it, but it was the first time Latisha had told her story live and in person. It made for fucking great television.

And Hal realized he never wanted to speak of it ever again.

After the first segment, the show pivoted to issues that he knew nothing about. Or, at least, couldn't talk about without sounding like an opinionated ass.

"Never share your opinions with people unless they are the majority's. Fringe opinions alienate audiences. Right now, everyone loves you. Say the wrong thing and you'll be a leper the rest of your life." That was Sally again, over drinks or at home or in bed. "The rules of being a public figure are sometimes easy to forget, but it only takes one fuck-up, so pay attention."

Topics came fast and furious, and with little to no conversational structure. Latisha, unlike Hal, had no problem being opinionated, and the audience ate it up. Being a nurse, she felt she was on the front line of a number of women's issues, from abortion to equal pay, birth control, maternal rights. She was able to talk intelligently about sexual assault statistics in the city, and how the NYPD and Transit Authority were starting a new initiative to protect late-night subway riders.

After the second question where Hal didn't provide an answer that got applause, the panel kept him out of the conversation. He was grateful.

By the time the show was finished, he still got a great response. Thanks from the panel, a hug and kiss from Latisha, and a nice send-off from the audience.

Sally was waiting, a smile on her face. Twenty feet away, she gave him a big thumbs-up. He smiled as the audio guy took his mic off. A producer came over and shook his hand, clamped his other hand on Hal's shoulder, gave it a squeeze and said, "You should have shot them or stabbed them or whatever. Something. Or the police should have. But, anyway, we need more people like you."

Hal nodded, said thank you, walked over to Sally who hugged him. He closed his eyes, decided to take the leap and whispered, "That was the last one. No more."

She was smiling as she took his arm and waved to people she knew or wanted to know. Smiling when they got into the full elevator, and smiling when they were out in the lobby.

By the time they got outside and he started down the street, he wasn't surprised when he turned around and saw she was gone.

He spent the day walking, seeing the city with a new perspective. As a human being wearing a suit, not worn-out clothes that hung on him like he was an old, warped hanger. It was the first time he'd been alone in two weeks.

People ignored him, but for different reasons.

He got lunch, walked around some more. Sat for a bit, bought a hot dog bun from a street vendor and fed some pigeons. He got dinner—tacos and a beer—and then hiked back to Sally's place in the hopes that she wouldn't be home.

She was.

He buzzed and she let him in. The visit was short.

"You're making a mistake," she said.

"Maybe," he said back. They stared at each other in the foyer of her apartment. "Or maybe I've done enough."

"Enough for who?"

She'd packed a bag for him, handed him an envelope with five hundred dollars, and said good luck.

He was grateful. He hugged her.

After a while she hugged him back.

Three days later she was in the news as the Good Samaritan who took in a local hero, and they were still good friends. "In the end," she told Nancy Altman during a one-on-one segment, "Hal felt, in his heart, that he had to find his own way. And I respected that."

He'd watched the interview in a diner, a cup of coffee perched at his lips the entire time, waiting for the other shoe to drop. Whatever it might be.

It didn't.

Sally went on to become a famous face and voice within the national news scene. A mouthpiece for both the downtrodden and the endless fight against corruption. She would also go on to win the Pulitzer Prize.

Nineteen years later, their paths would cross again under terrible circumstances.

CHAPTER ELEVEN

In Carla's third year of nursing school, coffee became the official staple. Alcohol became the coping mechanism.

Four days of classes, one day of clinical. Classes were 9 a.m. to 4 or 5 p.m. Clinical ran ten to twelve hours, starting at 7 a.m. each Thursday.

"You show up late for classes, that's on the teacher to decide what to do with you. Show up for clinical late? The first time we'll reward you with some extra hours. The second time, we'll just bounce your ass out of here. No ifs, ands, or buts. Got it?"

That was the long and the short of clinical orientation.

Classes.

Pharmacology, Science of Nursing Fundamentals, Ethics, Pathophysiology, Evidence Based Practice, Health Policy, and Physical Assessment, or what her fellow students called Molesting 101.

She fell in with a group straight away. No sob story about Greg, no nothing. She was just a transfer from the oppressive heat of Tampa, Florida. Most people in her class were from up north and they equated the south with two things: heat and stupidity. She didn't argue the point, especially after they gave her a pass for the presence of mind to "get the fuck out of that shithole."

She didn't argue that point, either.

The group got along well enough and shared in the fun times, the drama, the frustration. They leaned on each other when they could. All of them were working on little to no sleep, with slight reprieves solely during late nights and weekends. They worked hard. They partied hard. They paid for it in the morning and repeated the pattern. It seemed the only way to survive.

Carla was the only one working odd nights and a weekend shift when she could get it. Her first job in Philly had been at an ice cream shop in Old City, serving tourists who were in town to see Independence Hall and the Liberty Bell. She got the job on a lark, walking down Market Street after she treated herself to dinner at the Reading Terminal Market. She'd gotten a cheese steak and some fries and a beer.

The shop had a "help wanted" sign in the window. They didn't even ask her to fill out an application.

Shakes, cups, cones. Tourists asking for samples and then saying: "OK, thanks anyway," after the fifth tasting. She was on her feet for six hours a shift. She split tips with five teenagers who acted as though they had fantastic lives in store for them.

She was making a little under $200 a week. Just enough for rent and food. Her mom sent her an extra $50 a month. "You know. To help."

Carla couldn't thank her enough.

Alex was true to his word. They stayed friends and got along better than she expected. Sometimes he'd keep her company at the ice cream place. He was working his way through the flavors alphabetically. He was on Eggnog.

She rarely got to hang out with him outside of the shop, but talked on the phone with him a few nights a week. When they did get together, he would introduce her to his friends. None of them were accounting majors. "Honest," he said. "I don't get along with any of them. They're all so... stiff."

She tried to get six hours of sleep a night. It rarely happened.

If classes were the bane of her existence, clinical hours were hell on Earth.

7 a.m. was bad enough after her workload. Walking into the hospital where it was all action or stress or screaming all the time... it

felt like a war zone. The Hospital of the University of Pennsylvania was the lower right of a triangle of hospitals in one of the worst parts of Philadelphia. Belmont Behavioral was at the top of the pyramid. Mercy was on the bottom left. In the center was West Philadelphia, at the tail end of the crack epidemic.

Tampa seemed like a walk in the park compared to Philly. Greg had never said a thing about how bad things had gotten in his hometown. Odds were, where he lived, he never saw a thing.

Sue Caruthers was the faculty liaison who handed out the assignments for third years. Two students, Brian Langford and Brenda Coolidge, showed up three and four minutes late. They were assigned to Psych straight away. Carla thought she saw a hint of satisfaction when Caruthers sent them off into what could only be described as the great unknown.

Carla got sent to Med Surg, a floor dedicated to those who'd already been through their surgery or had been diagnosed successfully and were receiving treatment.

Her nurse preceptor was Abigail Bowman, a tall, slightly overweight Black woman who looked thirty, acted fifty, and had the energy of a teenager. Carla and three other nurses followed her as best they could as she went from room to room and handed off patients to each of them.

"Now listen, you hear? I take you under my wing it means I'm responsible for all the shit you do to these fine people. You have a question, ASK. Even if it's something you've done a hundred times. I get it. You've got your classes and your personal lives and whatever. We've all been through it. You come here exhausted, honey, baby, sweet child, we're *all* exhausted. But we've got the experience and you don't. So ASK. Don't be stupid and think you know more than we do. You DON'T. Uh uh." She huddled them all up close. "You fuck up in here and get my malpractice premiums up? I'll find you and kill you and then haunt you in hell. You hear?"

Carla liked her straight away.

She was assigned two patients. Both Black. One old, one young. The old man, Mr. Castle, had gotten pneumonia and was receiving an IV of antibiotics, which was making him shit himself endlessly. He was constantly saying he was sorry. His wife sat there watching television, ignoring Carla while she did her work. The smell didn't seem to bother her.

"I figured I'd start you off in the deep end," Abigail said. "No pun intended. We don't have a bowel blockage for you to deal with today, but rest assured..."

The young guy, James, was there for knee surgery. He was nineteen and deeply depressed. His football career was basically over. He didn't talk much. He said hello. He held out his arm for Carla to take his vitals, opened his mouth when she took his temperature.

"Tragic," Abigail said as they walked away. "Got hit by a car in just the wrong spot." She pointed to her knee. "He played for Villanova. Just such a shame."

"What's he going to do now?"

"I don't know," Abigail said as they walked down the corridor. "I don't think it's the kind of thing people bounce back from. That's going to haunt him the rest of his life. I've seen it before." She stopped outside a room. "Now, him... this is something you're going to have to get used to. I'll deal with him today."

The kid had a gunshot wound in his arm—through and through, right below the left shoulder, severing his bicep. He was young. He was in high school. Ganged up. He was brought in wearing colors. The cops had come by the hospital when he got out of surgery. He was a bystander, they weren't arresting him, but they gave him a hard time to identify the shooter. He kept his mouth shut.

He had a girl that visited him. She was pregnant. He was seventeen. She was younger.

He cursed, he kicked the bed, he slapped Abigail's hand away when she went to take his pulse. He told her to fuck herself when she went to take his blood pressure. Carla looked inside and got a "What are you looking at, bitch?"

84

They took a coffee break after.

"You better get used to it."

"Used to what?"

"The violence. And the racism. We're in the Bermuda Triangle. At least, that's what I call it. We get some of the hard cases. Some go to Mercy. They send a lot of the crackheads up to Belmont because they don't know what to do with them here, *and* they're more equipped, personnel wise."

"It's that bad, huh?"

Abigail grabbed two mugs, started fixing them coffees. "Most of the time, people want to just get better and get home. They make for long shifts, but they're not bad ones. You'll always remember the bad patients, because they'll ruin your day like that." She snapped her fingers. "It's either older people or gang bangers like that piece of work. They're scared. They're vulnerable. They don't want to rely on someone like you. Or me. It's not like he almost died, but he could have. A few inches here or there, you know. He'll be home in a few days and it's not like he's got anything to look forward to. Not at his age. There's a good chance we'll see him again the way things are going out there."

Carla sighed, feeling for the first time that she might be in over her head. "Fucking Greg," she said under her breath.

"Fucking who?"

"Long story. I just... it didn't occur to me that it would be this rough here."

"Well, hospitals in places like this are like the sea wall. It's holding for now, but it won't hold forever." She handed Carla her cup of coffee. "Sometimes you WISH for the comments, you know what I'm saying? So you can at least be angry. Stay angry. You should hear some of the white patients. I've been called every name in the BOOK. You'll see. Stick around long enough you'll get a bingo card. Rows full of swear words. Winner gets a box of wine at the end of the week."

The shift was long. It was difficult. There was always something to do, and she knew she didn't see half of what she was supposed to. Most of the other nurses treated her like they'd never see her again.

By the second week, Mr. Castle and James were gone and replaced with two new patients. Same with the gunshot kid. By the third, she couldn't remember the names of most of the patients she'd helped.

Around the fourth week, Gerry, one of the guys in her classes, came and asked if she wanted some Adderall, like he was asking an everyday question. She'd never heard of it before nursing school. It was everywhere.

By mid-semester, coffee simply wasn't cutting it. By the end of the semester she was taking it three or four times a week.

He took pity on her with the pricing.

Carla secretly thanked God that Gerry was gay.

As the weeks went by, the nursing staff slowly warmed up to her. Abigail helped with that.

The doctors were a different story. They were either always frustrated or always flirting. She'd gotten four marriage proposals, some light harassment, and three outright propositions. None of them were even remotely appealing.

"If I threatened to cut Dr. Graham's dick off—"

The nurses' station burst into laughter.

"—do you think I'd still get to graduate?" Carla asked.

"Yeah," Nurse Pendleton said. "With honors!"

More laughter.

Carla found that the good times were few and far between, but gave them energy when they needed it most. She was running on fumes by that point, and the worst part was, Carla couldn't stand to look at ice cream any more, let alone eat it.

Abigail walked with Carla to her next patient. She gave her the sideways glance once-over. "What in God's name are you doing to yourself, girl?"

"What do you mean?"

"You look like you just WALKED a marathon. Twice."

Carla laughed. "Just... classes and clinical and the tests and the studying..."

"Yeah."

"And the job."

"The what now?"

"Yeah, I work at an ice cream shop down on—"

"You WHAT?"

"Yeah, an ice cream shop on—"

"OK, hold up, hold up." They stopped. "First off... why don't you bring any ice cream to work?"

"I, uh, I don't know..."

"And second, I honestly thought you were coming in here with a perfume that smelled like... what?"

"Bubble gum."

"That's it! For the life of me, I couldn't figure out why this bleach blonde—"

"Bleach... blonde?"

"At first I thought it was cotton candy—"

"We have cotton... have you ever even seen someone with bleach-blonde hair?"

"But bubble gum! Really? People eat bubble gum ice cream?"

"You wouldn't fucking believe it."

"Is it gross?"

"It's gross."

"It SOUNDS gross, my GOD. And so you work at night scooping ice cream."

"Yeah."

"For what?"

"So I can afford my apartment."

"No, I mean, for how much?"

"A little over minimum wage."

"Which is what?"

"Six dollars an hour."

"JESUS!"

People in the hallway stopped.

Abigail crossed herself. "Honey, you'd make more money sucking DICK!"

"I know..."

"Well, OK, don't go doing that now. You're on your way to a career and we don't need you getting bailed out and all..." Abigail smoothed out Carla's scrubs. "You're smart. You're punctual. You've got an attitude that says 'don't fuck with me.'"

"Yeah. It's perfect for the tourist ice cream trade."

Abigail laughed. "I bet. But I've got a friend down at the Trauma Center who needs a medical scribe."

"OK..."

"Know what that is?"

"Sort of."

"You'd be shadowing a physician, logging intakes. Basically a written record of everything that happens with a patient under the doctor assigned to you."

"OK... for how much?"

"I can get you... ten an hour?"

"What?"

"Ten an hour. At least."

Carla visibly shook. The words, the stress, the exhaustion. The extra $120 a week. She slid down the far wall in relief. "Abigail, if you could make that happen, I would have your children."

Abigail looked down at her. "Well, how's about I just give you the ones I've got, and we'll call it even."

CHAPTER TWELVE

"**B**oth of them were Irish?"

"No, just the one guy. The other guy was just... white. Non-denominational."

Gino was pissed. "You think this is funny?"

"What? No—"

"And what did he say?"

"Who?"

"The fucking Irishman!"

"'Open the fucking trunk.' That's a direct quote."

"That's it?"

"Well, he almost shot me, so, I don't know, maybe more, I don't remember." John had driven himself to one of Gino's doctors after the robbery. Two broken ribs. The tape on his chest was tight. Made it hard to move and breathe.

Gino studied his face. "And he took both briefcases." It was a statement, not a question.

Four years. John had been working with the D'Escopio family for four years, and not a hiccup. Not a problem on any level. "Yes, both."

"You'd recognize him if you saw him again?"

"Yeah, the dumbass didn't wear a—"

"OK. Paulie is going to take you fishing. You find him, you make sure you find his partner before you kill him, capisci?"

"What?"

"Yeah. Find him, and don't kill him until you find his partner. I can't stress that enough."

"Kill him?"

"Too many guys want to get it over with before finding out what they need to know. They get overly excited and—"

"I'm sorry, kill—"

"Yeah."

"You want me to kill him?"

"This is your mess. Yeah, I want you to kill him."

"I'm not going to kill him," John said, and sat down. His chest hurt. He'd been standing, hadn't asked to sit, hadn't been invited to. The three goons in the room looked half shocked with the breach of etiquette.

Gino looked at him and grinned. He was used to John's bullshit. "You're not?"

"No. That's not... Gino, that's not what I do here. This is a, this isn't a situation that I—"

"You didn't expect this to happen?"

"No. Not that."

"You never thought in your wildest dreams that the guy who takes a fucking muscle car the fucking long way every single fucking time would ever, and I mean ever, get caught with his pants down?"

"That's not what happened."

"It's not?"

"No, it's not."

Gino shook his head, sat down, sighed, got a cigar and did his routine. He rubbed it on his lips for a moment, then put it under his nose and sniffed. Then, more lip rubbing, then he clipped it, lit it, smoked it for a second until it caught, and looked at John. "So what happened? Dazzle me."

"You've got a mole."

"A mole?"

"Yeah."

"Where?"

"At the auto repair shop."

"I've got a mole at the shop."

"The fuck is a mole?" one of the goons asked.

Gino ignored him. "Why do you say that?"

"Because it was the first time I took the car out for a pick-up."

"So?"

"Well, how would they know what to look for if not for the car?"

"Maybe they saw you come out of Darby's." Darby's was a bar in Woodside that Gino owned. It was a drop for a handful of bookies under Gino's protection.

"Maybe. But that would mean they knew Darby's was Darby's, which means they've been watching it for weeks. Maybe even months. I can't remember the last time I took *two* briefcases out of Darby's. Normally it's an envelope; I put it in the glove box. How would they know I was going to be bringing that much back? How would they know it was *me* doing it? And how would they know what I was driving?"

Gino sat there thinking about it for a long time.

"Seriously, what the fuck is a mole?" the goon asked again.

John was steady but nervous. He didn't want to kill anyone. He was happy with the driving and the delivering and the occasional rough-up, but this…

"You're sure it's at the shop."

"Yeah," John said. And he had a pretty good idea who it was. "And I've got a pretty good idea who it was."

"Who?"

"Gordy. Maybe Juan. Maybe both."

"Gordy and Juan. Maybe."

"Yeah."

"OK." Gino leaned back in his chair. "If it's not what you say it is, you're going to find the Irish guy and you, not the guy behind you, not the fucking tooth fairy, you are going to torture him until he tells us who he's working with, and how they found out about this. *And*, who else was in on it. *And*, if he happens to spill as soon as you find him?

Well, you're going to torture him anyway. Then you're going to kill him, and get rid of the body. *Then* you'll kill the partner and the other guys behind this and you won't whine and complain, you'll just do it. And *then*, after all that, you and I are going to have to have a long talk about your place here. Because this, whatever it is you're doing here? It's candyass. And it makes me fucking sick."

CHAPTER THIRTEEN

H al left Sally's building and looked around. The sidewalk was empty in both directions. He was back in familiar territory, alone, and it presented some anxiety.

He found a hotel room through a website via an internet café for $60 a day, in Chinatown. It was a hole in the wall, smelled like used cooking oil, and had low watt bulbs throughout.

He booked it for a week.

He had a hard time sleeping that first night. It wasn't the situation or the unknown. It was the settling noises of the building in the quiet. Thumps, echoes, creaks. Hollow sounds he was unfamiliar with. The street noise didn't help either.

He woke the next morning, got a bacon, egg, and cheese sandwich, got a coffee, and took stock.

He had three outfits: one suit, one pair of jeans, two shirts, a couple of pairs of underwear, socks, a nice pair of shoes, and one pair of sneakers. It all fit in a gym bag.

He brought the suit to a dry cleaner, had them put a rush on it just in case. The lady behind the counter said come back after five o'clock. He said OK.

He had no idea what to do next.

He didn't have a phone or an email account or friends. The Sally thing—he knew the regret he was feeling was out of fear, but the situation had gotten out of hand. Run for office? Public service? What the shit...

He wanted a regular job where he got a paycheck and wasn't bored and could keep his head down. So, he grabbed a *Village Voice* and a *New York Times* and combed through the want ads.

He circled half a dozen jobs that he knew he could do, and that didn't require previous experience. Mostly they were retail register jobs, stock room, etc.

After the sixth interview, he felt his old rock-bottom status take hold. It had been for a stock person at a wine store. The guy who owned the place asked a bunch of questions about varietals, regions, what was dry, what was fruity.

"But it's a stock job, right?" Hal asked.

"Doesn't mean you shouldn't know what we sell. Can I see your résumé?"

Hal said he didn't have one. He had no idea how to make one, no idea what to fill it with. The last real job he had was working at a shitty pharmacy when he was sixteen, stocking shelves, taking out the garbage, baling cardboard. His cousin had gotten him the job. And it wasn't like he could put down the under-the-table jobs he'd gotten when he came back from prison.

The wine store guy gave him a look, that same look he'd gotten from the others. Slightly amused, with a definitive no on the horizon.

He left in the suit that he was starting to hate, thinking public service wasn't sounding so bad any more.

Three days later, no job, no prospects, no résumé.

He was walking west on Canal Street until he hit Mulberry and decided to take a right up through Little Italy. It had been more than a decade since he'd walked through that neighborhood. Not being Italian, or a tourist, he had little interest in the area, but his brain was fried *and* scrambled. He couldn't get the idea of pasta out of his head, like a pregnant woman with a craving.

As he walked past each restaurant, hosts and hostesses called out, trying to entice him to eat at their establishments. He wasn't sure what he was looking for, but he hadn't found it yet. The smells coming out of the restaurants, though... my God.

Passing Hester Street, he saw a line of limousines outside of a restaurant. Angolo's. Yellow tinted stucco and windows with ornate double doors made the place look like an Italian villa. The effect worked. Had the place not looked packed to the gills, he might have given it a shot.

Drivers were here and there, a handful of young Italian men standing outside of the restaurant bullshitting.

Hal walked through the throng, past the limos, daydreaming. He couldn't imagine a life where he had a driver, took meals wherever he wanted, and had enough money to never worry about anything, ever.

He felt another pang of regret.

Sally could have made that happen. He'd flirted with the idea of calling her, of trying to get back together, but he could hear her answer. *"If we're going to do this, it'll be for keeps. I mean the full boat. Like marrying someone for citizenship. Otherwise, that ship has sailed."*

It took a second before he realized someone's hand was on his chest.

"Holy fucking shit!" It was a kid, early twenties, jet black hair, thick eyebrows, slightly tanned, thin, and about half a foot shorter than Hal. Sweating in the late July heat.

Hal stopped, stepped back half a foot, and was surprised to find himself practically surrounded. "Excuse me," he said, and went to move around them.

Jesus, not today, please...

"No, you're the guy, the fucking guy!"

"I'm not—"

"You're the... this is the guy who beat the shit out of those fuckers on the subway!"

Hal was immediately rushed by a throng of young men, all of them slapping his back and arms.

"Hey!" and "Way to go!" and "You should have shot those fucking—"

"Jesus, Marco, you're acting like you've got a hard on!" one of them yelled.

Big laughs.

"Oh, the boss has *got* to meet you," Marco said, took his arm, and dragged him into Angolo's.

The restaurant was longer than Hal had imagined from the outside, with the same yellow stucco walls covering the interior. Most of the tables had been moved from the sides to the center, to allow for family-style serving. There were more than twenty men seated around them.

A dozen waiters were constantly moving about, filling water glasses, wine glasses, removing plates, bringing plates, and generally fussing over their guests.

There was a lot of talking going on in small and not-so-small groups. The men were all dressed in suit jackets with matching pants and white shirts. Hal noticed, strangely, there was not a single tie among them.

Except one.

"Hey, boss," Marco said as he walked over to a particularly large man, whose stomach was slumped down between his legs in a spectacular fashion. "Boss," Marco said again. The guy looked up, mid-conversation.

"Marco, what did I say?" the fat man asked. His face was a mask of consternation, dotted with food.

"But boss..."

"I swear, the grief you give me is not worth it. You *and* your mother. The fuck you interrupting me for?"

"Nardo, I don't have time for this," the guy next to him said. He was smaller, as in thinner, and yet seemed infinitely tougher. He had a comb over, dark eyebrows, square head.

"Paulie, I'm sorry—" Nardo started.

"Don't 'sorry' me," Paulie said. His tone began to quiet the room.

Marco tugged on Hal's arm. "But boss, it's the guy," Marco said, his voice wavering.

"What fucking guy!?" Nardo's voice was cracking. "He looks like he sells fucking tampons. Get him the fuck out of here," he said, trying to get back some of the respect he'd lost.

The table had quieted down full now as heads were turning towards Hal. He felt his body start to shake a bit. His palms were getting sweaty, and he realized that he was witnessing something only prosecutors, district attorneys and FBI agents wanted to be party to. No one else.

Marco tried one last time. "He's the guy! The guy who—"

A hand slammed the table. The entire restaurant went quiet. Even the staff. A man stood up. He was short. Much shorter than Hal. He was immaculately dressed in a three-piece suit of Italian silk, wearing big, square sunglasses. And a tie.

He's the boss, Hal thought to himself. *Of all of them.*

"Nardo, who is this man who's interrupted our meeting?" the tie man asked.

Nardo's eyes widened, turned his face up to Marco, pleading to either get the fuck out or save his life.

"M-my apologies, Don D'Escopio," Marco said to the whole room. His voice echoed off the walls. "This is Hal Shipley. He's the guy who beat the shit, the, uhhh, the crap out of those three guys on the subway. Saved that Black lady's life."

"The one on TV?" Paulie asked, and arched an eyebrow, looked up at Marco.

"Yeah, Paulie. Paul. Mr. Grasso."

Paulie turned to Hal. "That you?"

"Uh, yes. Yes, sir."

"Yes sir? The guy's known me two fucking seconds, I already get a 'sir' out of him. You can't buy that kind of respect!" Laughs down the table. Paulie turned to Nardo. "How is it possible that this guy, this fucking stranger off a street, has more respect for me than someone I've known since we was five, huh, Nardo?"

"Paulie, I'm sorry," Nardo said. He looked at the tie guy. "Gino, I... things got out of hand and I couldn't stop them."

"Couldn't stop them? Or you didn't want to…?" Gino D'Escopio said, shaking his head. He walked over. When he got to Nardo he looked up at Hal's face with half contempt, half humor. He made his way around the table. "You've put me in a position, that's for sure."

"I didn't know they were skimming!"

"Nardo…" Paulie said, putting his hands together, as if he were about to start praying.

"Please, don't kill me," Nardo said, looking like he was ready to shit himself.

Gino turned and looked at him, almost as if wounded.

Paulie was smirking, shaking his head.

Marco, meanwhile, had let go of Hal's arm. He knew his boss had been worried about the meet. Driving into the city, Nardo had been completely distracted… but the idea of him being taken out hadn't crossed Marco's mind. He had no idea things were that bad.

"Kill you? You owe me money, Nardo," Gino chuckled. "Why would I kill you? No. Paulie's going to take over your territory. He's going to run things. You're going to be responsible for getting him up to speed on the day-to-day until we're whole again. You'll be responsible for the…" he looked at Hal, back to Nardo… "for the mess. And the clean-up. Then we'll figure out what to do with you. You've got a week to take care of it. Now get the fuck out of here so I can enjoy my lunch."

"Thank you, Gino. Thank you." Nardo stood up. His back was drenched in sweat. He went to go shake Gino's hand, but he got waved off. Nardo took Marco and left the restaurant.

Gino bent down and said something to Paulie in a whisper. Paulie nodded, took out a cell phone and walked to the back of the restaurant.

Gino straightened up, looked around the room, looked over at Hal and walked over.

His men watched.

Gino stuck his hand out. Hal shook it. "So you're the guy they're talking about in the papers and on the TV."

"Hal Shipley, yes."

"Just yes? No 'sir' this time?"

"I—" Hal said and stuttered, looked around.

After a second, the table broke up in laughter. The men in the room went back to their conversations.

"You eaten?"

"No, sir."

"You can cut that out. Sit down." Hal grabbed a seat by his side. "No, over there. I've still got business to take care of. Lorenzo?" The host came out of nowhere. "Bring him a plate of chicken Fiorentina; it's my personal favorite, and pasta with vodka sauce. Some wine, too." Lorenzo nodded and double-timed it to the kitchen. "You ever eaten here before?" Gino asked.

"No."

"Well, today's your lucky day." And he walked away, back to mid-table.

Hal sat away from the men and watched, listened. A waiter brought him a glass of water. Another brought him a basket of bread and a small dish of olive oil. A third brought him a bottle of red wine, opened it, poured it, left the bottle.

Around the main table, the men didn't speak to anything specific, and when they did, it was in hushed tones that didn't travel.

A plate of food was put in front of him. Rigatoni with vodka sauce. A second plate of food was put in front of him. Steaming, sizzling. Breaded chicken with a slice of eggplant and prosciutto, a slice of mozzarella on a bed of spinach.

It was the best food he'd ever tasted.

CHAPTER FOURTEEN

"**S**he was covered in blood…" That's what Carla heard when she came back with a round of drinks. It was a Friday night. She'd found out earlier that her classmate Brenda had left the program. Michelle, a nosey pain in the ass who loved to gossip, was telling the story. She was from Newark, New Jersey. Carla loved her accent.

Alex was there, along with Tina, Gerry, Madeline, and Conroy, all Carla's classmates. It was two months before the end of their third year.

"Wait, who was?" Alex asked.

"Brenda, I told you—" Carla said.

Michelle said, "OK, so this woman was pre-eclampsia, you know, so she was getting induced."

"What is pre…?" Alex asked.

"Pre-eclampsia. It's when the baby isn't getting enough oxygen and so it releases these chemicals to put pressure on the mother's body for more oxygen," Carla said.

"God," he said.

"But, that pressure puts stress on the mother's vital organs…"

"Fuuuck…"

"And so your blood pressure goes up—"

"Yeah, but she was also getting magnesium," Michelle said.

"OK…" Alex said.

"It lowers your brain excitability, but it also lowers your muscle excitability," Carla said.

"So that's good, right?"

"Not when you're getting induced," Gerry said.

"Jeeeeeeesus—"

"This went on for three days," Michelle said. "Brenda came in on that third day. She was brought up to speed. The physician said it probably wouldn't happen that day. The birth. I mean, this woman was locked UP, you know? Brenda's doing her bed checks, it was her last week of gyno, and all of a sudden, this woman starts crowning. Like, from nowhere. And Betsy, up on three there, she gets Brenda and the two of them grab the woman's legs because this kid is *stuck*. So picture Brenda, right? She's got the woman's leg over her fucking shoulder, 'cause they're trying to—"

"Wait, what?" Alex asked. "Over her what?"

"Like this," Michelle said. She made a motion like she was lugging something heavy over one shoulder.

"You're shitting me."

"Nope."

"But... what about the stirrups?"

"That's some movie shit, boy! Or the world's easiest fucking pregnancy. Like those Catholics who keep breeding..." laughs around the table. "When you need to get a greater angle, you pull those legs apart." Michelle knew she was getting to Alex.

"Jesus."

"Like a wishbone, baby!"

Alex started going a little green.

"Your boy here... not really the cast-iron stomach type is he?" Michelle asked Carla.

"Hard to say. We don't talk about vaginas much. But that is a new shade on him..."

Alex smiled weakly.

Michelle winked.

Carla sat back and watched.

"Don't worry baby, you get sick, I'll take care of you. Now, where was I?"

"Wishbone," Carla said.

The whole table yelled "WISHBONE!"

Except for Alex.

"Yeah! Well, they're holding her open, and the fucking doctor isn't around! A nurse was playing catcher, and the woman is pushing and pushing, and she's thrashing, even though she's on the drugs and all, 'cause she's fucking terrified. And the doctor comes in and at that exact moment... well... the mother got loose and kicked Brenda in the head. Hard. Knocked her right out."

"Fuck! That's awful!" Alex said.

"Oh, look at him, concerned," Michelle said, looking at Alex. "He's so sweet. Yeah. No. That's not even the worst part. Brenda hit the floor just as the kid came out, directly underneath it all, and was covered in blood and afterbirth and shit."

Alex made a noise, covered his mouth and swallowed hard. Even Carla had thrown up a little in her mouth when she heard it the first time.

"She woke up to Betsy and Angela... you know Angela? They were trying to clean her up, but it was too late. She started screaming, threw up and passed out. She had a concussion, too. When she woke up she was screaming again, like she was reliving it, right Maddy?" Maddy nodded. "And that was it. She said fuck it, she'd had enough. Abigail made her wait a day before she quit, just in case she changed her mind. Brenda said she took a three-hour shower and used all the soap and shampoo in her apartment, *and* her roommate's. Next day, she said she could still smell it. Still feel it. She packed it up. So long, Brenda."

"She'd already been struggling," Conroy said. "She wasn't sleeping much, and she had to retake an exam two weeks ago after she failed. Pullman gave her another shot and she passed, but it wrecked her."

102

"How many does that make?" Tina asked. She was on her third martini, and still talking straight.

"Seven this year. Abigail said that wasn't even close to the record," Carla said.

"You've had seven people drop out of the program this *year*?" Alex asked.

"Yeah, and that's just in our class," Gerry said. "I almost quit after that Presidents' Day weekend. Second most violent day in Philadelphia the last ten years. The ER was just gunshot victims and ODs. I slept fourteen hours that Tuesday. Missed all my classes. Went in Wednesday, no one said a word, so…"

"I didn't know that," Carla said, surprised. Gerry shared everything. "You can't leave. I won't get through this shit without you."

"Oh, honey, you know I got you. This woman," he said, touching her shoulder. "With classes and the tests and clinical and her JOB. I just don't know how you do it, Carla."

"I'm a masochist."

"Ooh, really? Did you know that Alex?" Michelle asked.

"No, but I had my suspicions," he said, and smiled at Carla.

"You two been going out long?" Michelle asked coyly.

"We're not going out," Carla said, just a bit too fast.

Alex didn't notice, nodded. "Yeah, we met when she got into town. Been friends ever since."

"No kidding," Michelle said, and turned her body towards him. "So who are you dating?" She arched an eyebrow.

"No one," Alex said, and looked around. "Just living the life. As an accounting student. Trying not to die of boredom."

All eyes were on him.

He finished his full beer, peeking at everyone over the glass rim. "What?"

Carla was in the bathroom examining her face when Michelle came in. She saw Carla, slowly walked up to her, looked at her in the mirror and smiled shyly. "Tell me I can fuck him," Michelle said and laughed out loud, covering her mouth. She was drunk.

"You can fuck him."

"Really?"

"Sure."

"Oh, thank you!"

"You're welcome. Not that... I mean, I don't think this should become a habit."

"What, fucking him?"

"No, asking me permission to fuck guys."

Michelle laughed. "That's not what I was doing."

"It wasn't?"

"Well... OK, it was. But I was asking just in case, you know... you were waiting to get with him."

"I'm not."

"Because if you were—"

"I'm not."

"—I'd forget him."

"No need. Fuck away," Carla said.

"OK, great."

Carla smiled at her, grabbed her bag and left the bathroom.

Michelle looked at herself in the mirror. "Bitch. I don't need permission to fuck anyone."

A woman in one of the stalls said, "Get that dick for me, girl!"

"I'm gonna head home," Carla said to the table. Alex stood up. She put her hand on his shoulder. "Nope, you stay."

"No, I'll take you home."

"Trust me. Stay. I'll see you all Monday." She hugged and kissed around the table. "Have fun," she said to Alex, and left the bar.

She walked the two blocks to the station, waited for a northbound line train. The platform was half full of people heading out or heading home on a Friday night. It was a quarter to ten.

Tell me I can fuck him.

104

Jesus.

Carla's answer had been quick, and she knew it was the right one. It wasn't one of those "flip a coin and while it's in the air you'll know the outcome you really want" situations. She wasn't torn when it came to Alex. She was happier being his friend than anything else. And Michelle was attractive and reasonably nice, and so Alex deserved... well, whatever he gets, right?

Right.

She felt the air shift in the station as her train made its way down the tunnel. She sighed.

You'd never see him. You wouldn't be able to give him a normal relationship...

"What's normal?" she said under her breath.

Don't. Don't do that shit. You know what normal is. You think you have time for some guy with this course load? With the job? He's the only real friend you've got. You trust him. You want a fuck buddy? They're all over the hospital. Literally. But it's not what you need. Not now. You have a monogamous dildo for God's sake. What you're doing is too important.

"It's not what I need," she said as the train came into the station. "Too important."

Fuck. Fine. Whatever.

Yeah. Alex was cute. He was funny. Kind. And if she knew nothing would change, she'd have taken him already. She knew it. Sitting in the train car, her body reminded her that it knew it, too. "Fucking hell," she said under her breath, and adjusted her seat.

She got home that night and dropped her clothes on the floor as she slowly circled the studio apartment. It was a sometime ritual. She kept the lights off and waited for her eyes to adjust to the streetlight, the moonlight coming through the windows. She grabbed a glass from a kitchen cabinet, filled it with water, drank. Some dribbled onto her chest. It was cold and felt good against her skin. She took another drink and let water fall from the glass, out the sides of her mouth. It dripped down her cheeks, her neck, onto her chest, down her stomach, and spread to both of her legs.

She masturbated that night thinking of Alex, thinking of a porn video she'd seen a few days before, thinking of other men. She came twice, breathed it out, covered herself with the comforter, turned on her side and emptied her mind before falling asleep.

An email from Alex the next morning: *So, what, you're my pimp now?*

She fixed a bowl of cereal, trying to think of the perfect response. She typed back: *Guess so.*

Meh.

He wrote back: *Guess I should thank you then.*

She wrote back: *You're welcome. Hope you wore a condom. Now where's my fucking money, bitch?*

CHAPTER FIFTEEN

John was at the auto repair shop. The same shop he'd borrowed the flatbed truck from. The same shop he'd been fixing up his baby at. The same shop he felt the leak came from. He stood out in the sun, his eyes closed, wearing his coveralls and reflexively wiping his hands on them. It was a gorgeous day.

John turned, looked at the back end of his baby, and sighed. The deep indentation, half a foot into the trunk, the bullet holes, the taillight busted, the chrome that used to be so uniform and polished was scratched to hell, or just plain torn.

It would take him at least six months and a shitload of money to fix it. *This time*, he thought, *I'm going to add some improvements*.

But they would have to wait.

Juan came up and put his hand on John's shoulder. He'd known the guy practically the entire time he'd worked for Gino. Ran the place. And he didn't seem the stupid type. "It's a fucking tragedy, man."

"Yeah."

"Easy to fix on a newer car. This… can't just buff it out."

"Yeah."

"And the fucking taillight! I mean, I remember when you found it, you had a hard-on—" they both laughed. Juan measured one out, a foot long—"Like this! Like she was the most beautiful woman."

"Yeah. Listen," John said, and turned to Juan. About five foot seven. Thin. Handlebar mustache, mid-forties, three kids. Every once

107

in a while, his wife Lucinda would bring enough food for the whole garage. John didn't know where to start. "There's a... Juan, this is a problem."

"Yeah, it's a fucking problem; you love that car more than I love my kids!"

"Not the car." John said, his face turning serious. "What was in the car."

Juan shook his head slowly. "I don't know nothing about that."

John sighed, unsure of how to continue. He looked around to see if anyone was watching. Paying attention to make sure he'd do the job. Or to see if Juan was gesturing to anyone.

He didn't see anything out of the ordinary.

"Juan, they told me I have to take care of this. You understand?"

"Sí."

"And if I don't take care of it, they're going to come in here and hurt people until they find out what happened. You see?"

"Sí."

"No, not sí, that's not what..." John shook his head. "Never mind. You don't know anything about it?"

Juan took a breath, trembled it out.

"Juan..." John said, and tilted his head in a fashion that said, trust me.

Juan wrung his hands in a dirty rag, looked at the ground.

John grabbed him by the shoulder. "You gotta tell me. Did you know? Did you tell anyone about the—"

"Puto idiotas, it wasn't me!" Juan yelled, and then checked himself. He looked around the shop, hung his head. "It wasn't. I keep my head down. I know the people who own this place. I've been working here twenty-five years. You think I no hear things? Know things? I'm not a stupid, John."

"I know you're not—"

"Gino remembers my kids' birthdays! I don't, I wouldn't—" He was getting very agitated. The notion of a gun to his kids' heads... "—because I'm not like that. I'm happy here!"

"OK, OK. Cálmese."

"Cálmese? Cálmese usted!"

"Just… Juan, you have to tell me what you know."

Juan made a noise.

"You tell me what you know, this goes away."

Juan wrinkled up his face.

John gave it a beat. Another. Let the guy build up the courage to—

"Gordy. It was Gordy. He came in drunk yesterday and he said something about quitting and fuck this job, fuck Gino, fuck me, fuck *you*… I didn't know he did it beforehand, comprende?"

"Yeah."

"Shooting his mouth off, I thought it was just talk, and then he was on the phone and I heard him say…"

"Say what?"

Juan shook his head, made the sign of the cross. "I'm sorry, my friend." He walked over to the stall the Charger was in and motioned John to come over. He did. "By the time you brought her back, he was gone…"

Juan grabbed the frayed rope connected to the garage door and pulled it down. He went over to the passenger-side front wheel, reached up into the wheelhouse, and retrieved a small black box that had a green LED lit up.

"You've got to be fucking kidding me," John said, and grabbed it from Juan.

"I found it last night. I was going to tell you, I just—"

"You just what? The fucking guy had a… and you found this last *night*?"

"I'm sorry, John. I am. I didn't sleep. My wife beat the shit out of me when I told her. I was a scared. I'm sorry."

John looked at the machine. It was small, had a powerful magnet on one side. The LED was pinging on and off.

"Where's Gordy?"

"I don't know. He didn't come in today. Are you going to tell Gino what—"

"I'm going to tell him everything. It's the only way you don't get shot in the face, Juan." Juan made the sign of the cross again, twice. "Is that it? Is that everything? Because if he finds out something else—"

"I swear! I swear, that's it." He grabbed an actual cross on a necklace, kissed it, lifted it to the sky, and looked legitimately frightened.

John decided to tack some on. He grabbed Juan by the shirt, pushed him up against a wall and leaned in. "You see him, you call me. Understand?"

"Sí. Yes. I call."

"You find out if any of these other fuckers knew about it—"

"I call! I'm sorry, my friend."

John went and put the tracker back in the wheelhouse. He grabbed the garage door, threw it open, and walked to his back-up, the car he'd been using the last four years.

Something made him stop before he got in.

He walked to the front of the car, checked the wheelhouse of the driver side, the passenger side. He walked to the back passenger wheelhouse and found another tracker.

"Motherfucker," he said, and put it back.

CHAPTER SIXTEEN

Hal watched the meeting break up. He got a handshake here and there. Some kind words. Some not so kind with their descriptions of others.

Gino sat and watched as the last of them left. He sighed, loosened his tie, and slicked his hair back. He grabbed a glass of wine in front of him and took a big sip. Then he turned his attention to Hal.

"How was the food?"

"Fantastic," Hal said, and meant it.

"Good. That's good. You know who I am?"

"Just your name."

"Nothing else?"

"No."

"You from around here?"

"Yeah, and Texas for a few years... but I don't really follow local politics or... family businesses."

"Cute. That's cute. Come here. Have a seat."

Hal walked over, sat down. Not too close.

"Lorenzo, two brandies."

"Yes, sir." Lorenzo, the host or owner who'd been hovering, nodded to a waiter who'd been loitering. He went to the bar. The other waiters were finishing clearing off the tables.

"I saw the news, the report on you. I talked to my guy at the 1st. He said you were legit."

"Thank you."

"Why'd you do it?"

"Why?"

"Yeah. Why stick up for some nurse? Why get involved?"

"Because she was alone."

Gino made a noise somewhere between not good enough and barely acceptable.

"And there were three of them."

Gino nodded slowly. "*That* I can appreciate. One on one, I say kill or be killed. Though, you're never really lucky enough for it to be one on one. Not these days..."

Two brandies appeared in large snifters. Gino grabbed the closest one and handed it to Hal. Hal reflexively put it under his nose. It smelled fantastic.

Gino picked up the second and held it out for a toast. "To White Knights. No pun intended."

They clinked glasses.

"I've been in this city my whole life, and there hasn't been a day, not a single day that a piece of shit hasn't tried to murder or rape someone on the subways. Not one day. It attracts them, I think. The underground. In the 70s, the police chief got it in his head that it was better to lie to the public than do his job, so he made sure that transit cops didn't report crimes from midnight to six a.m., if you can believe it. He was more concerned about public perception than he was about fixing the problem. Although... well, there *was* no fixing that problem. At least, not in the 70s. Or the 80s. The Blacks were well into their second coming by that time. With education. And politics. They were also the country's new boogiemen... the way the news portrayed them. But, a lot of them were really finding themselves. That type of evolution... it's always violent, no matter what skin color you are." He took a sip. "Not much was being done about the subway problem. Or, I should say, whatever *was* being done, it wasn't working. So, we took care of the N and the R trains as best we could. From Astoria, down to the Plaza, and over to Forest Hills. It was a pet project of my mentor's before he died, and it made him a lot of friends in the neighborhood." Gino nodded, remembering distant memories, drank again. "But, boys will be boys. There was an incident in about '85, a year or so after Bernie Goetz. You know that guy?"

Hal nodded.

"So, three guys gang raped a woman coming home late one night, from a party or from work or whatever it was—I don't remember—on an F train headed to Coney Island. Well. She was white, they were Black, and the whole fucking world came to a halt. The papers went nuts, the news stations. There was a protest down at City Hall. Everyone was there. Reporters doing live news coverage, some heavies from the police unions, a bunch of reverends, actors... Blacks, whites, Asians, Hispanics... and all of a sudden, the mayor remembered he had a job to do. From then on, it was a show of force. There was a cop on every fucking train, every line in the city for six months, day and night. They said it helped, too. Not that anyone could verify it actually did anything. After six months, they toned it down. From what I heard, it played hell on the city's budget, which, let's be honest, will always be a bigger issue to these people than one white woman." Gino loosened his tie some more. "The one and only time I've been arrested, I was on my way home, two in the morning, and I spit, just spit in the subway car. Something I'd done a thousand times, which was stupid, I know, but I was a punk kid whose boss was a big shot. They brought me out at the next stop in cuffs, had three cars waiting for me, the works. Shot my mouth off, and got a crack, right here." He leaned back, felt the back of his head, and remembered. "It's good those days are gone. Well, mostly gone."

"Yes, it is." Hal drank some of the brandy. He had no idea if it was the good stuff or not, having never drunk brandy before. It went down smoother than any alcohol he'd ever had.

Gino smelled his, twirled it in his hand. "Perception's a strange thing. My business—and I'm not going to get into the particulars, but I hire the best lawyers, I get the best financial firms, the best PR people—and I can't wash this stink away. Shit my boss did forty fucking years ago, it's still here, around my neck. Not that I don't appreciate everything he did for us."

"Of course."

Gino sighed. "You have a college education?"

"No."

"Ever been in prison?"

"Yes. But you knew that."

Gino smiled. "Ever kill anyone?"

"No."

"Not for lack of trying, or…"

"Never came up."

"Uh huh. So you're barely clean."

"Well, that depends on—"

"I can't use you."

"Excuse me?"

"I can't use you. Publicly. I have a PR problem, and I can't use you. I thought I could, you know. Hometown hero, all that shit they were saying about you. But it won't work. I can't use you. Not a felon. Not even a hero felon."

"I understand. Listen, I just got pulled off the street, I wasn't—"

"You don't want a job?"

"A job?"

"Yeah. Something I ask you to do, you get paid to do it, and then a day or two later I give you something else to do. A job."

"Is it illegal?"

Gino sighed, closed his eyes and shook his head. When he opened his eyes, he was smiling. "Seriously?"

"Well… I just figured I should ask," Hal said.

"Well… let's say it's a grey area."

"A grey area."

"Yeah, but, you know… a darker grey."

CHAPTER SEVENTEEN

Carla sat at the bar and looked at her glass of beer. It was half full. Suds were slipping down the side.

She couldn't believe it was over.

Two years in a new city. Two years of classes, tests, clinical work. Hospital time. Working thirty hours a week, detailing patients and procedures.

She felt like she'd been moving a mile a minute while the rest of the planet was standing still. And here she was. June of 1997. Her world had finally slowed down.

She smiled and gave herself a mental pat on the back.

She was sitting in the same bar she'd met Alex in.

The same bar she went to after calling *him*.

She'd run into Greg once in those two years. He was with a stringy dark-haired waif of a woman with wild eyes and a periodic twitch that shook her body. Carla figured it wasn't a tic, but some kind of physical arrogance, like people who thought it was chic to say they were OCD, when all they were was an asshole.

"Jacqueline, I presume," Carla said, and stuck out her hand.

"No," she said. "Lindsey. Who's Jacqueline?"

"No one," Greg said, and began to walk away.

"Lindsey!" Carla yelled, calling after them. Lindsey turned. "Get the Jacqueline story! It's a fucking whopper!"

She took a sip of beer. That was a good day.

She pressed the cold glass against the inside of her wrist. It was already unbearably hot for June. It was just 3pm.

Carla slid her hand up her face and back down again. Four hours to kill before a bunch of her classmates were going out to a fancy dinner. She'd decided to pregame, and way early.

She'd received her Authorization to Test for the NCLEX, to receive her nursing license. She'd hear from them in thirty days about a test date. Then she'd cram, hard.

End of her third year, Abigail took her aside and said, "Girl, you better get ready. That test will eat you up and shit you out. It's dozens and dozens of questions, and it's run on a curve, OK? But not like a regular curve, like in high school. This test, it takes into consideration what you get right and what you get wrong, and then asks the next question. And then the next. You keep getting them wrong, they keep feeding you the low-end questions. You start to get them right, you start going into the upper echelon questions. And then..." she snapped her fingers. "Just like that, the test might just be over."

"How many questions are you talking?"

"Don't know. Could be seventy-five. Could be over two hundred. It all depends."

"So, if I only answered seventy-five, and it shuts off, that's a good thing, right?"

"Not if you got them wrong!"

Carla nodded.

Everyone told her the test was a bitch. Anxiety about it, even a year out, was at an all-time high.

Summer of her third year, she worked full time at the trauma center. She took on extra shifts when she was able, and saved as much money as she could. Alex, meanwhile, went away to California, Nevada, Hawaii. He flew down with his family to the Bahamas. He sent postcards from them all.

Whenever he got back, they'd hang out, go to movies, eat dinner, talk about whatever.

One night, after finishing her third year, they were out celebrating Alex's graduation. They'd been having a great evening. Dinner, drinks, some of his friends, some fellow graduates. The night ended up at her place. They were both particularly drunk and he asked if he could kiss her.

Carla turned him down, and regretted it right away.

She watched him go from not having a doubt in the world to being completely embarrassed, instantly. "I thought…" he said, and got up. He stared outside for a moment. "Sorry," he said, and went to leave.

"Alex, wait." It was half-hearted. Her apartment was a furnace, and she was sweating and drunk. All of her windows were wide open. She didn't have an air conditioner.

"No… you're right. We shouldn't. This… it's too good, right? People hope for friendships like this."

She nodded.

"Who says men and women can't be friends?" He grabbed his dinner jacket, turned, and looked throughout the apartment. "You know, I should really buy you an air conditioner. Friends do that, right?"

"I don't know. No one's ever bought me anything before. You're my only real friend," she said.

He laughed. He laughed and braced himself against the doorjamb of the apartment's front door. "Jesus, Carla. You're so full of shit."

And he left.

She shook her head. It was a bad memory. She'd had friends. Good ones.

She wasn't sure what she'd been afraid of. If they'd tried it and it didn't work out, and the friendship didn't work out, it's not like she'd just be alone… and it wasn't like she was leading him on.

"Could have been nice," she said under her breath. The bar was practically empty. She took another sip and stared straight ahead.

Later that same summer, Alex started dating a woman named Gabby. Redhead. Polish. Looked like a model. *Was*, in fact, a model.

They met at a rave.

For Alex's graduation summer, he went full bore. "I'm rarely sober," he said. "And I've never been happier."

Carla thought it might have been a reaction to her rejecting him. Still, it looked and sounded like Alex was having the time of his life.

And she was jealous.

Alex brought Gabby around one night when he invited Carla out with some people. Sports bar. Chicken wings, chicken tenders, mozzarella sticks, beer specials, twenty-eight televisions.

Samson's Bar and Grill.

Alex introduced them, and Carla was more than cordial. It felt like a test. Or a snub. She sat and watched them together and laughed when people laughed and stared at the TVs when there was a lull.

Alex was paying a lot of attention to two basketball games that were on, which seemed strange. He wasn't a sports guy. Not really. Gabby would ask questions and Alex would answer them, fully engaged. It seemed he'd mastered the ability to do two things at once.

Carla didn't drink that night. She was trying to prepare for the eventual *slight* Adderall addiction that she knew was going to come with her final year.

Her comedown at the end of year three hadn't been particularly bad. She was able to taper off two weeks after the semester ended. Some sleepless nights. The shakes. Her attention span had gone to shit, but it wasn't affecting her job performance, thank God.

Gerry, her classmate and dealer, applauded her. They were at their end-of-year party. "You're Iron Will Carla in my book. Most people need an intervention to get off this shit. And other shit. This shit usually turns into other shit, on TOP of this shit, so... consider yourself lucky. I'm around if you need anything," he said. She kissed him on the cheek and said thank you, again.

Gabby had been wearing a blouse, no bra, three-inch heels, and jeans that seemed to have had the air sucked out of them. With hips, my God... and a thin waist. Carla watched her walk to the bathroom, turned to Alex and said, "OK, look—"

"Here it goes."

"No, listen, I'm serious. *How* does she get those jeans on?"

Alex turned and watched Gabby walk towards the bathroom. "Honestly?"

"Yeah."

He turned back to her quickly, eyes wide and smiling. "It's fucking unreal to watch. She starts off in like a squat, and then launches herself up into the air and pulls with all her might on the belt loops, and inch by inch they get over those—"

"Those hips!"

"—hips. Yeah. Takes her like three minutes. It's ridiculous. And awesome."

"Well, record it next time, for posterity's sake."

He laughed. "I'll see what I can do. How are you doing?"

"I'm fine. Just... nervous. One more year. And if it was like last year, I think I can do it. But I'm told it's not, and... I just have to... I'm just nervous."

"You're going to ace it. I know you are."

"Yeah. What about you?"

"Me? I start my new job first week of September. Corporate tax stuff that I don't understand *at all*. But the starting salary is pretty sweet, and I get three weeks of vacation and ten sick days and benefits and my own office..."

"You get an office?"

"Yeah, I mean, well, a cubicle is an office, right?"

"No, it's not."

"Well, I'm going to think of it as an office. You and your elitism can't hold me back."

Gabby came back and sat down, started talking to Alex straight away. Carla watched them. He looked happy, and she looked legitimately content with the guy.

Carla had a hard time not wondering what might have been. As hard as she tried to see it, it wouldn't come. Her fantasies about a life with Alex weren't boring. They were blank.

She couldn't tell if that was a good thing or a bad thing.

Carla would pass the NCLEX. She would stay on at the hospital as an RN with a good starting salary, two weeks of vacation, and seven sick days. She kept her apartment for another year before moving into a one-bedroom with an air conditioner.

Alex and Gabby were together for over four years.

Carla would stay single for a long time.

CHAPTER EIGHTEEN

Ivan Sokolov was six foot five and weighed 290. Most of it was in his chest, shoulders, and stomach. And legs.

He sat in the passenger seat and was quiet the whole way to Gordy's mother's house, which was the last place on a list he could've been hiding out.

The fucking car was leaning. John could tell.

Ivan was a loan-out from some of Gino's friends in Brighton Beach who wanted to make a good impression. He spoke reasonable English.

"I am hungry," Ivan said, and tried to stretch. His knees were high up near the top of the dashboard. He'd leaned the seat back as far as he could. His head was angled against the roof.

"We ate lunch. Twice."

"So?"

John sighed and turned the car off. "Ten minutes, we'll get some hot dogs."

"I live near Nathan's. We are not to getting shit fucking hot dog. It would be like getting cannoli from Cuccio's and saying Hostess Twinkies is best."

"OK, Jesus Christ, we'll get some sandwiches or whatever, just relax."

"I am perfectly relaxed."

"Yeah, you *sound* perfectly relaxed."

"Good."

"Jesus. And what the fuck are you eating cannolis for?"

"What do you mean?"

"You're fucking Russian. What kind of desserts do Russians make?"

"Vatrushka."

"Vatwhat?"

"Is ring of dough with sour curd in middle."

"Christ—"

"Delicious with espresso."

"Of course it is..."

"And Syrniki. Zefir. Sushki are mini bread rings, sweet."

"OK."

"Ptasie mleczko, chocolate covered soufflé. Delicious with espresso."

"Yeah, I got it."

"But none beat cannoli from Cuccio's. I buy dozen. My mother loves them. She get six, I get six. I eat mine, then I eat half of hers. She loves watching me eat."

"I bet."

"She make best kulich, but only at Easter."

John stopped listening. He saw Gordy come out of his mother's house and start walking down the block.

"I beg her to make at Thanksgiving, but—"

"Shut up."

Ivan looked over at John at the slight against his mother.

"That's him." John pointed at Gordy just as Ivan opened the car door. "What, where are you going?"

"To get him."

"Just wait, he's on foot. He's not going anywhere. Let's follow him, maybe he's going to the guys who ripped me off."

Ivan made a noise and closed the door. "Am hungry."

"Yeah, well, just wait."

Gordy made his way down the street and crossed to their side. John started the car up and pulled out, slowly. A rolling tail of a guy on foot, in the middle of the day, on a busy street, with a psychotic Russian.

On a Sunday.

Gordy didn't seem too worried as he walked down the block, took a right, crossed the street and headed around a corner near an abandoned string of houses.

John pulled up close enough to peek down the street and saw Gordy head into a particularly shitty building. Boarded-up windows, cracked foundation, broken fire escape. A van was parked out back.

"We go?" Ivan asked.

"I don't like it," John said. "We don't know who or what's in there."

"So?"

"Jesus, what do you mean 'so'? You want to see your mother again?"

"Of course."

"Then just relax."

"You keep saying for me relax. Look at me. I am."

They sat there and waited.

A full minute went by when, all of a sudden, a noise grew from Ivan's stomach. An alien noise.

"Are you fucking kidding?" John asked.

"I tell you—"

"Just go get a slice of pizza from the place up the block. He leaves, I'll call you. He gets in a car, you can fucking explain to Gino that you were thinking with your stomach. I'm sure he hasn't heard that one before."

He watched Ivan's face as he tried to figure out who he'd get in trouble with more, Gino or Vadim, his brother.

The Sokolov brothers had been in country for three years. Originally from Gatchina, just south of St. Petersburg, they'd been in the arms business, a family business, until a regime change saw their father murdered. They had no choice but to leave the country. Money got them, their mother, their two sisters, and some other immediate family to Finland, where they got new identities, fake passports, and came to Brooklyn by ship.

The brothers were independent contractors who did mostly wet work, and some strong arm and torture. They had been working with Gino on and off for about a year, and this was their third job.

"I wait."

"Good. There's a, Christ, there's a fucking protein bar in the bag in the back. I don't want you to fall over from low blood sugar."

"Is serious problem," Ivan said and reached in the back, grabbed the bag, grabbed the bar, ripped the packaging off, and stuffed his face.

"Better?"

Ivan nodded. It was the second time he'd worked with Ivan, and while he appreciated the guy and his talents, he was always wary of people significantly larger than he was. Especially those who got paid to hurt people.

Four men exited the building, including Gordy.

John turned to Ivan, smug, smiling.

"What?" Ivan asked.

"See?"

"See what?"

"See wha... there's four fucking guys there!" They made their way to the van, opened the back of it, started talking.

"So? I take four guys easy."

"Bullshit."

Ivan looked at him, smiling. "Twenty dollars."

"Are you fucking kidding me?"

"Twenty dollars." Ivan stuck his hand out.

"Twenty dollars." John shook his head, looked at the four guys, looked at Ivan, looked at the four guys. "Sure, fuck it. Twenty dollars." John shook it.

Ivan smiled, opened the car door and started to walk over to the four guys. He turned back to John. "Record. On camera."

"What?"

124

"To show my brother," he said and grinned. Ivan took out a mini-camcorder from his pocket and handed it to John.

"You have your own... fuck, OK." John rolled the driver-side window down full, hit record, and pointed the camcorder at Ivan, who fucking *waved*.

The sun was setting, and John could see Ivan's shadow slowly creeping up on the four men.

Their confab over, the guys were closing the back of the van. By the time they saw Ivan, it was too late.

Ivan grabbed the closest guy, lifted him straight off his feet, and threw him into the wall of the building they'd come out of, face first. The guy didn't get up.

The second guy tried to go toe to toe. Ivan grabbed the first punch thrown, swallowing it with his enormous hand, and bent his wrist until it broke. There was a split second between the crack and the scream, and it echoed back to John, who started to get queasy. "Oh, fuck," he said quietly, half forgetting he was filming.

The third guy put up more of a fight. He got in two punches before Ivan kicked his knee out, almost snapping it backwards. The guy grabbed his leg and did a quick shuffle before falling to the ground.

Ivan grabbed Gordy by the face and smashed his head into the back of the van's rear window. It shattered. Gordy slumped to the ground and tried to crawl away. John could hear some kind of animal noise coming from him. From all of them...

All the conscious ones, anyway.

Ivan grabbed Gordy by the pant leg and dragged him across the street towards John. "What the fuck..." John said, looking around the street. He kept filming.

"Twenty dollars," Ivan said as he got there and dropped Gordy's pant leg. Gordy looked up from the ground and saw the camcorder, saw John. His face was a literal mess of glass, dirt, and blood.

"Shit," Gordy said with some difficulty.

"'Shit' is right." John shut the camcorder and got out of the car. He grabbed a twenty from his wallet and handed it and the camera to Ivan, who stuffed both into his pocket.

"Ask questions. Be right back."

"Where the fu—" He watched Ivan head back to the van. "Jesus, forget it." The guy who'd been thrown into the building still hadn't moved. Wrist snap was sitting on the ground, blankly staring at his hand. Knee break was screaming in agony.

The block was curiously deserted.

"Where's the redhead, Gordy?"

"Tijuana by now, you fucking—"

John stepped on his chest. Hard. "Where?"

"He's in Monte Carlo fucking your mother up the ass!"

"The Irishman is fucking my mom's corpse in the ass in Monte Carlo? Gordy, that seems highly unlikely."

"Fuck you!"

"You..." John chuckled. "You don't seem to understand the situation, man. Which is really fucking unbelievable. Take a look." John looked up. Gordy craned his head. Ivan was on his way back holding a large black duffle bag and a small dog.

"Fuck," Gordy said and squirmed under John's foot.

"You think he's going to appreciate your stories of mother ass-fucking? Or is he just going to rip off one of your arms and beat you to death with it?"

Resigned, Gordy laid back down. "Probably the second..."

"Probably you're right. Why don't you just tell me what you know and I'll make sure you live through this."

"You serious?"

"Yeah."

Ivan came over, handed John the dog, a white terrier.

"What the fuck is this?"

Ivan looked at John as if he had two heads. "Is dog." He walked past him, opened the back door of the car, threw the duffle in, came over and took the dog back. "He talk?"

"Not yet."

"I should rip arm off now?"

"I guess so, yeah."

"No, fucking no! Just wait. Jesus!" Gordy got comfortable. As comfortable as he could, lying on his back with a broken face and a foot on his chest. "His name is Finn, he's a friend from the pen, from way back. I needed the money, John. I'm sorry. He was going to do the job without me and it was so stupid."

"How'd he find out about Darby's?"

"We'd been tracking you for a while now. Finn made friends with a bartender there and said he'd give him a heads-up when it was a big pick-up."

So, Darby's was compromised, too...

John shook his head. What a mess. He looked around. "The fuck are you doing here?"

"We were going to leave town and wanted some protection."

John looked into the back seat. The bag was full of guns.

"Where were you headed?"

"Atlantic City to start."

"Atlantic... Atlantic City?" John took his foot off of Gordy's chest and bent down. "Are you fucking kidding me? What the fuck is wrong with you? Gino's got a whole fucking family down there!"

"Does he? Shit." Gordy sounded so disappointed in himself.

John shook his head. The guy was too stupid—"Just tell me where Finn is, and the other guy, the bartender."

"They're in Hoboken. See, we were going to take 78 to the Parkway and—"

"Shut the fuck up," John said, and rubbed his face.

"I told them not to hurt you!" John looked down at Gordy, who had his hands up pleading. "I swear, I told them to not hurt you, John. Seriously. They were just going to shoot the car up and I said you were a stand-up guy. Not the violent type like Andre the fucking Giant here."

John looked over at Ivan, who shrugged and said, "I cannot go to Hoboken." He rubbed the dog's face and kissed the top of its head.

"No one's asking. You're just going to take the dog?"

"Yes. Can't leave here to die. To get run over."

"OK. Put Gordy in the trunk."

"No, John—" Gordy started.

"Just do it." John held his hand out for the dog. Ivan handed it over again, grabbed Gordy by the jacket and deadlifted him off the ground. John reached in through the driver-side window and popped the trunk. The car rocked a bit, then some more as Gordy complained. Ivan slammed the trunk down and wiped his hands on his pants.

They both got into the car. Ivan took the dog back.

"You going to name it?"

"Is not it, is boy."

"So?"

Ivan thought about it for a few. "Max?"

John turned the car on, put it in gear. "Yeah, OK."

CHAPTER NINETEEN

Two weeks after the lunch with Gino, Hal stood outside of a Queens' fortress not knowing what to do, how to act, or who to talk to. He was dressed in his suit, a charcoal-grey piece with a white shirt and grey paisley tie, black shoes, black socks. He'd gotten his hair cut the week before and he'd shaved that morning. Taking the train on a Saturday into Queens wearing a full suit, he felt awkward. Even more so in the heat.

The place was buzzing with activity. Three catering trucks with people going in and out of the house. Guards strategically placed. He thought he recognized a few from outside of Angolo's restaurant. All of them had the look of business and wariness of the world.

He'd gotten the call three days earlier.

Hal and Gino had gotten along well at lunch, and, after some back and forth, Gino said he'd be in touch. He asked if Hal had enough money to get by. Hal said he thought so. Gino slid him three hundred dollars, had Hal write down the name of the hotel he was staying at, the room number, shook his hand and left.

Hal extended his stay for another week and waited. He'd spent the next two days in the hotel room, leaving only for food and some fresh air every once in a while. On the third day he was sitting on the bed watching football with the sound off when his phone rang.

"You own a suit?" Gino asked. No hello, no nothing.

"Yes."

"Take this down." Gino relayed an address. "This Saturday, one o'clock. Bring an appetite."

He got another week's extension on the room.

Hal spent a few days wandering the city, wondering what the occasion might be. He saw a couple of movies, ate in a few different restaurants, went to the Met. He spent some time in the hotel room watching TV, sleeping, showering, or jerking off.

He was in that place where boredom meets opportunity. Maybe.

Another thing he did to occupy his time: he learned about his new acquaintance. He went to the public library and got microfilm on the D'Escopio family.

There was a lot of material... and the more he read, the more fascinated he became.

The place was two levels, with gorgeous full-length windows that showcased an enormous living room with a spiral staircase, all decked to the nines in white lace and streamers. It sported brick outer walls, with an iron gate and a guardhouse. Hal shook his head in wonder.

The whole street was blocked off. Security guards were at both ends, letting in and denying cars.

It wasn't until a woman holding a tray of full champagne glasses walked by and offered him one that he realized it was someone's wedding day. He said no thank you.

It was August 9, 2000.

He made his way to the front where a guy with a stiff upper lip, goatee, slicked back hair, and a tuxedo was waiting to receive guests. "Invitation?"

Hal patted his coat for some reason. He knew he didn't have a physical invite. "I'm sorry, I never got an invite."

"You never got a..." he motioned to someone. A man in a tux, definitely security, walked over.

"Name?"

"Hal Shipley."

130

The guy looked at his clipboard.

"I'm sorry, I don't see you here."

"Well, I was invited. Kind of last minute, I guess." The security guard came over, grabbed Hal by the arm. It hurt. "Hey—"

The host smirked. "Yeah. Listen, you're going to have to—"

"I was invited by Mr. D'Escopio. Personally."

They both stopped.

"You better ask," Hal said. "You know. Before there's trouble."

The security guard let go of Hal's arm. He moved away, keeping an eye on Hal, and spoke into a microphone. He looked over. "Name?"

"Shipley."

He spoke into the microphone. After a second he turned, nodded, went back to his post.

The host bowed. "I'm so sorry for the confusion, Mr. Shipley. Welcome. Do have a wonderful time." He made a flamboyant gesture with his hand towards the front door, which was flanked by two white columns, satin drapes, sparkly shit here and there, and half a dozen papier-mâché cherubs floating in the air.

Seriously.

Hal smiled, nodded.

He walked inside to find another waiter with a tray of champagne. He passed, again. The first time he ever drank champagne, he puked. He was fifteen. Hadn't touched it since.

The house was air-conditioned, with the windows and doors open.

Hal entered the living room with the big windows, the spiral staircase, and an unbelievable smell. There were three enormous tables full of food, and a flurry of catering staff adjusting and primping displays and trays. Some of them were assisting guests with their plates in an effort to keep the buffet as neat and tidy as possible. And moving.

Hal grabbed a plate, a thick off-white ceramic with a floral pattern, held it out for one of the attendants who took it and asked, "Would you like anything specific?"

"I'm not picky," Hal said as his stomach grumbled. It was the smell. It was overwhelmingly, overpoweringly delicious. He watched as spoonfuls of colorful foods were dished onto the plate. Ziti, chicken parm, eggplant parm, a piece of flounder. "Lemon?"

"Sure, and some of those, the white balls there, the cheese."

"Mozzarella," the attendant said.

"And the tomatoes. Thanks. What's this?"

"Prosciutto and melon."

"And?"

"Delicious."

"Sure, OK."

Hal moved away with a full plate and watched the crowd as he ate, piece by piece, just standing there. He saw the bar and decided it was his next stop.

There was wine, red and white, vodka, scotch, rum, some dessert drinks, like anisette and Sambuca. He finished his plate, handed it to some geek with a tray, walked over, got himself a glass of red, and meandered.

No one paid any attention to him. A party like this, Sally would have had him moving from group to group, sniffing out the one person who it would've been of benefit to talk to. "The Alphas," she'd say. "Either they're leading the conversation, or the person speaking is waiting for their approval. Listen, and look for body language cues, like exacerbation or interruptive energy. Eye contact, too."

No thanks.

He was happy for the relative anonymity.

As he moved from room to room, one thing he did notice... it was a pretty diverse crowd for an Italian mobster's daughter's wedding.

Dotting the landscape was a Latino guy and his date, a gaggle of Asians in a corner, and not the fresh-off-the-boat kind. Businessmen. Foreign businessmen. They were not speaking English. There were also two Indian men in hand-tailored silk suits talking amongst themselves, completely comfortable in their surroundings.

Hal also saw an older Black man talking to Paulie Grasso, who was laughing.

While the party was semi-diverse, he noticed that most of the Italians stuck to their own, and he made an observation. It wasn't a race thing. It was a family thing. The wives of all these Italian men, these mobsters, they were huddled in the kitchen together, talking, laughing, yelling, a cacophony reserved for geese heading south for winter. Like the kitchen was a homing beacon. Hal could hardly make out single words, let alone actual sentences.

Other women, the dates, were either attached to their man's arm, or in small groups with other ladies, happy for the short reprieve from the everyday conversations they were used to. And for the food. And the alcohol.

The Italian men were spread out, huddled in their own groups, joking around, and genuinely having a good time.

They were all on their best behavior.

It was early and no one was drunk. Yet.

CHAPTER TWENTY

"I'm sorry. What?" Carla was mid-drink and coffee spilled out of her mouth.

Alex hadn't touched his coffee.

"I lost eight thousand dollars."

"Like, lost it lost it? Like, you can't find it?"

"No, like I had to give it to someone else."

"Well, then it's not lost, is it?"

"OK, smartass."

"You owed someone eight... *thousand*... dollars?"

"Yeah."

"Have they been mowing your lawn for the past decade?"

"No."

"Did you buy a fuck-ton of Girl Scout cookies?"

"Carla, I—"

"I know. You borrowed five dollars from a friend in the fourth grade, and the interest came to seven thousand nine hund—"

"I lost it gambling, OK?"

Carla nodded slowly. She leaned back and just basked in it. It was one of those rare moments when she knew, no matter what she'd done in the past, she'd never been stupid enough to gamble. At least, not more than she could afford to lose... which was always very little. "Tell me it was a back alley dice game."

"Jesus."

"Or that guy, the one who kept yelling MAO in that movie... you were playing Russian roulette, right?"

"Carla, for fuck's sake."

"It was one hand of five card stud. THAT I could understand. Kind of like that game where you say you can name a song in five notes. 'Oh, well, *I* can name it in four...' The ante just kept going up and up, right? Tell me it was something majestic that you simply couldn't pass up and not a fucking basketball—"

"It was on a basketball game."

"Oh, for God's sake, Alex—"

"I'm sorry—"

"Just lie to me! Just lie! That's all I asked. I'm not your mother. I'm not going to tell you what to do with your money. But you come here and tell me you lost more money than almost ten months of rent... dazzle me just a bit next time, OK? Please. Pretty please." She put her hands together like she was praying.

He smiled and nodded. "OK. Next time it'll be something a bit more grandiose."

"It's all I ask. Now," she said and squared herself off to him. "What the fuck is wrong with you?"

"I know."

"You know? Do you even have eight thousand dollars to just give up like that?"

"Yeah, of course."

"Oh! Mr. La-di-da..."

"Not *of course* like that, like I'm fucking rich. But I would never place a bet where I didn't have the money to pay up. That's what I mean."

"OK. OK. That's... better. At least you're not a total moron."

They were in a coffee shop. The place was like heaven. She could smell butter and chocolate and powdered sugar and all of the things she was constantly telling her patients not to eat.

"I have to get a cookie," she said.

"So get one."

135

"I'm going to. But I know you haven't told me everything."

Alex sighed. "I... I didn't have all of it."

"And the penny drops."

"Carla..."

"Or the shoe. The other shoe. Is it both shoes?"

"Would you just listen?"

"I am listening."

"I had to borrow it from my folks. They weren't happy about it, but I told them I can pay it off in four months."

"Please tell me that you don't owe them two thousand a month."

"No, Jesus, I just said I didn't have all of it."

"Please tell me that you don't owe them one thousand nine hundred a month."

"Would you stop it? I owe them a grand a month. And I can do it. And I will. I just... I fucked up."

"Well, I'd say that knowing you have a problem is the first step, but screw that. You're smarter than that."

"It's the first time I lost that big, ever, OK?"

"Have you won anything?"

"Of course. I win all the time."

"So what do you do with the money?"

"I gamble—"

"You gamble it."

"—it... yeah."

"Nice. Smart." She got up and bought herself a chocolate chunk cookie. It looked ridiculous. She got back to the table. "So, I have a question. What's the end goal?"

"The what?"

"To gambling. What's the end goal? I mean, you're not saving what you win..."

"I was."

"OK, you saved four thousand dollars from gambling winnings?"

"Yeah."

"Not from work."

"Well… yeah, I mean, it's all the same money."

"Uh huh…" she bit into the cookie. Her mouth had an orgasm. She chased it with some coffee. "I never want to leave this place."

"That good, huh?"

"You didn't answer my question."

"Yeah, I know, I was trying to change the subject." She just looked at him. "What my goal is?"

"Yeah."

"I don't know. The big score, you know? That lock that you look for. Or the long shot that pays off fifty to one."

"How likely is that?" she asked.

"Pretty likely. It happens all the time, all over the world."

"Does it?"

"Yeah, it does. And I don't need you judging me right now."

"You don't? Then what the hell did you tell me for?"

"I… I don't know. You're my friend. We share things."

"Yeah, we share things so we can be judged, you moron." He looked at her. "Or for help…" She shook her head. "Yeah, OK… I'm waiting to hear the…" she gestured with her hands. "You know. So, ask already."

"Oh, hey. No. I would never come to you for money. Not ever. I know what you make. You *just* live within your means."

"Hey!"

"You know what I mean. It's not like you're socking away half your paycheck."

"I wish."

"You've got a good job and a pension and I'm never going to put you in a position to fuck that up. Not ever. This? This shit? It's not going to get the better of me. It's for fun, and with a little luck I'll make some real money. But beyond that? It's just a… a hobby."

"A hobby."

"Yeah. Something to pass the time. Trust me. You won't hear about my hardships when it comes to gambling ever again."

Carla shook her head. "Alex, those seem like famous last words."

"They are!"

"Do you... do you even know what famous last... forget it. What did Gabby say about it?"

"She doesn't know."

"Really? So, three and a half years in, that's the secret-keeping stage."

"More like year one. She doesn't know I gamble."

"Wow."

"Yeah."

"So, she's a moron."

"No, I'm just a really good liar."

"Uh huh. OK, well, I have to go—"

"No, not yet. I have to ask you something," Alex said.

"OK."

"I'm starting up a side business. So that this doesn't ever happen again."

"A side business."

"Yeah. I'm doing personal taxes. One hundred a filing or ten percent per return, whichever is more."

"OK..."

"That's standard, by the way," he said.

It wasn't.

"I've got a couple of clients. I want some more. I want you to tell your friends at the hospital—"

"Alex, come on—"

"It's just some extra cash. It gets me out of hock with my folks, gives me back my cushion. That's it. And I'm good at it. I do yours..."

"Yeah...?"

"Well, I suspect your friends would want the kind of returns I've been getting you these past few years."

She looked at him. He looked matter of fact, not eager. "You're not going to fuck over these people, right?"

"Are you serious?"

"I have to see them every day, Alex."

"Jesus, if you're serious, forget it. I'm just trying to make some extra money, not get people audited, or, God forbid, steal from them. But if you're uncomfortable letting them know—"

"No, no, I'll tell them. Just tell me you're on the level."

He held his arm out in front of him, stiff. "I'm on the level. I promise. See how level?"

She took another bite of the cookie. "Mister, you better be." She chased it with some coffee. "Please put your arm down."

CHAPTER TWENTY-ONE

Max was roaming around the back seat, sniffing the satchel of guns. They were stuck at a red light. "I hope to Christ none of those are loaded," John said as he snuck a peek into the back seat. He tried to shush the dog away. Max persisted.

"They are. I check safety before I take them."

Ivan was eating his third lunch, a calzone with ham.

"You must have been anorexic in a previous life," John said, and put the car in drive as the light turned green. They were heading back to Queens for an update. If there was one thing Gino hated more than anything else, it was technology. He refused to use a computer. He barely liked talking on his cell phone. Face-to-face meetings were the only way he conveyed next steps when it came to violence. And they were definitely in next-step territory.

They were headed to a construction site in the Rockaways. Gino always said, "If you're coming with a body, live or dead, don't bring it to my house."

They pulled into a huge lot. In the center was the shell of an office building. Steel girders going up six floors. Concrete forms and foundation walls. The ground was torn up for sewer, gas, water, and electrical. Off to the side were four white trailers. There were no workers on site. Stalled because of union problems. Gino was going to make a fortune over the negotiations.

Ivan got out of the car, grabbed Max and the bag of guns, brought both to his own vehicle, a massive Escalade. Black, chrome, recently polished. Gleaming in the sun. As he walked towards it, he noticed there was fresh bird shit on the hood. "Fucking damn... I deal with this every day from seagulls!" he yelled as he threw the guns into the back seat. It was part of the deal he'd made with Gino. Keep what he found.

Ivan put Max in the front seat, closed the door, went around to the driver side, opened the door, put the key in the ignition and cracked the windows. John shook his head, rolled his eyes at the new father. "You cannot be too careful," Ivan said. He took the keys out, closed the door, blew a kiss to Max, and straightened his jacket and hair. The two went to the second trailer on the left and knocked.

Gino's body guy Eddie opened the door. Eddie was young, fast, tough, in great shape, and an asshole.

"Where you been?"

"What?" John asked.

"Where you been? He's been waiting all day."

"He hasn't been waiting – shut the fuck up and let us in." John didn't particularly have a bad history with the majority of Gino's guys, but he knew that giving them an inch, especially when they were lying, well... it meant grief forever.

Eddie smiled out of half his face and tilted his head waaayy back to look at Ivan. "What's up comrade?"

"I got dog."

"What? You ate a dog?"

"Long story," John said, and made his way through the trailer. It wasn't a normal one. More like an expensive motor home. To the left was a kitchen and dining room. To the right was a seating area. Behind that, an office.

Paulie Grasso was frying up something. There was a lasagna pan on the counter with layers of eggplant, sauce, and cheese.

Ivan made a noise.

"Don't *even* fucking say you're hungry," John said, and walked to the back where Gino's office was.

Gino was behind a desk. Not as nice as the one in his home, but still... he was on the phone, scratching his nose when John and Ivan walked in.

"Uh huh," Gino said, and acknowledged them. He didn't motion for them to sit down. "Yeah. Well, I don't give a shit about that." Long pause. "Or that." Pause. "I feel like I'm going to start repeating myself." Pause. "Yeah, well, that's because everything that comes out of your mouth is bullshit. You've got three more days or I'll hang you upside down, cut out your dick and your balls, and dump rock salt into the hole, and *then* I'll phone your wife and let her hear you scream while the salt slowly eats your insides." He hung up, shook his head and sighed. "Do you know, I have to come up with scarier and scarier ways of killing people just to get them to do what I ask? Does that make any sense? I mean, who ever thought you'd have to work so hard just to get people to do the right thing?"

"I don't know," John said. "But that shit would work on me."

Gino barked a laugh, motioned to the chair across from him. Ivan stood in the back. "Give me some good news. It's been a while since I've heard some good fucking news."

John sat down. "It wasn't Juan."

"You told me that. Jesus."

"It was Gordy."

"Yeah, you told me that too. I'm not fucking senile."

"We got Gordy."

"Where?"

"Here."

"Here where?"

"Here, here. Here, like, in the trunk of my car."

"Jesus fuck... he's in the trunk and you brought him here? Since when?"

"Since... now. We found him an hour ago."

"He's still alive?"

"Yeah."

"Why?"

142

"Because he's a fucking moron, but he didn't—"

"Stop," Gino said, and held his hand up. "Don't do that."

"Do what?"

"Make excuses."

"He's the reason they didn't kill me, Gino."

"What?"

"Yeah."

"He told you that?"

"Yeah."

"And not to save his own skin?"

"Well, they *didn't* kill me..."

Gino nodded. "Where are the keys?"

John took them out of his pocket, went to hand them to Gino, took them back. "You going to kill him?"

"Me? No. Ivan is."

"But I have dog—" Ivan started to say.

John shook his head. "Gino..."

"Listen, you did what I asked you to do. You found the guy who made it happen. Thank you. My faith in you is restored. Really. You don't want to get your hands dirty, I respect that. But, John, I have to do this. He's not going to tell me the rest unless I—"

"He told me the rest."

"What?"

"Yeah. The Irish guy and his partner, they're in Hoboken."

"Hoboken?"

"I cannot go to Hoboken," Ivan said.

John turned around, wide-eyed at Ivan, like, *shut the fuck up.*

"Oh, boy," Gino said. "Who's the partner?"

"Bartender at Darby's."

Gino nodded slowly. "So, you *were* right."

"Listen, they're waiting on Gordy, they're going down to A.C."

"Are you fucking kidding me?"

"No," John chuckled. "I even said—"

"We've got people down there!"

"I know." John smiled and sighed. "What about Juan?"

"What about him?"

"Gino—"

"He's fine. His wife will do more damage to him than I ever could, save killing him. But you," he leaned forward. "You need to stop collecting people. Like pets. You never know what they're thinking. Not *really*. And if they do something stupid, and I'm not even talking colossally stupid, I'm talking anywhere on the stupid scale... they just don't understand the repercussions. They'll bring you down. It's inevitable."

John nodded. "Understood. I'm not going to get in your way here. You have to do this, OK. But if we're square, I'd just as soon go home than have to see this guy one last time."

"Give Ivan the keys. Take a cab home. I'll get you a replacement ride tomorrow."

John handed the keys to Ivan.

"You got a dog?" Gino asked.

"Yes."

"What kind?"

"White dog."

Gino sighed, resigned. "OK." He leaned back, massaged his eyes a bit while Ivan walked out with John. "Eddie?"

Eddie came into the office. "Yeah, boss?"

"Get Sal on the phone from Hoboken; tell him I need a favor. John!"

John trotted back to the office. "Yeah?"

"You're coming to the wedding next Saturday?"

"Am I coming to the... well, let's see. Free food, drinks, hot women who, you know, get wet at weddings? Of course I'll be there."

"So... don't put you down for a plus one?"

"Nah."

John had already put in a request for a tux rental. He'd figured the personal invite was coming. Gino had just been crazed, and pissed about the Gordy/Irish/Juan situation. The invite meant all (or most) was forgiven.

He picked up the tux and made sure the bowtie was a clip-on. Bowties were the moon to him.

He drove over to the wedding reception (the ceremony was family and close friends only), left the new loaner with the valet, gave his name to the host, grabbed a glass of champagne off a tray, drank it, grabbed a second, and entered the house.

The place was packed. He saw plenty of recognizable faces, but was only really concerned with the food. He walked over, got a plate, handed it to a staffer and said, "Some of everything."

He waited patiently and looked around, saw four pain-in-the-asses he would just as soon ignore.

Lenny, Max, Mike and Benny came up together in Bensonhurst. They'd all been hired around the same time by the Scorpion in 1989. Running numbers, picking up drops. Like all beginners. They graduated to full-time hits when Gino was on the fence about their usefulness. They decided to hit up a pool hall in Sheepshead Bay, where a rival family, the Spinellis, was shaking down local businesses for "insurance." They were also running women, drugs and numbers out of the pool hall.

The four of them showed up with machine guns they bought off a Black guy Lenny knew from high school, Jerome Freemont. Jerome was known for not having the most reliable merchandise.

Three of the four guns worked. Benny got the short straw and spent most of the time yelling at his, while the other three shot up the place, killing most of the Spinelli people. Benny found the last one hiding behind a pinball machine, took a 7 ball and hit him in the head until it split open.

The guy's head, not the 7 ball.

They'd been working hits for the D'Escopios ever since, and they barely tolerated John.

Lenny yelled over, "Hey, make sure you don't put any meat on that guy's plate. He gets plenty when he lets queers fuck him up the ass!" The crew laughed.

John shook his head. It wasn't even low-hanging-fruit funny. It was bottom of the barrel—

Low, from somewhere, was a clearing of the throat. Lenny, Max, Mike and Benny looked over to see Gino staring at them. They went from smiling to cowed right quick.

"Sorry, Gino."

"Sorry."

"Sorry."

"Sorry, Mr. D'Escopio."

And they moved on.

Gino was standing there with a tall Black man, and either the guy's wife or his date. John had never seen him before. Gino waved him over. John nodded, turned to the guy fixing his plate and said "That's good enough, thank you," grabbed the plate, a peach-colored napkin wrapped around a fork and knife, and walked over.

Gino smiled, grabbed John's arm. "Here he is, this is the guy I was telling you about. Ray, this is John. John, this is one of my best and oldest friends, Ray."

John didn't let the surprise register on his face.

"Oldest?" Ray said, mock hurt. Gino actually laughed. Ray held out his hand. John shook it. It was unbelievably dry and calloused. "Nice to meet you."

"Nice to meet you, too."

"I'll be back," Gino said, slapped them both on the arm, and walked off.

"This is Bella, my wife."

John smiled. "Pleasure to meet you."

"Hello," she said.

Ray touched her shoulder. "Baby, can you get me a drink?"

"Sure. Can I get you anything, John?"

"No, thank you very much."

Bella walked away.

The two men sized each other up. Similar height. Similar build. Ray looked like he was in his mid- to late fifties. What he really looked like was unassuming.

"So you're the new me," Ray said.

"Pardon?"

"You're Gino's new problem solver."

"Well, I—" John looked around. "I guess that's... yeah. Some problems. So you used to—"

"Back in the day, yeah. I got back from the war and I didn't have anything to do, or much to come home to, so..."

"Marine?"

"That's right."

John put his hand up and clenched his fist. "Semper... fid... something."

"You a marine?"

"No, sir."

"Then never do that again."

"Yes, sir."

Ray smiled. "So, anyway, then this guy," he nodded towards Gino, "and his brother were trying to take on the entire city, and they needed some help. I figured it couldn't be any worse than what I just left."

"And was it?"

"Oh, he doesn't look like it these days, but that man was a bullet *magnet*." Ray's face changed when he realized what he said. "Shit, I... uh, he told me what happened. With you and..."

"Don't worry. I know exactly what you mean."

Ray nodded. "Well, the 70s were tough. The 80s... Jesus. You get him drunk enough, you ask him about the Great Cocaine War. It's what we called it, anyways, and nowadays, compared to that? Night and day, man. I don't think the new crop would last long." He looked around, lowered his voice. "Whole room full of pussies."

John barked out a laugh, covered his mouth. "Well, can't say I disagree. There's an epidemic of tough guys around here who are constantly in over their heads."

"So, nothing's changed."

Bella motioned for Ray.

"You're being summoned," John said.

"Yeah, that happens."

"Well, maybe we can get together some time. Share stories."

"Stories, huh?"

"Yeah. Like how you survived."

John stuck his hand out. Ray smiled, shook it. "Definitely. Keep your wits about you around here, young man. And always, always remember that even though you might be the smartest guy in the room... you can't think of everything."

John nodded as Ray walked away, turned and faced what he thought at first was a wall. A black and white—

"Hello, my friend," Ivan said.

"Big guy. Jesus. Where in the hell did *you* get a tuxedo?"

"Custom made. Domenico Pucci. Five thousand dollars."

"Well, it looks great." John looked around the room. "So, what's shaking?"

"I spend morning dumping bodies into caustic agent. Family recipe."

Jesus fuck.

"OK, look," John said, put his plate on a nearby table and steered Ivan outside. "Don't talk about that shit at a fucking wedding, man."

"You asked."

"Not... OK, I deserve that. Just... people want to have fun. Not—"

"*Was* fun."

"Not that kind of fun, goddammit." John went to go inside. "Wait... what bodies?"

"Men from Hoboken. I cannot go to Hob—"

"Yeah, yeah, I know—"

"Transported by Paulie and his men last night. Redheaded man. Other man, not sure who. And man who snitched. The bad men."

"Yeah, the, uhh..." John closed his eyes, pinched them with his fingers. "The bad..."

"Getting food before gone," Ivan said and walked inside.

John sighed and leaned against one of the caterer's cars. "Fuck."

CHAPTER TWENTY-TWO

Hal made small talk with people who recognized him, happy to shake some hands. He was on his third glass of wine and second plate of food.

Prosciutto and melon was fucking delicious.

He'd tried a balancing act with the glass in the crook of his arm while attempting to get food onto his fork, but gave up. His priority was to not make a mess of himself, of the suit, and he was doing OK with that. Nothing a little club soda wouldn't get out when he had the chance.

He made his way towards the back of the house, the glass and the plate in separate hands, and found a seat at a table where a younger white guy was sitting, nursing a scotch. He was in a tux, with a bow tie lying unclipped around the right side of his neck. He wasn't drunk, he was bored. Or he'd gotten some bad news.

"How's it going?" Hal asked.

The guy didn't look over. His eyes were glazed over with thought.

"That good, huh?" Hal said, mostly to himself.

The guy looked over. "Excuse me?"

"Sorry, I just asked how's it going."

"Fucking terrible. You?"

"Not so bad."

"Well good. I'd hate to know that people weren't having a good time at a wedding. Excuse me." The guy stood up and walked away.

John's head hurt as he moved away from the stranger. He thought maybe some caffeine might help.

Fucking Gordy. He liked the guy all right. Loud, terrible sense of humor, but a good mechanic, and reliable at the shop. A fun drunk.

And so stupid.

He rubbed his temples and turned around, looked at the guy who'd just talked to him. He looked familiar. John stopped a waiter. "Can I get a cup of coffee?"

"Yes, sir."

"I'll be over there," he said, and pointed back to the table. He made his way over, sat down. "Sorry about that. I just got some bad news earlier and it put the zap on my head. I'm John Moore."

"Hal. Hal Shipley."

"You're shitting me."

"No. Shipley."

John laughed. Louder than he'd expected to. Hal grinned and continued eating. "I saw you on TV. That was... that whole thing was something."

"It was something, all right."

"What the fuck are you doing here?"

"That's a really good question." Hal leaned back, took a drink, and started the story.

The waiter brought John his coffee. "Let's make this Irish, huh?" he said to the waiter, who nodded. John winced after he said it.

Irish. Fuck.

The two sat there for a while, chatting.

An hour later, the bride was walking through the rooms, smiling, waving, hugging. Tipsy, but not in an overly embarrassing way. She had a throng of bridesmaids trailing her that looked like the best thing John had seen in a long time.

And they were all taken.

"I thought weddings were where you went to *get* laid," he said. "You know, like funerals." Earlier he'd tried to find an in, but they were all attached, recently or otherwise. The remaining prospects at the house were so deep within the family it would have made a mess. He just decided to give up.

Hal beamed a smile. "Not mafia crime family weddings," Hal said. He leaned back and watched them all walk away. "Not unless you want to get shot."

"Yeah. Too much of that in my life as it is."

Hal looked at him questioningly, looked back at the women. "Might be worth it for the one in pink, there." Her outfit was tight in all the right places. She reminded him of Sally. From behind.

John looked at the half glass of mediocre scotch in his hand. It wasn't cutting it. "Let's find a next-level bottle. We're not plebs. Or, well, I'm not a..." he stood up. "Yay or nay?"

"Lead on, Macduff," Hal said, stood up, left his plate on a table, and followed.

As they got to the kitchen, Paulie stopped John, slapped him on the back hard and hugged him. Didn't say a word.

John smiled, looked at Hal like, *this happens all the time.*

"How are you doing, you fucking hump you?" Paulie asked. "You hear about that little job, huh? No one steals from our boy. No one! And you..." He reached up and pinched John's cheeks. "You did a man's job with the mammoth, who is currently eating Gino out of house and fucking home. I knew you had it in you." He looked around. "You see all the fucking trim around here?"

"Yeah, Paulie. It's all taken though. Taken trim."

Paulie was mid-sip and spit it out laughing. "Taken... hah! You just have to know which are the real whores, and which are the... well, they're all whores, aren't they?"

John nodded just because.

Hal nodded, half reluctant.

Paulie wasn't the guy you disagreed with. He was an underboss who loved to cause fear and pain. He'd been Gino's right-hand ever since the Scorpion had been killed. He was the one who found out who was responsible. An independent outfit from Baltimore that was looking to co-opt the new Chinese heroin source the D'Escopios had found. Paulie took ten guys to Maryland, rounded the crew up in an old warehouse, and kept the ones they didn't kill outright alive for four days.

Paulie came back from the trip a new man, as if he'd been on vacation.

He looked over at Hal, then at John, then at Hal, and laughed again. "I don't fucking believe it. What are the odds you two lily-white Anglo Saxon motherfuckers were going to meet? Oh, Gino's going to *love* this."

He hit John on the shoulder, laughing, and walked away.

John went to say something.

Hal held up a hand, shook his head.

John nodded.

They walked through the kitchen, through the ever-continuous noise of Italian housewives, into the small hallway that would lead them to Gino's private office.

Hal seemed concerned. "You sure this is OK?"

"Sure. We're like this," John said, making a big deal of trying to cross his fingers. He opened the door to Gino's office.

Pacing there, back and forth, was the groom. With him, two low-level men, Alfonso and Mike, who could have been brothers, but weren't.

"Sorry," John said and went to back off. The groom, Arnold Bridgeman, dentist, was in his late twenties. Reasonable face, thin, not a douchebag frat boy or a nerd. A middle-of-the-road kind of guy.

Arnold looked like he was having a panic attack.

John had heard the story of how he and Gina, Gino's only daughter, had met.

She was one of his patients.

CHAPTER TWENTY-THREE

Arnold Bridgeman breezed through high school with straight Bs and got a free ride to the University of Pittsburgh's School of Dental Medicine because his father Earl, a successful oral surgeon, was a big-shot alumnus. While he'd heard horror stories of the trade from his father, Arnold also grew up experiencing the wealth it provided.

Earl was cavalier with his money, flirted incessantly with his staff, bought them gifts, went on lavish vacations with his family, had three cars, and would retire a multi-millionaire.

Arnold had been to his father's practice hundreds of times as a kid. It had been nothing but smiles and hugs from the staff. Cleanings, the occasional cavity, braces for a year and a half, and sugar-free lollipops when he was good. The first day Arnold went to work with his father, some of the other dentists in his practice went out for dinner and drinks to celebrate.

"A toast," his father said. "To Arnold Bridgeman, whose long road led him here. I couldn't be prouder."

The group toasted, drank.

"Now, son, rule number one at the office," Earl said. "I don't care how attractive the woman is in that chair, OK? Trust me. Don't touch her unless she's unconscious."

Arnold went to talk, closed his mouth. He looked around the table, for some cue that they were joking. Earl's oldest friend Tom cracked a smile and then laughed.

"You!" Earl said, mock angry. "You always ruin that joke," and grabbed Tom's shoulder, shaking him.

"Jesus, the look on his face," Tom said, tears coming down his cheeks.

Laughs all around. Arnold smiled.

"Seriously, though," his father said. "Keep away from the patients. Malpractice insurance doesn't cover the fucking nightmare that comes with the bad PR of sexual harassment, molestation, etcetera, etcetera."

"It's what whores are for," Tom said.

"That's *right*," Earl said. "You take a quick trip down to Atlantic City, or wherever... hell, there are plenty up here."

"I'll give you some numbers, kid," Tom said. "Just wear a condom, for chrissake."

"Now, the staff...? Eh. We try and keep a don't-shit-where-you-eat policy, but sometimes... I mean..." He looked at Tom and another dentist, Jerry.

Seriously.

They shrugged, smiling.

"Sometimes they just... I mean, if they're up for it," Jerry said. He was fifty and absurdly handsome for his age. "But not at the office."

"No," Earl said. "No fucking at the office."

Arnold nodded. His parents had divorced fifteen years back. His mother wouldn't talk about it. His father said they were just unhappy.

Now he knew why.

Arnold had always respected his father. His mother would sugarcoat their relationship whenever he would ask what had happened. Then she'd change the subject. He had no idea his father had been such a... well, scumbag.

The conversation devolved from there.

He sat there at the table listening to them talk. He hatched a plan. Two years and out. Two years and he'd build his own practice. He could stomach two years for the money, for the experience. He'd keep his head down. He'd keep his hands off the staff, and he wouldn't get involved with any of his patients.

He'd been working at the Bridgeman Dental Group for about a year when Gina D'Escopio walked in.

Gina wasn't a classic beauty. Her head was a bit on the narrow side, her nose was a bit too big for her face. She had a long neck. She had one mole on her left cheek and another on her forehead, top right. She'd plucked her eyebrows into two thin curves, wore a bit too much jewelry, had jet-black hair, and a voice straight out of Queens. She was curvy but fit, wearing a tight skirt and a shirt that had the top three buttons undone.

But it was her eyes that did Arnold in. Eyes that stayed on his the entire time he was giving her a cleaning. Eyes bright with humor, with real interest in what he was saying, and filled with dirty thoughts, all at the same time.

By the end of her appointment, he knew he was going to break that rule. He didn't make the first move, out of professionalism. But he somehow knew she would.

He left that night, went home, ate dinner, watched a movie, found some porn star that looked exactly like her, jerked off, and fell directly asleep.

The next day, after a long shift of extractions, cleanings, and two cappings, he got to his car, a used 1994 BMW, and found a note on the windshield.

Chelsea Lounge, 8 p.m.

She was there when he got there, even though he was fifteen minutes early. Evening dress, classy, low cut, hair done up in a beehive, if you can believe it, and looking like she just vamped out of a 70s *Playboy*. She was twenty-four years old and the sexiest thing Arnold had ever seen.

Arnold was a reasonable looking guy, and had been with a handful of women, but in his life, he'd never been ridden as hard as she rode him that first night.

It was a whirlwind romance and he went in with his eyes completely closed. Gina rarely discussed her family. Arnold never bothered to pry. He was addicted to her. Her sounds, her smell. There was a devotion—obsession—there that he'd never experienced before.

He asked her to marry him on their two-year anniversary, after he'd gotten permission from her father. He'd gotten along with Gino quite well, he thought.

Gino would say he tolerated the man. For who he was, for what he was, but more importantly, that he wasn't anywhere near the life.

CHAPTER TWENTY-FOUR

Arnold was pacing back and forth and stopped when the door opened. Light from a skylight haloed him briefly, causing deep shadows across his face, and he turned in slow motion, aghast.

"Sorry," John said, and went to leave.

Hal pushed in. "What's going on here?"

"Who are you?" Arnold asked.

"Nobody. Sorry. Thought it would be empty," John said. "Come on, Hal."

Hal didn't move.

Arnold nodded, went back to pacing.

John turned to Alfonso with a questioning look, who said, "Babysitting."

"What?"

"Cold feet."

"Cold..." John said.

"But they already got married..." Hal said.

Alfonso nodded slowly, smiling. A glint from inside his jacket. A gun in a shoulder holster.

"Arnold, Arnold, Jesus, are you thinking of leaving *now*?" John asked. He couldn't believe it.

"I can't do this," Arnold muttered, and began wiping his forehead. He checked his fingers for sweat. Then he started taking his pulse.

"You got to be shitting me, man." John made his way into the room.

"Don't—" Arnold said and stopped pacing, put his hand out, a finger extended. "Don't. Please don't do this."

"Do what?"

"Don't kill me."

"Don't what?" John asked. He could hear a low chuckle out of Hal.

"Look, this was all a mistake, OK? I made a mistake and I just need to leave. Please." Arnold put his hand down, tried to take a deep breath. It didn't work. "Oh my God, I can't breathe."

John looked around the room. All smiles. No help. "Arnold, Arnold, Arnold. You got married. Of *course* it's a fucking mistake. But you can't just turn it off. You can't just leave."

"I don't know what I was thinking. This is... you know, it's these *people.*"

"Whoa, easy with that—" John said.

Hal snickered again.

"I thought maybe she was exaggerating, you know? Women do that. My dad's this, and he's that. I get it. *My* dad's a serial cheater. On my mom, on his taxes! But then I found out what she was talking about and oh my God!"

"Serial cheater?" Hal asked.

John waved him off. "Dude... it's been like three years. You're just figuring this out?"

"What am I going to do?"

"I... listen, it's not that bad," John said.

Snicker from Mike.

"Seriously, this, here... they... it's not that bad. The papers blow things all out of proportion, you know." John tried to be as convincing as he could.

"It is that bad! He's in the news, and the lawsuits and jail and the DEAD BODIES, and my mom did a Google search and had to go to the hospital!"

"The fuck is a Google?" Hal asked.

Alfonso covered his mouth.

"Arnold, calm down," John said.

"You calm down!"

Hal half turned away, shaking from laughing.

"You've got to just take it easy. Deep breaths," John said and slowly moved over to him. "What are you worried about?"

"I'm scared."

"About what?"

"What if I hear things? What if I find out things? What if Gina talks in her sleep?"

John turned to Hal and mouthed, *talks in her sleep?*

Hal snorted.

"I've heard the stories, OK? I've heard the stories and I've watched the movies and—"

"The movies?"

"Yeah."

"Like what?"

"*The Godfather*," Arnold said.

"The what?" John said.

"Never heard of it," Hal said.

Alfonso barked a laugh.

"Listen, what if the cops come and bother me? What if we have kids and they use them as leverage? What if—"

"Stop," John said, and put his hand hard on Arnold's shoulder. "You're hysterical. Relax."

Arnold's eyes had gone wide by this point, and he was barely breathing.

"Someone get him a drink," John said, and he saw Arnold's eyes go wider. "What?" John asked, seriously concerned.

"That's a line from *The Godfather*!"

"Arnold, Jesus, this is not a horse head kind of family! Sit down a second, OK?"

Arnold sat down.

No one had noticed, but Gino had come in the side entrance. He stayed against the wall, in the shadow of a corner, watching, listening.

John got in close. "No one is going to involve you in the family. No one. You know why? Because of all this shit right here. You've successfully removed yourself from ever being trusted by the family, ever. Seriously."

"Really?" Arnold asked as Mike brought him a drink.

"Yeah. Hey, don't be too happy about it. Not being trusted is a big fucking deal."

"It is?"

"Yeah. Everyone in this room? All trusted people. Like this guy here. Hal. You recognize him?"

"No."

"Hal, you want to jump in here? He's the strong, silent type, but..."

Hal walked over and sat down. He looked at Arnold sternly for a long time before—

"I was homeless and your new father-in-law took me in. Now I'm beholden to him forever, and if he tells me I have to shoot you in the face, I'm gonna do it."

John swallowed hard, his eyes bulged, and he had an impossible time keeping a straight face.

Hal nodded. "Consequences be damned. You know why? Because there are two constants in life that will get you through it all. Family and loyalty." Hal motioned to one of the guy's for his gun. "Give me your piece." The guy handed it over. "Now, listen," Hal said, and cocked the gun. He put it to Arnold's cheek, who started to cry. "Is Mr. D'Escopio asking you to join the family business?"

"N-n-no."

"Is he asking you to do anything illegal?"

"N-n-n-no!"

"Does Gino want you to take care of his baby girl?"

"Y-yes!"

"You going to fuck that up?"

"No!"

"You do drugs?"

"No!"

"You drink?"

"No! Yes!"

"You get drunk?"

"No!"

"You cheat?"

"No!"

"Don't lie to me! Are you a cheating piece of shit like your father?"

"I don't cheat!"

Hal tried to think of something else to ask. "You going to talk to the cops?"

"Oh, Jesus!"

"Are you?"

"No! Jesus!"

John had tears streaming down his face. He wiped them off.

"Then calm the fuck down and just do as you're told. You're a fucking dentist. What in the holy fuck could you possibly do for the family except clean everyone's teeth? Which you're going to do, right?"

"Yes!"

"It's not like they offer dental here, you know?"

"No! I mean yes!"

Hal grabbed both of Arnold's shoulders. "Gino's thrilled his daughter married a fucking nobody who wouldn't know one end of a gun from the other. He's got a hundred guys for that job. But he's only got one guy who he'll point to and say 'take care of it' if he finds out his new son-in-law hurt his baby girl. And that's me."

Whimpers.

"So, you're going to keep it in your pants. You're not going to fuck your assistant or your secretary or whoever the fuck it is dentists fuck. You're not going to go on a junket and fuck some stripper—" John mouthed the word "*junket*" and made a face. Hal caught himself "—or a convention or whatever. Right? You're not going to bring home a disease from some skank you found. You're going to fly right and stay clean. You're going to get Gina pregnant. You're going to shower them both with gifts, spoil the living hell out of the kid, and you're going to keep your head down and your nose clean."

"Yes, sir."

"Good." Hal held the gun up. Mike took it away, eased down the hammer. Hal stood them both up. Arnold's knees started to go out from under him. John steadied him. Hal squared off with the young man and straightened his suit. "Now go enjoy the party."

Arnold hugged Hal, who patted him on the back and rolled his eyes. John covered his whole face with both hands.

Arnold broke the hug, turned to John. John offered his hand. Arnold shook it, nodded, wiped his face, smiled, and left the room with Alfonso and Mike.

John fell down on his knees, laughing uncontrollably.

"Too much?" Hal asked.

It sent John into another fit of laughter.

"It depends…" Gino said from the back shadow.

John instantly stopped laughing and got up off the floor. "Oh, shit," he said under his breath.

"Yeah. It depends on if my wife finds out or not."

"I'm not going to say anything," Hal said, which got John giggling.

"Guys…" Gino said, and shook his head.

"I'm sorry, Gino. It just… I mean, the guy was talking crazy," John said.

"Yeah. Sorry," Hal said.

Gino looked at both of them. They were acting like they were in high school. "You know, I'm going to get a lot of shit from people about you two. My son-in-law, not so much. The further away from all this my daughter is the better. And times change. I've hired outside the family before… people don't like it. Especially non-Italians. Even

163

at the start of the twenty-first century, it's kind of a big fucking problem. Don't make me regret it."

"We won't, Gino," John said.

Hal rolled his eyes and said, "*You* won't."

Gino sighed, nodded. "Now, tell me the truth," he said and put both hands on the back of his chair. "You were in here for the good booze."

"It was all his idea," Hal said, and pointed to John.

John laughed, his face mock angry. "Jesus, you fold! At the first sign of trouble, you fucking asshole!" John smacked Hal on the shoulder.

Hal laughed, smacked him back.

Gino went to a glass cabinet, opened it, took out a bottle of bourbon. He cracked the seal, took out three glasses, poured three mean pours, handed one to John, one to Hal, took the third. "Salud," he said, and drank the full glass. John looked at Hal, who shrugged. They both knocked it back.

"I'm tentatively thanking you for setting him straight, with the option to retroactively kick the shit out of both of you. Time will tell." He handed John the bottle. "Knock yourselves out." Gino went to a mirror, did a once over, liked what he saw, and left the office.

Gino found John and Hal in his office two hours later, drunk off their asses, hysterical. The bottle was almost finished, food plates discarded here and there.

In the future, when Gino would describe their friendship, their first meeting, he would say it was a match made in heaven.

And for the next eighteen years, John and Hal worked together, solving problems for the mob.

CHAPTER TWENTY-FIVE

Carla sat in the lunchroom at work, looking at the text she just got from Alex. It read: *Gabby dumped me.*

"Shit," she said.

It was early May, 2002. Carla had convinced eighteen of her fellow nurses and staff members to go with Alex for their taxes. There wasn't an unsatisfied customer in the bunch. Alex raked in over three grand, and gave it all over to his parents. Carla watched it happen. Alex had insisted she be there.

Abigail walked in, sat down, brown bagging it. "If I eat peanut butter another day in a row, I'm going to come in here and go postal."

"Just do it on my day off."

"Uh-uh bitch. You're the first one I'm going to come find. Put you out of your misery."

"You think I'm miserable?"

"Miserable might be the wrong word. Forlorn, maybe."

"That basically means the same thing as miserable."

"Well, then I was right the first time." Abigail bit into her peanut butter and jelly sandwich, made a face.

"Let me see if I can work this out."

"Do it," Abigail said, and washed down some sandwich with a small container of milk.

"I live to work."

"Yup."

"I have no social life."

165

"True."

"When I do go out, I don't talk to anyone."

"You see what I'm saying?"

"Yeah. There's more, right?"

"There is, but does there really need to be?"

Carla shook her head no. "Alex just got dumped."

Abigail's eyes went wide. "Oh, honey, you have GOT to hit that."

"What? No. Fuck no."

"Why not?!"

"Because I'm not screwing a friend on a rebound. That would be worse than a pity fuck. No, absolutely not."

"But he's so vulnerable and sad and he'll be crying—"

"You should go fuck him."

"I would if I could…" Abigail drifted for a second. Carla watched, smiling.

"Was it nice?"

"Nice isn't the word. Transcendent. That's the word to use."

"See? That doesn't mean the same as nice."

Abigail tapped the side of her temple. "Word-a-day calendar. That's what it is."

Carla nodded.

Her shift was over around seven. She found Alex at Samson's. He was sitting at the bar, not looking like a guy who'd just gotten dumped, watching a baseball game.

"Hey!" he said, and slid a chair out for her. "How's it going?"

"It's… going," she said, and sat down. "How are you doing?"

"Fine. Good. Great. Want a drink?" He motioned to the bartender.

"Sure, uh… just a… what, a Guinness?"

"You got it," the bartender said, and walked away.

Alex watched the television.

Carla adjusted herself in the seat and looked at his face. It was a mask of concentration. She moved her hand close to his face. Closer. Closer. She snapped her fingers.

He looked at her. "Hey! When did you get here?"

"Are you fucking serious?"

"No, I'm not, Mrs. Guinness. Jesus. Just, you know, invested in the game."

"How invested?"

"A hundred or so…"

"Or so, what?"

"Five hundred."

"On a baseball game?"

"Yeah."

"Who's playing?"

"The Phillies and the Astros. Myers was pitching—it's why I picked them for the win."

"Why Myers?"

"You're going to think it's stupid."

"No. Tell me."

The bartender brought over her drink. Alex watched him walk away before he said anything.

"Because of Breyers."

"Breyers… what, the ice cream?"

"Yeah."

"OK…"

"And you used to work at the ice cream shop—"

"Oh God."

"And I just thought it was a sign, you know?"

Carla covered her face. "Are you serious?"

Alex started laughing. "No! Jesus! You never bet against your home team. Ever. It's bad fucking luck. Breyers… Jesus, Carla!"

She laughed. He laughed. They shared a moment when their eyes locked. It was brief, and Carla knew in that instant she was going to stick to her guns.

"Tell me what happened."

"With who?"

"Alex, come on."

He drank his beer. She drank some of hers.

"Yeah, uh, I couldn't keep up," he said, wiping his mouth.

"What?"

"I couldn't keep up. She, uh, she was doing a lot of drugs. A lot. And then I got all those clients, you know?"

She nodded.

"Thank you, again. And I just couldn't do both. And so she was going out all the time and was coming home fucked up... made for some interesting nights. Waking up to this woman on top of me, kissing me and getting me har—"

Carla put her hand up and said, "I get it."

"Yeah. It was... pretty amazing. But she started staying over a 'friend's' apartment. She kept saying she was out too late and wanted to just crash and her friend's name was Sasha and I thought OK, I know Sasha. I've met Sasha. She's great."

"OK."

Alex smiled, finished his beer. "It was a different Sasha. Yeah. A guy. Taller than me. More muscles. Has a big place in Chestnut Hill. He's an 'artist.' Not sure what kind. Anyway, she comes home and she's... well, exhausted. But the kind of exhausted I'd seen before, you know? Like when we first started... and I just knew... and so we got into it the next morning and she said yeah, she'd been fucking him the past two or three months and that it was no big deal."

"She said that?"

"Yeah. I think he was part of like a tantric sex cult or something? I don't know, because she had this whole new philosophy on what was acceptable, and fucking other people was at the top of the list. Still, she said it was time for us to re-evaluate our inner energetic priorities."

"Jesus. That sounds right out of the tantric sex cult pamphlet."

"Right? That's what I thought, too."

168

"So what did you do?"

"What else could I do? I joined the cult."

"Stop it. Come on…"

He laughed. "I told her to grab what she could, and get the fuck out."

She nodded. "Nice. Simple. To the point."

"Yeah. I feel… not so bad, to be honest. I mean, I feel fucking terrible, but I don't feel suicidal. And I honestly thought that was part of the process of getting dumped by a Polish model. Or any model, really."

"I've never heard of that before."

"Oh, yeah. It's totally a thing. There are support groups and everything."

"Huh. Well, here's to you and escaping the dreadful thoughts of taking one's own life over believing they're *so* pathetic that they need someone else to make them happy."

Alex looked at her. "Jesus… that… where did that come from?"

"A few years of harsh introspection."

"No shit. Well, cheers to that." They touched glasses and drank. "Hey. You have some vacation time coming up, right?"

"Yeah. Well, I mean, I have to put in the time, but yeah."

"Three weeks from now. Memorial Day weekend. A three-day party at a friend's place in Cape Cod."

"Cape Cod? Are you serious?"

"Yeah. Woods Hole, specifically. His place is awesome. There's going to be like thirty people there, it's going to be great. It's right on the water, tons of stuff… and people to do…"

She smiled. "Uh huh. Should be nice, having a rebound weekend."

"My thoughts exactly! Or a 'I'm thirty'—"

"Fuck you!"

"—'and my hymen grew back,' weekend. You have to go. Please. Please go."

"I'm twenty-eight and my hymen—fuck you, talking about my… I'll think about it."

"It's going to be so much fun. A friend of mine is going. Well, sort of friend. He dated Michelle for a while." Michelle was Alex's older sister.

"Oh, shit. The man's been through hell."

"Yeah, well, we always got along and I told him about it, so he's getting on the train in New York."

"Train? Shit."

"What?"

"Nothing, I just sort of swore off… never mind. OK, so, this guy got a name?"

"Yeah, he's got a name. Hal."

CHAPTER TWENTY-SIX

The first time John and Hal worked together on a job was the fall of 2000, two months after the wedding.

As he did with particularly delicate situations, Gino brought John on to solve a problem. The lone surviving member of the Capreze family, Angelo, had been indicted for tax evasion and was out on bail. He was seventy-six years old and needed to disappear. There had been several attempts to get him out of the country, but the man was under constant surveillance.

"I need to see the layout," John said. It sounded like a logistical nightmare.

Angelo lived in a large house out on the Island, in Great Neck. The man hadn't been part of D'Escopio business for over fifteen years, but still had interests he looked after. And, like most Americans, he hated paying taxes. He'd filed fraudulent tax returns for decades, and an intrepid FBI agent, in conjuncture with the IRS, had decided to use him as a career maker.

Victorian-style houses dotted the block, all with large lawns. Red brick and white paint as far as the eye could see, as if the residents were given strict guidelines on what their homes could look like.

Roads on both sides of the block went to side streets, which emptied to a main road that would get you in the general direction of the LIE, and then anywhere. He looked at a map first, but was having trouble visualizing it. Then he tried to plan his way out of the neighborhood with MapQuest. He was having trouble.

Finally, he drove out east to see it in person.

It *was* a logistical nightmare.

Stop signs, stop lights, and speed bumps, not to mention heavy traffic during the day. Water to the north, and an eight-minute drive to the nearest thoroughfare, Northern Boulevard. Three churches within two miles of the place would make doing it on a Sunday impossible. Not to mention, the Great Neck police station was half a mile away.

He spoke with their guy, a captain who got regular Christmas presents from the Caprezes for years, who told him the deal. Two cop cars on either side of the block. Three shifts of state police and an in-person visual I.D. of the suspect twice a day.

"For a seventy-six-year-old man?"

"The guy's a flight risk."

"Oh, come on," John said, and rubbed his mouth. "They bringing the Feds in on this too?"

"Would they tell me?"

"Jesus, I would fucking hope so."

"This is a mess," John said. He had photos, some blown-up maps with lines for potential routes.

"We can just pay the cops off," Gino said. To him, the printouts looked like blobs of shit.

"They're not cops, they're state police, and they're doing three shifts, twenty-four hours a day. That's twelve guys, and they all have to keep their mouths shut."

"So just pay four of them and make it happen during that window."

"Look, even if we did, we'd just be leaving them high and dry, and it'd come back to us eventually. Even if we used proxies, it's not like your friendship's a secret. We have to make it a real fuck-up, not a paid one."

"So?"

The trial was in three days, and all signs pointed to a quick one. Once taken into custody, he'd be sequestered to a hotel room near city hall, then the trial, then straight to the tombs under the courts, and then to God knows where.

"Why aren't his people taking care of this?" John asked.

"He doesn't have people any more. They got him on a bullshit charge that's going to stick, and they're going to try and flip him. Not that the fucking guy knows anything, but some asshole's trying to make a career out of him, and he'll provide color. Maybe fill in some gaps..."

Once a year, Gino spoke with Angelo to catch up. It was coffee or lunch or dinner, and never more than an hour.

"So? Wouldn't it be easier to kill him?"

Gino looked at John. "Just like that? Coming from Mister I Don't Want to Get My Hands Dirty?"

"I'm just saying—"

"He was my father's best friend's brother. He's not a rat. He doesn't deserve prison. He deserves a nice retirement in a non-extradition country with women and lobster and fruity drinks, not having to look over his shoulder for the rest of his fucking life. Got it?"

"I got it. I'm working on it."

"Work faster."

Sal's Bar and Grill was a relic of the 1970s that still had the neon, still had the Formica and the red stools, the nicotine stains since forever, and those wall mirrors that had the gold leaf designs in them. John sat there with a headache, eating a hamburger and steak fries, drinking a beer and wondering how the fuck he was going to solve this particular nightmare.

Mid-bite he decided to bring in an outside perspective. He got up, swallowed the rest of his beer, went to the bar. "Carrie, can I have the phone?" Carrie the bartender, tall, thin, flared-out black hair you only got by using an entire can of hairspray. Thick eyebrows, fake blue contact lenses, spray-painted make-up. She handed him the bar phone. "I love what you've done with your—" he said, and motioned to his own face.

She smiled. "When are you going to ask me out?" She knew who he worked for. Sal's was a magnet for people in the life. Carrie was a bit nutso. She'd spread herself thin with some of the clientele about a year prior. It ended up costing a guy his life after a fight over who was going home with whom.

She'd shrugged the whole thing off with a c'est la vie attitude.

"As soon as you dump your boyfriend." John dialed.

"He's not my boyfriend, he's my husband." Her husband was a... something. She'd told him one time, maybe. It didn't stick. She'd met him after the trouble and used the marriage as a Band-Aid, still took on side guys.

John looked at her and winked. "Oh, well, in that case..."

A half an hour later, a medium well done steak in front of him, Hal listened to John while he sawed into it, took a bite.

Sawed, took another bite. "Sounds ridiculous," he said, half chewing.

"It is ridiculous."

"So why not just kill him?"

"Because he's not the bad guy. He's the good guy going to jail for the wrong reasons." Hal looked at him. "OK, bad reasons. Stupid reasons. I don't know, but they're not worried about him flipping, they just want to save him the grief."

"OK. And you can't buy off the cops?"

"No."

"And you can't sneak him out of the house?"

"You mean like over fences and shit? No. The guy's got a bum leg and he's pushing eighty."

"How about a disguise?"

"A what?"

"You know—"

"Like a Groucho mask?"

"Yeah. That's exactly what I meant."

"They know how many people are in the house, and who. Put him in a fake wig and walk him out, they're going to know."

Hal cut another piece, chewed, leaned back. "What we need is a diversion."

"A…" John thought about it. "Like a bomb?"

"Do you know how to make a bomb?"

"No."

"Then, no, not 'like a bomb.' Jesus. You can get in there?"

"Yeah, I think so."

"They know your face?"

"No."

"You have a record?"

"No."

Hal thought about it a minute. "Good. You won't even be breaking any laws… just gotta…"

"What?"

"We need a getaway car."

Gino didn't look happy. "You two have got to be fucking kidding me."

"Listen, Gino—" John started.

"This is what you came up with? You've had this a week now, and this—"

"You've had this a week?" Hal asked John.

"Well, yeah, but—"

"And you just came to me with this?"

"Jesus," John said. "Look, we can't get him out of there without anyone seeing—"

"Buy the goddamn cops!" Gino slammed his hand down on his desk.

"It's not going to work, Gino! The State Police Chief is a hard ass, he hates the Italians on the Island more than anyone else, and his brother-in-law is a state representative."

"Which should make him infinitely easier to bribe!" Gino yelled.

Hal tapped his finger to his lips. "That's true…"

"Would you just look at the plan?" John spread his arms out, showing the printouts, the diagrams.

Gino took a deep breath and folded his hands under his chin. "You want to hear the kinds of ideas I'm getting? Cop assassinations. Seriously. Kidnapping their families. One of my guys said we should roll up to the blockade and use a bazooka." John laughed. "Now, when I originally said no idea was too stupid, I should have realized—"

"Yeah, never a good thing to say that," Hal said, smiling.

"Probably those four idiots," John said, referring to Lenny, Max, Mike, and Benny. He'd had a few run-ins with them since the wedding. It was never cordial.

"Which?" Gino asked.

"Mike and Ike and the… their friends."

"That was the best you could come up with?" Hal asked.

"Shut up," John said.

"Yeah, it was them," Gino said. "What's the problem?"

"Honestly Gino, I don't know why you keep them around."

"I keep them around because they do things you don't want to do. Serious things. Things that allow me to protect my family, and my interests. Capisce?"

John nodded, kowtowed.

"Listen fellas, you think I want that kind of agita? I've got a responsibility to this guy. The other families are telling me to let him go, and I can't. You're supposed to be the smart ones—"

John interrupted him. "Gino, I go in the night before. I bring in the clunker. We bring him out of the house with a diversion up the block, people coming in for a party or something—we're going to work out the details. He spends the night in the trunk and in the morning we drive him out of there."

"And if they check the trunk?" Gino didn't sound convinced.

"They're not going to," Hal said.

"And why's that?"

John smiled. "They'll be too busy."

John stared at himself in the mirror. "Dye my hair… that wasn't part of the fucking plan."

Hal rolled his eyes. "Please, you love it."

John sat in the chair of a ladies beauty salon, a recommendation from Carrie the bartender. "See Gail," she'd said. "She's phenomenal."

Gail was tall, frosted-blonde hair, make-up out to here, with huge nails and a fake tan. But cute. "We doing a trim, too?"

"No, just the dye," Hal said, taking control, like the husband who says *she fell down some stairs*.

"'Just the dye,'" John said and rolled his eyes. "How long does it take for this shit to wash out?"

Gail shrugged. "Couple of weeks."

"Fuuuuck," he said, and slunk lower into the leather chair.

Hal sighed. "Look, it's easier for you to go darker than it is for the other guy to go lighter, OK?"

"Easy for you to say."

"It's the truth. And plus he said no."

"He said no, huh?"

"His exact words were 'fuck no.' Not to mention, he'd look like shit as a, well, dirty blonde, I guess."

"We call it 'dark blonde' now," Gail said. "Dirty doesn't sell well."

John looked at her through the mirror. "Uh huh." He turned to Hal. "Who are we using? Minnow?"

"Milo. He's a cousin of someone, or a nephew. I can't remember."

"Fantastic."

"Same build, same height, that'll be enough. Just relax. This is going to work."

Gail took two hours. By the time it was finished, Hal was calling him Ponyboy. John punched him on the shoulder, grabbed his things and left.

When he got home, he kept looking at himself in the mirror. It took a while to get used to it. He looked meaner. More confident. He never told Hal that the black hair looked pretty fucking good on him.

That evening, John made his way out to Great Neck in a four-door piece of shit with a souped-up engine, just in case. He filled the tank when he was close and drove down to the cordon, left side of the house. The cop who stopped him was what one would expect. Muscles, hat, sunglasses at dusk, professional attitude. "Evening, sir. Can I help you?"

"I'm here to see Michael Snyder, number 302. Has something happened?"

"No sir, just routine."

Routine.

It took every ounce of will power for John not to roll his eyes.

"I'm going to need to see some I.D. They're expecting you?"

"I would hope so, I'm his dinner guest. Jacob Sherman." John handed the trooper his new fake I.D., reflecting the hair color, change of name, address, the works. The trooper took it, went to his car and was replaced by a clone, another cop who stood there watching, waiting.

John had made the arrangements with Michael Snyder a few days before. He was a contractor who did mostly dock maintenance, and had worked with Angelo Capreze on and off for the last two decades. It was one of the businesses Angelo still kept tabs on, the docks out in West Bay Shore, and it was the reason Snyder could afford a house in one of the most expensive parts of Long Island. John did a face-to-face with the guy at his office and told him as much as he needed to hear.

Snyder took some convincing. "What the hell am I supposed to say is the reason?"

John told him he would be there to seal a "deal" over a home-cooked meal.

"What deal?"

Jesus fucking Christ...

Snyder sent his wife out of town to her mother's, and had her leave her car in front of their house. She didn't understand why. It

178

caused a half-hour fight. Shrill, on the way out the door. "*We* complain when the neighbors park on the street! I don't understand why—"

The trooper came back and handed John his I.D. "Thank you, sir, you can go on in."

"Thanks very much."

The clone officer moved his patrol car and John drove through. What he thought was going to happen, happened. He got an escort.

The patrol car followed him to the Snyder house and waited as John drove into the roundabout. He pointed the car towards the street, got out, waved to the officer. John took a quick look around. He was pretty sure the trunk couldn't be seen from either cordon. As he walked to the front door to ring the bell, the lights came up on the front of the house. There was an auto-sensor.

And the cops had seen it happen.

Michael Snyder sat across from him at the dinner table and ate in silence. His maid had cooked a pot roast with potatoes, onions, and carrots, with a side salad. It was delicious.

John sat there for a while until the silence got to him. The two made small talk about Snyder's business, his family.

Neither of them brought up the job, or Angelo.

"Hey. Can you disable the light sensor out on the front yard from in the house?"

"Yes."

"Good. Do it."

Snyder got up in the middle of his meal, walked over to the front door, opened a small panel and clicked a switch. "We get deer, sometimes. Front yard, backyard. They set off the sensors so much, most of the time I just leave them off. I turned the backyard one off, too." He sat back down.

Once dinner was done, Snyder said goodnight and went upstairs. John wouldn't see him again until morning.

It was 8:00 p.m.

He had seven hours to kill before the next police shift change.

He grabbed a backpack he'd brought with him. It had the printouts, maps and all, and he went over the plan again.

He took out a pair of binoculars and stealthily looked at both cordons, which he could see just past the tall, thin trees that marked the property line.

Business as usual.

He watched TV, read a pile of *Newsday*s the guy had sitting around.

He made some coffee.

By 10:30 p.m. he was exhausted. He set his phone's alarm for 12:30 a.m. and took a nap.

He dreamt of women with frosted blonde hair slicing his head open with their ten-inch nails, and massaging his brain.

He was thankful when the alarm went off.

John sat up on the couch and got his bearings. His side hurt from how he'd been sleeping. His head was swimming a bit from the dream, and he had to piss. He sat there for a bit, letting his body adjust, and the used the ground-floor bathroom.

He drank some of the leftover room-temperature coffee and stood by the front living-room window, waiting for the 1:00 a.m. shift change. As the clock on his phone ticked off the remaining minutes, he saw headlights and shadows moving up the street.

On cue, a car full of women pulled up, asking for directions at the left cordon.

He pulled out the binoculars again.

John had gotten bartender Carrie to get some girlfriends to help out. One of them was already so drunk, she puked out the back window, unplanned.

John chuckled, grabbed his phone and sent out a one-word text:
NOW

A few seconds later, the trunk of John's car opened slightly. Milo climbed out wearing a suit jacket, slacks, a white button-down shirt and a tie, and made a crab-like run for the Snyders' backyard. He ran to a glass sliding door off the patio and waved at John who let him in.

"Where's the fucking bathroom?" Milo said, pleading.

"Down the hall," John said.

"Fuck! And whatever that smell is, I want some."

John took a plate out of the oven he'd saved for the kid.

A few minutes later, he got a text from Carrie. *You owe me the fucking of a lifetime.*

Yeah, she was married. So, OK.

John wrote back, *I'll think about it.*

Milo ate and didn't talk much.

"We have to be fast," John said.

Grunt.

"And he's old, so we have to be careful, too."

Grunt.

"You have the route down?"

A *yes* of a grunt.

"Tell me."

"Listen, just let me finish this, OK? I feel like I spent the last day in a fucking fish can. Like the, uhh…"

"Sardines."

"Those. I know the plan. We'll go over it, just, Jesus, give me a minute."

"OK."

"There any booze around?"

"No booze," John said.

"Some wine—"

"It's 1:30 in the morning—"

"So?"

"—and I don't need you drunk. We need to go over the plan. The sun's going to be up soon. Soon-ish."

Another grunt.

Milo finished his food, leaned back and stretched. John heard a couple of pops, felt some sympathy for the guy.

He looked him over, saw some similarities. *Maybe this will work...*

"OK," Milo said, pushing his plate away. "Let's go over it."

3:00 a.m.

Sneaking out the back of the house, John and Milo went through two backyards before they got to Angelo Capreze's house. A short, old man opened the patio door, looked at them both, shook his head and allowed them inside.

"Translate," John said to Milo.

"What?"

"He doesn't speak English very well."

Angelo made a *comme ci, comme ça* with his hand.

"Fuck, OK, my Italian's rusty."

"Better than mine."

"Fuck, OK."

"We're going to put you in the trunk now, Angelo." John lowered his voice after he realized he was doing that thing, like talking to deaf or old people, raising his voice for no reason. "Are you ready?"

Milo talked. Angelo nodded.

"You'll be in there about eight hours. OK?"

Milo talked. Angelo said something. Milo chuckled.

"What?"

"He said, no, it's not OK, but it's better than prison."

"That's exactly right," John said. "You need to eat something? Go to the bathroom?"

Milo talked. Angelo shook his head.

"OK. Tell him to bring a coat."

Twenty minutes later they made their way out the back of the house, over to the Snyders and around to the front. A combination of the dark, the trees, the hour meant they were able to make their way to John's sedan without being seen.

John popped the trunk quietly and waited as Milo slid Angelo inside. He said something to him. Angelo gave a thumbs-up.

They closed the trunk slowly, quietly, and went back into the Snyders.

They sat in silence for almost four hours.

By the time 8:15 a.m. rolled around, they'd switched clothes. John spent twenty minutes ironing what Milo had come in.

The in-person check was scheduled for 9 a.m., but could happen half an hour on either side. Or maybe an hour. Snyder kept a lookout, just in case.

John handed Milo his keys and his backpack. "You know where you're going." It was more of a statement.

"Absolutely."

"And you know the guy you're handing him off to."

Milo nodded. He was nervous.

"Relax, we do this all the time."

"Really?"

John nodded, feigning confidence. He was terrified.

Odds were he was going to spend some time in prison. After the embarrassment, the finger pointing, the bad press, the cops would do their best to jam him up, make something up so it'd stick.

If the kid got stopped with the old man in the car, well, they'd all get sent up. But that was the least of John's worries. If the plan failed, Gino would look weak in front of the other families, and it was possible he wouldn't come back from it.

The three of them ate cereal for breakfast. While Milo was in the bathroom, Snyder asked, "So, what's going to happen to me?"

"Nothing. I think."

"My business, my employees..." he shook his head. "They're going to figure this out. The cops, I mean."

"They might, sure, but they can't do shit to you. Or me. Our goal is to make sure he—" John pointed to the bathroom "—doesn't get stopped. That's it."

"They're going to call me in for questioning."

"So?"

"What do you mean 'so'?"

"What do you know? You loaned your wife's car out to some guy who got drunk the night before."

"Why?"

"Why what?"

"Why did I loan you my wife's car?"

"I don't know, make something up." John realized he hadn't thought this far ahead.

Snyder looked incredulous. "Make something u—"

"Tell them my car wouldn't start and I had to get to a meeting. OK? You let me stay over, a business associate. What else is there to say? You don't know me. I overdid it at dinner with the wine and all... this big business deal you and I agreed to last night, right? It was a celebration."

"Yes, I remember," Michael said. He didn't look convinced.

"So, what are you worried about?"

"Just... all of it."

"Well, don't be. There will be so much confusion and finger pointing... it'll be a clusterfuck. And after this, you won't hurt for jobs or money. Whatever you were doing with Capreze, the new guy, the guy who's taking over his businesses... that's my boss. And he won't forget this. And if it goes south, he still won't forget that you helped. You just have to stick with the story. There are six people who know what's really happening here. You, me, the guy in the bathroom probably puking his guts out, my boss, Capreze, and my..." he struggled for the word. "My partner. That's it. *And* the married bartender."

"That's seven—"

"But she doesn't know shit."

"The *married*—"

"Listen, five of us... no, six of... the... *no one* is going to say a fucking word other than the *story*. I promise, this is all on you."

For some reason, there was a bit of relief on Snyder's face. "OK, I got it."

"OK," John said.

Milo got out of the bathroom looking a little peaky. He held his stomach, said, "I'm fine," before John could ask.

"Keys," John said, and held his hand out. Snyder got up, grabbed his wife's car keys and handed them to John, who nodded. "See you when I see you."

John left the house first, walked over to Snyder's wife's car, a late model SUV, opened it and started her up. He looked at the clock on his watch. The timer ticked closer to 9:00 a.m. Up the block, the opposite direction he'd arrived in, he could see four state police cars instead of two, and four officers shooting the shit.

One of them got into his car.

John put the SUV into gear and hit the gas.

He was about a hundred yards away from the cordon, which was now opened up, when the cops turned towards the noise of the SUV's engine and started waving their arms. One of them had his gun pulled.

John blew past and continued straight. In the rear view, the cops all got into their cars and came after him. He took a right at the next stop sign and then a left, drove for about five minutes until he came to a four-lane street.

They stopped him about half a mile up the road.

Four days later, John sat there savoring what could only be described as the most delicious thing he'd ever smelled. It was a snifter full of Macallan, 1952. Gino brought it out with a flourish and poured four glasses.

John gave the toast. "To people. It's amazing what they think they see."

John slammed on the brakes as one of the cop cars got in front of the SUV, and spun around to a stop. Officers came out with guns pointed at him.

It wasn't much of a stretch for John to act scared.

"GET OUT OF THE CAR!"

"HANDS UP!"

"Which is it?" John asked, putting his hands up.

One of the cops came around and, knowing he had back-up, pulled the SUV driver-side door open. He grabbed John, yanked him out and threw him to the ground.

"What the hell is going on? I didn't do anything!" John said. He still had his hands up.

The cop that grabbed him checked the back seat. Empty. "Sanders, check the fucking trunk!" One of them went to the back of the SUV and hit the trunk sensor button.

"Jesus, I'm late for a fucking meeting!" John yelled, hands still above his head.

"Shut the FUCK up!" the cop said, waiting.

Sanders pulled the trunk open, flanked by two additional officers with guns drawn.

"Uhh, sir?" Sanders said.

"What is it?"

"I think you better see this..."

"Someone lost their job over this," John said and chuckled.

"A few people did," Hal said and leaned back. He took a deep breath, let it out. He wasn't normally a scotch guy, but Jesus...

"Seriously?"

"Yeah." Hal pointed with his glass to Gino. "*Including* your guy in Great Neck, if you can believe it."

For some reason, this was hysterical to Gino, who shook with laughter.

"You going to take care of him? Not *take care* of him, take care of him. You know." John asked.

Gino smiled. "Why, you volunteering?"

John went to say something, stopped.

"He's taken care of."

John nodded, left it at that.

Milo just sat there. He hadn't realized it when he first met John and Hal, but the men in the room were way above his pay grade.

"So?" John turned to Milo. "Spill."

Milo left the house scared out of his mind. Shivering because of the cold morning, because of the adrenalin. He watched one of the cop cars from the left cordon peel out and follow the SUV. He got into the clunker, turned the car over and drove out slowly. He'd almost forgotten which direction he was supposed to turn and was about to make a right when he hit the brakes, hard. There was a bump, and he could hear cursing come from the trunk. "Shit," he said under his breath, and turned the wheel left.

He got down to the end of the block and a police officer held up his hand.

Milo stopped and rolled the window down. "Officer."

"Sorry. You can't leave, sir." he said, and looked at Milo closely. Then he looked down the block to all the fleeing cop cars.

"Why? Just leaving the Snyders. Spent the night, I completely overdid it at dinner, so I... spent the night." He swallowed hard. The officer didn't notice. "But I guess that's what happens when you make a five million dollar deal." Milo went to get his I.D.

"Stop," the cop said, and went to pull his gun.

"Hey, hey. I... I got in last night. My name is Jacob Sherman, I'm sure there's a record of me having come in last night..." Jesus... "I was a guest of Michael Snyder, and I was just going to show you my I.D."

The cop looked at him a long time, almost as if he was trying to discover a tell. "Don't move," he said, and walked towards the patrol car. He reached inside, got out a clipboard and walked back with it. "I.D."

Milo grabbed his wallet and the fake I.D. they'd set him up with. Same name, same address. Different picture.

He handed it over.

"Jacob Sherman," the cop said.

"Yes, sir."

"Seeing the Snyders."

"That's right. Just locked down a five million dollar construction project for my—"

"Shut up," the cop said and double-checked the log. Then the I.D. Then triple-checked the log. He handed Milo the I.D. back. He looked in the back of the car.

Empty.

He grabbed the mic that was attached to his shoulder. "Martin, copy?"

"Copy!"

"You get him?"

Brakes screeching. "We got him!"

Through the speaker they heard *"GET OUT OF THE CAR!"*

The cop looked at Milo, who said "Wow. That sounds crazy. Glad they got him... whoever 'him' is."

The cop held his I.D. out. "Get out of here."

Milo took the I.D. "Yes, sir." He put the car in drive, swallowed hard, and made a right. He drove the speed limit and took the route John had made him memorize.

Once he was on 25A he relaxed a bit. He got off, took Glen Cove Road south down to the LIE, got on to 25 just west of Jericho and took that straight to Syosset.

Milo pulled into an auto repair shop on Jackson Avenue. A mechanic closed the garage door and stayed outside. Milo got Angelo out of the car, had him piss in a bucket, and then into the trunk of a black Honda Accord that was in the next stall. He said, "Sorry."

Angelo shrugged, nodded.

Milo honked. The garage door opened. He drove out, got back on 25, straight to Commack, then took the Sunken Meadow Parkway up north, got back on 25A and headed east. It took just over two hours for him to drive to Port Jefferson, a drive that should have taken 45 minutes.

John had figured that, once Milo got out of the cordon, he'd have ten minutes before the Capreze house got spot-checked. Maybe another minute before an island-wide APB went out for the sedan.

He was right on the timing. Nassau County got locked down quick.

Milo, meanwhile, found the address, 400 Springer Street, pulled into the driveway and into the open garage.

He shut the car down and was finally able to breathe easy. He rested his head on the steering wheel, gave himself a minute, got out of the car, closed the garage door and opened the trunk. Angelo was lying there, looking a bit worse for wear. Milo helped him out and got him into the house.

"Never again," Angelo said in Italian, and waved his hands. His back hurt, his legs hurt, his eyes hurt. But he was smiling, relieved.

They got in the house (spare key was left under a potted plant), and Angelo took a shower while Milo made them some cold cut sandwiches (the food had been left for them).

Once they'd eaten, they made the short walk to the Port Jefferson–Bridgeport, Connecticut ferry. They bought tickets and boarded, waited for it to take off. Once the horn blew, they both breathed a sigh, smiled, and enjoyed the trip from the observation deck.

The trip was about an hour and fifteen minutes.

Hal was waiting on the other side. He'd prepped the car at the garage, the house in Port Jeff, the key, the food, and waited for them to dock. He gave Milo keys to a Nissan Altima, what Hal would later call the world's most unassuming vehicle. It was parked in the ferry's lot. He gave marching orders for the kid to drive out to Danbury. "Leave the car, bring the keys back with you."

"Leave it where?"

"At the train station." He handed Milo a one-way Amtrak ticket to Penn Station. "Tell Angelo we're going for a boat ride. Tell him it'll take three or four days, unless we hit shitty weather. Tell him we're going to the Dominican Republic, and then he'll be taking a flight out

189

to Libya via Frankfurt." Milo relayed it all. Angelo sighed, nodded his head. "He'll be met at Frankfurt and will travel with a guy to Libya. It's all set up, and it's the closest we could get him to Italy that was a non-extradition country. After that... it's up to him if he wants to go home." Milo told Angelo that, too. Again, he nodded. "There's food and wine and magazines and some money and shit on the boat, and, uhh, sunscreen, yeah. So, let's get going."

Milo shook Angelo's hand Angelo grabbed him, hugged him, and kissed both cheeks with tears in his eyes. Milo got a bit choked up, smiled, held his hand out to Hal. Hal looked at it, sighed and shook it. "You're not getting a fucking kiss out of me," he said. Milo nodded and left.

The two went down to the South End Yacht Club, a ten-minute walk from the ferry. Hal and John had found a charter for the trip with Captain Dan Rivers, who owned a 56-footer with two beds, a half-kitchen (fully loaded), and a bathroom with a shower. Dan was cordial and kept to himself. He slept in a hammock on deck.

The trip down to the Caribbean was uneventful. They barely talked. Mostly, they ate and drank and slept and watched the sea. There was no time for fishing. Dan suggested they trawl, you know, for fun. Hal shook his head, said they were on a deadline.

They traveled during the day and anchored at night. Hal pulled out a chess set and they'd all play a few games before bed.

They stopped every few hundred miles to refuel—once in Woodbridge, Virginia, and once in Key Largo, Florida. With every stop the weather got nicer. Hal could see that Angelo was getting a little buggy by the third day, so they got off the boat during the second refueling and took a walk. They ate lunch at a hole-in-the-wall called The Key Lime Café. Hal got the fish basket with fries and coleslaw. Angelo got the cracked conch. They both drank two beers. They brought Dan back a fish sandwich.

Dan got them down past the Bahamas, past Duncan Town, which was a small island in the Ragged Island chain. Dan said the population was only about eighty people.

They passed dozens of small islands. Or maybe they were simply rock formations. It was hard to tell. Everywhere Hal looked there was some kind of land mass sticking out of the ocean.

They made their way south past the Inagua Islands until they finally landed in Puerto Plata where they said their goodbyes to Dan.

They each got a hotel room at the Grand Paradise Resort. Hal's room was massive and white and air-conditioned. Later that evening they had oysters and crab cakes for appetizers, charred Mahi-Mahi for dinner, polished off two bottles of wine, dessert, espresso, and then gambled at the casino.

Angelo found—and figured out a way to communicate with—a hooker, and went off to bed.

Hal slept alone.

They got up for breakfast, ate, checked out, took a cab to the airport, and checked in for separate flights.

Hal got Angelo situated at his gate. He shook the man's hand.

Angelo grabbed him and kissed both cheeks. "Thank you," he said.

"Any time," Hal said, and meant it. He nodded goodbye, walked off, found his gate, and waited for his flight back to JFK.

John, Hal and Gino looked at Milo with a bit of pride, raised their glasses and drank.

Milo left shortly after. It was the last time the D'Escopio family called on him. He spent the rest of his life at his family's meat shop on Bleeker Street. He got married three years later, had two children, and retired at the age of sixty.

"And you?" Gino asked John.

"Seventy-two hours in lock-up, then they let me out. Snyder kept his mouth shut... I think they're just going to let it go."

"They are," Gino said and leaned back. "Another week, maybe two, my guy at the D.A.'s office says it won't be worth anyone's time. They're all name-makers there, anyway, and this was small potatoes.

The FBI guy who put it together is going to be filing paperwork in Dubuque the rest of his life. Plus... I paid a little extra, so they lost your file."

"Thanks, Gino," John said.

"Thank *you*, boys. I didn't see a way out for Angelo. Not a peaceful one, anyway. But you did it. You fucking did it." Gino smacked his table.

John smiled, nodded. Hal finished his drink.

"I've got another job for you two... if you think you can stomach each other some more."

"Sure," John said, and looked at Hal.

"Forget it," Hal said, and laughed. "I'm not here to be a babysitter."

Gino got up, put the scotch away, came up behind John and put his hands on his shoulders. "See, now, here I was thinking *he* was going to be the babysitter."

"Oh," Hal said.

John laughed. Gino winked.

Hal smiled at them both. "Well then, sure. OK."

PART II

Confluence

CHAPTER TWENTY-SEVEN

"**M**emorial Day? Are you shitting me?"

"What? What's so special about Memorial Day?"

Abigail looked at Carla deadpanned.

"I mean besides the obvious," Carla said.

"Everyone wants that weekend off! Half of these people don't even go anywhere, they just sit at home, happy to Christ that they're not here."

"I can see that."

"Yeah. They should just shut the hospital down for the weekend, you know? Because nothing bad ever happens when you mix a national holiday with drugs and alcohol and some fireworks. Like Fourth of July."

"Quietest day of the year." Carla couldn't look at Abigail. "So... problem solved."

Abigail got up and shook her head. "Give me one good reason why I should let you—"

"I'm going to get laid."

Abigail stopped and sat down fast. "Are you fucking with me?"

"No."

"You're going to take that tall drink of water—"

"No, he's my friend—"

"That slightly lazy Adonis—"

"And he's not that tall—"

"With those puppy dog eyes—"

"Those don't work on me—"

"And you'll ride him until you break his dick off?"

"I... guess? Is that what guys want these days?"

"Wants got nothing to do with it. NEED is the word. It's what I'd do." Abigail fanned herself. "OK. You got your days off. Hell, I'll even cover for you. But I want proof."

"Proof?"

"Yeah. Photos, audio, hidden video, I don't care what. Just as long as I can keep it and live vicariously through your shamefulness."

"I wasn't going to bring a camera..." Abigail started to get up. "But I'll see what I can do."

Carla met Alex at the Amtrak Station.

She stood there waiting and thought about Greg for the first time in a long time. They weren't pleasant thoughts. "The fuck is wrong with you?" she said under her breath, and shook her head. "That was years ago, for God's sake."

The station was cavernous. It was the only word she could think to use. Conversations echoed throughout the great hall. Even the quiet ones meshed with the footsteps of people coming home. People leaving town. She couldn't imagine it ever being completely quiet.

It was a Friday morning, eight o'clock. The train to Boston was five and a half hours, originally coming from Washington DC. It would continue to New York City, then on to New Haven, and finally Boston, where Alex had some friends who'd rented a passenger van that sat fifteen. From there, they'd drive the hour and a half to Woods Hole.

She hadn't had breakfast yet, and her stomach was giving her a good reminder when Alex walked up holding two tickets. "Business class!"

"Seriously? You didn't need to do that," Carla said.

"Hey, I invited you," he said, and looked around. He seemed nervous. Or exhausted. It was hard to tell. "I'm starving. Did you eat?"

"No. I'm starving, too. Are you all right?"

"I'm great. Why, what have you heard?"

"Nothing, I—"

"I'll get us something for the—"

"No, *I'll* get us something. You've done enough. What do you want?"

"I don't know… a bacon, egg and cheese sandwich, and a coffee."

"Watch my stuff."

"You got it," he said, and watched her go. "Hey! There's a dining car for lunch, so, breakfast will do."

Carla got two coffees, two breakfast sandwiches, two bottles of water, a pack of gum, two granola bars, a bag of almonds, an apple, a banana, and a chocolate chip muffin. She came back to where Alex was and handed him a coffee.

"Jesus, you're loaded for bear."

"You ever travel long distance by train before?"

"No."

"Trust me, this is nothing."

The train left on time at 8:36 a.m. They sat in a two and two across from each other.

Alex had his headphones on. He showed her a white brick. "It's an iPod. Five hundred songs on this thing. Unbelievable." He was fidgeting a bit, and would concentrate on taking deep breaths every few minutes.

Carla took out a *People* magazine to read. She flipped through the first few pages and realized she'd already devoured most of it at work. She kicked Alex's foot. He took his head phones off.

"Tell me you brought something to read," she said, and tossed the magazine aside.

"I did." Alex pulled out a worn paperback. Red cover, block letters, with illustrated flamingos on it.

"What the fuck is this? *Rum*—"

"*Rum Punch*. Elmore Leonard. Trust me. It's fantastic, just don't lose my spot. You like crime novels?"

"No."

"You ever read a crime novel?"

197

"No."

"Then shut the fuck up and read it."

She scoffed, turned to page one. Alex put his headphones on and leaned back, keeping an eye on her.

By the time they reached New York, an hour and a half later, she was almost a third of the way through the book.

The train pulled into Penn Station. Alex nudged Carla's foot as the train slowed and stopped, her face practically buried in the pages. The doors opened. Some people got on, some got off. Carla people-watched, curious as to whether she could pick out Alex's friend.

Two minutes later, the doors closed and the train started moving.

Alex looked around. "Huh."

"Huh?"

"Well, I mean, he could be anywhere, you know? It's a big train."

"But you let him know where you were."

"Yeah, I sent Hal a message."

"You sure he's got one of those fancy phones?" Alex had a Blackberry and constantly reminded her of it. Whenever they got together, he would send her emails that she couldn't check until she was home.

Carla had left her pager at her apartment. She knew the only messages she'd get would be Abigail wanting updates, every hour on the hour.

"Trust me. Hal's probably got a fancier phone than I have."

A man lumbered up carrying a knapsack and two plastic grocery store bags. He was shortish, receding hair line, glasses, reasonable looking. Smiling, but clearly not a morning person.

This is either going to be fun, or a nightmare, she thought.

"Hey!" the guy said.

"Hey, Hal!" Alex said and stood up. They hugged. "Hal, this is my friend Carla."

Carla stood up. "Hi." She held her hand out. Hal took it, shook it warmly. "Nice to meet you."

"You too," Hal said.

He put his bags next to Carla and sat down next to Alex.

"So," Hal said, and they all just looked at each other for a moment.

"Yeah," Carla said. "So."

There was a long awkward silence that Alex let go on for long enough. He smiled at Hal, smiled at Carla as the train found its way back outside. "We've got another three and a half hours of watching the lovely Eastern Seaboard... sort of... not to mention what can only be described as riveting conversation..." He went into his backpack and pulled out a glassine bag. "I think we owe it to ourselves to experience nature as it was intended."

"Through chemistry..." Hal said, groaned, and leaned back.

"Exactly," Alex said, and took out three pills. There had to be at least fifty pills in the bag. More.

"Oh boy," Carla said. "Where did you get all of those?"

"It's not polite to ask," Alex said.

Hal looked at Carla, leaned in and said, "If I knew it was going to be this kind of trip..." Alex smacked him on the shoulder. "Ow...! I still would have come."

Carla smiled.

Hal reached over into one of the grocery bags and pulled out a six-pack of beer.

"Oooh boy," Carla said again.

"Yeah, well, they'll sell you two things at Penn Station in the morning. One is train tickets, and I didn't have breakfast this morning, so..." Hal peeled off cans to give to Carla and Alex.

A conductor came by and Hal froze, just as he was giving a beer to Alex, who had the presence of mind to hide the bag.

"Hey... officer," Hal said.

Carla laughed out loud. Alex was too nervous to do anything but hold his breath.

"We, uhh... well, my buddy here—" Hal smacked Alex "—just found out he's cancer free, and so we're celebrating."

"Uh, yeah. Ball cancer," Alex said and gave a thumbs-up. "Yeah, it's a miracle. Got to keep it, too. Not like a souvenir. I mean, I still have it. Inside."

"Uh huh," the conductor said. He looked around the train car, looked back at Hal. "Tickets please. And a beer."

Hal arched an eyebrow as the others gave their ticket to the conductor. He reached into his pants pocket and handed the conductor his ticket. He peeled off a beer for himself and handed the conductor the rest of the six-pack. "Enjoy," he said.

The conductor took the three cans off the six-pack ring, put them into his coat pockets, put the plastic ring into one of the grocery bags, tipped his hat, and strode off.

Alex watched as he left. When the coast was clear, he took out the three pills, handed one to each of them. They opened their beers almost in unison. Carla was a bit late, and the two men looked at her and shook their heads.

"For shame," Hal said.

Carla started giggling. It had been a while since she'd done anything like this.

Alex held out his pill. Hal followed. Carla held hers out and they cheered them, swallowed them, and chased them with beer.

There was a nervous energy. Carla could feel it. Hal settled in, put his feet up on the seat next to her.

Alex smacked both sides of his face lightly. "This is going to be fun," he said.

Carla leaned back, bent an ear on the page she was on, closed the book and waited.

There was small talk for half an hour and then the Ecstasy hit.

She felt like the seat was closing in around her, in a good way. The car was temperature controlled. She could smell food and coffee and perfume. The beer was halfway to lukewarm, but she still drank it, a sip here, a sip there.

The landscape raced by, and she imagined all of the people in their homes, in their cars, barely moving.

Carla puked about an hour in. She could feel her anxiety level getting the better of her and purged what was still in her stomach.

Hal did the same. "This shit feels like it was cut by some Russian who's trying to restore communism across the globe."

"It's speed, you pussy," Alex said.

Hal nodded. "Communist speed. Not that I'm complaining."

"You ARE complaining," Alex said, who seemed unaffected by it.

Carla sat there most of the trip and listened to them talk about things that made both sense and no sense to her. Like they were speaking in code. It wasn't what they were saying, it was how fast, and how much of it drifted to her ears through the noise of the train. She fashioned whole sentences together with fragmented words, and tried to follow along.

They were sometimes too loud and were sometimes contemplative, and always philosophical. They talked about great big things and small things simultaneously, as if the world was simply chaos, but in the best possible way.

And maybe they'd figured it all out.

As she listened, as the train moved closer to Boston, as she relaxed and ate the chocolate chip muffin, Carla realized her life was pretty great. And she was in good company.

They were two of the goofiest-looking motherfuckers she'd ever seen.

But they made her laugh.

CHAPTER TWENTY-EIGHT

By the time they got off at Boston, they were getting along swimmingly. The van was waiting for them on Causeway Street, half full. Brad, Alex's friend from high school, was in the driver's seat, along with a mixed bag of people.

"Please tell me you've got some food in here," Alex said, as he poked his head through the passenger window.

"I've got food, I've got beer, scotch, wine, vodka, that gold cinnamon sludge that women seem to love—I don't know why... uh, there's chips and some hot dogs and hamburgers in the igloo for tonight. What else..."

Hal muscled his face through the window. "Do you have any fucking sandwiches, man?" He was blitzed out of his mind. His eyes were all pupils.

Brad laughed, turned to Alex. "You just couldn't wait, could you?"

"Don't look at me..."

"Oh, I *am* looking at you. You just better have saved me some." He turned to Hal. "Yeah, man, I've got some sandwiches. If we run out, we'll get some more. Hop in!"

Alex got into the front passenger seat. Carla and Hal got in all the way back, huddled, whispering and laughing. Hal reached behind them and grabbed sandwiches from a cooler, and bags of chips. "I'll replace what we eat," he said to no one. "I promise," and he tore open a bag of tortilla chips. They went everywhere. "Oh, shit."

Everyone in the van looked at him.

"You're making a fantastic first impression," Carla whispered.

"Really? Thanks. I was getting worried."

The two of them burst into laughter. Other people in the van who'd heard him joined in.

Alex turned to Brad, who was shaking his head. "They're good people, I promise." Brad laughed, hugged his friend, put the van in gear and took off.

Hal grabbed a roast beef sandwich with lettuce, tomato, Swiss cheese and Russian dressing. Carla grabbed a grilled chicken sandwich that was still a bit warm. Hal passed Alex a tuna sandwich on toasted whole wheat with lettuce and tomato.

They got on 93 South to Braintree and switched to MA-3 South. Once they hit Sagamore they got onto US-6 East.

Hal tried to get the van to stop in Plymouth. "You know, to see the rock! Birthplace of America?"

Carla said, "I, uhh, think that's Phila—"

"The fucking *Mayflower*? Anyone?"

Everyone ignored him.

"Fuck it, I'll get John to drive me."

"Who's John?" she asked.

"He's nobody."

"Nobody. Fun."

"Oh, so much fun. Yeah. He'll be here tomorrow night."

The entire van got into a fit of giggles when they found out they were on Sandwich Road.

Sandwich got them to MA-28 South.

Even high, Carla and Hal could appreciate the view as they took Palmer Avenue down and around to Sippewissett Road, into Quissett Avenue, and saw the vastness of Buzzards Bay. It was a beautiful day and, as one would expect, the bay was full of sailboats.

The van crept along until it finally pulled into a driveway. The two of them had a hard time seeing the property until they finally got out of the van.

It was enormous.

"Holy shit," Carla said.

The front yard was well-kept and modest, clearly to showcase the front of the house. It was easy to picture what it had looked like in its heyday.

"Yeah, thanks," Brad said, and started unloading the van. "It's been in the family for fifty years. Built in 1901. The original owner made his fortune as a publisher. He was my great-grandfather's best friend. Bought it with a heavy heart when the guy went bankrupt."

"Wow," Carla said, and looked back at the house. Two stories. Dark shingles spread from the roof to the foundation. They were worn by the sun, by the weather, and salt water. Faded and cracking white paint covered the window panes. Potted plants on the porch were alive and in good condition. There was a smell in the air that was almost too inviting. A tan welcome mat lay beneath a freshly painted white front door.

The place was right on the water.

Hal took a few photos on his Blackberry, sent them to John, and called him.

John was silent a long time before saying, "I'm never going to have that, am I." It was a statement.

"You don't know that," Hal said. He looked around to see if anyone was near. "Who knows where we'll be in a couple of years, working with Gino. Oh, and by the way, that shit... when you get up here, we keep to ourselves, right?"

"Yeah, of course. Hey, listen..."

"Yeah."

"I heard Whatsherface was in France with—"

Hal hung up, looked at the phone, shook his head. He put it in his back pocket, gave the exterior another once-over, got his knapsack, grabbed the beer he'd brought, grabbed one of the bags from the back of the van, and made his way into the house. "Oh, fuck you..." he said as he got into the front door.

The inside looked like it was part of the Kennedy compound.

The foyer was enormous, and about the size of the apartment Gino had set him up with. White walls and ceiling, dark-wood floor. Rugs here and there, and a fireplace directly opposite the front door. To the right was a large living and dining room.

The kitchen was off to the left. It was wide and deep, with a large island in the center. There was one double-door refrigerator and one separate freezer. Dishwasher, double sink with a garbage disposal, and a trash compactor. There was a light-wood table that sat ten, with white chairs surrounding it. Along the wall facing outside were five matching stools tucked underneath a counter.

The walls were lined with white cabinets with glass windows, filled with white plates and bowls. An entire cabinet was dedicated to mismatched glasses of all sizes.

Above the cabinets, nailed here and there, were dried starfish, the jaws of a small shark, and some local knick-knack signs. On one of the counters were two mason jars filled with sea glass.

Hand-blown glass windows looked out over an acre of backyard. Large shrubs bracketed a gorgeous view of the Great Harbor. In the center was a white stone path to a private beach.

Hal unpacked the groceries, shaking his head. It wasn't his dream house. It wasn't even close to what he'd originally imagined his dream house would be. He'd never seen the like. But it was giving him a fuck-ton of ideas about his future.

He opened the fridge door.

Cool air blasted him and chilled the sweat on his body. "Oh, God..." he said, stretched out his hands and just stood there.

After thirty seconds, he noticed he had an erection.

Carla found a perfect spot in one of the five bedrooms on the second floor. Brad had had the presence of mind to set up some cots here and there. They looked like army surplus.

"Yeah, my grandmother bought a bunch of them," Brad said as they walked through the house. "Not that she had a ton of grandchildren, but she said 'you never know,' so... I think most of the people coming tonight will be showing up around dinner. Beds will probably be two to one, so I'd grab a cot."

"OK, great. Thanks. And, you know, thanks for letting me come here."

"Of course. It's a wonder we've never met before. Alex has told me a lot about you."

"Oh, great," she said, and blushed.

"Good things. Honest. Dinner's going to be around six. Make yourself at home." Brad patted her on the shoulder and left her to decide on her own.

The bedrooms were different colors, matte finish, as if white chalk had been added to the paint. There was a darker blue room. A maroon one. A pink one. A yellow one, and a green one.

Carla found herself gravitating towards the darker blue room. She put her bag on a cot that was there, grabbed one of the folded-up blankets that was on the bed, grabbed a bottom sheet, made the cot up and sat down. It was reasonably comfortable.

She spent the next five minutes rubbing her hands up and down the patch quilt blanket. Her fingers kept finding the seams and traced them, back and forth. The shag carpet had her making fists with her toes.

For some reason, it was turning her on.

"I am high as fuck," she said after a while. Her body felt both energized and tranquil. She could feel her heart pulsing. There was an almost zooming affect at the edges of her vision, in sync with the beats.

She got up, stretched—God, that felt good for some reason—and walked on her tiptoes to the window facing the backyard. Some people she hadn't been introduced to were milling about. She waved to no one in particular and grinned.

Then she saw the pool.

"Oh, come *on*," she said. "Just look at that..."

She hadn't brought a bathing suit.

Maybe I can get one in town, she thought. *Or I'll just go in in my underwear. I don't care. I can't imagine what water must feel like on this shit...*

Before she left the bedroom, she checked the bathroom. It was reasonably sized, with a stand-up shower, toilet and sink. "Everything a girl needs," she said, and grabbed her purse. She didn't know where Alex or Hal were, but she was on a mission to get into that pool.

CHAPTER TWENTY-NINE

There were only a few areas in New York City where you could actually smell the ocean.

Hal wasn't big on sunshine. When he was younger, his trips to Coney Island or Brighton Beach or even the Rockaways were short-lived, and more of a hassle than anything else. It had been years since he'd spent more than an hour on a beach. He didn't realize how much he'd missed the smell until he breathed it all in.

He was a long ways away from where he'd been two years prior.

He remembered taking the D train one afternoon down to Stillwell Avenue, and he could smell the water as soon as the subway doors opened. Sand piled up here and there around the concrete of the station, even that far away from the beach.

He hadn't slept in a long while, had about four dollars to his name, and in two days he'd get into the fight on the subway.

He'd made the mistake of walking by Nathan's and just sat there, smelling it all. He watched a family of four dump their food in a can next to him. It was the first time he'd ever grabbed garbage and eaten it. Two half hot dogs, a half-eaten plate of cheese fries, and an almost full soda.

All of it resting on top of the other garbage.

His first thought was to check and see if anyone was watching, but he'd decided to keep his head down and just enjoy it.

Afterwards, he found a bench on the boardwalk and people-watched for a while, until his eyes drooped and he fell asleep in some shade. By the time dinner rolled around, he'd waited by Nathan's for another family to finish their meal. Grabbed a half-eaten hamburger, another half a hot dog, more fries, and a half-finished Sprite.

Found a public restroom, used it, washed his hands, washed his face, splashed water under his arms and aired them out as best he could, then made his way back onto the subway for the night.

Hal shook off the memories, walked back out to the van. Everything was brighter. Sharper. Crisper. More saturated. He could feel the hairs on his arms standing up. The muscles in his neck felt like they were constantly flexing. Then he realized he was biting on his back teeth, over and over again. It was the speed. He stopped.

The house was something, yeah, and Hal knew the kinds of friends Alex had, that they could afford such a place. Ivy League graduates, all of them.

He was thankful that Michelle, Alex's sister, wasn't joining them for the weekend.

"Tell me she's not going to be there," Hal said as he paced his apartment. He pulled on the cord of his landline. His apartment got shit cell reception.

He hadn't seen or heard from Michelle in more than a decade.

"Who? Where?"

"Michelle, goddammit, for the Memorial Day weekend thing."

"Tell you she won't be there? Or just, you know, tell you the truth..." Alex said in his ear.

"Both."

"She's not going to be there. She's in Europe with some movie star."

"No shit. What, like a B-movie star?"

"No. Like a fucking A-list movie star who's taking her to the south of France to his enormous villa and vineyard."

Hal was silent for a moment. "Is it someone I would recogni—"

"Yes, you would recognize him! And then you'd kill yourself. So don't ask."

"Yeah, OK, that all sounds about right."

"Hey, listen. Consider yourself lucky. She said that only two months in, the guy wants to marry her. Without a pre-nup."

"Jesus fuck," he said. "Fine, you sold me." He shook his head, went to hang up. "And Alex? I'm bringing a friend."

Hal sighed as he stared at nothing. He and Michelle had never really gotten along, except in bed. Every weekend she'd take the train back and forth from Philly, their relationship lasting solely from Friday night to Sunday night. They were notorious during the 80s club scene, even as teenagers. They fought and fucked constantly, sold drugs, met movie stars and musicians, scammed dumb bridge-and-tunnel kids, and were fixtures at The Limelight, The Tunnel, and CBGB for a long time.

At least, it felt like a long time.

One night, they were on their way to breaking their own personal sales record. He handed her the cash he'd made. She said she'd be right back. Next he heard she was on her way to Amsterdam.

Six months later, he was on his way to Texas.

And he still missed her. Sort of.

He brought a cooler from the van into the kitchen, dropped it on the counter, patted Alex on the shoulder. "Do something with that, will you?"

"What, like hit you with it?"

Hal drifted through the house.

The dining room had a barren twelve-foot dark-wood table with matching chairs. The living room would fit three of his *current* living rooms, and then some. Two massive L-shaped couches, along with three recliners, all facing a large stone fireplace. A 42-inch plasma screen mounted on the long wall. Floor-to-ceiling windows with a sliding door that went out to the back patio. To the right was a large crystal-clear pool. The deep end was ten feet. There was a diving board four feet off the ground.

Stone paths crisscrossed the backyard and collected at the entrance to the beach. Hal decided to wait until later to check it out.

He sat down in the living room. The temperature in the house was quite comfortable for a sunny May afternoon. He felt himself sink into the couch. He held his breath for a moment and shut out the noise in the house.

He closed his eyes and just... was.

The guests were all college-educated, all in the vicinity of rich, and all there to have a good time and relax. They did not act as though their days were full of stress. They weren't working in an emergency room, or doing jobs for the mob, or owing money to bookies in Philadelphia.

Hal, Carla, and Alex had come down from their first dose. Alex offered seconds. They both refused. Alex decided to take the lead.

It was going to be a long weekend.

Dinner consisted of anything and everything that could be made on a grill. Hotdogs, hamburgers, sausages, chicken, corn, and three different kinds of seafood.

Two men, Jack and Gary, had come down from New Hampshire. They owned a financial consulting firm and had gone to Yale with Brad and a number of other guests.

"We decided to make a quick detour to Scarborough," Jack said, and opened up the back of his Land Rover. Inside were six enormous cardboard boxes, stacked inside two large black plastic garbage bags. The boxes were soaked. Inside were thirty lobsters, five to a box, all on ice.

"Jesus, you shouldn't have!" Brad said.

"I mean, we're just down in Portsmouth, it's such a quick trip, and anyway, it's where we go to get all our lobsters. You know, at Pine Point."

"The co-op they have there. It's amazing," Gary said.

"Well, I'm glad you did," Brad said.

Brad was grill man and host. His wife, Vanessa, dished out food and freshened drinks. People were kind and courteous. There was enough of everything to go around... twice.

The majority of partygoers got there just as dinner was cooking. All in all, almost thirty men and women, all in their late twenties.

Music played from a CD and stereo receiver system that was connected to speakers all over the house, inside and out.

Carla and Alex sat in the living room on one of the massive couches, staring at Hal, who was smiling and making satisfying smacking noises as he ate.

"Look at him," Alex said.

Hal looked up, smiling. Butter was dripping down his chin.

"Can't take him anywhere."

"Please. This is the happiest I've been in years," Hal said with his mouth half full, and wiped his face with a soaked napkin.

"Those must have been some years," Carla said smiling.

Hal looked away, swallowing hard.

Carla noticed it.

Alex was looking towards the kitchen at a woman who could only have been an underwear model. She was wearing a bikini in the house, and seemed perfectly comfortable being the center of attention.

Hal looked back up at Carla and nodded, somber. "Yeah. Not great." He looked down at his plate of lobster and corn on the cob. It was covered in butter. "But all this sort of makes up for it," he said and looked up smiling. "What about you? How's your last few years been?"

"OK, I guess. Constantly settling in. I think the life of a nurse... it's pretty much just repetition. Most days you'll see something, like a wound or an infection site or something, and you know the treatment, you've done it a hundred times, and so you just let your muscle memory take over. Most of the doctors know what they're doing, and the other nurses are great, so, you have people to lean on, just in case. Patients become a blur. That's both good and bad, you know. I just try and be nice to everyone, and go with the flow."

"You love it," Hal said.

"She does?" Alex asked, and chuckled. "That's not what I just heard."

"I do," Carla said, and smiled.

"Well, I don't know what *you* heard," Hal said. "But I heard pure satisfaction. It might be twenty years of more of the same, but there's nothing she'd rather be doing. Am I right?"

"Well..." Carla said. "I mean, I wish I was in the south of France..."

"Oh, fuck you," Hal said.

"With just the dreamiest of leading men..."

"You just couldn't keep your mouth shut," Hal said to Alex.

"What? She fucking reads *People* magazine!"

"Oh, for chrissake..." Hal got up. "Who wants a beer?"

"I want one," Alex said.

"Me," Carla said.

"OK, great. Get it yourself," Hal said and walked away.

"Oof. Touchy," Carla said and smiled. Alex nodded.

They watched Hal get a beer from the fridge and walk outside.

After a few seconds Alex said, "Wait, did he mean I have to get *my* beer myself, too?"

Hal found himself alone on the beach around nine thirty that night. He sat there and listened to the waves lap back and forth. He could hear conversations happening in the backyard of the house. A few people were walking up and down the sand. Residuals from the Ecstasy had him taking deep breaths and holding them for as long as possible.

He couldn't remember the last time he'd been this relaxed.

Way down the beach, some guests had built a bonfire. He walked over, said hello to some people he recognized, and asked if he could grab some beer from the cooler they had out with them. Someone said, "Of course."

Hal grabbed two, thanked them, made his way back to his spot and watched the night sky for two hours. He'd counted eight shooting stars when he took his last drink of beer. The fire was still going. People were migrating in and out of the house.

Hal called it a night when his bladder felt like it was going to explode. He got into the house, tossed the empties, grabbed a glass of water, looked around to see if he saw Alex or Carla to say goodnight to. He didn't. He went upstairs, found his bedroom, found his cot. He went to the bathroom, drank half the water, took off his pants and his shirt and lay down.

The windows were open in the bedroom. It was closing in on midnight at a house party in Woods Hole on a holiday weekend, and he could barely hear the people outside.

He was asleep five minutes later.

By eleven o'clock, people were off in little cliques, or on their way to sleep. Carla had made sure throughout the evening that her spot to sleep was still hers.

At around midnight, she was having a lovely conversation with Jack and Gary about all the wonderful things to do in New Hampshire, when she felt the first tinge of exhaustion.

"If there's one thing you HAVE to do," Gary said, "it's the Telephone Museum."

"The... telephone...?"

"It's wonderful. Such a rich history this country has with the telephone. Plus, there's Santa's Village. And, of course, there's Robert Frost's home."

"Oh, I get chills whenever I go there. I get the same thing whenever I go to Hemingway's house in the Keys," Jack said. "Honey, whenever you need a break from whatever it is you do, just give us a call and come out. We have plenty of room."

Carla smiled. "You live together?"

"Seven years now."

Gary took Jack's hand. "And as soon as they legalize gay marriage around here, we'll go through the motions. But for now, we're living in sin."

"Marriage is overrated, anyway," Carla said.

"Isn't it, though?" Jack said. "Want to smoke some pot?"

"Yes!"

Carla called it a night around 2 a.m., after she stuffed her face with two chocolate and caramel brownies and a large glass of milk.

She couldn't remember the last time she'd gone to bed that satisfied.

CHAPTER THIRTY

Hal woke up around seven the next morning when he heard a clanging noise coming from the bay. The room he was in was full of people sleeping. He hadn't heard them come to bed.

He went into the hallway bathroom, peed, washed his face, brushed his teeth, and went down to the kitchen. He found the coffee maker, found the coffee, found the filters, and put on a fresh pot.

After a night of thirty or so people eating and drinking, the kitchen was spotless.

He poured himself a cup of coffee, put some milk in it, stirred it with his finger and licked it clean. He opened the fridge to see a bunch of leftovers from the night before. None of it appealed to him. He looked on the counter and saw a bag of English muffins, took two out, used the tines of a fork to split them open, plugged in a toaster oven and placed them inside. He grabbed butter and a container of orange marmalade and smeared them all once they were toasted. He grabbed a plate, took his coffee, and walked out to the beach.

A couple were sleeping under a large blanket, close to where the bonfire had been.

Hal watched the water and the sailboats that were already making their way out for parts unknown.

Around nine o'clock he went back in the house to find Vanessa cooking up enough food for a platoon.

"I fried up some tomatoes, too," she said. "And mushrooms. And peppers and onions. Don't you just love a six-burner stove?"

"Love them," he said. "You a chef?"

"I am. Brad and I own a restaurant in Beacon Hill. Three years now. She's my baby. It's called *Hillside*, if you're ever in the neighborhood. How do you want them?"

"Uhh, scrambled?"

"Scrambled it is. Would you mind making another pot of coffee?"

"Happy to." Hal took out the used filter and dumped it in the trash. He saw that there had already been three pots of coffee brewed.

"Toast?" she asked.

"No, I already had some earlier." She handed him a plate with three scrambled eggs and the works. "Thank you very much." He grabbed a stool and sat by the window, facing her. "So. What's there to do around here during the day?"

"Well, Brad's going to take people out on the boat for a bit."

"Boat?"

"Yeah, his family has an eighty-footer that was just brought out of dry dock. It's out in the bay there. I think you can see it. Dark blue and white, it's got a grey canopy... there it is," she said and pointed.

"Holy shit..." It was massive.

"Yeah. It's Brad's father's pride and joy. If he could live on it, he would."

"I bet."

"You get sea sick?"

"No. Yeah. I mean, maybe."

"Ever been on a boat before?"

"Yes." The trip down to the Bahamas with Angelo Capreze hadn't been too bad. He only threw up once.

"Well, there's Dramamine and all that on the boat. Brad's aunt hates the water, but she never passes up an opportunity to drink, so... Uhh, let's see. There's the Woods Hole yacht club. They'll *teach* you sailing, if you want to learn. There's the ferry that'll take you to the Vineyard. That's a nice trip. You can go visit the lighthouse, or take a

217

bike along the Shining Sea path. There's the aquarium, or the Oceanographic Institution..."

"So, basically all the boring parts of *Jaws*."

"Basically. I mean, it's no Plymouth Rock..."

"Jesus," Hal said and smiled.

"Or, you know, the south of Fran—"

"Don't," he said, and held up his hand. "You... you cooked, and it's delicious... nope. Goddammit, you were turning into my favorite person, and you just fucked it up."

Vanessa laughed, drank some coffee. "If you like to fish, you should join Brad. They're going to try and catch us some dinner. I think he's hunting black sea bass this time around. Should be a great day for it."

"I'm not a big fan of the sun."

"I hear you, me neither. It's so dangerous for you. But, we have sunscreen, and there's the canopy, like I said, and there's a living room..."

"A fucking what?"

"Yeah, it's pretty sweet. And there are rooms below and it's only supposed to get up to seventy today. I honestly think you'll regret it if you don't go..."

"I honestly think I'll regret not stealing it," Hal said.

She laughed.

"No, I'm being serious."

"I need to buy a bathing suit."

"So buy one," Alex said. He was shoveling breakfast into his face.

Carla watched. It was half fascinating, half disgusting. She'd already eaten. "Yeah, but where?"

"At the bathing suit shop."

"Where the hell is there a bathing suit shop?" she asked. "Would you slow down? You're going to choke."

"Boat's leaving," he said, got up and started out of the house.

"What boat?"

"Brad's boat. I'd invite you, but I forgot to. See you later!" he said, and ran for the beach.

"Brad has a boat? Brad has a boat but he doesn't have bathing suits lying around?" She sighed. "Must be a small boat."

"Actually," Gary said, walking through the kitchen. "It's enormous."

"Of course it is. Hey, you know where the bathing suit shop is?"

"The what?"

"You have to go to Falmouth to get anything around here," Vanessa said. She was lying outside on a beach chair.

"Great," Carla said and walked outside holding her coffee. "Where the hell is Falmouth?"

"You passed it on the way in. They have a few shops and all. I'm sure you'll find something there. I'd loan you one of mine..." She gave Carla a once-over. "It'd probably fit, too, but I only brought the one. Sorry."

"It's OK. Falmouth. OK. Easy to get to?"

"Very. Woods Hole Road to Locust to Main Street. They have a Main Street. Isn't that crazy?"

"Crazy. Yeah. OK. Don't suppose I could walk it..."

"I mean, you could. If you were a masochist."

"I am."

"Then, yes. You can. Walk the bike path. Don't forget sunscreen. Shouldn't take you more than an hour each way. Or just take a bike. There are some in the garage. You'll have a gorgeous view of the sound."

"Great. Thank you." Carla looked out at the Bay. "Where's the bike path?"

Vanessa laughed. "When you're ready to go, come get me. I'll show you."

Hal took the last skiff up to the yacht at around 11 a.m. As it got bigger and bigger, he felt like he'd made a mistake. Not to go fishing, but for coming up for the weekend. It was all so intimidating.

This was not his life. At all.

The skiff went to the back of the yacht. There were stairs that led up to a landing, where two men were preparing a dozen fishing poles. There was a freshly bloodied table with four knives stuck in slots. There were chum buckets set up, four large coolers filled with ice, and two large coolers filled with beverages. Hal saw stairs leading to the upper deck.

Past the landing was the living room. It was full of people.

"Jesus fucking Christ," he said under his breath.

Two large couches on either side of the room. Beyond was an oval table with six chairs. Beyond that the bridge, where the captain was sitting and talking to guests. On the right were stairs that led to the roof deck, which was also full of people. There were couches in blue felt, a white retractable canopy, a few plastic tables, and a second set of ship controls.

But it was the view that really got to Hal. Behind him was the harbor. In front was an island. To the left was Martha's Vineyard. To the right, across Buzzard's Bay, was mainland Massachusetts.

"He's right," Hal said. "We're never going to have this." He turned around to make sure no one heard him.

He walked back downstairs, made his way to the left side of the boat, and came across an open door that led to a kitchen. A woman in an outfit matching the captain's was putting food into a fridge. He saw sandwiches stacked here and there, along with chips, pickles, bowls of potato salad, macaroni salad, regular salad, and drinks. "Welcome aboard," she said.

Hal smiled and said thank you. He saw stairs past her. "Do you mind?"

"Nope," she said and shifted as he walked by.

Down the stairs were living quarters. One master bedroom that looked nicer than any apartment he'd ever lived in. Three additional bedrooms, two bathrooms. The master bath had a shower and a bidet.

Hal felt the boat shudder as the engines kicked on.

"This is going to be a long day," he said, and sat down on the master bed.

Carla's knees started creaking even before she began peddling. "This is a terrible idea," she said, and started biking down the street. The Shining Sea Bike Path was two blocks from the house. She hadn't been on a bike in... well, since high school. As she got to the path, she looked left and right. Her sense of direction was useless. There was water simply everywhere.

She took a right. Three minutes later, she was at the beginning of the bike path, looking out at the Vineyard Ferry.

"Shit," she said, but chuckled. The path was reasonably flat, well paved, and there was a gorgeous breeze coming off the water. She took a deep breath, turned the bike around, and started peddling.

Other bikers were moving past her at a faster clip. She could feel the muscles in her legs fighting each push on the pedals, so she lowered the gear until it became easier. The path was flanked by rocks, sand, and patches of grass. To her right, water as far as the eye could see.

She figured she would bike until she was tired. Maybe find a place for lunch, swing around to Falmouth and pick up a bathing suit.

More importantly, she let her mind empty. She kept breathing in the air, let her legs get used to the exercise, and tried to forget as much as she could. She knew she'd left behind patients that she cared about. She knew the staff would treat them well. But there was always the feeling that the place would fall apart without her.

She told Abigail that one night during drinks. Abigail laughed in her face. "Girl, we were fine without you before we even knew there *was* a you. But that doesn't mean we're not glad you're with us. You might not be the best, but you're better than most."

"Oh yeah? Who's the best?" Carla asked.

Abigail rolled her eyes. "Please."

Fifteen minutes later, Carla was passing Main Street. She saw a bunch of shops, including a sports clothing store.

She decided to keep going. Her legs were no longer stiff, and she was enjoying the sunshine. The path took a turn to the left, and then continued to the north, past some inlets and ponds.

On her right was a large piece of fenced-in land. Grass, trees, a farm, with a sign that read "Bird Sanctuary." There was a densely wooded area on the left, another pond, some houses here and there.

Twenty minutes later she saw a yellow and grey house with a café sign on the front. She had a light sweat, she was thirsty, her legs were getting a bit tired and, for some reason, she was hungry again.

She got off the bike, walked it over to the café, propped it up outside the railing to the front door, and walked in.

The place smelled like heaven.

"Hi, good morning," a woman in her fifties said. "Anywhere you'd like."

"Thanks. Good morning," Carla said, and sat in a booth. Wood seats, wood table. White cotton tablecloth and a light wood Roosevelt placemat under beige plates. Two glass and two mugs. Mismatched silverware made her chuckle.

"Just you this morning?"

"Yeah, but I feel like I'm eating for two," she said and patted her stomach. "Not that I'm... I mean, I'm not. God forbid. But I already had breakfast, and I'm starving."

"That's what we like to hear. Sort of." She handed Carla a menu. "Coffee?"

"Yes, please."

"Juice?"

"Sure."

"What kind?"

"Surprise me. My brain is barely working."

The waitress smiled, left.

Carla looked at the menu. Pancakes, French toast, omelets. They all came with potatoes and toast. The pancakes and French toast came with homemade whipped cream.

"Fuck," she whispered to herself. "Fucking second breakfast..."

The woman came back. "Surprise. Grapefruit juice."

"My favorite," Carla said. "So, it's a toss-up between the pan—"

The waitress put a hand up. "Get the French toast."

"Sold. Then I can spend the next hour biking it off so I don't hate myself later."

The waitress laughed, sighed. "Sweetheart, I don't think an hour's going to do it."

Hal watched one of the hired hands lay out a chum line.

OK, he thought. *Some of the better parts of Jaws.*

The yacht was moving slowly out towards Long Island.

"You ever fish?" Brad asked.

"Not for a long time. Took a charter out of Jones Beach for bluefish one time when I was a kid. But I don't remember much."

"Well, we're after sea bass today. The season just opened up, so, fingers crossed. They'll make for a delicious dinner if we find some. Probably some tautog, too. Vanessa does great sea bass. Randy will set you up with a pole. I'm sure we'll be stopping soon. We're looking for the wrecks, mostly."

"Wrecks?"

"Yeah, old ships, maybe some reefs. It's where they gravitate towards. We'll use the depth sounder, see what we find. The captain's really aces, he's been with us since dad bought her." He patted the ship. "Knows what he's doing."

"Sounds good," Hal said.

"So, I heard you know Alex because of—"

"Yes. Yes. And I know she's in France with whatshisface... I'm fine with it."

"That's good. It's good you two stayed friends. You and Alex."

"Yeah. He's a good guy. And thanks, by the way, for…" Hal motioned with his hand.

"Don't mention it. I wish we could do this kind of thing more often. There aren't enough national holidays, if you ask me."

Hal nodded. He didn't know what to say.

"So what do you do for a living?" Brad asked.

"Me?"

"Yeah."

"I, uhh. It's hard to explain, really. It's like consulting."

"Nice! Financial consulting?"

"Sometimes…"

"So, investments? Banking? Commodities?"

"It, uhh, varies. Some… commodities. My client is very particular. His moods change."

"You work for only one client?"

"Yeah. Family… fortune kind of… person."

"Old money."

"You could say that."

"Well, that's Massachusetts all over. Couple of people here have that kind of lineage. It's a burden."

"Yeah… I can see how that could be a… burden."

"The old guard really doesn't like outsiders around here. The islanders, you know. But, they love the business. The old families… they're dying off. It's like an oasis around here for some of them. No, not an oasis. Like a time capsule. Something. Anyway, they want to keep it to themselves… but, it's just not sustainable. Not anymore. Houses are going for… well, a lot. You live in the city, right?"

"Yeah."

"Rent or own?"

"My client has a number of properties around the city, so…"

"Wow. That's very generous of him."

"Well, he's… generous. That's a word. For him. Uh, what do you do, Brad?"

"I help manage my family's business interests. Me and my father. Vanessa and I have the restaurant. That's just a hobby for me, but it's her life. The *family* business has its hands in real estate, like your client, and some publishing. That's from way back. We own some newspapers and the like. A few local television and radio stations. We own a chain of grocery stores in New England. Let's see… a few other things. It's all very autonomous. Which is good. Allows us to come out here and enjoy ourselves."

"That's great."

"But our real money comes from banking. My family bought a few small banks that were struggling in the late 70s, turned them into a chain. New England Trust. To hear my father talk, banking was like the Wild West in the 80s and 90s."

"I can imagine," Hal said, who couldn't imagine it.

"Yeah, it's a bit over my head. I stick with a lot of the media. A bit more glamorous, hah. But still… you ever want to make money hand over fist for your client? I mean, I don't know how much capital he has to work with, but banking is one of the last real bastions of capitalism, where they're still making up the rules as they go along."

"No kidding." Hal leaned forward and listened.

"Yeah. No one's paying attention. I mean, not *really*, and we're a legitimate institution. My dad is way too loyal to the legacy of his family to screw around, but you can't help but hear the industry horror stories. Laundering is a big problem, but that's been forever. Lobbyists are fighting congressional regulations tooth and nail. Those are the big, you know, commercial banks. *Small* town banks practically own their communities. You stay under the radar? The world is your oyster."

"No shit." Hal's mind started working overtime.

"Hey. You should talk to… Reggie, that guy over there. He's our COO. Reggie! Come here for a second, meet Hal."

Reggie walked over. Tall, Black, solidly built. He looked like he played squash exclusively. He was wearing khaki shorts and a full white button-down shirt. Definitely not there for the fish. "Hey Hal, nice to meet you."

"Reggie, nice to meet you. Brad was telling me some of the ins and outs of the banking world."

"Oof. I could tell you some stories."

"Tell away," Hal said, and smiled. "And let's catch some fucking fish."

CHAPTER THIRTY-ONE

Carla sat at the café for an hour after finishing second breakfast. The French toast. It was ridiculous. Covered in slivered almonds, homemade whipped cream, and real Vermont syrup. She licked the plate clean when she was sure no one was watching.

She had the grapefruit juice. It was freshly squeezed. She drank two cups of coffee and three glasses of water.

She went to the bathroom for a second time, paid the check, left a good tip, thanked the waitress and walked the bike back to the path.

It took her a few tries to get back on the bike, and finally she headed down to Main Street. She left the bike outside of the sports clothing store, found a one-piece in her size, didn't bother to try it on, and paid with a credit card. She got back on the bike trail and made her way back to the house. More than half the guests were on the boat.

Vanessa was where she'd left her. Sunning. "I was going to send out a search party. You find it?"

"Yes, thank you."

"You walk it?"

"No, I took the bike."

Vanessa looked at her a bit strangely.

"Oh, I stopped off at this café... I can't remember the name. Yellow house—"

"Shelly's. Yup. We go there whenever we get the chance. Tell me you had the French toast."

Carla nodded, smiled. "I need a nap."

"I bet." She turned over and lay back down.

Carla went up to her room. She changed out of her clothes. She put both hands on her belly. "Oof," she said. Carla was in pretty good shape. The belly was all breakfast.

She put the bathing suit on. It fit well enough. She pulled the tags off, grabbed a towel from under the bathroom sink, and went back outside.

She walked over to the pool where there were three people lounging about, grabbed a bottle of sunscreen and covered herself wherever she could.

She put the towel down on an empty chair and began the slow walk into the pool. Each step was excruciating, the water was so cold.

Carla decided to just jump in. She went under and pushed her tired legs as far as they would go. She resurfaced and saw she'd gotten about five feet.

"Oh, boy," she said, and put her feet down. They barely touched. She treaded water to the far end of the pool and grabbed the side. The entire pool was in the sun. She drifted over to the diving board and moved her head into the shade.

She floated for a while, enjoying the cool water and the sense of weightlessness.

Thirty minutes later she got out, dried herself off, went into the kitchen, grabbed a handful of chips and a glass of water. She went back to her room, took a shower, dried off, got into a pair of shorts and a T-shirt, and took the first nap she'd had in over a year.

By the time Hal got back to the house, he was ready to die.

The sun had done a number on his head. The waves had done a number on his senses. The smell had done a number on his stomach... and *not* the smell of the sea.

One of the mates, Malcolm, had handed Hal a reel with something called a diamond jig, said, "No need to cast, you're just going to drop it in the water."

Hal had figured it was going to be one of those trips where everyone tries, and nothing happens. Or someone, the least likely person, lands one of those ugly fish that you only see in *National Geographic*.

It took thirty seconds for Hal to feel a pull on the pole, and he almost lost it in the water. He grabbed the bottom of the handle just as it slipped out of his hands, and yanked back. Then he started reeling it in. People cheered him.

"This is fucking ridiculous!" he yelled as he kept trying to turn the reel. He had no practice. It went slow, then fast, then slow. He couldn't find a rhythm.

About a minute later, he pulled up a six-pound sea bass that was roughly 22 inches long. It was the third one caught in the first ten minutes of fishing.

Hal hadn't seen what happened to the other two.

Malcolm grabbed the fish, took it off the lure. He grabbed what looked like a sharp screwdriver and slid it into head of the fish. Then he used one of the knives and cut the fish, put his hand inside and scooped out its guts and gills.

Hal felt saliva bubbling in the back corners of his mouth.

Malcolm then put the fish in one of the containers filled with ice. He grabbed a ladle, dipped it into the water, and dumped it into the cooler.

He threw the guts and gills into the water.

Brad walked over, slapped Hal on the back, handed him a beer. "First catch, first beer," he said. "Keep it up! There will be a lot of hungry people tonight."

Hal smiled and nodded. He drank some of the beer, hoping it would stave off the nausea.

Alex was across from him—drinking, laughing, fishing. He seemed very much at home.

Hal dropped the lure into the water and turned in time to see another fish get skewered. His mouth went slack. The boat seemed to drift. The air got a little thick. The sun seemed focused solely on him.

A few moments later, he caught another fish. He reeled it in easier this time. The bass was about the same size.

Malcolm came over, removed it from the lure. "Well done!" he said, and repeated the procedure.

Hal threw up a little in his mouth. It was hotter. The boat rocked a bit more. The air was salty and close. He was sweating and chilly at the same time.

Hal put the reel off to the side. Malcolm saw him, came over, secured the reel, secured the lure. "Need a break?"

"Something like that," Hal said. "Gonna..." he pointed towards the living room.

"No problem, man. I get it. Sometimes people, when they see the process... I get it."

Hal nodded. He walked into the living room where people were in the middle of conversations, eating and drinking. He walked past them, set the beer down, walked through the kitchen, down to the bedrooms, found an empty bathroom, and puked his guts out.

They dropped anchor four hours later. Hal was the last on the skiffs back to shore. Brad found him asleep in one of the bedrooms.

"Thought you jumped ship, buddy," he said as he waited for Hal to adjust to waking.

Hal got to the house, bypassed everyone, grabbed a couple of bottles of water and a sandwich, and went to his room. He was feeling light-headed. His forehead felt warm. He wasn't sure if it was because of the sun or not. He found a thermometer in one of the bathrooms and made sure he did not have a fever. He didn't.

He was asleep an hour later and didn't wake up until four in the morning, just as people were coming to bed.

Just as John was coming down from his peak.

CHAPTER THIRTY-TWO

"Vanessa, you're a genius."

Carla watched as the assembly line for dinner moved from the kitchen to the grill outside. She was back in her bathing suit, with a towel wrapped around her waist.

Brad and the rest of the guests had come back with two coolers full of sea bass, cleaned and ready to go.

Vanessa had thirty pieces of tinfoil laid out on the counter. She had a large saucepan going with butter, garlic, onions, paprika, pepper and salt. She'd place a piece of fish on the tinfoil, bend the sides, pour the mixture in, and then fold it up. She'd pass them on to Brad who had a timer next to the grill. Seven minutes a side.

Vanessa had cooked rice. Brad had grilled a ton of vegetables.

Carla grabbed a plate and got a pouch of fish dumped onto it. She got a glass of white wine and settled in. It was delicious.

She talked to people she'd been introduced to, but never got to know. They asked what she did for a living, asked where she lived. They asked about funny stories from the ER. The only half-funny story she knew was what happened to Brenda. She left out most of the gory details. She didn't want people to lose their appetites.

There were two triple-chocolate layer cakes for dessert. Carla was relieved when she found out Vanessa hadn't baked them.

Alex came around and sat down. "Having fun?"

"I am. This was just what I needed. Thank you." She hugged him.

He hugged back. "You're welcome." He looked at her. She looked back.

"What?" she asked, feeling just the slightest flutter.

"Nothing, just... I rarely get to see you like this."

"Like what?"

"Happy."

"I'm happy most days, Alex. I'm stressed and tired a lot, but I'm happy. I rarely get to see *you* happy."

"Well, I'm high," he said, and took out his bag of pills. They were more than half gone. "You want one?"

"I absolutely want one," she said. "Looks like they're selling."

"Yeah."

"Give me one for Hal, just in case he wakes up."

As Alex handed them to her, the underwear model came over. She stood there with her hand out. "You better have saved me one. Or two. Or three," she said in a cutesy voice that made Carla want to punch her.

"Oh, I did," Alex said to her, kissed Carla on the cheek and said, "Have fun."

"Oh, you too," she whispered. "Wear a condom."

"Ah ha... you're funny," he whispered back. "Kelly!" he said to the model. "Let's go find something to wash these down with," and they walked away.

Carla watched them go.

It wasn't a moment, she thought. *It wasn't. It was you talking to practically the only person you know here. And now he's gone. And he's going to do God knows what, and so what? You could have any of these guys, if you really wanted them. Except the ones with wives, or girlfriends. Which is basically all of them.*

Fuck.

She got up, went to the kitchen, found another bottle of white wine, filled her glass, put the pill in her mouth and drank.

All you need to do is get the feeling back of having a good life. That's it. Half an hour or so. You can survive for half an hour.

She turned to go just as the front door opened.

In walked the most uncoordinated person she'd ever seen. Mid-yawn he stepped on a pair of shoes and went tumbling. He grabbed for a shelf in the foyer and slid along the wall to the floor. He went to get back-up, saw he didn't have the strength, and slid back down the wall.

She walked over and held a hand out to help him up.

"No, thank you. I think I found my new home." He didn't sound drunk.

"You OK?"

"Yeah, yeah, I just... I've been driving for fifteen hours straight and I'm exhausted."

"Jesus, where are you driving from?"

"South Carolina."

"You live in South Carolina?"

"No. I live in Brooklyn. But I'm originally coming from Miami. Spent last night in Charleston."

"You're driving from Miami... on purpose?"

He chuckled. "Yeah, for work."

"What the hell do you do for a living?"

"I... well, it's hard to explain. I drive cars for people. Back and forth. I deliver them."

"You deliver cars."

"Yeah."

"That wasn't hard to explain at all."

He chuckled again. "That's true."

"It was just three words, in fact."

The guy counted on one hand. "'I deliver cars.' Shit, you're right."

"So, to who? Rich people?"

He paused for a second. "Yeah. They're rich... people."

"You have a car outside that you're delivering to someone?"

"Yup. It's the piece of shit sedan. But it has sentimental value for the owner, who's up in Boston. Normally I would have taken a break

233

after ten hours, but I wanted to get here to enjoy the party, you know… I have to be out of here by eight tomorrow morning."

"To deliver a piece of shit."

"Yeah, then errands, and then back here to pick up his highness on Monday."

"His highne… you mean Hal."

"Yeah."

"You must be John."

"Yeah. And you're… Yolanda."

"No. Do I look like a—"

"Rita."

"No."

"Melanie? Janet? Carrie. You have to be Sara."

"Nope."

"I swear, they told me there was going to be a Helen here to greet me."

She laughed.

He yawned, got onto his side, pushed his way up onto his feet. He was tall. Reasonable looking. Nice face, nice body. Nice smile. "Boy, I don't know if I'm going to make it."

"Well, there's a… there's coffee inside."

"No. I've already had too much coffee. I think I need something a bit stronger… so that I can enjoy the rest of the evening. You know?"

She smiled. "I think I can help you with that." She pulled out Hal's pill.

"You don't say… are you already…?"

"Yup."

"Most people are…?"

"Yup."

"And Hal is…?"

"Asleep."

"Of course he is." John put the pill in his mouth and started chewing it. It was disgusting. "Ugh! These aren't the chewable ones for kids?"

She laughed again. "Get you a drink?"

"Lead on, Macduff."

"Who's Macduff?"

"I have no idea."

They went into the kitchen. Brad was grabbing a bunch of things from a cabinet and putting them into a straw bag.

"Brad, this is John. Hal's friend."

"Hey man! Nice to meet you. Welcome. I'm just heading out to the bonfire."

"You have a bonfire?"

"Sure do." Brad lifted out graham crackers. And marshmallows. And chocolate bars.

"Are you fucking kidding me...?" John said.

"What?"

"S'mores?"

"Well, yeah. It's a tradition."

John said, "Where the hell am I?" with a straight face.

Carla started laughing.

Brad chuckled. "Yeah, we get that a lot. Next you're going to wonder—"

"You're in a cult," John said. "This is a cult weekend, and you're recruiting."

"Actually, I was going to say church group, but... yeah, cult works."

"Well, I'm in. What time is the blood sacrifice?"

"Uhh, hah, it is at ten. You won't want to miss it."

"Wouldn't miss it," John said. "Virgin? Non... virgin?"

Brad opened his mouth to say something, smiled and left.

"I think you scared him," Carla said.

"Yeah, well, blood sacrifices are scary."

"And messy."

"And messy." John went into the fridge, grabbed a beer, popped the top and drank. "So! S'mores?"

"Oh, absolutely."

They went out to the beach and sat around and chatted. John asked her who she knew up there. She told him about Alex and how they met. "Alex, who is… somewhere," she said. "And I came up on the train with Hal."

"Nice. And what do you do?"

"I'm a nurse. In Philadelphia."

"Ah, the birthplace of America."

"Yes!" she said and started laughing.

"What?"

"Nothing, just, Hal said Plymouth Rock was the birthplace of America." She took a drink of beer.

"Jesus. Well, he *was* homeschooled…"

Carla spit her beer out and laughed.

"I'm serious. He got kicked out of seventh grade for running a prostitution ring… what?" She was silently shaking. "Have you heard this story already?" She laughed. "And so his mom started working her way up the teacher chain, you know, year by year, brought them home once a week and, well… traded services for his education."

"That is awful."

"I know! Just awful. But true."

She laughed again.

"Imagine my surprise when he was named Valedictorian."

Carla collapsed with laughter.

Fifteen minutes later, Brad handed them both plates filled with gooey goodness.

"Thanks, Brad!" Carla said. She was salivating

"Thank you, man," John said. He was in a daze. For the last few minutes, his hands had been massaging the sand in a way that could only be described as pornographic. And he couldn't stop.

"Wipe your hands, they're filthy," Carla said, taking his plate away.

He wiped his hands on her shoulder. She laughed again.

"What? It's working," he said and smiled. He took his plate back.

236

"Uh huh." She could feel the warmth coming off the fire, and she could smell the burnt wood and ash and sea salt in the air. There was a light breeze out. Her eyes were wide, and she could feel every stray hair that was moving on her face and her shoulders.

She kept making fists with her toes, again, and rubbing her heels back and forth in the sand. She could feel herself getting turned on, and knew that her nipples were hard. The plate was covering them. They were driving her nuts.

None of that compared to the first bite of the s'more, though. She got a trifecta bite and drool dripped out of her mouth as she tried to savor it all. "Oh my fucking God," she said.

John was staring at the fire while chewing slowly. His face was a mess. Chocolate was spread all over his cheeks. "This is what God must taste like. You get up to heaven and he says, 'Taste of my flesh,' or whatever the hell he says, and you take a bite and you're like, 'Motherfucker, you taste like s'mores!'"

Carla giggled. "I'd start going to church if communion was s'mores and wine."

"Me too."

They finished eating and leaned back on their elbows. John looked up at the stars. Carla looked at John.

"This is... exactly what I needed," John said. "To be high as shit, and eating chocolate on a beach with a bunch of rich people."

"You want to go in the water?"

"Fuck yes," John said, and started taking off his clothes.

"Uhh... don't you want to put on a bathing suit?"

"Who just has a bathing suit lying arou..." he looked at her. "Oh, well. No, I'm fine with going in my underwear. I'll just go commando tomorrow."

"OK..." Carla said and stood up.

John took his boxers off.

"Oh boy..." Carla said.

"Yeah, I changed my mind," he said, and walked towards the shoreline.

Carla watched him go. She didn't realize she was biting her lip or sliding her hand down to her stomach.

She heard people yelling and clapping, and turned to see everyone at the bonfire watching John go into the water.

"People of... of the Earth!" he said as he turned around to face them. He walked backwards. "What say we christen these waters in the name of all that is good and holy fuck it's cold!"

John turned around, ran into the water and dove in.

Most of the people from the bonfire joined him. Half of them took off their clothes.

Carla walked over slowly, watching for him to resurface. When he did she waded into the water, went under, came up a few feet away from him.

"Well, that happened," he said.

Carla wrapped her arms around him and kissed him.

He kissed her back.

He was able to stand where they were. Carla wrapped her legs around him.

They broke off their kiss and touched foreheads.

"That was... incredible," he said.

"It was." She kissed him again. She forced her tongue into his mouth. He reciprocated, and moved one of his hands down her back to her hip, and then cradled her ass and pulled her closer to him.

"I don't know your name," he said.

"No names. Except your name. You get my name tomorrow."

"I'm leaving tomorrow."

"Then do you really care what my name is?"

She kissed him again. She reached down to his crotch, started slowly massaging him.

He grabbed her by the back of the hair and pulled her head back. She groaned as he slid his lips from her ear down to her shoulder.

"Oh my God," she said and yanked the bottom of her bathing suit to the side. "Please, just—"

"Seriously?"

"Yes."

"Are you sure?"

"I'm on the pill."

"OK, but—"

"Do you know where your dick has been?"

"Yeah. In my pants."

She laughed. "When was the last time you fucked someone?"

"Like a year ago. Bartender. *Definitely* wore a condom."

"I'll take my chances." He held onto her hips while she worked him inside.

Once she did, she wrapped her legs around him, put her head onto his shoulder, and worked her hips.

John held on for dear life.

He walked them further from the bonfire and the group. He moved them into slightly shallower water and she was able to lean back while he held her, just above her hips. From there he was able to help her move.

She kept making a sound through her teeth, knowing she had to be quiet. When she was about to come she brought herself up close to him, wrapped her lips on his shoulder and made an animal noise while her body clenched up.

John started panting as he held onto her. He'd never had sex in the water before. It was exhausting.

Carla wrapped both arms around him, wiggled her hips so he was fit snug inside of her, and laughed while she breathed it out.

"That was... exactly what I needed," she said.

"Good," John said. "Good."

She broke the clinch and looked at him. They were both wet and breathing heavily and smiling.

"Listen, I'm sorry to bring this up now..." John looked ashamed.

"What?"

"I, uhh... I only take cash."

She laughed out loud, grabbed onto the back of his neck and kissed him.

They had sex twice more. Once again in the water, and once in a bedroom.

The Ecstasy was making it hard for John to finish. Carla was having no problems at all.

He finally came in the bedroom while she was on top. He had his hands on her shoulders and she had her hands on his wrists. She worked her hips until his head finally went back and he said, "Oooh fuuuuck..." and gripped her hard. His hips arched off the bed.

She doubled her efforts and finally he begged her to stop. "OK, OK, OK, stop," he said giggling.

She didn't. "Just hold on a second more," she said, and pushed down hard, rubbing herself against him.

She made that same noise through her teeth and held her breath. After a few seconds she opened her eyes wide and stared straight ahead.

She saw something out of the corners of her eyes. Like flares. She could hear him breathing. She could feel him staring up at her, and she could sense what he was looking at. It was the first time she ever felt truly dissociated.

She started breathing again. She lessened up and dropped her hands. "Oh my God," she said.

He dropped his.

She collapsed on him and just kept breathing.

"You OK?" he asked.

She nodded. "You?"

"I'm better than OK. Rachel."

She chuckled.

"Sally? Arlene?"

"Keep guessing."

"Am I close?"

"Nope."

Ten minutes later, after they'd relaxed and traced fingers back and forth on each other, John said, "I have to take a shower."

"Help yourself," she said.

"You want to...?"

"No, I'm done. My legs are Jello," she said and giggled. "But thank you."

"Sure."

He got up and stretched. She took a long last look at him. She could feel sleep coming. It was three in the morning, and he'd be gone soon.

"Tonya, listen—"

She laughed.

"—I'm not sure what this was..."

"Don't spoil it," she said. "It was fun."

He nodded, waved to her, walked into the bathroom and turned the shower on.

Carla stretched out on the bed and listened to the noise of the water before closing her eyes.

She didn't hear him leave the shower, and he was gone when she woke up the next morning.

CHAPTER THIRTY-THREE

Hal woke up around 4 a.m. and made his way down to the kitchen. Most people were asleep. Two were lounging around the living room, talking.

He found John out by the pool, staring up at the night sky. He had a plate of barely eaten food on his chest and was drinking a beer. He was half naked.

"How long have you been here?" he asked.

"I don't know. What day is it?"

"Wise-ass." Hal went into the kitchen, got himself a beer, came back out. "You get the car?"

"Yeah."

"What did you do with it?"

"It's out in the driveway."

"You... you brought the fucking car here?"

"Yeah, of course I did."

"Are you fucking...?" Hal looked around to see if anyone was listening. "You brought a car full of cocaine to a... the fuck is wrong with you?"

"What do you mean? What else was I supposed to do with it?"

"Deliver it to the guy who bought the stuff maybe?"

"Yeah. Tomorrow. He's not expecting it until tomorrow. I'm not going early and surprising the guy with a carload full of fucking coke *before* the drop off. The fuck kind of... that could get me killed, man. These people are already tense as it is."

"They're *drug dealers*. Tense is in the job description."

"Fuck that. I'm sticking to the plan, all right? Overeager means cop or snitch or fuck-up, so quit worrying," John said.

"I'm not worried about anything."

"You *sound* worried..."

"I'm not, I just... there's got to be a better way to do this."

"It's not a big deal."

"It's a fucking huge deal. We're taking all the risk. And for what? How much is in the car?"

"Fifty."

"Fifty what?"

"Kilos."

"You have fifty... in the car? Just out there?"

"Yeah. I retrofitted the trunk. False sides, false bottom. I even doubled up the buffers with coffee grounds and sealed baggies of gas."

"No shit. Gas. That's good."

"Yeah, man. I'm not worried about getting stopped, I'm just fucking exhausted. Or I was. Whatever they cut this E with..."

"Speed."

"Yeah. I figured. My teeth are wiggling." He massaged his jaw. "Listen, I have to leave in a couple of hours, get up to Boston around ten, meet this guy at some warehouse, drop the load, bring the money back to Gino, come *back* up here on Monday—"

"We have to go to Plymouth Rock."

"Yeah, fuck that."

"It's on the way."

"It's *north*. How can that be on the way? No. I have to come pick you up, bring you back down so *you* can drive the cash down Monday night back to Miami, and *then* I have to do the whole run again on Tuesday." He sighed. "Gino's got six hundred k's just sitting there."

"Are you shitting me? That's twelve trips!"

"The car fits more—"

"Why doesn't Gino just sell it in Miami?"

"He *is*. The six hundred is like a third of what he brought in."

"Six hun... Jesus. You didn't tell me that."

"I just fucking found out Thursday. You ever walk into a warehouse that's got almost two thousand kilos of cocaine in it? They had to give me a fucking gas mask to wear. This guy up here, Gino said it's a good faith buy."

"So then make him fucking pick it up!"

"Gino doesn't trust the guy."

Hal rolled his eyes. "Are you fucking—"

"Not in Miami. He doesn't want a Boston hothead down there. *Or* his guys. Gino's not ready to give him all of it. He's new, the city's locked up by some crew on the South side, I don't know, this guy I'm meeting... Gino said he's who's next. He asked for fifty to start. The drop goes well, in two weeks he'll double the order."

"Then you drive a tru—"

"I'm not driving a fucking truck. Trucks are goddamn cop magnets, and I don't mind the drive."

Hal shook his head. "You have to figure a better way. *We* have to. We're more than just delivery guys. You better be careful, going in there."

"Please. The entire town would get savaged if anything happened to me."

"That's not the point. This shit is below our pay grade. We're better than this. Gino's going to run into real problems one of these days. We can't be worried about some Boston dick-licker, or driving through Savannah Fucking Georgia and having to worry about dumping a car when time is of the essence. *And* have no backup. Safe havens up and down the East Coast might work, but it means too many mouths to feed. You tell them too little, they get ideas of their own. Tell them too much, and they'll throw you to the wolves when they get pulled over for drunk driving."

"So what do you suggest?"

"I don't know, man. I've got to think about it."

"OK. You let me know when you come up with a plan." John sighed.

Hal looked at him a long moment. "You look relaxed."

"I am."

"No. *Too* relaxed. Too relaxed for going into the lion's den tomorrow morning."

"Boston isn't the lion's den. You can't have Harvard and MIT be in the fucking lion's den." John settled back and relaxed, smiled.

"What?" Hal asked.

"What?"

"You've got a look on your face."

"What look?"

"Like you just fucked a soccer mom."

"Oh, she wasn't a soccer mom."

"Jesus, are you kidding?" Hal rubbed his face with his hands. "You just got here!"

"What can I say? Women just—"

"Goddammit." Hal walked away, walked back. "They put me on another fucking boat, man."

"They what?"

"Yeah, I had to catch fucking dinner. With the sun and the water and fish guts. I got back and was sick like a dog."

John started giggling. "That's why you were asleep?"

"Ugh, the smell... fish and blood, it's disgusting."

"I can imagine."

"So I missed out on... you know, there are barely any fucking women... ah, man. Shit. What's her name?"

"Why, so you can finish the job? Not that I didn't finish the—"

"I'm not going anywhere your dick's been. It's so I can stay away from her."

"I don't know her name."

"Bullshit."

"I swear. She said no names."

Hal looked at him a long moment. "You lucky son of a bitch."

245

"It's why I've got this look on my face."

"Fuck. Fine. You're an asshole, but fine." Hal got up. "I'm gonna get something to eat."

"OK."

Hal walked into the kitchen.

"Oh, you know what? She said she came up on the train with..." John turned and looked, but Hal was gone.

John was still feeling trippy when he got up, threw the food away, took the beer and went for a walk down the beach. He turned back when he saw light creeping over the horizon.

By the time he got to the house it was almost seven thirty, and he couldn't find Hal. The place was quiet. He put on the rest of his clothes, made himself two eggs and some toast, got in his car, and drove to Boston.

The drop went as expected.

CHAPTER THIRTY-FOUR

Carla woke up around eight that Sunday morning. Her back hurt. Her legs hurt. Her stomach hurt. Muscles she either hadn't used in a long time, or just simply overused.

She got up, took a shower, brushed her teeth and went downstairs.

No sign of John.

She felt like the cat that ate the canary, except no one knew there was a canary to worry about. Or eat.

Most people were still asleep. She made some scrambled eggs and an English muffin. Coffee was already made and she fixed herself a cup.

She spent an hour relaxing by the pool.

She didn't have any photos, but she thought telling Abigail about her rendezvous in the sea would be enough to get her by for at least six months.

Six months of, "Tell me he held you close and whispered sweet nothings in your ear after every damn thrust."

Six months of, "Tell me you rode him like a Texas rodeo rider who just found Jesus."

Six months of, "Tell me he treated you like a rag doll and you slapped him when he stopped to take a breath."

Carla went back upstairs and saw the remnants of the night before in her discarded bathing suit. She hung it up in the shower, went outside, got back on the bike, and went to Shelly's for more French toast.

Hal watched John walk down the beach wearing only a pair of boxer shorts. He ate some cold fish, some leftover salad, and started up the coffee maker.

He paced around the house, walked out the front door, touched the four-door he knew was John's, and took to the street. Quiet, a little chilly. A dog barking somewhere. It was an hour before a car drove by.

By 6 a.m. he couldn't decide if he should go back to sleep or wait it out. He made his way back into the house, walked through the kitchen, grabbed another cup of coffee, walked into the living room, through a pair of double wood doors, and found himself in a study.

Books lined all four walls. Directly in front of him were two brown leather couches that faced each other. Between them a long coffee table and a lamp. Just beyond was a window facing the backyard, which was open and screened.

There was a grand oak desk with gold-plated hardware in the far left corner. An ornate lamp was on one side, and an antique perpetual calendar on the other. It was set on July 21, 1969.

He slowly made his way around the room, looking at the spines of hundreds of books, touching them with his fingertips. He found a copy of *The Old Man and the Sea*, sat down on one of the couches, and started reading.

He went back and forth from the kitchen three times. Once to get his reading glasses, once to get coffee, and the third time to fix himself breakfast. By 9 a.m. the house slowly began to wake.

It was half past noon by the time he finished the book. He put it back where he found it, made his way back into the kitchen. Carla was sitting there with Alex, who looked a bit worse for wear.

"Morning," Hal said.

"Afternoon," Carla said. She looked well rested and ready for the day.

"Oh, shit, yeah," he said. "What's up with him?"

"He doubled up last night. Got the shakes, threw up a few times. I put him in a cold shower this morning when I saw he had a fever. He's doing OK. Just what?" She tapped Alex on the shoulder.

"Keep cool," Alex said in a voice that came from deep space.

"That's right. Are you hungry, Alex?"

Alex shook his head no.

"When was the last time you ate, man?" Hal asked.

"Don't remember."

"OK, let's just... you have to eat something. What do you like?"

"I don't know."

"Well, what do you hate?"

"Food."

Carla rolled her eyes.

Hal laughed. "OK, man. Eggs it is."

Hal cooked. Carla sat with Alex, put a cool washcloth around his neck, and had him drink a cold glass of water, slowly.

Alex ate the food and sat there with a zoned-out look on his face. "God, this stuff tastes weird. Like cooked worms."

"It's not worms. Don't go there, OK? It's just eggs." Hal looked at Carla. "Anything we can do for him?"

"He just has to ride it out. I think the worst is behind him."

"OK," Hal said and put his hand on Alex's shoulder.

They brought him into an empty bedroom and laid him down.

"You sure he should be, you know, alone?" Hal asked.

"I'll check up on him. You should join the others on the boat."

"Oh, *fuck* no. No. I'll just... I'll just hang. Go back to the library and read something."

"There's a library?"

"Yeah. Off the living room."

"No kidding. Well, I've got a book, I'll join you. We can both keep watch."

"Deal."

249

Hal made them sandwiches. Turkey, Swiss cheese, lettuce, tomato, some mayo. He grabbed handfuls of potato chips and put them on each plate.

Carla sat on the left-hand couch and continued to read *Rum Punch*.

Hal put their plates down on the coffee table and started looking for a new book. "What do you think? You think I can finish a copy of *Moby Dick* in one sitting?"

"Absolutely."

"Yeah... maybe next time." He brushed past a copy of *Slaughterhouse-Five*. "What about this?"

"Never read it."

"Seriously? Whew. This is..." he looked at the book closer, put his glasses on. "No, wait. Never read it."

She chuckled, bit into her sandwich.

Hal sat down across from her with the book, opened it while grabbing his own sandwich. He took a bite while reading the first page. "Holy shit, check this out. 'A fourth-generation German-American now living in easy circumstances on Cape Cod.'" Hal arched an eyebrow and looked over at her. "If that's not serendipity, I don't know what is."

"I guess this weekend was meant to be," she said and smiled. She lifted her book up to eye level, reached over for some potato chips, and started reading.

Every half hour, one of them went to check on Alex. His temperature was gone. Color came back to his face around five that evening. He was still jittery, but his appetite was back. He said he was still tripping, but it had mellowed to a constant over-saturation of color, sound and touch. Not panic.

Dinner was standard barbeque fare, which fine with everyone. People took turns on the grill. No one let Brad near it. Vanessa was banned from the kitchen.

Hal and Carla ate in the library and finished their books roughly at the same time.

"Holy shit," Carla said. "This was... it was fucking good. They should make a movie out of this."

Hal held up his book. "This was... it was fucking weird. But really good. I think they already made a movie out of this. You should read this."

"Yeah? So give it to me."

Hal handed *Slaughterhouse-Five* to her.

"This was nice," she said.

"Yeah. Kind of like we've been married for twenty years, and can just enjoy each other's company."

"So we got through all of the terrible shit."

"Oh yeah." Hal ticked off fingers. "The fighting, the kids, money stress, only seven more years on the mortgage."

"Seven. Nice."

"Both are kids are in college."

"Two kids?"

"Oh yeah. One of them is doing well, the other's the fuck-up."

"Which one is the fuck-up?"

"You tell me."

Carla thought for a second. "The girl."

"Really? So, one of each."

"Yeah. She rebelled early. Smoked when she was younger, got into pot and drinking by the time she was fifteen. Lost her virginity to some punk rocker kid named..."

"Kyle."

"Oh, fuck Kyle for what he did to my baby."

"You remember that time I picked him up by his throat and slammed him into a wall?"

"We renewed our vows the next day."

Hal laughed. "What's our son's name?"

"Robin."

"OK, so, androgynous."

"No, Jesus, that's a unisex name."

"OK, what did I say?"

She laughed.

Hal smiled. "And what's he going to college for?"

"Creative writing, of course."

"So... we're going to support him forever," Hal said, and shook his head.

"Absolutely. Sheila—"

"Fuuuuck... practically a stripper name."

"I'm from Tampa, so it's a family name. Kind of. She's going to fall into something by accident, like fashion or interior design, and she'll become rich and famous and will tell her friends quaint stories of how she grew up with parents who simply didn't understand her."

"Jesus, she sounds just like Michelle."

Carla clapped her hands onto her cheeks. "Oh my GOD, she does!"

They both laughed.

"We don't see her on holidays anymore."

"Who?" Carla asked.

"Your daughter, Sheila, jeez..."

"Oh yeah. But, we get a card on—"

"Easter. Robin says it's her way of being ironic."

"Poor Robin... his writing is terrible."

"It's SO bad."

They both laughed.

"You want anything?" Hal asked.

"I'd take another hamburger and a beer if they have one."

"You bet." Hal walked out.

Someone was still manning the grill. He put in an order for two burgers, went to the kitchen to get some beers. The fridge didn't have any.

He went to one of the coolers by the grill. Empty.

He went over to the last remaining cooler he knew about, by the pool. He found it half full. He grabbed two beers.

When he looked up, he saw Alex and Brad sitting near the back of the house, talking.

CHAPTER THIRTY-FIVE

Hal made his way back into the house, walked into the library. Carla was sitting where he left her. The window behind her was still open. She was curled up, biting one of her fingers. He walked over, handed her a plate and beer. She took it, distracted. Hal could hear Alex and Brad talking from outside as he sat down.

"... just unlucky," Alex said.

"Or stupid," Brad said.

"Listen, don't start in, OK?"

"Well, I get to start in a little. I'm not judging you, man. I've been there. I have. But, Jesus. Eleven thousand?"

"And I just paid them back a shitload..."

"So I'll lend it to you."

"No. No. I don't want... no."

"Well, why did you tell me if you didn't want—"

"I'm just venting, OK? I come up here, you know, to relax, and it's on my mind... so I needed a little, you know. Release."

"Kelly's good for a release."

Carla bit into her hamburger.

Alex made a noise. "Don't get me started about Kelly, OK? I could barely get it up..."

"I'm sorry, man. That really sucks. And, about the rest... you're sure you're OK?"

"Yeah. I can do this on my own. I can. Borrowing money from friends... that's a sure way to lose them. No. I'll take care of it."

"OK," Brad said and stretched. "Hey, what's up with your friend?"

"Who, Carla?"

"The guy."

Hal bit into his hamburger.

"Hal. Yeah."

"Yeah. He was on the boat and we got to talking... I mean, he seems like a nice guy, but... he's not..."

"What?"

"Here to, you know, keep an eye on you, is he?"

Alex laughed. "No, man. No. It's not that bad. No."

"So who is he? What does he do?"

"Don't ask."

"Why? Is he dangerous?"

Carla looked over at Hal. Hal shook his head.

"No. He's just... nothing. He got into some trouble... he's harmless."

"Well, he said he only has one client. Some businessman in New York and you know what that means..."

"What?" Silence for a second. "Oh, come on," Alex said. "No. Hal's not the type. He's a... the guy's practically a saint."

Hal mouthed the word "*see*" to Carla. She ignored him.

"OK, OK, fine," Brad said. "I'll take your word for it. Listen, come tomorrow, what do I owe you for the stuff?"

"It's twenty a pop."

"And how many did you bring?"

"A hundred."

"And what's your cut?"

"Jesus, nothing man. No. This is just to shave off some money I owe."

Brad nodded. "OK, well, I'll pay for half, OK?"

"You don't have to do that."

"Well, I will. You've been getting paid, right?"

"Yeah."

"You got any left?"

"A few."

"Well, someone will take them off your hands. You just... you give them what you owe them, and give them some more so they lay off for a while, OK?"

Alex sighed, held out his hand. "Thanks, man."

Brad shook it. "Hey. It'll be fine. Don't worry about it."

Carla looked at her hamburger. She dropped it on her plate, got up and left the room.

Hal followed.

"Hey," he said. "Hey, wait."

"Fuck you."

"For what?"

Carla walked out the front door.

Hal followed. "What?" he asked.

She stopped in between some parked cars. "Tell me."

"Tell you what?"

"*Are* you here to keep an eye on Alex?"

"The fuck are you talking about? I didn't know anything about this."

"You didn't know Alex has a gambling problem?"

"Of course not. How would I know that? Did *you* know he had a gambling problem?"

Carla went to talk, closed her mouth. "That's not the point."

"I don't... I don't know what the point is. I got invited out here to have a good time. Alex and I talk once a month, maybe. That's it. An email here and there. I had no idea he was in hock."

"That seems like a gambling term."

"It just means you owe something..."

"I *know* what it means!"

"OK, OK."

"Tell me the truth."

"About what?"

"Who do you work for?"

"Who do I work for?"

"Yes."

"A… guy. Just a guy."

"And John? He just delivers cars for people? Even pieces of shit cars?"

"Sort of…"

"Hal. Leave me alone." Carla walked out into the street. It was almost nine o'clock. Streetlights were on and spread out along the coast. Carla made it about ten feet before she realized she was barefoot. She stepped on a pebble and yelped.

Hal shook his head as he watched her hop for a second, turn back, saw him, remembered she was pissed, and kept walking. "OK!" he yelled. "OK."

She stopped.

"Come back before you cut your feet up, for chrissake."

She turned around slowly. She walked back over to him, folded her arms.

Hal half-thought she was going to start tapping her foot. "Inside," he said.

"Why?"

"Because it's a long fucking story."

They walked into the house. In the kitchen Hal grabbed a half-bottle of scotch on the counter. He said to a guy perched next to it, "I'm taking this. You want any?"

"No, thanks. Help yourself." Hal walked off with it. The guy called after him. "Hey, you want a glass?"

"Nope."

They got back into the library, where there were a couple of people. Their food was still there. Hal grabbed their burgers and they headed upstairs. The bedroom Hal had been sleeping in was empty.

"Have a seat," Hal said.

"No, I think I'll stand."

He sighed. "Please." He motioned to the bed. "Look, it's not a power play. I'll sit with you, OK?"

She looked at him for a long couple of seconds, sat down across from him. Then she grabbed her burger and took a bite.

Hal put the bottle of scotch down, did the same.

"First things first. I didn't know about Alex. That's the truth. Bookies don't have guys followed, even with product, and that's a slippery fucking slope of a situation for Alex to put himself in. It's easier for bookies to either just beat the shit out of their deadbeats... or kill them. Because there's nowhere for them to go. Their name is forever on a list, and their debt gets bought by someone else, usually someone worse, and those people have a vested interest to find *that* person, and bad things happen to them, OK? And their families. I don't do that."

"Well, then what do you do?"

Hal sighed. He grabbed the scotch, took a big drink from the bottle.

"Up until about two years ago, I was homeless."

"Yeah, right."

"I was. Before that, I was in prison."

"Jesus—"

"It was nothing, believe me, in the grand scheme of... anyway, then I got into a fight with a couple of guys on the subway and—"

"Holy SHIT!" Her eyes went wide. "I've been trying to figure out where the hell I knew you from. I thought I was fucking imagining things... You... oh my God."

"Yeah. Well. That's the only good part of this story."

"What does that mean?"

He took another drink. "About a month after, with the news and the TV and all that, I was walking in Little Italy, and Jesus, this already sounds like a fucking bad movie."

"What? Tell me."

Hal studied the scotch bottle for longer than he should, then looked up at her. "I work for the mob."

Carla arched an eyebrow, went to speak, closed her mouth, went to speak again, swallowed hard and smiled. "You what now?"

"Yeah. I work for the mob."

"You... work for the mob, and you didn't know about Alex and his—"

"Jesus, it's not like it's a fucking sewing circle, Carla. Even if his bets were with a guy who was connected, he's in Philly. Do you know how many fucking sports gamblers are out there? Why do you think most of it's controlled by the fucking mafia? For fun?"

"OK, OK. But... how? How did it happen?" Hal smiled. He went to take a drink. Carla took the bottle away from him and drank some. "Get to talking," she said.

He did.

It took a little over an hour to tell her everything. The more he talked, the easier it was. When she had questions, he answered them. More often than not, she sat there and took it all in.

"And so, John..." she said.

He nodded. "He's my partner."

"Fuck you!"

"He is."

"Oh, so his 'I deliver cars' bullshit—"

"Oh, no, that's actually true. John's a driver. He loves it."

"OK... OK." She looked at him. "So, should you be telling me all this?"

"I don't know. Are you going to tell anyone?"

"No. Who would believe me?"

"Alex would. He knows something's up, but he doesn't know what."

"I'm not going to tell Alex. I don't think I can trust Alex at this point."

Hal nodded. "Gamblers are tough. They're usually not out to hurt anyone, but it's hard to differentiate between their own self-destruction and the trail their actions leave. My cousin was a gambler. After a while you just come to expect them to fuck up. Every single time."

"Can you help him?"

"Help him? How?"

"I don't know..."

"No, I don't... I don't know. Can't start a turf war over one guy, and asking a favor from another family is... it's a big fucking problem."

"OK."

"Plus, I don't even know if the guy he's working with *is* connected... it's too messy."

"OK."

They sat there in silence. Hal was on his way to actual drunk.

Carla took a drink from the bottle. "Why me?"

"What? Because you fucking asked!" He laughed at her.

She shook her head. "You could have let me walk away."

Hal looked at her closely. She was right. He nodded, lowered his head. He looked visibly exhausted. "Because I don't know anyone. Not anymore. John's in deeper than I am, but I think he enjoys it more. No, not 'enjoys it.' Tolerates it. He was doing this before I came along, and, well, he's seen some shit. Me, I... I think I made a mistake."

"You're in trouble?"

"No. Not yet. And I don't plan on getting into trouble, but people like me don't have that long a shelf life. At least that's what I'm told."

"So you're telling me because you're scared?"

"No."

"Good, 'cause you don't look scared. Resigned, maybe..."

"Resigned. Resigned is the word. It's funny, I'm working for the types of people I should be scared of. But... I think I'm smarter than they are. I think. Maybe not our boss, but the rest... yeah. Definitely. And the rules are pretty simple. Don't steal from them, and don't fuck up. Even I can handle that."

Carla thought for a second, turned to him. She wasn't sure asking him this question was a good idea. "You ever kill anyone?"

259

"No. No, that's a rule we won't break, John and I. We're more like problem solvers. We beat people up sometimes. Well, one person so far..."

"Did he have it coming?"

"Yeah. Yeah he was a bad guy. Not that it made me feel better about it after. They're not all going to be bad people. Some are just going to be stupid. Some will just be in the wrong place at the wrong time. Strong-arming people... it takes a lot out of you. Unless you're psychotic which... well some people are."

"Is John psychotic?"

"No. John's a teddy bear."

Carla visibly relaxed.

"I mean, a teddy bear who gets shit done, but no. In fact he talked his way *out* of killing someone, which just doesn't happen if you want these people to trust you. But he did, and he's still here so... Not that we couldn't kill someone if we *had* to. But, that's anyone..." Hal took another drink. His breath shuddered out of him. He could feel the weight of confession relaxing him, but speaking it all out loud... "You know, I didn't realize just how fucked I am until tonight." He started tearing up. "This isn't what I wanted out of life. I didn't want to be homeless, or in jail either, but this... I'm afraid I sold my soul for cheap. And one of these days I'm going to have to do something terrible, and then they'll really own me." He looked at her. "And I think someone should know the story just in case my life doesn't work out."

Carla took the bottle from him and drank what was left.

"Aww," Hal said.

She put the bottle on the side table by the bed. She looked at him for a long time.

He looks like a goddamn puppy.

"Oh, boy," she said.

Real tears rolled down his cheeks. "Sorry," he said. "I didn't mean to unload on yo—"

She went to kiss him.

Hal got up from the bed. "No, no, no. Listen. I'm..." he started pacing. Carla watched him. "I'm not the kind of guy you should get mixed up with. Jesus. I think you're great, and you're beautiful, but this kind of life, it's... I can take care of myself, *and* John, but I can't take care of someone else, too. OK?"

She stood up and walked over to him. She took his hands. "Hal, you're the first guy I've met in a long time who told me the truth. This here... it doesn't have to be anything more than that. I'm someone you can always tell the truth to. OK?"

He nodded. "OK."

"OK," she said.

She took his glasses off with one hand and led him over to the bed with the other.

CHAPTER THIRTY-SIX

He fell asleep first. She stared up at the ceiling for a long while. Not with regret, just of absolute wonder at how the world works. She fell asleep around two in the morning and felt him stir around eight.

He kissed her forehead, kissed her cheek.

"I'm glad you didn't leave without saying goodbye," she said.

"I'm not that kind of guy." Hal got up, put his clothes on. He looked on the bedside table and saw the copy of *Slaughterhouse-Five*. He grabbed it, wrote his telephone number on the inside back cover. "I'm going to be *way* out of town for a few days. I'll be back Friday, if you feel like calling."

"Maybe I will," she said.

"Maybe OK," he said. He took out his wallet and peeled off some money. "I need you to give this to Alex. Tell him thanks for the ride."

Carla fanned ten hundred dollar bills. "Are you sure?"

"Yeah. It's the least I can do."

"Thank you, Hal."

He nodded. "Listen, I'd kiss you, but, you know, morning breath."

"Such a gentleman."

"No, I mean yours. It's awful."

She threw a pillow at him. Hal grabbed it, came over and kissed her. "Thank you for listening."

"Thank you for trusting me."

He nodded, squeezed her hand and walked out of the room.

Carla curled up in bed and waited until she heard a car door close. Then she went to the bathroom and sighed. She took a shower in a daze.

Breakfast was the usual. The weekend had wound down and people were dreading the trip home.

Alex looked in better shape. He was talking to Kelly over coffee and empty plates.

By eleven, the passenger van was practically full. Carla was in the back, leaning against a window. Alex had his arm around her. "Thanks for taking care of me yesterday."

"Of course. I'm just glad you're feeling better."

"I am. Won't be doing that again. Ever."

"Good."

They got to Boston in an hour and a half. Goodbyes for ten minutes or so. They had half an hour before their train back to Philly.

"Hungry?" Alex asked.

"Starving."

"My treat. What do you want?"

"Anything but egg salad. I think I'd legit throw up if I smelled any more eggs."

"You got it."

Alex walked towards a deli in the terminal.

Carla sat down with their stuff and tried to put the weekend in perspective.

Why? For who? The fuck are you doing?

She nodded.

Did you have fun? Yes. Did you hurt anyone? No. Was it smart to have unprotected sex with two men you barely knew? Ehhhh...

She leaned back and sighed.

OK. You're a dummy. Don't make a habit out of it.

She nodded again.

Alex came back ten minutes later with two sacks. "I got us tuna sandwiches, OK?"

"Great."

"And chips and some fruit and some drinks and some other shit—I don't know. I just had him throw it in a bag."

They got down to the track, found the business car and grabbed a two-and-two, sat across from each other.

"You make out OK?" she asked.

"With who?"

"That's not what I meant, but it's good to see where your head is. I meant with the E."

"Oh. Yeah. Not bad. Kelly took the rest off me, so..."

"Did she pay?"

"Sort of..." he said, and winked, but very exaggerated.

"Uh huh. Well, Hal told me to give you this." She handed him the money.

Alex looked at it for a long time. "Why?"

"He said thanks for the weekend."

"Are you serious?"

"Yeah."

Alex smiled. "Awesome. Fantastic. Oh my God, OK." He stuffed the money into his pocket, ripped open his bag of food, grabbed his sandwich and started eating.

Carla watched him. Again, it was both fascinating and disgusting. He was making a mess. "What?" she asked.

"What?"

"Well... I mean, you look like you just got a life preserver."

"No, hey... I'm just so glad he had fun, that's all."

She nodded. She grabbed her own sandwich and a bag of chips, started eating.

"Uh, you didn't happen to bring back that copy of—"

Carla reached into her bag and handed him his book back.

"Thanks."

"Sure."

He watched her for a moment. "Everything OK?"

"Yeah, why wouldn't it be?"

"I don't know, you seem... upset."

"Nope. Just hungry."

"OK."

Carla pulled out the book she'd stolen and started reading it.

"I thought you didn't bring anything to read."

"I didn't. Someone left this behind, so I took it."

"Huh. OK."

They barely spoke for the rest of the trip. Alex would ask questions. Carla would limit her answers to one or two words. Any longer, and she wouldn't look at him while answering.

After a while, Alex stopped talking.

By the time they got to Philly, Alex had done some actual thinking. Chronological thinking.

By the time they got out of the tunnel and back up onto North 30th Street without a word spoken, he'd figured it out.

"Stop," he said.

She didn't stop.

"Carla, please."

She stopped. She turned around. "What?"

"What are you doing?"

"I'm going home. I'm tired."

"Why don't you come over?"

"No."

"I'll get a cab and... what did I do?"

"Alex, I'm tired. And this... this isn't going to just go away, no matter what we say. I'm going home before I say something I'll regret."

"Brad told you and Hal about the money I owe."

"No. He didn't. I heard you telling him. So did Hal."

Alex nodded, lowered his head. "OK. Sorry. Bye, Carla."

"Bye."

She turned and walked away.

Carla got into a cab and headed home. She was pissed off, but was relieved she had one more day (Mondays and Tuesdays were her days off) before she had to go back to work.

265

CHAPTER THIRTY-SEVEN

Wednesday morning, Abigail walked up to Carla and didn't say a word.

"What?"

Abigail just looked at her.

"What?" Carla asked again. She moved down the hall with two bags of plasma for two different patients. One who had liver disease, and one who was going in for heart surgery.

"Don't act like you don't know," Abigail said. "Video. Audio. Pictures. Cave paintings. Whatever you have to share, I want it."

"Well, I have parts of the cave in the car..."

"Bitch, you can't afford a car."

"That's true."

"Don't mess with me, woman. I just went through Hell Weekend for you, OK? And if you want me to make you feel bad, I can talk to you about Mr. Goodall, whose son shot him in the jaw after he wouldn't give up the TV remote."

"That happens..."

"Or Patty Buchanan, who weighs four hundred and eighty pounds, and hadn't bathed in two months."

"Oh God."

"Yeah. We found some necrotic tissue in a fat flap. Poor Aaron puked his guts out. Dr. Carter had to drag him out of the room after his face went white. Poor Patty started crying because of it, and said she was going to sue the hospital for emotional distress. You ever heard of such a thing?"

"Not until today."

They kept walking.

"PLEASE—"

"OK, OK. I will. At lunch, OK? I promise."

"You better."

They found a spot, just after noon. A park bench, down the block, under a large tree. It was sunny out, mid-eighties, not humid. There was a nice breeze.

"So?"

"So what?"

"*Girl*..."

Carla sighed. She looked left, looked right, looked behind them. No one was around.

She held up three fingers.

"Ooohh! You had sex three times?"

Carla shook her head no, then nodded. "Technically."

"Well, what..." Abigail's eyes went wide. "You had... you were..." She crossed herself. "What in the *hell* kind of *Eyes Wide Shut* party did you go to?"

Carla laughed and then started crying.

"Sweetheart, it ain't nothing to be ashamed of. Why are you crying?"

Carla wiped tears from her face with both hands. "I'm not crying because I did it."

"You do it with Alex?"

Carla nodded.

"Was he the first...?"

Carla shook her head.

"Second?"

Carla shook her head.

"Oh lord. Does he know about the—"

"No."

"Well, don't tell him."

Carla shook her head no. She started crying again.

"Honey, what's wrong?"

"We got into a fight... sort of. I found out he was gambling again."

"Oh, for the love of... what is WRONG with that boy?"

"A lot," Carla said. She took a deep breath.

"So what happened?"

Carla sat in bed that Monday night after the uncomfortable train ride. She'd ordered Chinese take-out. Moo shu beef with scallion pancakes, and vegetable lo mein. Food for days.

She opened up a bottle of red that she had lying around. She drank a full glass after unpacking and taking a shower.

She sat on her bed, slowly building a moo shu sandwich, when her buzzer rang.

She stopped. Stopped food-building, stopped moving, stopped breathing.

She slowly looked up at the buzzer.

It buzzed again.

"You've got to be fucking kidding me."

Her phone started ringing.

"Jesus Christ," she said, and put her plate down.

She walked over to her phone. It said ALEX.

She declined the call, put the phone down and went back to her food.

Her phone buzzed. A text.

"No. I'm not doing this. I'M NOT DOING THIS!" she yelled, hopeful that it was loud enough he would hear it.

"I'm not leaving!" she heard from the street.

She rolled her eyes.

The door buzzed again. Then again. Then it buzzed to the tune of "Shave and a Haircut."

Carla closed her eyes and sighed. She went to the door, buzzed it open.

Moments later there was a knock. Carla walked over, opened the door.

Alex was out of breath. "Thank you," he said, and came inside. "I've been trying to call you."

"So?"

"Well, I mean, the least you could do is answer."

"Actually, the least I could do is what I was doing. Which wasn't answering. Answering would actually be the most I could do. You see the difference?"

"Jesus, what is up your ass?"

"Is that what you're here for? To ask me what's up my ass? I finally give you what you want, and that's what you ask me?"

"I fucked up, Carla! I fucked up. I fucked up again, and you can judge me all you want. But this isn't your problem, it's mine. And I'm not asking you for anything. I'm just... I just need my friend."

Carla nodded. "Uh huh. Yeah. Do you have any idea how difficult it is to watch you flush your fucking life down the toilet? Do you?"

"You're over-exaggerating."

"Am I? How much money do you owe them?"

"That's irrelevant."

"It's perfectly fucking relevant to this conversation, Alex. It's the only fucking thing we're talking about."

Alex sighed. "Eleven thousand."

"And? After you give them the money from the weekend? How much then."

"A little over nine."

"Nine thousand dollars. That is more than a year's worth of rent for me—"

"What is it with you and rent—"

"I don't know what your problem is—"

"Did your rent go up or—"

"—throwing away your money—"

"It's not like this is a habit—"

"*Jesus*! What the hell else would you call it? I've seen you here before. Where you had to dig yourself out of the same hole. And you didn't learn a goddamn thing."

"I got unlucky, Carla, Jesus, give me a break."

"Unlucky."

"That's it. It's not an excuse. I fucked up. I'm right back where I was, with the same people, yes. The only thing I have going for me is they know I'm good for it."

"Well, that's a load off my mind. You can leave now."

"Please..."

"*Please*? Please what? What do you want from me? What am I to you except someone who, up until tonight, didn't give you too much shit for all the stupid things you do? It's almost like you have me as a back-up to constantly say 'eh, don't beat yourself up. These things happen.' I'm not that person, Alex. Terrible things happen to people every day. That's not hyperbole, I actually witness it! And most of the time, they don't deserve it. They were just in the wrong place at the..." She suddenly remembered what Hal said the night before. "But sometimes, people actually do deserve it. Because they did something they shouldn't have. Or they were just stupid. I never thought of you as stupid, Alex. I really didn't. Not until last night." Carla sat down on the bed. She looked at her food. "Stay, go, whatever. I'm fucking starving." She finished building her dinner. She bit open a container of hot yellow mustard and dumped it into the middle of the moo shu, folded up the pancake and took a big bite. She looked up at Alex, who was staring at the food. "Jesus. Just help yourself already."

He did. Alex grabbed a scallion pancake and dipped it in soy sauce. He dished out some lo mein and ate it with a pair of chopsticks.

Carla rolled up another moo shu pancake, dumped more hot mustard. "Taste OK?" she asked.

Alex nodded.

"You want some wine?"

He nodded again.

270

"Fine, just don't play that wounded soul shit with me, all right?" She got up, grabbed a glass for him, came back to the bed and poured him a glass.

Carla stopped her story to sigh. She looked at her watch. They had about ten minutes before they had to head back in.

Abigail was riveted.

"I have never had good luck with men. Ever."

"No. No. Do NOT interrupt this story with some philosophical shit. Please."

"It's not philosophical shit. I'm just... over three days, I met three men who I... I really liked. What are the odds of that happening?"

"Pretty damn slim."

"Right?" She took a bite of her sandwich.

"So? What happened?"

"Alex told me he loved me."

"He what?"

"He told me he's in love with me."

"He told you..."Abigail put her food down. "He *told* you...?" She got up, walked away. Walked back. Carla watched her as she ate her sandwich. "Why? Why do men *do* that?"

"You know what my favorite memory of you is?" Alex asked around a mouthful of food.

"No, but I have a feeling you're going to tell me."

"I am. We went out drinking one night. After you graduated. We were at that... that shitty club on Ludlow and you saw a woman come out of the bathroom with a bloody nose. You remember?"

She nodded.

"We were in the middle of talking and all of a sudden you just stopped and walked over to her, and then you walked her outside. And she was crying and just... I mean, she was just beside herself. I followed you out, I thought something was seriously wrong with her, like a fucking aneurism or something, the way she was screaming and

271

crying." Carla chuckled. "I mean it! And you asked her what happened and she said—"

"'All I did was some coke,'" Carla said.

Alex started laughing. "I couldn't fucking believe it. And you just nodded like, 'yeah, OK. I get it.' And you said 'I need you to just relax, OK? I'm a nurse.'" He looked at her. "And she calmed down, just like that. And you put her in a cab and had her friends take her to the emergency room. You told them what to say, and they all looked so... *relieved*. And you watched the cab go, and you put your hands on your hips like fucking Wonder Woman—"

Carla laughed, drank some wine.

"I swear to God, you did. And you turned around, patted me on the shoulder, went back inside, and drank three shots of tequila. You danced for an hour, and then I dropped you off at home. And you gave me a hug, and kissed me on the cheek, and then we had brunch the next morning. And you didn't bring it up."

Carla blushed a bit. She brushed her hair out of her face and looked at him.

"It's the day I realized I was in love with you."

It didn't hang in the air for longer than a second before Carla said, "God*dammit,*" and shook her head.

"What?"

"You really know how to ruin a good story."

Carla and Alex stared at each other. The room was quiet. There was no noise coming from the street. The only sound was a hum from her refrigerator.

"I think you should leave," Carla said.

"What?"

"You heard me. I don't think it's funny—"

"Funny?"

"And I don't think it's fair."

"What are you talking about?" he asked, and moved over to her.

Carla put her drink down and stood up, moved away from him. "This is one of those moments that... I'm sorry, Alex, but that weak people come up with for sympathy. It's such a grand gesture, in the hope that maybe I'll forget your other faults, because you know that, after all these years, there's a chance I feel the same way."

"You think this is a ploy?"

"It isn't?"

Alex laughed. Actually laughed. He put the wine glass down, wiped his mouth with the back of his hand. "Fuck you, Carla. I mean it. All these years...? Yeah. Doing what you asked. Being your friend. I didn't come over here for you to forgive me my, whatever, my *sins*. I came here to tell you I love you. And I've been in love with you for a long time."

"Oh yeah?" She could feel the anger building up inside. "How did fucking Kelly fit into your grand scheme here?"

And then, suddenly, the air felt like it was sucked out of the room.

The look on his face said it all. Crushed was the only word that came to her mind. Carla stopped looking at him. She knew that, as soon as she said the words, she'd made a mistake. If he'd seen her with—

"I didn't fuck Kelly."

"No, that's right. You couldn't get it up." Even worse—and she couldn't stop it. For some reason, she was incredibly angry at him.

It's because he said it first.

Don't you fucking start!

Alex stared at her, then lowered his head. "Boy, you heard everything."

"That's right."

He nodded. "Well, a lot's happened since then. Wouldn't you agree?"

She couldn't tell if she was being baited. "No, I wouldn't."

"Well, you found out about what I owe, we barely talked the whole way home. I've been trying to piece together exactly what you knew, how you knew it, and how to explain it to you. Maybe not a lot's happened to *you*, but I've been overwhelmed with guilt and

273

stress and feelings and this... this terrible desire to just tell you the truth. And not just over the weekend. For months. Longer. This isn't me looking for a way out, or for you to just forgive me. The only thing I want to do is spend the rest of my life with you."

She shook her head. "I don't think that's a good idea, Alex."

"Why?"

"Because I don't think I can trust you. Because look what it took for you to tell me the truth."

"I would have told you the truth..."

"But?"

"I thought I could handle it. Like I handled it before. I didn't take into consideration you were listening in on a private conversation."

"Don't get indignant now. You don't get to do that."

"I'm not. But if you hadn't heard me, and I came to you today, tomorrow, a week from now, and I told you I love you... what would you have said?"

She swallowed, hesitated. "I... I don't know."

She knew her face betrayed her, instantly.

"Now who's talking out of their ass?"

She stopped and took a breath, nodded. "Maybe you're right. But I still wouldn't have known the truth."

Alex nodded. "You're right. You wouldn't have. And I'm sorry. I'm sorry for fucking up *and* for not being honest with you." He looked around the room. "And I'm sorry for showing up here and springing this on you. It's not how I wanted it to happen." He sat down, drank his wine and cradled the empty glass. Carla grabbed the bottle and gave him a refill. "Thanks." He drank some more.

"You're a fucking idiot," she said, and drank from the bottle.

"You said that to him?" Abigail asked.

Carla nodded.

"Good for you. Could have been a perfect moment..."

"Yeah, it could've."

"So what happened?"

Carla sighed. "I had him stay over. For pity's sake."

"Sounds about right."

"We finished eating, we watched half a movie. We were both exhausted. So he slept on the floor and I slept in the bed, and then I couldn't get to sleep…"

"Oh God. I know where this is going."

"It's pathetic, right?"

"It's kinda pathetic… but only *kinda*."

"One in the morning, I'm lying there. And I get up, and I peek over to see if he's asleep, and he's looking right at me. And I just shook my head, lifted the covers…"

Abigail made a noise and rubbed her hands together, smiling.

Carla chuckled. "Boy, oh boy. You know, I feel like I'm going to go to hell and I don't know why."

"Honey, if you're going to hell over this? Humanity is FUCKED."

Silence for a long while. Cars passed. Birds chirped. The sun moved lower in the sky.

"Was it good?"

Carla nodded. "It was." She looked around. "They all were. Different, but good. Alex and I spent the day in bed together. Yesterday."

"That's nice." Abigail said. "You tell him you love him?"

"No. Hell no. Jesus."

"Good, 'cause it's the only ammo you got left."

"Don't I know it."

They both sat there, taking it all in.

Abigail looked at her watch, looked at Carla. "You OK?"

"Yeah. I'm OK. Thanks, Abby."

"Whew! Well, I would have preferred pictures… but I'll take what I can get." They got up and walked back to work. Abigail looked over at her. "So, now wait. Who were the other two?"

"Just two guys. Two friends."

Abigail stopped. "Just… two… at the…" She pointed her fingers at each other. "At the same…"

"No. No! Jesus. No."

Abigail fanned herself. "Thank God. I don't think my heart can take any more."

PART III

All in the Family

CHAPTER THIRTY-EIGHT

Making up for taking off on Memorial Day weekend, Carla worked four six-day weeks in a row. It wasn't until she finally had a weekend to herself that she realized she'd missed her period. It had happened before, mainly due to stress, and she quickly forgot about it.

A week later, she was in an elevator going from Med Surg to emergency, when she threw up her breakfast.

She was so embarrassed she used her scrubs to clean it up. She tossed them into a bin and went to rip open a new pair when she put two and two together.

"Oh, no," she said.

It was the first and only time in her life she would have a panic attack.

She threw up again.

Carla walked out of the locker room in a cold sweat. She made her way back up to Med Surg and found Abigail, who had her head in some paperwork.

"I need to talk to you."

"OK, just a sec—"

"Now. Like, now, now."

Abigail looked up at Carla. She was white as a sheet.

"Girl, you're white as a sheet!"

Carla swallowed excess saliva that was creeping up from behind her back teeth. She was going to throw up again, she could feel it.

"Garbage can," she said.

"Say what?"

Carla motioned with her hand. Abigail gave it to her. Carla threw up.

"Oh, no," Abigail said.

Carla nodded. "My pulse is around 140, shortness of breath, I feel like I'm going to faint, I need something, Abigail, something, or I... I'm gonna pass out."

"OK, one sec, one sec." Abigail looked around and grabbed a set of keys from a drawer, walked over to the medicine cabinet and took out a pill wrapped in foil. "Don't make this a habit," she said.

Carla nodded. She snapped open the foil, walked over to the floor's water fountain and swallowed the pill.

"I gotta check," she said.

"I'll get you a—"

"No. Not here."

Carla took the same elevator down. She could still smell her puke. She walked out of the hospital to the nearest pharmacy. She bought a pregnancy test, walked back to the hospital, and found an empty bathroom on the third floor, near Pediatrics.

She closed the door behind her. The pill had started working. She wasn't panicky, but she broke down anyway. Her whole body shook as she took the EPT out of its container.

She sat down, peed on the stick, and waited.

And waited.

She watched the indicator as it slowly developed a double line. She started shaking, crying harder than she'd ever cried in her life.

She said "Oh my God" over and over again. She didn't know how long she was in the bathroom before she got up, tossed the test and the box in the garbage, covered it with some paper towels, and walked out.

Carla's face was a mess. She got back up to Med Surg, where Abigail was waiting.

"So, uhhh... good news?" Abigail asked.

Carla started crying again and threw her arms around her friend.

Carla was shaking when she opened the door to her apartment. Still shaking when she attempted to make pasta, and ended up letting it cook too long. It was a rubbery mess when she dumped it out of the pot into a colander.

Alex came over around 7 p.m. He buzzed, as usual, even though he had a key. "Out of respect," he'd said to her two weeks earlier. "It's still your place."

She buzzed him in, stood by the door to let him in.

"Hey," he said, and kissed her hello. He dumped his bag and coat onto her bed and sat down. "What's for dinner? I'm starving."

Carla hadn't moved.

"Hey. What's the matter?"

She turned to him, tears in her eyes.

"Honey, what's wrong?"

She started crying. Her body heaved and shook as she held her arms out for him. He got up and walked over and hugged her.

"Baby, what's the matter?"

"You're going to be so mad," she said, muffled by his shoulder.

"What?"

She lifted her head a bit. "You're going to be so mad."

"Mad? What would I be mad about?"

She wiped her face with his shirt.

"What the... OK, that's OK, I have to get it dry cleaned anyway. Honey, tell me. What's going on?"

"Sit down," she said.

"Jesus, sit down? It's sit down news? OK. OK." He sat down. "Now tell me. What's going on?"

Carla didn't know how to say it. "I... I'm... I..."

She touched her belly and started crying.

"You... you're sick? Constipated? You're crying because you're constipated? What? That happens to every—"

"No, goddammit…" and she mimed making her stomach bigger.

"You're fat? Baby, you're not fat…"

She gave him a look.

Alex's face slowly changed. It went from confusion to doubt to comprehension to nervousness to excitement in about ten seconds.

"Oh my God," he said and stood up. "OH MY GOD!" he grabbed her and lifted her off the ground in a hug. "I'M GONNA BE A DADDY!"

He bounced around the room with her. She was still crying. Not good tears.

"This is the best fucking news of my goddamn life!" he said and let her go. "Oh, I have to call my parents. My mom's going to *shit* that she's going to be a grandma before she turns sixty."

"No—"

"She can't *stand* getting old!"

"Wait," Carla said, kind of weakly.

Alex stopped. He walked over to her. "Honey, baby, sweetheart, this is unbelievable!" He kissed her. "Isn't it?"

She started crying again. She covered her face with her hands and sank down to the floor.

"Carla? It's good news, isn't it?"

"I don't know," she said in between sobs. "I wasn't… I didn't… I'm on the pill, Alex."

"Christ," he said. "I know. I'm sorry. You're right. This… fuck, OK, I didn't realize how much of a shock this must have been for you. When did you find out?"

"Around lunch. I threw up in the elevator."

"Jesus."

"Yeah."

"Was Abby there?"

"Yeah."

"Good. Good. I'm glad that you had someone to… I'm sorry, honey. I wasn't thinking."

"It's OK," she said, and pulled her knees up to her chest. "I just… this wasn't the plan."

"Right."

"I mean, we just started going out and—"

"No, I get it. I do."

They sat there for a long time.

"Well, say something," she said.

"Like what?"

"I don't know. Anything."

He thought about it a long moment. "Are you hungry?"

Carla stared at him like he'd asked the dumbest question in the world, then said, "Yeah. I ruined dinner, so, we have to order something."

"OK. OK. Pizza?"

"Yeah. Double cheese, double pepperoni."

"OK." He went to her phone, grabbed the menu they always ordered from off the fridge, and called.

He sat back down with her and held her hands.

"We might only have just started going out... but we know each other. We're best friends. Right?" She nodded. "OK. OK." He looked around the apartment. "Listen, I, uhh... OK. I'm not going to pressure you. I'm sorry I flew off the handle there when I found out. I know it might seem like I'm all for just one option, but... listen, if you're not ready, you're not ready. And I won't be upset. I mean it."

"Really?"

"Yeah. Of course. It's your choice, Carla, and I'll be OK with whatever you end up deciding. I'll love you no matter what."

She started crying again. After a day of stress and sickness relief hit her. Her stomach started grumbling and she thought, *Jesus, I'm eating for two*, and she started crying harder.

The food got there. She had three slices. They barely talked. Alex watched her eat and would occasionally reach over and wipe her face, whether it was tears or sauce.

When she'd had her fill, she got into bed. He got in with her and turned to be the big spoon. "Let's just lay here and take it easy, OK?

We'll just relax and digest this greasy, disgusting… I mean, really, who needs double cheese?"

She laughed. "It's the only thing that was going to make me feel better."

"Well, you get what you want, OK? You want dessert?"

"No."

"Because I want some ice cream."

She turned to him and said, "I want some ice cream," but grabbed his arm and wrapped it around her. "I'm scared."

"I know. It's OK. I'm going to be here, the whole time. OK?"

"Well, not the whole time. You have to get us ice cream."

Alex smiled. He squeezed her and got up off the bed. "What would you like?"

"Rocky Road."

"Perfect. I'll be back in a bit."

"OK."

Alex made his way to the door, opened it.

"Alex?"

"Yeah."

"I love you."

CHAPTER THIRTY-NINE

A week later, Carla made the decision to keep the baby. She sat down with Alex at a diner and laid down the law. "I'm not going to marry you until the debt is cleared."

"Marry me?"

"Yeah. The kid's going to need a father. We're not doing whatever hippy it-takes-a-village shit that some people think is acceptable."

"Are you asking me to marry you?"

"No. Not yet. But it'll happen eventually, and if you want to be in this kid's life…? The debt has to go."

Alex nodded, smiling. "OK. That's fair."

"Fair?"

"I meant of course, that's the way it should be. Not like we're negotiating."

"We're not. That is non-negotiable. You've got seven months to get your shit together, Alex. This kid isn't going to be born in the red. You get me?"

"I get you."

"And I'm not taking your last name?"

"What? Seriously?"

"Yeah, seriously. Holsfer? It's impossible to pronounce."

"So?"

"Or spell. Wait, what do you mean, 'so'? You agree it's impossible to pronounce?"

"Well, yeah, but… it's my last name."

"Uh huh. You know what you're going to eat?"

"A burger."

"Me too. OK. Next thing... and this is to help. You should move in with me."

"What?"

"You should move in with me."

"Why would I... why don't you move in with me?"

"Because your rent is more than mine. And because I can afford my own rent. So, I'll pay rent, you pay down your gambling... your debt."

"Carla, I don't think that's a good idea."

"Why?"

"Because your place is too small for three people."

"That's right. It is. As soon as you're done paying these people off, we'll get a bigger place. But until then... these are the rules."

He nodded, not smiling this time. "But I love my apartment."

"Well, you can continue to love your apartment and never hear from us again..." she shrugged. "Or, you can be a grown up and—"

"OK, enough of that shit. How's that for a rule? Quit patronizing me, like I'm some fucking asshole who hasn't learned from his mistakes."

Carla arched an eyebrow.

"You know what I mean. This... that..." he said, pointing to her stomach "is way more important than basketball to me, OK? I'm not going to put us in a situation where we're... I'm not going to fuck up again."

She sighed, looked around for the waitress, who noticed and nodded. "Alex, I want to believe you. I really do. I want to trust you. Do this for me. Move in. Pay them off. I won't question you or patronize you again. I promise."

The waitress came over. "Ready to order?"

"Yeah. Honey, you first," Alex said.

"I'd like a burger, medium with cheddar cheese, French fries, and a chocolate shake."

"And you, sir?"

"The same. Thanks."

The waitress took their menus and walked away.

"The same..." Carla said. "We're not going to wear matching outfits, for God's sake."

"Might be fun."

"Might get you pushed in front of a bus."

"Yeesh, OK, OK." He looked around the place. It was half empty. "You tell your mother?"

"No. Not until the first trimester. I don't need her up my ass, just in case... you know."

"Yeah."

"So don't tell anyone."

"Who am I going to tell?"

"Your parents."

"Besides them."

"Your friends."

"Besides them."

"The people you work with—"

"Jesus, I'm not going to tell anyone!"

"Don't."

"I won't."

They sat in silence. The diner was full of diner noises. Patrons eating. Line cooks slapping grills with metal spatulas. The ringing of the line bell. Waitresses moving back and forth with food and drinks. The shake machine was whirring. Busboys were cleaning off tables.

"I told my sister."

"You WHAT?"

The place went quiet. Heads turned.

Carla reached across the table and grabbed Alex by the tie. "You did what?"

"She called from France out of the blue and she was drunk and high and there's a real chance she won't remember any of it."

"Are you fucking kidding me?"

"Well, see… we were both drunk and—"

"Alex, this is the kind of thing that gets you killed."

"I know, but I was so excited and… I wasn't thinking."

The waitress came over with their food. "Here you are," she said. Carla let go of Alex's tie. The waitress put the food down. "Everything OK here?"

"It's fine. He's just got a big mouth."

"He must be friends with my husband," the waitress said, and walked away.

"See? She gets a bigger tip for that," Carla said, and grabbed the ketchup.

Alex smoothed his clothes and smiled.

"Don't smile. You're not out of the shit just because our food is here and it smells delicious."

"You're very funny, you know that?"

"I'm not trying to be funny."

"I know. That makes you even funnier."

"Alex…"

"I won't tell another soul. I swear." He put his hand up with two fingers in a V. Then three fingers pressed together. Then he did the Vulcan salute. Then Mork's—

"Enough," she said, smiling. "I get it." Carla dumped ketchup onto her plate next to the fries. She handed the bottle over to Alex, who dumped ketchup onto his burger. She dipped her burger into the ketchup and took a bite. Then another. Then sipped her shake. Then ate some fries. "I'm going to get fat," she said.

"So am I," Alex said. "That's a thing, right? Sympathetic weight gain?"

"Yeah, but I mean, like…" she mimed getting huge. "Especially these," she said, and grabbed her breasts.

Alex drank some of his shake, came away with an ice cream mustache. "Well, I don't know about you, but I can't wait for that."

CHAPTER FORTY

With what Alex brought in from Cape Cod, breaking his lease, and taking some side work, he was able to pay off his debt in six months.

His sister did, in fact, forget the conversation.

Carla called her mother at the beginning of her eleventh week. She was just starting to show. Her mother broke down crying, thanking God for the miracle. Her grandchild.

Alex's parents were less than thrilled. "Well, you can't stay here," was the first thing his father said. His mother scolded him for that, but doubled down on the fact that there was simply no room for them. Not that they weren't wanted.

They lived in a three-bedroom house with a full basement and a two-car garage.

Alex told them they'd be fine, and that maybe, someday, they might want to spend some time with their grandchild. "No pressure, though, OK?"

He left shortly thereafter, feeling angry and frustrated. He was still paying off the money at that point. Jerry, the guy who ran the book, kept asking if he wanted to try and pay it off a bit sooner, with more drugs. Alex said no thanks. They capped his vig at twenty percent. "We usually don't have guys come in here who do what they say they're going to do," Jerry said. He was covered in tattoos. "Normally we'd break your arm or your leg or something, which is

289

fun, don't get me wrong. But you're like a homing pigeon. Once you're done paying, you'll be back."

"No, I won't," he said.

"You've got the itch. I've seen it a thousand times. You'll be back. And maybe next time you'll actually win."

The conversation bothered Alex. Not because Jerry was making fun of him, but because he wished, like all gamblers, for the big one.

Still, he was true to his word.

Carla's place was cozy. Not too small, but neither of them was used to living with someone. It took some adjusting.

Her mood swings were legendary, and quick to subside. She craved strange foods, and Alex did his best to cater to her whims. He found himself eating along with her every once in a while. None of the taste combinations made any sense. Some were downright disgusting.

Carla always seemed satisfied in the end.

Because they were still in the honeymoon phase of their relationship, they were still having sex multiple times a week. Carla found that her appetite for it was all over the place. Sometimes the thought made her sick. Other times, no matter what they were doing, she would drop everything and attack him.

They went in for an ultrasound after the sixteenth week and their doctor asked if they wanted to know the sex of the baby.

They said yes. They'd already picked out a name, regardless of whether it was a boy or a girl. Jesse/Jessie.

Alex was over the moon about having a son. Carla had been on the fence, but came around when she realized she would have another ally in the house. She was sure Alex would have been the type of father to become the hands down favorite if they'd had a girl.

Once the debt was paid off, they started looking for a new place. They found a fantastic two-bedroom that was equidistant from both of their jobs, and the rent was manageable. Good neighborhood, too. Carla broke her lease and they moved in a month before the baby was due.

A week later, they were married at City Hall, in a large room with painted portraits of famous men and women on the walls. Carla ended up taking his last name. They were one of eight couples, and the entire room cheered whenever someone got married. Abigail was her maid of honor. Alex had invited Brad and Vanessa, along with some people from work.

Their parents were there, too. Michelle was a no-show.

They spent the evening at Vetri Cucina, and ordered the kind of foods they normally never would. The bill was astronomical, but no one seemed to mind.

Alex's father sprung for a bottle of champagne. Carla had half a glass.

A week before Jesse was due, Carla's water broke at work. Alex had asked her to stop working after the eighth month. Carla said, "What better place for me to be if something happens, than the hospital?"

"OK. I'm going to tell you this, OK? Not because you're right, but because I can admit when I'm wrong."

"OK."

"I feel stupid for not realizing that," he said.

She patted him on the cheek. "As you should."

The entire hospital staff, one at a time, came into her room, asking if she needed anything. It was like a clown car procession. When Sam, one of the janitors, came in with a catcher's mitt, she said, "OK, that's enough of that!" It got a big laugh.

She was scared, but excited. Her doctor was someone she'd worked with on numerous occasions. Alex was there in scrubs and a mask, blotting her forehead and feeding her ice chips. She'd gotten an epidural and everything was happening exactly as it should.

Abigail was in the room and gave a play by play while recording it on a camcorder.

Jesse was born after three hours of labor on February 9, 2003. Six pounds, twelve ounces.

With sandy hair.

Throughout the pregnancy, Carla and Abigail kept the lone secret. Carla had gotten good at pushing it away when it crept up on her. She was secretly thankful that John, Hal, and Alex were not only all white, but had similar hair color. They ran the spectrum of dirty blonde to light brown.

Still, there were bound to be unmistakable characteristic differences that might get Alex thinking... *if* it wasn't his child. He'd never said anything about where she was or what she had been doing that weekend. The second night, she was too high to care. The third night... well, anyone could have peeked into that bedroom and seen her with Hal. Whether they would have mentioned it to him in passing...

In nine months, he'd never said a word. But, if there was one thing she knew about Alex... he could be an excellent actor when he needed to be.

"He looks like you," Abigail said as she laid Jesse in Carla's arms.

"You think so?" she asked.

"I wasn't talking to you," Abigail replied, and looked over at Alex, who took his mask off. He was smiling, tears streaming down his face.

Carla looked at Alex, who came over and touched Jesse's face with his fingers. She looked up at Abigail, who winked.

It took only a moment for her to realize what had just taken place, and Carla started crying. She was tired, she was in pain, and her best friend had just made the save of a lifetime.

CHAPTER FORTY-ONE

The hospital gave her three months paid maternity leave. Carla stayed home and took care of Jesse. Alex worked and stayed away from the bookies.

Friends would come over and hang out and help before their shifts. Carla's mom left a week after the birth. She was still working, still slowly socking away money for her retirement, and a week was all she could spare.

"I can take off some time around August, maybe?" she said on the way out to catch her cab. "You send me pictures. Every day, you hear?"

"OK, Mom."

Once, during those three months, Alex's parents visited. They'd given them $5,000 as a wedding present (on top of helping pay for the wedding dinner), and bought them a crib and some baby supplies when Carla and Jesse came home from the hospital.

Carla figured they would come around even more.

Alex said, "Don't hold your breath."

By the end of her leave, she was ready to go back to work. Carla had originally planned to switch to night shifts, but was talked out of it by literally everyone she asked. "You *think* you're not sleeping now. Switch shifts and you will want to die," Abigail said.

Carla said OK, and got back on an 8 a.m. to 4 p.m. rotation.

"You have to talk to your mom," Carla told Alex. She was feeding Jesse.

"Nope."

"Alex, we need her help. We can't afford a full-time nanny."

"She's not going to help. She's the most stubborn person I've ever met. She *hates* you."

"Why?"

"You know why."

Carla waited him out.

Alex sighed. "Because she's an elitist bitch who thinks I married below my, my—"

"Status."

"Yeah." Silence for a second. "*I* said she was an elitist bitch, you know. She probably thinks you sabotaged your birth control."

Carla started shaking from laughter.

"Right? She's nuts," Alex said. "It's a wonder I turned out as well as I did."

Carla decided not to ruin the moment by mentioning the gambling. "Yeah, well, she can hate me all she wants, she can't hate her grandson. Listen, you talk to her, or—"

"I'm afraid of her, OK?"

Carla looked at him. He was spooning cereal into his mouth, milk dribbling down his chin. Just a big kid. "OK," she said.

She drove over the following Saturday and knocked on their door. Helen, Alex's mother, opened it with a surprised look on her face. "Carla, hi. Sorry, I... I was expecting a friend," she said.

"No, I'm sorry. I have a mountain of errands to run and I cannot take him with me and get it all done. Alex had to go into the office, and couldn't take him with, of course. I'm in desperate need of someone to just watch him for a few hours, and you were literally the last person on the list. I tried, I promise. But I could really use your help."

Carla didn't wait for an answer. She held Jesse out to his grandmother, who took him reluctantly.

Helen stammered. "I... we..."

Carla said, "Great, thank you!" She kissed Jesse. "Bye, sweetheart." She dropped the baby bag and walked to her car. "Everything you could possibly need is in there. I'll be back around five!"

By the time she got back that night, Jesse was the center of attention at the Holsfer house.

"My God, he has such an appetite, and so much energy! He's a giggling and babbling machine and then—" Helen laughed.

Chuck, Alex's father laughed, too. "He just passed out. He was sitting up and then he just fell over and started snoring. Just like Alex used to."

Carla smiled. "Well, that's babies for you."

"Are you staying for dinner?" Helen asked.

It was the first time she'd ever been invited. It was the first conversation she'd had with Alex's parents without him being in the room. It was the first time she'd seen them smile for longer than ten seconds.

"Sure, that would be great."

Helen made meatloaf covered in bacon strips, green beans, and mashed potatoes. Chuck popped a bottle of pinot noir. They talked for two hours, and had apple pie for dessert.

She left that night with a pledge from them both. "Any time you need help with this little bundle of joy, you let us know."

"Thank you, Helen, Chuck. I'm going to take you up on that."

Kisses all around.

Alex said, "No fucking way did that happen," when she got home that night.

"They were quite lovely, actually." Jesse was on her lap. She turned his face towards hers. "Weren't they lovely?"

"I knew this was going to happen," Alex said.

"Bullshit, you—"

"This is exactly what I expected would happen when the fucking Body Snatchers got to them."

295

"Language."

"What? Lang—no, we've got, like, years before... kids don't start talking until they're like five, right?"

She rolled her eyes. "Something like that."

"Yeah, no, then fuck that. Jesse, look at me." Carla tilted Jesse's head towards Alex. "Fuck. Fuck, fuck, fuck. Shit. Fuck. See?" he asked. Carla laughed. "OK then. Back to my parents. In no universe do Chuck and Helen Holsfer act cordially. Unless they're fucking *aliens*."

"I told you, they aren't going to hate their grandson, are they?" She turned Jesse around. "No they aren't. Who could hate this little sausage, huh?"

"Maybe that's why they love him. So they can eat him."

"Stop. We had a great time, and they're going to help. We can do a nanny three days a week to start. Ease them into it."

"Babe—"

"Alex, there's no other way. They're going to be happy to help. Helen doesn't do shit all day. *All day.* Asking for two days a week from her... trust me, she's going to love it. It'll give her something to live for."

Two days a week turned into three pretty quickly. Helen loved her grandson, pure and simple. Chuck Holsfer worked most days and came home with an energy that he hadn't had in a long, long time. Jesse was the new light of his life, and everyone at the office knew it.

A financial burden partially lifted, Carla and Alex were still able to keep on their trusted nanny Karen, who had her own newborn, to watch Jesse two days a week.

Nevertheless, adjusting to baby life was difficult. That first year, they barely slept. They were exhausted. They were stressed. They fought. They found a middle ground where it was understood the fights were based on shit they were both going through, and their only outlet was each other. There was a severe lack of sympathy in the apartment, and they learned to cope without it.

Carla was breastfeeding Jesse, and would pump for the days she wasn't around. Her body was sore all the time. She found her co-staff were very accepting of her lack of sleep and the random slip-up. They'd become a tight-knit family, and Carla was one of the anchors. Half the staff had children. The other half learned, long ago, not to judge.

Six months after Jesse was born, Alex got a promotion at work. It came with an extra week off, some more personal days, and a twelve percent raise.

They celebrated with a family nap on a Sunday afternoon. It was raining and windy and they were all exhausted.

Carla woke up before them both and started preparing dinner. Mac and cheese. It was all they had in the house that remotely appealed to her. And it was easy.

She multitasked while the water was on the stove, and started sorting laundry. There were three bins in the apartment. One in the bedroom, one in the baby's room, and one in the master bathroom. She was quiet as she went from room to room and put clothes into a laundry basket.

She grabbed whites and stuffed them at the bottom of the basket. She started going through the pockets of all the pants and came across a slip of paper in the back pocket of Alex's jeans.

WASHINGTON, AT HOME, -7.5 SPREAD - $100

She looked at it a long moment before she went to the kitchen table, put it where he would see it, grabbed one of the pots from underneath the kitchen counter and slammed it onto the stove top.

She heard Jesse wake up.

She grabbed the laundry, grabbed the detergent, and went to the basement of the building where the laundry room was.

She fumed the entire way and started running scenarios in her head of the bullshit he would lay on her.

It was just a hundred dollars!

It wasn't my bet, I was laying it for someone else!

It's my money, I can do what I want!

She sighed and leaned against the washing machine, filled two of them up, paid, started the machines, and made her way up to the apartment.

Alex was at the kitchen counter, opening up the box of macaroni.

"Laundry already?" he asked. He took out the cheese packet.

"Don't change the subject."

"What subject?"

"That," she said, and pointed to the piece of paper.

"What about it?"

She moved over to Alex. Jesse was in his living room crib, bubbling and making strange kid noises.

"You'll want to make this easier on yourself," Carla said.

"It was one bet."

"Bullshit."

"It was," he said, smiling.

"This isn't funny, Alex! You promised me—"

"I know, and like I said, it was one bet. A bunch of us went by the bar and that guy Jerry was there—"

"Jesus."

"And it was just for old times' sake, OK?"

"That guy is a fucking asshole!"

"Language..."

"Don't get cute."

He dumped the pasta into the boiling water, turned and looked at her. "Carla, I haven't laid a bet in over a year. I swear it. The money wasn't burning a hole in my pocket, I just... it was just for some fun. OK? And I won. That's it. Won't happen again."

"Please don't do this to us."

"Stop overreacting, for God's sake."

CHAPTER FORTY-TWO

Four months later, Carla was sitting at a coffee shop across from Hal. She was crying. She hadn't spoken to him since that weekend. So much had happened since their night together, and it just didn't seem right to get in touch.

She got his number from the *Slaughterhouse-Five* book, dialed it, prayed it still worked.

Hal came down from New York straight away.

Jesse was at his grandparents.

Alex was just gone.

"I don't believe it. I don't believe it. I'm so stupid. I thought he would change, I swear I thought he would."

Hal sighed and shook his head. "How much is he in for?"

"He wouldn't tell me."

Fuck.

"That's not a good sign," Hal said.

"He's scared, and he's not eating. He's barely sleeping. Neither of us is because of the baby, but now... Hal, it's bad."

"When did it happen?"

"I don't know. But he hasn't been himself for a month. He came home one night and he had bruises on his chest—"

"Leave him."

"What?"

"You've gotta leave him."

She cried and covered her face. "I can't. It's just one thing. He's such a good father and... I'm not going to leave him just for this. Where would I go?"

Hal went to say something, and reeled it back in. The way things were going, the last thing he needed was a woman with a kid. "I don't know. But I don't see how you can trust him, when he... he just doesn't learn."

"You have to talk to him," Carla said.

Hal shook his head. "No."

"You have to. You have to find out how much he owes and who he owes it to." She reached over and she grabbed Hal's hands. "I need your help. Please."

Hal tried to think of a play. There wasn't one. Not without violence or compromising his relationship with Gino. "Where is Alex?"

"I don't know. He told me he was in trouble, he was so upset, and he was hysterical, crying. I've never seen him so scared and angry. He punched a wall... I'm pretty sure he broke his hand. I tried calling him, but—"

"Who's he bet with?"

"He goes to this bar on Sansom and 19th. It's a sports bar. He places bets with this guy Jerry. I don't know if he's the boss or not, but Alex is afraid of him."

Hal ran his hands over hers. They were cold and smooth and shaking. He looked in her eyes and there was that same connection, that same look from Woods Hole. He reached over and touched her face. It lit up his entire body.

"I'll take care of it."

Samson's Bar was dingy, even in the daytime. Half a dozen patrons. Mostly old boozers with nowhere to be. Hal walked in. There was a smell of peanuts, sawdust, old beer, and the faint tinge of puke.

Wood walls covered in sports posters, news clippings, photos, and banners. Wood booths with leather seats. Wood stools here and there. One bartender, who looked like he owned the place. One waitress, waiting for customers.

There were dozens of televisions mounted throughout.

Hal walked over to the bar and sat down.

"What can I get you?" the bartender asked.

"Nice play on words," Hal said, indicating the Samson sign behind the bar. "Being on Sansom. Unless your name is Samson."

"It is."

"Well, shit. You should probably come up with a better story. I'm looking for Jerry."

"Who's asking?"

"A friend of Alex Holsfer."

One of the boozers grabbed his beer, got up from the bar and walked away. Hal watched him. He sat down in a booth at the far end of the room.

"I'm guessing that's not Jerry," Hal said to the bartender.

"Oh yeah? Why's that?"

"Well... 'cause he looks like a miserable, broke, fucking asshole."

Silence in the place. Everyone watched Hal.

The bartender leaned on the bar. "Mister, I don't like people coming into my place and insulting my regulars. Especially when they didn't order nothin'."

"Sure. I get that." Hal looked around the place, made eye contact with everyone. "OK. I'll have your cheapest, shittiest beer, please. In your smallest glass."

The bartender looked around at his regulars. He didn't know what to do.

Hal smiled. "Now, what I meant to say about that guy over there was, he's pretty much the dumbest fucking person I've ever come across. I mean, I say I'm looking for Jerry and this fucking, hah... this fucking guy does the *least* subtle move I think I've ever seen. Like we're in a shitty fucking Western, you know? The bad guy walks in and everyone leaves? But he's still just right there." Hal turned and pointed to him. "In fact, he's in fucking walking distance. He didn't leave the bar… even though I'm the bad guy." Hal turned back to the bartender, who finally looked nervous. "He knows who Jerry is. *And* he knows Alex. Now, I can walk over there and put the screws to him, maybe shove that glass of his down his throat until it breaks… but what I really want to know is, which one of you is Jerry?"

"I'm Jerry," one of the guys said, and stood up. Tall, wiry. Tattoos going up and down his arms. Mid-thirties. Half a growth of beard on him. Bloodshot eyes. "Who the fuck are you?"

"I'm Hal. Let's talk." Hal got off the stool and turned to the bartender, who hadn't moved. "Hey. Where's my fucking beer?"

Hal called Carla after he was done. They met at the same coffee shop.

"I can't stay long, Jesse's home with my friend. Alex is at the hospital. He did break his hand."

"Fucking moron."

They sat there in silence. Hal stared off into space. Carla waited for him to say something. When he didn't she asked, "So?"

"So… they're not going to kill him."

Her face went white. "They were going to kill him?"

"Well, not right away. It's, uhh. It's bad, Carla."

"How bad?"

"Sixty thousand."

Carla's body heaved. She clamped her hand over her mouth. "Oh, God," she said.

"Outside," Hal said, and pointed.

Carla got up and walked out of the coffee shop, threw up on the sidewalk.

Hal looked away, shook his head. Some customers were watching. "Something she ate. Not *here*, just…"

Carla came back in, went to the store counter and grabbed a handful of napkins. She came back wiping her forehead, then her mouth. "I don't believe it."

"Believe it. The guy's practically a legend now."

"But how…?"

"Basketball. Three big bets on three different games."

She covered her eyes with her hands full of dirty napkins. "Jesus Christ. Oh, Alex. What are we going to do?"

"You're going to pay them."

"With *what*? We don't have—"

"Carla, stop. Alex is... well, he's really fucking stupid. But, he also pays up when he loses. It's going to take time, but... they sort of respect him. Sort of. It's why they let him place the bet. Now, he's got to go down there and talk to them and work something out."

"This can't be happening. What... what did you say to them?"

"I told them that he's got a family and that if anything happens to him and his ability to pay up... well, that they'd be making a mistake. They were worried about him skipping town, with or without you. So I told them I'd guarantee payment."

"What does that mean?"

"If Alex leaves town or... does something rash, like killing himself..."

"Jesus," Carla said and started crying again.

"That I'd cover it."

"Cover it? You'd *cover* it? Why don't you just *pay* them, Hal?"

"Well, for one, I'm not a fucking degenerate gambler. It's not mine to pay. Second, because I don't have that kind of money floating around. I can get it, but it'd hurt. Third, because I'm not his fucking father."

"You're his *friend*."

Hal looked wounded. "You think I'm here because of Alex?"

"I—"

Hal got up from his chair. "Listen, you wanted help, this is help. You think guys like Jerry just let someone walk away from owing $60k? Please, practically their whole business model is dependent on stupid people, OK? But *they* aren't stupid. I just stuck my neck out and namedropped, and I should have my fucking head examined, I swear to Christ." He wiped down his face with his hands. "Do you understand the position this puts me in? If this goes south, I'm going to owe, and when I say *owe*, I mean owe bad people. And not just money. You remember what we talked about? Right?" He sighed, took a step away from the table and looked out the window of the coffee shop. He saw people getting on with their lives. They had their own problems, but he had a feeling none of them owed money to low-rent gangsters.

He turned back towards Carla. "Look, I wanted to help, and I think I did, but I can't just pay it. I can't. What happens if he thinks he got off scot-free and does it again? Then, when I *really* can't help... they'd just kill him." He looked at her face. It looked defeated. "I also told them not to tell Alex about our little talk. You can't tell him. He's gotta do this on his own. Bailing him out would be about the worst thing I could do."

She scoffed. "Really? The *worst* thing? For him or you?"

He thought about it for a second and said finally, "For me."

Carla stood up, said "Jesus, fuck you, Hal," and pushed him in the chest with all of her strength.

CHAPTER FORTY-THREE

The fallout in the apartment was biblical. Lines were drawn. They weren't speaking. Alex was sleeping on the couch.

The routine was simple.

Wake up, take care of Jesse. Eat breakfast. Shower, maybe, if there was time. Alex would drop Jesse off at his grandparents, if it were one of their days. If he was spending the day with Karen, Carla would drop him off and pick him up in the evening.

One of them would cook dinner, the other would distract themselves with Jesse. Once dinner was over, Carla would find herself spending all of her time in the bedroom, worrying. She could feel the physical toll of stress on her body. She could only imagine what Alex was going through. She never asked. She felt the silence was punishment enough from her.

She wasn't sure how long it would last. She was thankful Jesse was young enough that he wouldn't remember any of it. She hoped.

The night Alex went to speak with Jerry, he came back hunched over and bleeding from his mouth. She got him on the couch, checked him just in case there were (more) broken bones. She cleaned his cuts and bandaged them.

When she was done she said, "I don't want to know specifics. I just want to know when it's done. Don't expect me to talk to you, or even listen to you. It makes me sick just to look at you, and I can't begin to tell you how sad that makes me. Did you tell your parents?"

He nodded.

"That couldn't have been easy. I'm sorry they had to go through that. I'll drop him off at their house when—"

"I'll do it. I'll do it. I need to."

"Fine."

Carla didn't tell anyone at work. She didn't say a word of it to Abigail. She learned to hide it. Work was where she could be herself. She found it ironic that her job was now less stressful than home.

A month into it, they were both sitting at the dinner table. Alex looked like a broken shell. The cast on his arm was filthy. She noticed his posture was just awful. His skin was slack. He had bags and dark circles under his eyes he didn't have before.

She'd made lasagna. She'd always loved making it before.

These days, anything she could make that was easy and could be cooked in less than half an hour, she was happy with. But something compelled her to make actual food that night. She stopped by the grocery store, bought all the fixings, came home and started. Alex came home with Jesse, walked over and let her kiss him hello.

They sat there in silence as she layered the food. Jesse was fidgeting in his crib. Alex was just sitting there, not moving, hardly breathing. He was staring into the living room with the TV off.

Before the food came out of the oven, Alex gave Jesse his bottle. When he was finished, he put him down in the crib and watched him fall asleep.

Carla dished out the food and sat down, barely looking at Alex, who sat in the chair and just stared at his food.

Carla dug in. It was delicious. She grabbed some parmesan cheese and dusted her food with it. She slid it over to Alex who looked at it for a long time before doing the same.

She felt compelled to talk to him. She was so angry, so scared. She didn't know how he was paying the men off, or how long it would take. She didn't know if he was going to come home once a week, having had the shit beat out of him.

Alex went to put some food on his fork and he stopped. His hand was shaking. The fork was bobbing up and down. She looked over. His arm was trembling.

No, not just his arm. His chest. His legs. His head.

She looked up at his face. It was a crumpled mask of skin, and it looked like he was hyperventilating. His whole body was wracked with it. Tears and snot were coming down his face. He dropped the fork, covered his eyes with his hands, and fell onto the floor.

"Oh, God, Alex," she said and got up and ran over to him. She got down on the ground and cradled him into her arms.

She could feel her whole body shaking with every breath he took.

"I'm so sorry," he said. Over and over.

It was the only thing he could think to say.

They slept together that night, holding each other. Three hours of crying and apologizing and fear had made Alex exhausted.

Carla didn't realize how much she had missed him until they were lying next to each other. She hated herself for ignoring him as long as she did.

They woke up the next day and had a talk before breakfast.

"Tell me how it works."

"Yeah. Uh... Well, I went and talked to them and they seemed... well, they were both angry, but nervous...? If that makes sense. It was weird. I have to come up with fifteen hundred a month—"

"Oh, God..."

"—and I pay it off for as long as it takes. They tuned me up, you know... but as long as I'm there, first of the month... it won't happen again."

"How are we going to be able to afford that?"

"My parents are going to take Jesse during the week. We won't need Karen."

"OK, but that's nothing—"

"They offered us to move in with them."

"What?"

"Yeah. Dad was going to give me his some of his savings, but I told him no. I think he was quite relieved about that, to be honest. So he said to stay with them until I get this sorted out."

"You want us to move in with your parents?"

"No. Fuck no, of course not. But it's how I can afford to... it's the only way I can afford to do this."

Carla got up and went to the fridge. She grabbed a carton of eggs and some milk and butter. She started up the range and put a skillet on the flame. Cut some butter, spread it around and started breaking eggs onto the pan.

"Well, they would be a big help," Carla said. She was trying to look at the bright side.

You sucker, she thought.

She closed her eyes and slowly shook her head. "How long?"

"How long what?"

"How long is this going to take?"

Alex sighed. "Three or four years."

"Jesus." She grabbed a spatula and turned the eggs. "Three or four... how did you...?" She felt tears coming. "How could you do this? Again?"

Alex braced himself on the counter and put his head down. "I thought I had a lock. I thought I... it was Jesse's college money and vacations for us and... I really fucked up. And I know I've said it before, but it'll never happen again. I swear."

Carla put some bread in the toaster. She scooped the eggs off the skillet and put them on two plates. She grabbed some ketchup, grabbed the butter, grabbed two mugs for coffee.

"Let me," he said, and fixed them both a cup. The toaster dinged. He grabbed the toast barehanded and let it burn his fingers. For some reason he felt it was the least he could do, punishing himself. He brought it over to the kitchen table, spread butter on both slices and gave one to her.

They ate in silence for a while.

"Are we in danger?" she asked.

"No. No, I swear you're not."

"If you don't pay, are we in danger?"

"That's not going to happen, Carla. Honestly, you and Jesse are the reasons I'll be working extra hours, and because of all the tax work I'm getting, it's going to help. All so I can pay them off as fast as I can, I swear. They know it. Nothing's going to happen to either of you. I won't let them hurt you."

"Alex... if they come snooping around? If they come around as a reminder that they're, you know, that they know where we are, and whatever stupid shit people like that do to intimidate people? You'll never see us again."

Alex looked over his half-eaten breakfast at her. Dead serious. "If they ever do that to you...? If they make me lose my family... I'll kill them."

CHAPTER FORTY-FOUR

The following Saturday, Carla went to scope out their new home. "We figured you'd want your privacy," Helen said as she walked Carla down the stairs. It was dark. That was the first thing Carla noticed. Barely any sunlight. She sighed.

Chuck and Helen had reworked the basement from storage space into a pseudo apartment. There was a bedroom, a bathroom (no shower), and a side room for Jesse and his crib. The kitchen was straight up the stairs. There was a mini fridge for Jesse's food, so they wouldn't have to go up and down all day and night.

"Thank you, I'm sure we'll all appreciate that when he starts crying at three in the morning."

"Oh, that won't bother me. Chuck snores so loud, I wear ear plugs."

"Fantastic," Carla said and walked to the bedroom. It was small and musty smelling.

"We'll get the smell out of here. I bought a dehumidifier. Just have to set it up."

"Very thoughtful of you," Carla said, and turned. "Listen, I'm sorry about—"

"No, don't you dare." Helen came over and grabbed Carla's hands. "*We're* sorry. For you. And so grateful that you're... well, standing by Alex, while he fixes this mess."

"Well, that's what wives do, I guess."

Helen shook her head. "They shouldn't have to."

The move to the Holsfers went reasonably smoothly. Carla took care of it herself, taking some slight pity on Alex, who still had two more weeks with the cast.

It was February.

She had a hard time looking at her apartment when it was empty. Too many good memories.

In the two weeks since she last saw it, Chuck had put down a fresh coat of paint. The entire basement smelled of it, even with the hopper windows open.

"We've got to close these," she said as the movers put boxes wherever they would fit.

"Sure, sure, I'll do it," Chuck said, and started closing them.

She thanked him and looked around.

Jesse was up on the ground floor with Helen.

Alex was at the office, eyeballs deep in year-end accounting and freelance clients.

Carla looked around at her new life. Boxes and new paint. A basement without any real light. Stress, and a détente with her own husband.

She sighed and wondered what was going to come next.

It took her a week to unpack fully. There simply wasn't enough room for all of their belongings. Their kitchen boxes were still unopened.

The priority had been Jesse's toys and clothes.

They bought some Ikea standing shelves for the living room. Put up some picture frames, laid out some books. She tried to make everything as neat as possible. They had one dresser and one closet for the two of them.

Things that should have been in closets or drawers were out in the open, like towels and bed linen. The dehumidifier only did so much for the dampness. She was thankful Jesse spent most of his time upstairs.

By the time April rolled around, Alex was a zombie. He was doing returns for dozens of people, individuals and businesses. He did the taxes for Samson's Bar and Grill, along with the entire staff, on the house. He found that the staff were not reporting a significant amount of their income.

He showed the paperwork to Carla. "It's a cash business, OK? So, the waitresses make like two dollars an hour because they're working off tips. So they pay taxes on their salary... but all of them think that they don't have to pay taxes on their tips. It's ridiculous. I don't know how they've gotten as far as they have without getting audited, but it's going to happen one of these days. I asked what they made for the year, and none of them knew. I explained what they should be doing, you know, as a group? They told me to go fuck myself. This is what I get for helping."

"They're taking advantage of you," Carla said.

"Yeah, well, I'm not in a position to argue. And the business... Jesus, what a mess. All cash. Thousands upon thousands of dollars each week... money from guys like me, on payment plans... they've got dozens of them. What they do, and it's pretty ingenious is, they're putting some of their book winnings into the bar as purchases, you know, like from customers, and they're paying themselves hefty salaries. They're washing part of their own money, and looking like respectable citizens while they do it."

"They're laundering money?"

"Yeah. They could be doing a hell of a lot more—"

"Don't even think about it."

Alex put his hands up. "I'm not. I swear. I'm not getting in with these guys more than I already am. I'm just doing their taxes. I promise."

"Good. The less you're involved in that kind of life, the better."

CHAPTER FORTY-FIVE

B eing alone in Gino's office was a strange feeling. The place was dark, with wood furniture and the smell of cigars and amber alcohol. A large humidor was against the right wall. The far wall had two floor-to-ceiling windows that Hal had heard were made of bullet-resistant glass.

The desk was old mahogany. Intricate designs along the front, sides, legs. A leather blotter covered most of the top. It was worn on the edges where Gino rested his forearms. There were a number of pictures in frames on the edges of the desk, including one of his daughter's family. Two kids. Still married to the dentist.

Hal smiled to himself.

The right wall also had three large framed pieces of art. Hal hadn't recognized the artists of the first two. The third was a piece by Picasso. *Femme Assise Dans Un Fauteuil.* "Woman Sitting in a Chair," Gino had told him one day after a meeting. "I don't see no fucking chair, but my guy says it's worth a fortune, so. Anyway, I like looking at her."

Hal sat there alone in the glow of a job well done. He had a glass of bourbon in front of him. He had his tie loosened. He was feeling calm and appreciated. Six months of trying to get Gino to take him seriously.

Six months.

"Listen. I met this guy…"

"Another guy? John's going to be jealous."

Chuckles in the room. It was Gino, Paulie, and Gino's lawyer Sal Lissman, who just happened to be there when Hal came to the house to tell Gino his big plan.

"Ha ha. Listen, I went on this trip to Cape Cod a few years ago."

"Love it up there," Paulie said. "Great fish. And boats. And sails. For boating."

Gino rolled his eyes. "Jesus. Go on, before he hurts himself."

"So this guy, his family owns a bunch of newspapers and shit—"

"So do I," Gino said.

Hal nodded, sighed internally. It was always a pissing contest with these people. "Well, his family also owns a bunch of banks. And so this guy who works at the banks, like the CEO or whatever, he starts talking about how banking is the best place to make money in this country."

The three of them just stared at him.

"Are you fucking kidding me?" Gino asked.

Sal got his suit jacket. "Glad I stayed for this..."

"This fucking guy," Paulie said and smiled. "We can't use a fucking bank account to launder money, you testa di cazzo." The room broke up in laughter.

"Just wait, Sal. Just... not a bank account. Jesus, I'm not stupid. An actual bank."

They weren't getting it.

"You *buy* a bank."

Paulie laughed out loud. Gino chuckled and leaned back, shook his head.

Sal put his jacket down.

"Listen," Hal said. "You buy a failing bank. Someplace in the tri-state area, you know, so we can drive the money up there. You find one that's in the middle of nowhere, in a small town and you *use* the whole town..."

Paulie shook his head. "He's still talking about it."

"You get real people to open up fake bank accounts. Start small. I don't know the particulars. But you make it a legitimate bank. You launder the shit out of whatever money you can. You use, what, buffers to buy it? Shell companies, I don't know. But all of a sudden... you have your own bank. Your own safety deposit boxes, maybe? They can transfer money all over the world, Gino. And you get the right guy in there... someone you own? They'll make it all look legit."

"You're serious?" Paulie asked. He looked at Gino. "Please tell me you're not taking this seriously."

"They've been doing that in Mexico for years," Sal said.

"This isn't Mexico!" Paulie said.

Sal sat down. "We'd just have to be a bit smarter about it." He looked at Gino, who looked back. "It's not the worst idea I've ever heard. I can ask around."

Gino leaned forward. "Quietly." He looked over at Hal. "Keep talking."

A month after that.

Sal and Hal sat across from Gino who said "You two should take your act on the road. You've got the names for it."

Hal chuckled. Sal just sat there.

"When Sal's not laughing, it's usually good news, which makes no kind of sense, I know. So what's up? I have my grandkids coming today, and I'm cooking lunch, so..."

"Well, I asked around. Quiet, like you said. I spoke with my contact at the New York FDIC office, and I have to tell you... it's not such a far-fetched idea as I first thought. In fact, it's a pretty damned good one."

"I knew it," Hal said to himself.

"Easy there, chooch. Buying a bank. That's what we're talking about?"

"Yeah," Sal said.

"To hide money."

"Yeah."

"And launder it," Hal said. They both looked at him. He decided to keep his mouth shut.

"Sal. First off, how in the fuck could this possibly work?"

"Well—"

"And second, why did it take a fucking mook to suggest it?"

Sal chuckled. "A better question would be why didn't this Jew think of it?"

"That *is* a better question. I can't believe this conversation has gone as far as it has. OK. What's next?"

"Find a location. Failing, but not failed. You want someone to sell it to you, not buy it outright. Brings less scrutiny."

"What's it going to cost?"

"A lot. You're not only buying the bank, but also its loans, foreclosures, potential for new customers. They look at the future dollar value, and depending on the seller... the real problem is the three-year wait."

"The what now?" Hal asked.

"Oh, you didn't know about the three-year wait?" Gino asked, leaned back and rolled his eyes. "Jesus."

"It's to give the FDIC time to suss out who really owns the bank. Hedge funds and investment firms come in with complicated contracts, and it's just to make sure they know what's what."

"Well, that's it then," Gino said and went to get up.

"Gino, wait," Sal said. "Three years is nothing. And it's 'up to' three years. This'll never get that far."

"Why?"

Sal made a face like, *please.*

"You think so?" Gino asked.

"I know so. You decide to do this, this is... it's the long game of all long games. A bank that passes the sniff test after three years? You'll have clean cash the rest of your life."

Gino looked like he was considering it, reluctantly. "So, what's next?"

"Let me find some locations. See what they look like, what their assets are. Can't hurt, and if I don't find anything, so be it. But if I do..."

Gino sat back down. "OK, do that. But, let's say you find a great location, and at a price I can afford... who do we get to run it?"

Hal raised his hand.

"You're fucking kidding," Sal said.

"What? No, not me. No. But I've got a guy... and I'm pretty sure he could use your help."

Two months later.

Hal was outside a bank in a small town in Upstate New York. Dingy looking. Quiet street on a spring afternoon. Pedestrians going back and forth, driving, walking. Clear sky, and it was in the low 60s.

He'd seen two other banks. One in Pennsylvania, one in Northern Jersey. The one in PA looked too good. It was in a real smart part of town, up and coming. It was going for a reasonable price because the owner was in his seventies and was moving to California to be near his children and grandchildren. He'd had a heart attack and didn't want the stress. Word on the street was a major chain was interested in the purchase. Sal said, "We're not getting into a bidding war with a brand bank, but go see it anyway. You might get inspired."

Sal was right. He was inspired. It was the exact opposite of what they were looking for. They wanted a town that was in trouble.

The bank in Northern Jersey wasn't bad. The price, the location, the surrounding area. The problem was it had been robbed three times in five years. Sal asked around and the family that ran the area simply didn't give a shit about the bank. He was concerned there would be pushback, but he had Hal go see it anyway.

"It's what we're looking for," Hal said. "Falling apart, shit town. Something a chain wouldn't give a rat's ass about. But we need a bank in a place that's been forgotten."

"Well, sonny boy... have I got the place for you," Sal said.

Sherborn, New York almost looked like it was out of *The Grapes of Wrath*... but not really. Dusty roads, farmland, businesses out in

317

the middle of nowhere. A place where land was still reasonably cheap. A small oasis in the center of town. Four streets with businesses. A tailor. A laundry. A diner. Grocery store. Gas station. A newspaper, if you could believe it...

And a bank.

Hal walked in and smelled ages of wear. The floor, the walls, the people. Tellers were talking to what few customers were there like they were neighbors. Stairs leading down into the basement looked lonely. It was the only way Hal could describe them to Gino later. "It was like no one had used them for a ridiculously long time."

"The fucking poet over here."

There was a closet for a vault, and an old man standing by it. He had a nametag that Hal couldn't see, but they nodded to each other.

"Can I help you sir?" a man asked from his right.

Hal turned to look at him. He was in his mid- to late fifties. Glasses. Pale blue tie on a white shirt, brown pants. "Hi," Hal said. "Just needed to change some bills."

"Sure, one of our tellers will be happy to assist. I'm Gary Hart, the manager. New in town?"

"Just passing through. To Syracuse."

"Well, welcome, and have a great trip. Nice day for it!"

Hal nodded, smiled. "Thank you, and yes, it is." He got two hundreds changed to twenties, continued to case the place. As he was walking out, he walked over to Gary, who was sitting at his desk. "Say, Gary. Where's a good place to eat around here?"

"You like diner food?"

"I love diner food."

"Well, I have just the place," Gary said standing up. "In fact, it's the only place in town."

Two months later.

Gino sat there a long time, staring at nothing.

Hal could smell the remnants of dinner. Marinara sauce. Garlic. Fish. Maybe flounder. Breaded, with lemon.

318

His mouth was watering.

"On a scale of one to ten," Gino said.

Sal had his legs crossed, was smoking a cigarette. "It'll work," he said, and smiled. "I don't know what an eight is on that scale. Pretty good, but not perfect... Who can say? But I know we can buy it. I've already started creating the chain for the money—"

"No one told you to do that."

"Preliminary stuff, Gino. You don't want the bank, I'll use it for something else. These are corporations we've used in the past. They're clean. It was money that was going to have to be moved regardless. It's still your decision."

"Well, I'm glad to hear it's still my decision," Gino said and rolled his eyes. He leaned back in his chair. It made leather and mechanical noises. "You're awfully quiet."

Hal arched an eyebrow. "Well, I—"

"For getting me into this mess, you sure seem... what's the word? Apprehensive."

"I'm not, Gino. I think it's a fucking great idea."

"Uh huh. I'll be sure to remind you of that when we're in prison. Or when I come visit you in prison."

"Neither of those seems likely," Hal said.

"I'll say something... you're smarter than I give you credit for." Gino sighed. "Let's say I pull the trigger. You said you had someone to run it."

Hal nodded.

"So, you going to keep him a fucking secret, or what?"

"His name is Alex Holsfer."

Gino looked at Hal, looked at Sal. "Please don't make me try and say that name."

"He checks out, Gino," Sal said. "Full background. No debts... at least no legal ones..."

"Here we go."

"No trouble with the police. No IRS trouble. On paper, he's squeaky clean."

"Uh huh."

Hal swallowed. "He's got a gambling problem."

Gino didn't move for a second. "Gambling problem. Gambling." He leaned forward. "You want to put a multi-million dollar operation in the hands of one of those fucking... am I hearing you correctly?"

"Gino—"

"We go through all of this bullshit, and the guy you want to run this is a fucking loser?"

Hal lowered his head. Sal shook his.

"This was a complete waste of time," Gino said, and stood up.

Hal started chuckling.

"The fuck is so funny?"

"Joey Lambini runs the book over there."

"What, in Philly? So?"

Hal said, "He's got a scam going..." Sal started laughing. Hal held out his hand to try and get him to stop. "You won't believe it."

Hal told him the story. Gino stood the whole time, and only laughed at the end.

Hal listened to Gino say goodnight to Sal. He sat there alone, in the glow of a job well done. He drank some of his bourbon.

Gino came back and sat down, grabbed his own glass. "Salud."

"Salud."

They drank.

"Tell me something. Where's John?"

"He's back at the garage."

"And he's not here."

Hal shook his head.

"He know about this?" Gino asked.

"No. I... this was just mine. Until, you know... I wanted to see it through is all. Besides, he's got other shit to worry about."

Gino nodded. "Well, keep John out of this. It's money, and I don't share money details with many people. In fact, only a select few, so... mum's the word."

Hal nodded. "OK. You still trust him though, right? John, I mean."

"Of course I trust him. But trust's got nothing to do with this. This is a the-less-people-know-the-better situation. And he doesn't."

"No problem."

"Yeah, we'll see. You two are like the sons I never wanted. But if you can keep a secret from him, then I know you can keep a secret." He drank some more. "So. What do you want?"

"What do you mean?"

"Please..."

"Oh, hey, Gino—"

"Don't 'hey' me. You did good. I want to know what you want."

Hal had expected the question. After six months, he still didn't have a good answer. "I don't know, Gino."

"Five percent, straight off the top. You babysit the guy, you make sure he doesn't become a problem. That's it."

"That's very generous, Gino. Thank you."

"I know it's fucking generous."

"What about Alex?"

"What about him?"

"For the work he's doing."

"Well, he doesn't pay off a debt for the rest of his life, at a usurious interest rate to a bunch of fucking pond scum assholes I wouldn't spit on if they were on fire. Not even piss. Just spit. They should be shot for what they're doing... but, well, it's a living."

"It is a living. Yeah. See, I just think that the guy will be more motivated not to fuck up if—"

Gino held his hand up. "Three percent. You're right. If he thinks he's being unappreciated and fucks up, it'll be a serious waste of time and money. Three percent. That's it. If he's not happy with it, well... you have to give it to these assholes who think it's a good idea to do really dumb fucking things *and* have a family. No one thinks anymore. Threaten to skin his wife and kid and keep them alive for, I don't know, however long. That usually works to get people in line."

Hal nodded. "You got it, Gino."

CHAPTER FORTY-SIX

Even with the extra money that Alex made with the tax returns from his regular clients, he was only able to pay off a little more than a fifth of what he owed. Less than what he thought he could pull off. The interest was killing him.

Carla had gotten used to the basement. Jesse's first birthday had come and gone. They had a big party. Jesse passed out in the middle of it all. She could see his personality evolving by the day. His first word had been "Momma."

Chuck and Helen were troopers. They loved the extra company and kept to themselves on the second floor when they wanted privacy.

Carla and Alex were on better ground. He was a doting father and husband, and every waking moment was spent trying to make things right. They barely argued anymore. As much as Carla appreciated it, she knew it came from a place of guilt.

In early May 2004, Carla was cleaning up the basement when she heard the familiar ring of an email into her AOL account. She walked over to the computer, woke it up, and saw an email from Hal. No subject line.

Her heart went a little haywire. She hadn't heard nor spoken to him since the last time she saw him. And yelled at him. And pushed him.

She clicked on the email.

It read: *You wanted me to help more, I helped more.*

She didn't understand. She wanted to write back. She wanted to call. She didn't know what to say or write or do.

Later that evening, Alex came home and was unusually quiet. Carla was in the living room with Helen and Jesse. Dinner was in the oven. Chuck was outside on the patio reading.

Alex sat down on the couch and watched them fuss with the boy, talking in child voices and tickling him.

"How was your day?" Carla asked.

"Fine," he said. "I need to talk to you."

"Sure, just—"

Alex got up and left, going through the kitchen and into the basement without another word.

Carla's stomach dropped. "Would you—" she started to say to Helen.

"Go," she said.

Carla got up and walked down into their living room. Alex was there, pacing back and forth.

"What?" she said.

He was rubbing his face. "This… fuck…"

"What?" she said. "Please tell me, I can't take any more bad news—"

"It's not bad news."

"Well then what is it?" she asked, and sat down on the couch.

"We're moving."

"What?"

"We're moving. To Upstate, New York."

"What? Where? How? What do you mean we're moving? Alex, what is going on?"

"It's a long story. But, suffice it to say, I don't owe them any more money."

"WHAT?"

"Yeah. I'm not out of the woods… in fact, it's just different woods and… shit. Just, OK, sit down."

"I *am* sitting down."

323

"Yeah, OK. Umm… do you remember Hal?"

"Hal?"

"From Woods Hole. He came up on the train with us—"

"Yeah, I remember."

"Well, he came to visit me today at work."

"OK…"

"Well, he, uhh… Jesus, I don't know how to explain this."

Hal made the trip to Philly as if it were a social call. He hadn't spoken to Alex in a while. An email here and there, a quick hello. Congrats on the kid, that kind of thing.

He called while he was on his way down, asked Alex if he was free for lunch, and said that he'd only be in Philly for a few hours. Alex said he wasn't sure he could do it.

"Make time, amigo," Hal said.

After a nice lunch that Hal paid for, some chit-chat, some laughs, the two of them went to a bar. They found a quiet corner and Hal said, "This isn't a social call."

"OK."

"I'm here to facilitate the acquisitions of certain debts."

"OK. Hah. Yeah, I'm an accountant and I'm not even sure what that means."

"Yeah. Listen, I know about what you owe, to Jerry and his guys."

Alex didn't speak, didn't look at Hal.

"And that payment plan? Yeah, you must not be too smart since you'll be paying that off longer than your student loans."

"I know."

"You know?"

"I had no choice."

"No, huh?"

"They beat the shit out of me."

"Yeah, well, they tend to do that."

"Oh, they do, huh? Well, what the fuck would you've done?"

"Well, not gamble in the first place—"

"Oh, fuck you."

"—and not get into hock with gangsters…?"

"I had a lock—"

"Oh, for chrissake—"

"Three locks! They were fucking golden, from the goddamn Gods, I swear."

"You sound like every other fucking loser—"

"This was different!"

"Sure."

"Hal, I swear, the guy who gave it to me—"

"Max Gemini."

Alex did a slow turn to Hal, his mouth slack.

Hal chuckled. "That's some name, huh? Max Fucking Gemini? I swear, when I heard it, I thought they were talking about some Edgar Casey motherfucker. Or the guy with the cult—"

"How—"

"In Jonestown."

"How could you possibly know about—"

"They set you up, you dumb shit."

"What?"

"Yeah. Gemini works for Jerry. They've been pulling that scam for years."

"Fuck you—"

"They even heard about it, all the way up in Queens. Yeah. Gemini makes it look like he's making bank off the guys. They were making it look like he was picking the winners, but only *after* the games happened."

"You can't be serious."

"Yeah, I am. And so Max looks like he's the God of gamblers, and gives you the locks. And you fell for it. You and a bunch of other morons."

Alex put his head in his hands. "Oh my God."

"Yeah."

"But... Max couldn't have known all those games were going to be losers..."

"Alex, these guys know who the losers are... not to sound harsh."

Alex had a look on his face like he couldn't believe it. "Not only am I a fucking moron for laying the bets, but they cheated me?"

"Yeah, that's about right."

Alex looked up. He had tears in his eyes. "Everything I've put Carla through. My parents... Jesse... I've been paying these guys for almost a year..."

"Well, come on, now. They didn't *make* you bet... but yeah, they fucked you over, pal. I'm sorry."

Alex wiped his face. "So, what now?"

Hal leaned back. "Well... now you kiss my fucking hairy ass for getting you out of this mess. I talked to my boss. I have this new idea... and, well, you'll be in charge of making it work."

"Your boss?"

"Yeah."

"Who's your boss?"

Hal smiled, cat and canary like. "Gino D'Escopio."

"You've got to be fucking kidding."

"Would I kid you?"

"You work for the mob?"

"Hey, better working for them than being into them for sixty grand, pal."

"That's a good point. But only just." Alex stared out the window for a full minute before turning back to Hal. "What's this new idea?"

"Money laundering."

"Of course it is..." Alex took a drink from his beer. "And that's not a new idea."

"It is the way I'm thinking."

Carla listened for half an hour. Alex was nervous and relieved at the same time.

"Those men cheated you?"

"Yeah."

"And they get to keep all of that money?"

"Yeah."

"And now… so you don't owe these mobsters money, but now you'll be working for them?"

"Different ones, but yeah."

"And this is a good thing?"

He chuckled. "I don't know. I don't think I have much of a choice at this point. They don't want my money. They want my help."

"To do something even more illegal than gambling."

"Yeah. They, uhh… they're buying a bank in a place called Sherborn. They're using a, well, a shell corporation, so they keep their boss out of it. Seems Hal talked to some people up in Woods Hole and got some ideas. And, hey, listen. I had no idea he was in to that kind of thing when he went up there. Believe me."

Carla dry swallowed. "I believe you."

"And I guess… it got him thinking on how he can help his boss with their… well, their money problems. Brad was talking banks because, well, his family owns some… and he told Hal some stories about how rampant the industry is with laundering and… and they want me to run it."

Carla stood up and paced. "Is it just me or do things keep getting worse for us?"

"It's not you."

Silence in the room.

"Alex, you don't know the first thing about running a bank."

"I know that. *They* know that. Hal didn't seem too concerned. He said they'd give me time to get it up and running and then… listen, the salary is double what I'm making now, and we'll be able to afford a house. A real home for the three of us."

"What about your parents?"

"They get their lives back! It's perfect, and it's only a four-hour drive. Not to mention, they can't take care of us forever."

"It wasn't for forever, Alex. It was a few years."

"Hal said that, at the rate I was paying, it would be like six or seven."

"Jesus."

"*More*. Six or seven *more* years. Yeah. Listen. This isn't... sit down, please." She did. "This isn't ideal. It's not even in the vicinity of ideal. But we can make this work. And we can get out of this fucking basement, and start over in a new place, just the three of us. It'll be better. It will."

"What about my job?"

He sighed. "Yeah... I'm sorry. I know you love it. I don't know..."

"What if you get caught?"

"I'm not going to get caught. These people... they don't take chances. They're not stupid."

"And you trust Hal?"

"Well, I trust him about as much as a guy who just got me out of hock with a bunch of fuckers who cheated me. So... yeah. I trust him."

"When is this supposed to happen?"

Alex looked at her somberly. "I have to go up there in two weeks to sign paperwork, meet the staff. Hal's giving me what he called a signing bonus, like a legit bonus, so we can put money down on a house. You have to come up there to help me find one because I'll pick something terrible, I know it."

Carla chuckled in spite of herself. "I don't know about this, Alex."

"I know. Listen," he said, and got close. "I was thinking. If you want to stay here... that'll be fine. I'll do like four days up there, three days down here. You can visit every once in a while and, who knows? Maybe you'll like it."

"What are you going to tell your parents?"

"I'm going to tell them that I got offered a great paying job in Upstate New York, and that I can't turn it down. That a friend bought a bank, and they want me to come manage it. They'll hate the idea at first, because of Jesse... but they'll be happy all this shit is over." He hugged her. "I know it's hard to look at it this way, but I think this is good news." He broke off the hug and kissed her, got up and went upstairs to tell his parents.

She sat there in the basement for a long time. She'd finally gotten comfortable in her own skin, in her in-laws' basement, and with her marriage.

She loved her job, and Jesse simply adored his grandparents. Now, after all the stress, the compromises… she had to give it all up?

It slowly occurred to Carla that she had helped put this in motion. She wasn't entirely convinced that things would be better, just different. Now, instead of owing money, Alex would owe something else. His allegiance. Except this time, she knew one of the players. She could rely on Hal to not put them in harm's way. She hoped.

She walked over to her computer, woke it up, opened the email, hit reply and typed, "Thank you."

She hit send, heard the familiar send-off noise and shut the computer down.

She looked around the basement, took a deep breath, held it for a moment, and let it out.

"OK."

PART IV

Upstate, NY

CHAPTER FORTY-SEVEN

First chance she got, Carla spoke with Abigail.

"Oh, you're not quitting," Abigail said as they sat at lunch. "You'll die before you quit. I know it, because I'll kill you."

It was not an easy conversation.

"Hal got a job running a bank."

"Who's Hal?"

She froze for a millisecond. "I mean Alex. Sorry, things have... sorry."

Abigail looked at Carla with an arched eyebrow. "Is Hal a daddy perhaps?"

Carla's eyes went wide. She looked around. They were alone. "Jesus, keep it down, would you? And, no, Hal is not...he's... Alex is the father."

"Wouldn't be too sure with that nose—"

"Abby, goddammit—"

"I'm just saying." She ate her peanut butter and jelly sandwich.

"I don't want to do this to you. I don't want to do this for me. But... it's a good opportunity for Alex. Sort of."

"Running a bank."

"Yeah."

"Which he's never done."

"Hey, I was never a nurse."

"Yeah, that's true. You took four years of college and a couple of years of shit from the staff here... but yeah, I can see how those two situations can be comparable."

"OK, OK. I get it. I know. Seems stupid. Let's just say... there's no shortage of stupid in this situation."

"Well, you still can't leave."

"Abigail—"

"Not until we find a replacement. Two weeks. I need it. I can't have a hole this big in the schedule."

Carla nodded. "Of course. I wouldn't have done otherwise."

"And we have a big party."

Carla smiled. "OK."

"With strippers."

"I don't... that's not really my thing."

"They're not for *you*, bitch."

Carla left Jesse with his grandparents the next day, borrowed Helen's car and drove to Sherborn. She took 476 North, up past Allentown, until she hit Wilkes-Barre, where she stopped at a Cracker Barrel for lunch. She got a chicken pot pie, buttermilk biscuit, and an iced tea. She bought a package of chocolate covered pretzels to go.

Back on 476, she drove through Scranton, got mixed up in Clark Summit where she was supposed to get on 81 North, and had to backtrack a full exit. She took out her MapQuest printouts and tried to figure out where she went wrong.

On 81, she drove for forty-five minutes listening to an Alice in Chains CD until she passed through Pennsylvania and hit New York. She sang "Rooster" at the top of her lungs.

She passed through Binghamton, which was one of the larger cities she drove through, kept on 81 until the exit for Sherborn.

She took the exit, looked at the directions, made a left on Washington Boulevard, a four-lane street that seemed to be a major thoroughfare for the area, and kept driving until she saw the Holiday Inn that Alex was staying at.

She pulled into the parking lot, got out, grabbed her overnight bag, went into the lobby and went to the reception desk. A woman at the desk said, "Welcome to the Holiday Inn in Sherborn. I'm Sandy. May I help you?"

"Yes. My husband is already here, he left a key for me."

"I can certainly help you with that. Name?"

"Holsfer."

"Uh, spell it please?"

She sighed. "H-O-L-S-F-E-R."

"Can I please see your I.D.?"

"Sure." She took her license out from her purse, handed it to Sandy.

"Great. One moment while I code your key."

Sandy walked away. Carla looked around.

Yep. It was a Holiday Inn.

Sandy came back, handed Carla her license and a card key. "Here you go. Room 302. Just go around the corner, elevators are on your left, and your room is on the third floor."

"What's this?" Carla asked. It looked like a credit card.

"It's a card key. Instead of actual keys, we use... you just dip it into the reader and it will open the door for you."

"OK. Thanks."

"You're welcome. Have a great day!"

"You too."

Carla walked around the corner, embarrassed. She hadn't been in a hotel room since forever.

She hit the elevator up button and the doors to her right opened. She got in, hit three. The doors closed and the elevator started up.

She got out, walked over to 302 and saw a black box just above the door handle. "What the shit," she said, and inserted the card into the top of the black box. She heard the door unlock, "You've got to be fucking kidding me," and opened the door.

The room was a mess.

The king-sized bed's sheets were off all three sides, somehow. Alex's bag was open, and clothes were thrown everywhere, haphazard.

"This is what happens when I'm not around. Sweet Jesus."

She put her bag on the bed and started straightening up, then stopped. "No. Nope. No. Uh-uh." She grabbed her cell phone and called him.

"Hey baby! You just get in?" He sounded absurdly happy.

"Yeah, to a goddamn tornado."

"Oh, shit. I forgot to clean up. I'm sorry. Did you have lunch?"

"Yeah, but I could eat."

"Great. Come meet me at the bank. I printed out directions from the hotel, but it's real easy. Just take Washington and hook a left onto Main Street. It's about two miles away."

"OK. You mentioned food."

"Ha. Yeah. I'll show you the place and then we'll grab a burger. Then we'll talk to the real estate agent."

"OK. See you soon. Love you."

"I love you!"

She ended the call and sat down on the bed.

Things were moving fast.

Carla parked on Main Street. It was practically deserted. There were a number of shuttered businesses around the bank. The buildings didn't look in great shape.

The bank was sandwiched between a tailor and a barbershop. The outside looked like it was straight out of a bad 70s TV show. She stared at it and had one clear thought.

It looks like an easy place to rob.

She got out of the car and walked over. The bank was called Sherborn Trust. The sign above the entrance was in large letters. The interior of each letter was filled with light bulbs, like you'd find at an old diner. Or a casino.

She went in and stopped, her mouth open.

As large as the place was... somehow, all of the furniture, the colors, the walls, the ceiling... she felt claustrophobic for the first time in her life.

The floor of the bank was a speckled Formica. To her left was a small cubicle with an even smaller folding table and a water fountain embedded into the wall. Past that, a set of stairs headed down to the basement, same Formica. There were dozens of spots where the floors had worn down to the wood beneath, all smoothed out over time.

To the right, two other cubicles, both with particle board desks and roller chairs that had seen better days.

On the long wall to the right, four teller stations. No safety glass. There were a few rope stanchions in the center of the bank to form a line for the tellers. They were all brass and going green. The rope threaded between the stanchions was something you'd find at a hardware store.

In the back was the lackluster centerpiece of any bank. Where a vault should have been, there was a metal Dutch door. Half closed, half opened. Beyond it, the bank's cash.

Sitting in a chair, minding his own business, was a seventy-year-old security guard with a nametag that said TIM. The skin around his mouth and jaw had tightened and wrinkled, due to lack of teeth.

There was one customer in the place. She was talking with a teller about her husband.

"—the laziest man I have ever met. If there was a contest out there, and I don't know how they'd judge it, but he'd win gold every single time. He'd be on a box of Little Debbie's instead of Wheaties, you understand what I'm saying?"

"Yes, Mrs. Swensen," the teller said.

Alex was in the back, talking with two men in business suits who looked extremely out of place. They were packing up their briefcases and shaking hands.

Alex showed them out, watched them leave, turned to Carla, spread his hands out and did a 360. "Right? What did I tell you?"

"That you were investing in asbestos?"

"Stop it. This place is great! Look at all the character."

She looked at the security guard. "I see a character."

"He's an institution around here. Trust me. This place is going to be fantastic."

"Yeah. A fantastic lemon."

"You have no imagination. Come on. Second lunch is on me."

"Where? Is there a prison in town where we get to eat meals? Because I didn't see a chain gang on my way here."

"I know just the place."

Murray's Diner was the restaurant everyone ate at because they didn't have a choice. It was clean enough. It smelled good. It was half full on a Thursday at 3 p.m.

An average-looking man in his thirties with black hair was in the back, cooking up a storm. A twenty-something waitress named Betty came by to take their order. She was all smiles.

"What can I get you?"

"Whatever you've been shooting up," Carla said, and rested her head on her hand. She was tired and depressed.

"Jesus," Alex said under his breath. "She just means how... energetic you are. It's been a long day."

"Oh, yeah, I get that a lot. I'm not sure what it is. Ever since I was a kid. Always happy." Carla looked up at her with a *please stop* look. "Just a clear, positive mindset in whatever you're doing," Betty continued. "Wherever you are, you're there for a reason. That's my motto, anyway."

"OK, Betty, what am I doing here?" Carla asked.

"You're here to... try our lunch special. Tuna melt with French fries... and... a black and white milk shake."

"Can I keep her?" Carla asked Alex.

Alex shook his head. "No. Two of those, please. Unless you see something else for me?"

"Nope. Two it is." Betty walked away.

Carla watched her. "I can't even... I miss the days when I felt like that for an hour. *Half* an hour."

"Just relax," Alex said, and spread out on his side of the booth. "Boy, do I love this place. The town, *and* this place."

"You're out of your goddamn mind."

"I'm not. It's like the new land of opportunity. I can't get over it. It's like... frozen in time. And we get to take advantage of it. In more ways than one."

"It's a depressed town, Alex."

"I know." He sounded gleeful.

"How does that help you and your new friends?"

"I'm not sure. Just have to take it day by day."

"Well, I thought the whole point of this was that you would take money in from the town. That's how you explained it to me."

"That's right."

"Alex... there's no town here. It's just some everyday businesses that people need to survive. It's not a boom town."

"Come on, *look* at this place."

"Yeah, it's the only one with a pulse." She rubbed her face with her hands. "I don't... I don't know if I can do this. I might have to take you up on—"

"On what?"

"Staying back in Philly with your folks."

He nodded. His demeanor changed. His face darkened. "Is that what you want?"

"Alex. Look around. What in the hell am I supposed to do here?"

"Take care of Jesse."

"Are you kidding me? I'm not a stay-at-home mom. I have a job. A career. You think I'm moving all the way up here to stay at home all day long?"

"Well, I... I thought maybe for a little while. Then you'd meet people and... get used to it."

She looked out the window of the diner. Across from them was a big empty lot. There was a sign that said 4 ACRES – COMMERCIAL

ZONING – FORECLOSURE – SHERBORN TRUST and a telephone number for the bank.

"I don't know, Alex. I just don't."

Betty came by with their food. "Now, who got the tuna melt?"

Alex and Carla looked up at her.

"Just kidding!" She gave them their plates. "Need anything else?"

Carla said, "Yeah, how about a chainsaw to—"

"Nothing. Thank you," Alex said and smiled.

Betty smiled and walked away.

"You never let me have fun," Carla said, and ate a fry.

"I always let you have fun. But we're strangers here, *and* new in town. Alienating people might not be the best thing to do."

"Says you." She took a bite of her sandwich. "Oh boy."

"What?"

"It's good."

"So?"

"I wish it wasn't, so I could hate this place." She drank some of her shake. "Goddammit."

They went back to the bank. Carla took some photos of the place.

"What are you doing?" Alex asked.

"I want to think about it. It needs something."

"Like what? I think it's perfect."

"It needs… elegance."

"What? It's not a…" he looked around. "A girl's bank."

"Not a… Jesus, Alex, you're showing your true colors with that statement."

"Sorry."

"This place needs to look professional. Customers need to come in here and think 'success.' All it says now is 'watch out for hepatitis.'"

"It does not."

"You're right. I'm sorry."

"Thank you."

"Yeah, more like rabies."

340

CHAPTER FORTY-EIGHT

W hen she got home the next day, she uploaded the photos she'd taken and emailed them to Hal, with a subject line that simply said: ARE YOU FUCKING SERIOUS?

He replied twenty minutes later with a phone number. A different one than the one from the book.

"That place is a joke," Carla said.

"Yeah, and we got it for a song."

"It's no Manhattan, Hal."

"What does that mean?"

"Manhattan was bought for a song."

"No it wasn't."

"Yes it was."

"It wasn't. What... who told you that?"

"I read it in... Social Studies."

"Where, in a communist country?"

"Fuck you, you were homeschooled."

"Homeschooled... what?"

"And you started a prostitution ring—"

"What the hell are you talking about...?"

She started laughing. "Forget it."

After a long moment, Hal breathed out the word "John." He sounded angry.

She stopped laughing.

"You talked to John. When did you talk to John?"

"At the—"

"Has he come to see you?"

"No, Jesus. No. He was at the Cape Cod party."

She could hear Hal breathing.

"And we were just hanging out while you were asleep—"

"OK."

"And he was joking around."

"OK. Listen, just... I'm sorry. He doesn't know anything about this, OK? It's between me and my boss, who's paranoid enough as it is about this plan and... I'm sorry."

"It's OK. I thought you knew..."

"No, it's fine. I'm sorry. I wasn't homeschooled."

"I know."

"OK."

"I never graduated high school. I just..."

"Hal."

"It's not a sore subject, you just caught me off guard there, that's all. Forget it."

"Are you sure? We can talk—"

"No. Forget it. Talk to me about the bank."

She got up and paced a bit. "OK. You sure it's safe to—"

"Just keep it vague."

"OK. The town is a joke. The bank is a piece of shit. It looks like it was abandoned and no one told the town. No one is going to do business there."

Hal didn't speak.

"Listen, Alex talks to me, OK? He has to, he's got no one else. Not to mention you and me are... well, you know. So just... look, the place is a dump. It's not going to get the clients you need."

"Sure it will."

"Yeah, people who live there and some of their businesses. But you're never going to get real money in there unless you fix it up. That place needs to be gutted. It needs a paint job. New ceilings. New floors. *Definitely* a new sign. I mean, if you're just going to be in and out after a year, fine. But if you need this to work for a while? Like *years*? I mean, Jesus, Hal. It needs a fucking *vault*. They have, like, a closet now, where they keep the money, and a cadaver watching it."

"Don't talk about Tim that way."

"Christ, between you and Alex—"

"How much?"

"How what?"

"How much?" Hal asked again.

"I... I don't know."

"Find out."

"Are you serious?"

"Find out. You're right. My boss won't need too much convincing. But I need a number. Get it to me quick. We need to get this thing up and running."

"OK."

They were both silent.

"How are you doing?" he asked. There was tenderness in his voice.

"I'm good. I'm good. You?"

"Surviving," he said, sighing. "Which means I'm doing OK."

Two days later, Carla was sitting on the bed of the hotel room folding her clothes while Alex was on the phone, pacing. She was leaving in the morning.

"Sure. Yeah. I can make that work." He looked at her with surprise. "Of course, I just..." he paused and nodded. "No, I got it. We'll find a crew up here... OK, *you'll* find a crew, and we'll have it up and running as soon as possible." He nodded. "Absolutely. OK. Thanks Hal. Talk later. Bye."

Alex hung his cell phone up and threw it on the bed. He looked at her with wide eyes and a smile.

"What?" she asked.

"He just told me they're going to pay to renovate the entire place. Top to bottom."

343

"Really? That's fantastic!"

"Yeah, it is. And… it's so strange. He wants me to buy a bank vault."

"What's so strange about that? It's a *bank*, Alex!"

"I know, but when he showed me the place he was fine with it…"

"I guess they have bigger plans for it."

"I guess so. I just… I've never done anything like this before."

"I think I've heard you say that before," she said and smiled.

"Shut up," he said, walked over and kissed her. "I almost feel like this is your fault."

"My fault? How?"

"You, like… put it out there. Into the universe. I don't know how that shit works. But boy… OK." He sat down on the bed and looked at her. "Did you…?"

"What?"

He made a face, like he was thinking crazy. "Nothing. It's stupid. So! You want to go down to the bank and help me figure this out?"

"I guess. Not sure how I can help."

"We're just going to—"

"How much are they giving you?"

"A lot."

"How much is a lot?"

"Half a million dollars."

"Holy SHIT."

"Yeah. Maybe more."

She had told Hal fifty thousand.

"Hal suggested installing new safety deposit boxes. He said we should add a night depository, too. I guess…" he swallowed hard. "I guess they're going to be giving me a lot of cash, so… he also suggested something called a class 2… something. I can't remember."

"The hell is that?"

"Some kind of vault, I don't know. But it's expensive, so… I guess he's been asking around. He's going to find a construction company to do the work. Hal said he wanted to make sure everything was top of the line."

"Alex... exactly how much money *are* they expecting you to launder?"

He shook his head. "I don't know. They aren't telling me yet. And I have to be honest, it's getting me worried."

"You *should* be worried," she said, and got up. "You're officially in the worry business." She looked at him. He looked... well, worried. "I'm sorry. We are. We." She held out her hand for him. He grabbed it. "Take me to dinner."

"You got it." He got up.

"Just not to the—"

"The diner it is!"

She sighed.

CHAPTER FORTY-NINE

A company from Syracuse that specialized in bank construction got in touch with Alex three days later. They said they'd been hired as a rush job and were bringing in four other companies to gut the building, put up new electrical, new plumbing, new walls, floors and carpets, new ceilings, new fire safety measures, central air and heat, new bathrooms, a small kitchen, and a security station with monitors and recording devices for their top-of-the line surveillance system.

Alex was beside himself. "Uh, yeah. Sure. Sounds good."

The basement was being reinforced to take the extra weight of the vault, which would sport a new Class 2 Modular door. A cement company came by, took measurements, and would have concrete slabs with reinforced steel rods made for both the vault and the walls lined with safety deposit boxes. They would be delivered in a week.

The contents of the eighteen safety deposit boxes (out of seventy-five) that were currently being used were stored at the police station. Alex made arrangements with the town sheriff, a Sheriff Briggs, to not only store people's valuables, but to also store the bank's cash reserves, and allow locals and businesses to continue their banking by placing a teller in one of the station's offices. All deposits were guaranteed.

As thanks for their help, the department was getting a new patrol car.

Carla and Alex had been fine with the original layout of the bank. They spoke with the foreman, a guy named Hicks, about it. He brought someone on his staff who worked with CAD. The next day they had a working set of blueprints, complete with accurate measurements.

Eight construction workers came in and ripped the place apart. The basement looked like a tornado had hit it. The fake wood panel walls were torn down. Behind them, layers of brick, from floor to ceiling. The guys took them down, too. Behind that was dirt. The bank was the only business on the block with a basement.

They ripped up the floor, took the ceiling tiles and its metal infrastructure out.

Same with the first floor. Everything went.

An interior designer who specialized in banks came by after the demo was completed. She worked with Carla and Alex on carpet and wall color, artwork, blinds, fabrics for chairs and benches, wood selections for all of the table tops, and more.

She suggested a wide U as a layout for the safety deposit boxes. She drew it for them and explained where the girders were going to go to reinforce the vault. They would be hidden in the center of the U, with boxes along the outside, plus along the two adjoining walls. They would have room for 200 boxes, including an entire wall of 10 x 10s. There was also space for two secure viewing rooms.

A security specialist gave them advice on equipment, electrical placement, camera and alarm system strategies, and the night depository location.

A graphic designer came in with more than a dozen options for the bank's new logos for stationary, a website, and the exterior signage.

Alex ran all of the suggestions by Hal before any decisions were made.

Infrastructure came next.

Six steel girders were installed directly under where the vault would be. They were encased in concrete cylinders, and finished with sheetrock, forming the interior of the U.

More than two dozen two-thousand pound concrete slabs were brought into the basement and secured along three walls. Electric came in and wired the ceiling and the outer basement foyer. Space for a doorframe was left for a security door connecting the foyer to the box room.

Plumbers came in and upgraded the water and sewage lines. Hicks worked with the heating and air guy to make sure the ducts were fed through to the basement, which originally didn't have heat or air. Vents were built into the basement ceiling on both sides of the U, and the basement foyer ceiling.

The vault was measured out to ten by fifteen feet. More reinforced steel concrete slabs were brought in to encase the sides and top.

They picked a Diebold stainless steel vault door with two combination locks and a hand wheel. The door alone weighed over four thousand pounds.

It was the most beautiful thing Alex had ever seen. "Next to my son, of course," he told Hicks.

"Shit, man, you should hear some of my clients. They love their vaults like they love pussy."

"Yeah, well... I... I'll stick with pussy."

"Good idea. Still, she's a beaut."

The vault opened to the left and had a reinforced acrylic and metal day-gate behind it.

Electric came in and placed outlets every ten feet on every wall of the main floor. Outlets were placed above the ceiling line wherever a camera was going to be placed.

Ballistic glass was fitted from the base of the teller counter to the ceiling. Lock boxes were fitted at every teller window.

The security station had room for four monitors, a lock box for a weapon, and was where the secure overnight deposit box would be located.

There were two security doors on either side of the teller station.

The front of the building was fitted with floor-to-ceiling glass windows and doors that were half frosted. From sunrise to sunset, the place would be full of daylight.

The alarm company came in and did their thing. They wired to windows, the front door, the rear emergency exit door, and the vault. There were panic buttons under every teller station, one in Alex's office, one in the box room, one in the basement foyer, one in the vault, and one by the security desk.

The carpeting was charcoal grey. The chairs matched. The desks for bank associates were a dark wood, as was the teller counter. There were abstract paintings on the light grey walls. The white ceiling tiles looked like stucco. They were washable and fireproof.

There was a full sprinkler system throughout on both levels, along with fire alarms and extinguishers at the security and teller's station, the vault, the basement foyer, and the main office. There was also a fire suppression system in the vault.

The day the place was finished, and the last piece of garbage was thrown out, Alex actually wept. Carla hugged him.

Hicks shook their hands and said adieu.

Alex ran his hand along the teller station. He touched the vault. He slid his feet across the new carpet. He breathed in the smell and realized he'd reached peak contentment for the first time in his life.

It was perfect.

And for the next fourteen years, Alex Holsfer laundered money for the mob.

CHAPTER FIFTY

While the bank was being renovated, Carla and Alex found a house to buy just outside of town. It was two levels, brick exterior with two white columns outside the front door. Two-car garage, a pool, big backyard for Jesse, and was surrounded by trees. It wasn't a mansion, but it was slightly larger than his parent's house, and they fell in love with it.

They put in an offer, paid cash (thanks to Hal's bonus), and Carla started the process of moving their belongings up straight away. It had three bedrooms, two and a half bathrooms, a large kitchen, living room, dining room, laundry room, a den, an office for Alex, and central air and heating.

Alex went out and bought an AMSEC home security safe: 40 by 24 by 20, B-rated, with four shelves that would fit upwards of 1.5 million... if it was in hundreds. The safe weighed 925 pounds, and took three men to bring into his home.

Abigail was true to her word. There was a party, and strippers.

Carla watched in amusement as Abigail got lap dance after lap dance from three different young men, any one of which could have been her son.

"Don't put that creepy shit in my head. I deserve this," Abigail said, and ran her hands down the muscular torso of a particularly buff one.

Carla wasn't really into muscles. She was more a fan of the slightly doughy variety, if she was being honest.

Still. She did give him a feel.

They closed the place. They closed it with drinking and stories and tears and jokes and must have hugged ten times. It was the saddest goodbye Carla had ever experienced.

"You're going to come visit me."

"I'm going to come visit you," Abigail said. "I have a shift in five hours and I think I'm going to go sleep on that park bench."

"I'll call you a car."

"OK."

She made sure Abigail was safely on her way home before she called her own car. She looked around Market Street, lost in thought, when she heard the car honk for her. She got in, went to her in-laws, stumbled down the stairs to the basement as silently as she could, and fell asleep on the couch.

Saying goodbye to Chuck and Helen wasn't as difficult as it had been with Abigail, but it was no cake walk. They hugged, there were tears. Jesse kept wanting to go into his grandma's arms.

Carla was nursing a hangover. The sun was blinding outside. The movers had finished and were already on their way up, with Alex waiting for them. She had a four and a half hour drive and was working on less than six hours of shitty sleep.

She finally pulled away from the house in her rental car. Jesse was in the back in his car seat. He was playing with his favorite possession, a white blanket with blue fringe and dozens of cartoon animals sewn in. Helen had gotten it for him the day after Carla first brought him by. It never left his side.

Two hours in, she made the same stop in Wilkes-Barre at the Cracker Barrel for lunch. A few waitresses came in and fussed over Jesse like he was a king.

They got back in the car. Jesse was passed out from the attention, from the food. She sat back and looked at him through the rear view and just let her body relax.

"You're not going to remember any of this," she said to him. "You're going to grow up in this new place and you'll have never known another. Not really. And you'll remember your grandparents, of course. They'll come visit you, I know they will. They love you so much. But I just wanted to take this moment to apologize. I'm sure it won't be the last time I'll have to do that. What we're doing? Your dad and I? It's not what we want. But unless I take you away, and you never see him again... and believe me, I thought about it... this is all we have, kiddo. At some point you're going to be put in a situation... and the options to get out of it in one piece will become narrower and narrower, until you don't have a good choice. We're going to do the best we can, OK? I promise." She turned to look at him. "I won't let anything happen to you. I swear to God."

She wiped tears from her cheeks, nodded, turned the starter, put the car in gear, and got back onto the highway.

CHAPTER FIFTY-ONE

The day of the grand opening, Alex, Carla, and Jesse were there to greet the customers. Alex kept the original staff. Barry Goodall was the manager. He was up on regulations and the day to day. Alex promoted him to COO. Gladys Tuscon and Kelly Ann Miller were tellers. Janice Hudson, who was in her late sixties, took care of the bank's books. Alex would spend most of his time with her in the coming months.

He had a consulting firm come in to talk with the staff about professionalism and dealing with customers. An instructor showed them how to use the new computer system for deposits and withdrawals. He had the security company bring an instructor down to show them how to use the system, in case of emergency.

He had them all signed up to a new health care plan, plus dental. He gave them all three weeks' vacation a year, plus sick days, and started a 401(k). He upped their salaries by fifteen percent, and with every decision, his heart was filled with glee.

"How are you going to pay for all that?" Carla asked, a few days prior.

"It's the price of doing business. All these people are... they're all going to be unwitting accomplices. The least I can do is compensate them for their clandestine criminality."

"That's too many big words, Alex. What's gotten into you?"

"I'm just excited, I guess... it's a new beginning, that's all." He sat down on the couch in the living room. The house was only half set up.

There was so much room, and they didn't have enough furniture. Their voices echoed when they talked. "We have operating income for three years. That's how long they're giving me to set up the laundering."

"And how are you going to do that?"

"I have no fucking idea."

A man came into the bank. Short. Nice suit. Sunglasses. Tie. Hair slicked back.

Italian.

"Hi, sir, and welcome to our grand opening!" Alex stuck his hand out.

The man looked at him and smiled. He took off the sunglasses, put them into his jacket pocket, and shook Alex's hand. "Thank you," he said.

"Would you like a cup of coffee? Some cake? Cookies?" Carla asked.

"No, thank you. Not a big fan of sweets. Now, who is this?" he said, and made a motion to hold Jesse's hand. Jesse pulled away, embarrassed, and dug his face into Carla's neck.

"Jesse. He's... well, he's shy. Sorry," she said.

"Oh, shy's OK. Better than whining and crying and throwing a fit, am I right?"

"Definitely."

The guy looked the place over. "Nice. Really nice. I've been in my fair share of banks, and this is really classy. Congratulations. It's yours?"

"Yes," Alex said, beaming.

"Well, again, congratulations."

"Thank you. Do you live in the area? Are you here to open and account?"

"Nope. Just passing through. Saw the sign out front, wanted to see what the hubbub was about."

"Well, thank you for stopping in. You're sure you don't want a—"

"No. Thank you." He waved at Jesse. "Bye, Jesse. Bye. Best of luck."

"Thank you," Carla said.

"Thanks," Alex said.

They watched the man head out of the bank, walk down the block a bit, get into a limo, and drive away.

"That was weird, wasn't it?"

"No, not really," Alex said. His complexion had changed. He was no longer smiling.

"What... Alex, do you know who that was?"

"Yes. Yes, I do." Alex wiped his face with his hands. "Excuse me for a sec."

He went into the bathroom and threw up his breakfast.

"He could have used some warning," Carla said to Hal on the phone.

"That's not how this works."

"Of course it does—"

"You think he just tells me what he's going to do? Listen, maybe you have an overinflated idea of what I am to this organization. I'm nothing. I'm new. I'm expendable. I came up with an idea that got tossed around by men who've been doing this for a living since they were kids. They talked to their advisors and their lawyers and people they trust and *then* they said yes. I'm helping run it. Barely. I make a suggestion. It gets taken or not. If not, I move on. If it does, I chalk up another notch of credibility. That's it. I got Alex out of a jam. I'm not sure I did him any favors. We'll see. My boss showing up? That should have been expected. He's got over twenty million dollars invested in this business."

"What?"

"Yeah. Construction was a drop in the bucket. That's why they were OK with it. There's six layers between my boss and your husband, and he's still taking an interest. That should give you all the information you need on how important it is for Alex to—"

"OK, OK. I'm sorry."

355

Hal sighed. "Don't be sorry. Just... don't be surprised by this shit any more. Weird things are going to happen. Weird is going to be the new normal. Just make sure he lives, eats, and breathes that fucking bank until it starts working autonomously."

"I will."

"Good. How's the kid?"

"He's good. He'll be two in a few months."

"And you? How are you doing?"

She sighed. Jesse was asleep. Alex was at the bank. She didn't know what to do with herself. She looked around the half empty house. "I'm surviving."

CHAPTER FIFTY-TWO

"Talk to me," Hal said. He and Alex were sitting down at a restaurant in Binghamton. Under Hal's legs was a briefcase. It was an exact duplicate of Alex's personal briefcase, which was next to Alex's chair.

"About what?"

"About your colon. What the fuck do you think I mean?"

Alex chuckled.

Hal was not laughing.

"Sorry, man. OK. Before I do, did you get me that name?"

Hal took out a piece of paper from his jeans pocket and put it on the table, slid it over to Alex. Alex unfolded it. Written there was the name Pamela Tully, along with her address, and social security number and a signature.

"Great. OK, great."

"And that's for what?"

"Safety deposit boxes. For the..." he looked around. "For cash."

"OK."

"And this is a real person, right?"

"Yeah."

"OK, good. Just, you know, just in case. And what about the gun?"

"It's clean, it's in the briefcase. Get to it, already."

"Uhh... well, so, the town's only got about three thousand people in it, and the majority of the stores aren't really doing crazy business except for the one diner in town. One of the motels has a business account, but their deposits are less than spectacular, and mostly by credit card transactions. There's a newspaper, too... could be worse. But I have to figure out a way to entice other businesses to come to town."

"How?"

"I don't know. Low interest business loans? Something. Cheap property, maybe. Or do what McDonald's used to do. Own the property, build the stores and rent them out? Might work." Alex looked around. "How much money do you need me to... you know?"

"Twenty."

"Twenty? Jesus. Twenty a year."

"A month."

"Shut the fuck up."

"I'm serious."

There was a long pause. What noise Alex had heard, just the general background milling about in the restaurant... it disappeared. All he could hear was the blood rushing through his head.

"That's impossible," he said. His mouth went dry.

"No it isn't."

"Hal, listen to me," Alex lowered his voice. "Twenty million dollars a month is impossible. I can't do it. I never would have said yes to... that would be almost a seven thousand dollars for every man, woman, and child in town. Per month. How the fuck am I supposed to allow deposits of that much money into a small bank?"

"I don't know. But that's why we hired you. To figure it out."

"I *can't*. That's... Hal, there are banks in major cities that don't do that kind of business. I can't do it."

Hal sat across from him, stone faced. They both had remnants of lunch in front of them.

"What can you do?"

"I don't know, I have to—"

"Do you know what you're doing?"

"What do you mean?"

"Do you know what you're doing? It's a simple question."

Alex leaned back and closed his eyes. The place was half empty. It was a Saturday at four in the afternoon. "Yeah. I know what I'm doing. The fundamentals of this business are pretty simple. The problem is, the amounts you're talking about, you can only do that one of... three ways, maybe."

"OK."

"No, *not* OK. Because it's impossible to launder that amount of money in a fucking podunk town, Hal. If you would've told me it was going to be that much money, I would have told you to buy in a major city, like Alexandria, or ancient Rome. Not fucking Sherborn, where it's going to become the mob equivalent of a fucking gold rush town."

Hal smiled. "It's not twenty a month. Calm down."

Alex started to say something and stopped. He smiled and visibly relaxed. "You were fucking with me?"

"What can I tell you? I'm a creature of habit. I don't know how much it's going to be. I just wanted to see your face."

"You're a dick."

"Yeah, I get that a lot. Maybe twenty a year."

"That's... maybe a bit more doable. Maybe. Jesus, man... storing it? That's one thing. But cleaning that much—"

"Tell me the three ways."

"Well, I mean, these are the simpler ways for hiding cash. First is, small deposits in fake accounts. In cash. Under $10,000. And more like eight or seven, if you really want to be safe. And not every day. Under $10k deposits don't get reported. They stay under the radar. The problem is, I need social security numbers, identities, all that shit for those accounts, right? After they passed the Patriot Act, they came up with *Know Your Customer*. Ten years ago, I probably *could've* moved twenty a month through there. No one gave a shit. Now... look, I'm sure someone in your organization can get me fake I.D.s to set up these accounts, but fakes will show up at some point in an investigation somewhere. Once a cop or a fed or the SEC or the fucking OCC gets their hands on a fake account, we're fucked. Plus, Jesus, this route would take forever."

"OK."

"But... you're talking about maybe fifty thousand a week in clean cash, with no loss."

"Nice. OK. He'll be happy about that. Keep going."

"Second are cash businesses. That would be great—if there were any fucking businesses in town."

"Right, we'll get back to that. And the third?"

"The third is real estate. Now, I took a closer look at the bank's foreclosure inventory, and it's pretty sweet."

"Explain."

"Well, the bank owns about fourteen lots around town, plus twenty homes. All foreclosures from defaulted mortgages. This is where we'll be able to wash a significant amount of whatever you send me. The good thing is, we can do that every other year or so, just keep rolling them over. We just have to show a legitimate chain from purchaser to purchaser. We can also buy some properties around the area, like other bank foreclosures or, you know, shitholes somewhere for cheap, but we don't want to make that too much of a habit. That's all public record, and unless we're buying off state officials left and right... see, it all depends on how much money you're talking."

"OK. Houses I get. How do empty lots help us?"

"Well, you buy an empty lot or whatever, and start building from scratch. Except you bring in your own crew, your own people, and you jack up the rates. You bring in non-union guys and pay them union wages on paper, and you pocket the difference. You up the costs of the materials, pocket the difference. You stop construction for a while, make it seem like there was a loss of revenue. You have *another* company come in and buy it for cheap. They do demo, and start the whole process over. Have the money come into the bank through the businesses, add some cash deposits in small amounts... pay actual taxes so the IRS doesn't come snooping around... you could do that forever."

"So do that."

"Slow down. It's a small town, man. People are going to catch on. This is like, once in a blue moon kind of shit."

"Why would the people in town care?"

Alex looked at him strangely. "It's their home, man."

"So hire local. They'll be happy for the work."

"Yeah. I can do all that, I'm just saying, it has to be timed. All of it. And I can't be the face of it. At least not for the real estate part. You'll have to bring in a lot of people."

"You tell me what you need, when you need it, and I'll do what I can. But you have to have something in place so that this, all this, is constantly working."

Alex nodded and sighed. "I got it. Now, I have a question. What is he expecting as a rate of loss?"

"It's one of the reasons we're here to talk, Alex. You tell me."

Alex gave it some thought before he talked. "The businesses and small deposits would be lower... maybe a few percent, just in case I need to pay taxes or transfer fees. For the bank, so it looks legit. It's a lot of moving money around, but if I don't do it right, it'll get noticed. The real estate deals? More like fifteen."

"Where is the fifteen percent going?"

"Property taxes, capital gains, closing fees. Real estate is tricky, because of the public records. Shell companies will help with that. Commercial property can trade hands without causing too much of a ruckus. Plus, you have to pay the people who are taking the chances. They have the clean records we'll need for this to make sense. If we start now, we can create the paper trails on where they're getting the money and where it's going to."

"Why would they get paid from us if they'd own the property?"

"No, *you* would still own the property. In their name. You'll be paying yourself with your own money for the property, but it's still on the books as theirs. You keep the property until you sell it to yourself again. Or, if you have a legitimate buyer, even better. And so... owning the property through a, a proxy... you want to keep them quiet, you pay them."

"We won't have to worry about these people keeping quiet."

"OK. Just as long as you don't send up people who are... different. Anyone out of the ordinary is going to stand out. Do you understand what I mean?"

"I can't promise you anything, but I understand what you mean."

Silence between them. The restaurant was quiet.

Alex looked around, looked at the remains of his lunch, pushed the plate further away. "We haven't talked about it, but... what about my cut?"

"Your cut."

"Well, yeah, I'm doing all the work."

Hal leaned in. "Let me explain something to you."

"OK."

"Don't ever mention your cut ever again. Not ever. Not to me, not to your wife. No one. Your cut is I got you out of a jam. Your cut from here on out is your salary at the bank. The house you bought. The cars you bought. Healthcare. Vacations."

Alex went to say something.

Hal leaned back, put his left arm out over the back of the chair next to him. "And... half a percent. That's it."

"Half a percent of... are you serious?"

"Very. And Mr. D'Escopio believes he's being quite generous with that."

"That's not generous, Hal," Alex lowered his voice, but still... "That's an ass fucking!"

"Yeah, well, you can tell him that and see where he leaves you." Hal sighed. "Don't make me threaten you, man. I don't want to be that guy. I really don't. We didn't pick you so *you* could make money. That was never the goal in all of this. Not for you. I'm a bit surprised you thought that was the way things were going to go. Especially since none of it is your money. Right?"

Alex shook his head. "Right, but... I mean, he's got to be getting the deal of a lifetime here."

"Maybe."

362

"Definitely! Hal... it's too much work for one person."

"How do you know?"

"I... OK, I walked into that one. What if it becomes too much work for one person?"

"We'll cross that bridge when we get to it."

"It's not enough, Hal."

Hal was tired. He was frustrated. He was doing this behind John's back, which made his stomach upset every time he thought about it. He sat across from Alex and felt a burning sensation crawling up his throat. The doctors said it was acid reflux. He'd never heard of it before. He tried to swallow it down. "What's half a percent of twenty million?"

"A hundred thousand dollars."

"Doesn't sound too bad."

"Are you fucking kidding me? Hal, I'm taking all the risk. Two percent. Two percent, you'll get the best of me. Half a percent... I'll be pissed off the entire time. No offense, it's just... come on, man."

Hal studied Alex for a long time. He kept his poker face, remembering Gino said to give him three percent. Hal had been thinking about what he was going to do with his money, long term. An extra percent was a reasonable bargaining chip with Gino... and he knew just what he wanted for it. He closed his eyes, opened them, looked dubious. "I'll talk to them. I'm not promising anything. You understand?"

"Yeah."

"I get you your two percent, you better become the fucking Rolls-Royce of money launderers, you hear me?"

"Absolutely."

"There're two rules here, Alex. One, don't fuck up. Two, don't steal from them. That's it. You keep your head down, you'll be a millionaire in just a few years."

A waitress came by with a fresh pot. "More coffee?"

"No thank you," Hal said.

"Yes, please," Alex said.

She poured and left.

"What's the first business you're going to buy?"

Alex smiled. "There's a gas station in town, run by a guy who's dying to move on."

Hal arched an eyebrow.

"Not literally. I mean, not... no. He just wants out. I've talked to him a bunch of times, and I know he's good to go. No one in town can afford it. It's perfect, and we'll get it for nothing. But I need a buyer."

"How much?"

"Three hundred thousand. Ballpark."

"Does it need renovations?"

"Not immediately. And when it does, the bank will give them a loan, at a reasonable rate of interest." Alex smiled, pleased with himself. "So, just to recap, I need the buyers to have an impeccable background. How they got that money... it's not going to matter with this guy, the gas station guy. But future dealings are going to require shell companies. LLC's out of Delaware, maybe. I can do some of that here, but I'll need legitimate front men or women. And no fly-by-nighters. I'll need people with significant capital, living in residences longer than two years."

"Anywhere?"

"Anywhere in the area. New England, tri-state... that'd work. They need to have real estate, personal holdings, stocks, whatever. As long as they fit the part of having the means to do this shit. Where they get their loans from... well, that's just more obfuscating, which is easy enough. But all this is hedged on the face of the people you pick. All of it."

"I'll get you a buyer for the gas station. Give me a week." Hal handed the briefcase over to Alex, who put it on the floor. Alex handed Hal his own empty briefcase. "See you in a month with another one of those." He got up from the booth, put two twenties down on the counter, and walked away.

CHAPTER FIFTY-THREE

Alex worked on the paperwork for Pamela Tully's safety deposit boxes that night. He practiced forging her signature before signing the actual paperwork. Inside the briefcase Hal had given him, there was a slip of paper in with the cash, detailing the amount. He counted the cash with a counter he'd taken from work. $714,860. It was correct.

Along with the cash was a Smith & Wesson Model 36 snub nose revolver. It used .38 Specials and had a five shot capacity. It looked like a gun from an old detective TV show he saw as a kid, but it was brand new. Alex had asked Hal for it, just in case. He put the handgun in the safe, and put the bullets in his desk drawer.

Alex would only shoot the .38 once in his lifetime.

The next day, before opening, Alex entered the bank, turned off the alarm, and went downstairs.

The security cameras that were in the basement had two blind spots, on purpose. One of them was at the back, where Pamela Tully had the entire bottom row of 10 x 10s registered. He used the key to safety deposit box number 1 and grabbed the box. The second blind spot was on a small table, just off the two secure viewing rooms. Alex placed the cash from the briefcase inside the box, replaced it in slot one, and went back upstairs.

He figured he had nine or ten months before he would run out of space.

Alex broke down a list of all of the property for sale in town. More than seventy percent of it was residential. The commercial properties consisted of two buildings on Clover Lane (two blocks north from the bank), a building on the outskirts of town that had been used by a printing company, a strip mall that never took off, and an entire block of stores on Main Street, across from the newspaper offices.

He found three parcels of farmland outside of town that could get picked up for very little money, and started researching property closer to Binghamton and Syracuse, where there were many more options.

He also priced out the gas station in town. Its present value was roughly three hundred and eighteen thousand, including the land. Alex looked into the business account the station had with the bank. It had cash deposits of roughly sixty-eight thousand dollars for the year. That number was steady for over a decade. Deposits were in the neighborhood of $400, every other day. Alex figured the old man had to have been pocketing some here and there.

Hal provided Alex with a buyer, a woman named Gloria Peligrino, who owned a condo in the Poconos and was "looking for an investment opportunity." She visited the gas station and talked to the owner, Leo Farr, who played it off as reluctant. He was in his mid-sixties. "I'm sorry to say, it's the only thing that's keeping me going these days."

"So run it for me," she said. "I don't know anything about the business, but I know people need gas, and your station is the only one for fifteen miles. I'll offer you four hundred thousand dollars, in cash."

Leo said he'd give it some thought, and said yes three hours later.

Gloria opened up her own business and personal savings account at the bank. Leo kept his business account at the insistence of Alex, who said, "You never know. Maybe you'll open a side business."

Leo would run the gas station another five years before dying in his sleep one night. He had no family, and left his money and home to a church just outside of Little York, a town about twenty minutes away.

Alex kept Leo's business account open after he died. It ended up being one of his major cash movers over the next decade.

Between the foreclosed properties, new properties, small deposits, the gas station, repeated construction jobs that went nowhere, and Alex's abilities to obfuscate, he had a steady stream of money flowing in and out of Sherborn. And there wasn't a blip of trouble from any of the regulating organizations, or the IRS.

The money funneled through to a dozen different accounts, all of them tangentially linked to Gino D'Escopio. All legit. All buffered.

Alex did, in fact, become a millionaire after two years.

He had three properties, including the strip mall, that changed hands once every two years. Construction jobs started and stopped almost immediately every time a new 'owner' came along.

He bought out the block of property on Main Street himself, had it renovated, and, at a town council meeting, set up a Chamber of Commerce, which he chaired. He took applications for businesses for the new storefronts and offered high interest rates for their checking and savings accounts, along with low interest loans and low rents.

Slowly but surely, businesses started coming to Sherborn.

Things were going smoothly. His family was doing well. His parents came to visit whenever they could. Carla got a job as an RN at a hospital ten miles outside of town. They hired Sofia Santiago, a woman in her forties who moved to town to be with her daughter, as their babysitter and maid. Jesse was growing up into a really great kid.

For more than ten years, Alex did exemplary work for the mob, and was a model citizen, father, and husband.

And then, one day, he completely fucked it up.

CHAPTER FIFTY-FOUR

In January of 2008, three years after they moved to Sherborn, Alex felt comfortable enough to start doing taxes for people in the town. He had multiple sources of laundering from cash businesses in the area. The gas station was one. There was a five-and-dime that opened on Main Street, along with a deli and a coffee shop. All in properties he owned personally. His tenants were very happy with the rents, with the help he provided for their shops. Alex was able to open up duplicate accounts for all of these businesses. He would have their deposits go into their own accounts, and he would deposit cash into the duplicates in similar sized increments. They were responsible for helping launder almost two hundred thousand per year.

He hired a down-on-his-luck CPA friend of his from college, Bob Murcer, to do the personal taxes of any bank customers that needed or wanted help. He paid the guy per hour, made only a modest profit on each return, and did the business returns himself.

He kept a ledger of the fake accounts and the real accounts. Like Hal asked for, the work was almost completely autonomous.

On the evening of April 12, 2014, Alex was receiving a blowjob from one of his tellers, Rachel Johnson. They'd been fucking for about a year. Alex was stressed, trying to get returns done on time. Rachel had stayed late to help out... and to help out.

It was quiet in the bank. Bob, who had gotten promoted to manager six months earlier, had left around 9 p.m.

"Half day?" Alex asked him as he packed up.

"Jesus, man. I'm gonna get it at home as it is. Judy's been up my ass, and it's like, this happens every goddamn year. Why is it a surprise when tax season rolls around?"

"Well, good luck, then. Maybe I'll see you in the morning."

"Night. Night, Rachel."

Rachel waved.

Alex got up and stretched. He'd taken his suit jacket and tie off, and unbuttoned the top two buttons of his shirt. They'd all been working steady for two months, no weekends off, and Alex's back had finally had enough.

He rolled his shoulders, rolled his neck, and they both heard it pop, loud.

Rachel giggled. "Boy, you need a massage."

"That would be nice."

"I could do one of those Asian massages on you."

"What the hell is an Asian massage?"

"You know. Where I pretend I'm massaging your back, but then you turn over and I massage your dick."

"So... that's all Asian massages, huh?"

"I think so. If not all, then most."

"And how much Asian do you have in you?"

"I don't know. Like, maybe, aren't we all two percent of everything?"

"Maybe."

"Then, two percent." She stood up and walked over to him. She grabbed his cock over his pants. "Already stiff."

"Yeah, well, sometimes you just have to look at me, honey, and I get all bothered."

"Oh yeah? Well, we don't have much room for a massage..." she looked at his desk. It had both ledgers, a bunch of folders, and the tax papers for Murray's Diner. "How about I just suck you off."

"Well, I mean, when you put it that way..."

She pushed him into his chair, got down on her knees, unbuckled his belt, and pulled his pants down.

She started going down on him. Alex leaned back and stared at the ceiling. It still had the same tiles that he and his wife and the designer had picked out.

Murray's Diner. They had a pretty damn good year.

What the fuck are you thinking about? Come on, man. Concentrate on what she's doing.

I can't.

Why?

Because, I'm tired and I'm stressed and this shit is never going to end.

What shit?

This. All this. I'll be doing this forever. Until they don't need me, or I get caught. Or they kill me.

He could feel himself getting soft.

You're not going to get caught. You're the fucking man. Now, why not instead of having her suck your cock, you bend her over your desk and fuck her like you're her boss.

So that's what he did.

While he was doing it, both ledgers got pushed off the desk. So did the paperwork for Murray's Diner, and a bunch of other folders. But he didn't care. Sex with Rachel had been spectacular from day one. There was the taboo part of fucking a subordinate. There was the part where she was only twenty-two. Eighteen years younger than he was. She was tight, she was up for anything. She wasn't Carla. She made different noises and genuinely wanted to rip his clothes off whenever they were even remotely in vicinity of each other. She was a good listener, which only mattered when he was feeling sorry for himself.

He could go on and on.

She was bent over the desk, making animal noises while he fucked her from behind. He grabbed her hair and she kept slamming her hands against the desk, over and over, with every thrust. Every time she came, she would hold her breath, let it out slowly and make a stuttered grunting noise, almost as if her body was shutting down. It always turned him on more. He'd heard it twice before he finished. He held onto her for a minute until he just collapsed onto the floor, exhausted.

She turned to look at him. "You are an unbelievable fuck."

And she said things like that.

He smiled and watched her adjust her clothing. She lifted up her panties that were taut between her legs. She flipped her hair back and smoothed it out. She buttoned up her blouse. She found her shoes and put them on, all while he watched from the floor.

"I'm going to leave you there," she said, and smiled. "Maybe you'll even be there in the morning."

"Maybe," he said, and looked at the mess. "Thank you."

"Thank *you*," she said. "I'll actually be able to get some sleep tonight. Two weeks without your dick is too long."

"I'm sorry."

"Don't be sorry. After the fifteenth, things better get back to normal around here."

"They will. Goodnight."

She came over, bent at the waist, leaned all the way down to the floor, and kissed him. "Night."

He lay there for a long time, breathing it all in. He felt almost untouchable. The stress left his body. He pulled his pants back on, tidied up and went back to work.

It took six months and an audit to find out Alex used the wrong account numbers for Murray's Diner.

CHAPTER FIFTY-FIVE

The way Carla found out her husband was cheating on her wasn't from seeing a different colored hair in their bed, or lipstick on his shirt or cheeks. It wasn't from smelling his clothes or catching him in the act.

Alex took to spending a lot of late nights in his office. She understood what he was doing... at least, she understood as best she could. She knew that all those numbers and figures and accounts had to mean something to someone at some point. He would talk about going over the books from scratch, once a year, just to make sure that everything either added up correctly, or was so confusing, no one would be able to figure out what money went where.

Except him.

Carla thought it would take more out of him than it did. Most days, Alex was in a fantastic mood. It made for a good home.

Jesse was growing up nicely. He was handsome and kind and fun to be around. He was twelve. His face was getting a bit messy from acne. He realized he liked girls. He was taking longer and longer showers. He was a bit of a late bloomer. His voice didn't start cracking until he was eleven. He'd talk back every once in a while. The first time he said the word "fuck" in anger, Carla and Alex laughed. It had been a serious moment for Jesse, and he got the wind taken right out of his sails.

"Watch your language," Carla said to him, still smiling.

"It's not funny!" Jesse yelled, and left the room.

Early on, it was Carla who convinced Alex to hire Sofia, to help clean the place while she concentrated on Jesse. After a few years, cleaning turned into babysitting so Carla could re-join the living.

There was a hospital outside of town, the Cortland Regional Hospital, about the same size as the Lourdes Hospital in Binghamton, save for some bells and whistles. She got put on the rotation straight away.

Sherborn was growing on her. Slowly. The people were nice. They loved her husband. His staff loved him. The businesses loved him. He was always willing to take a chance on them. The town council loved him. The police loved him. The library and the schools loved him.

And the mob loved him.

At least, that's what Hal said to her. They'd met one time, covertly, at a coffee shop in Cortland. He didn't ask any questions about Alex, which was a relief. Questions, she thought, would have meant problems.

She said he looked good. He said the same to her. She showed him pictures of Jesse. They talked about nothing in particular.

"I just want you to know that things are going well. With Alex. Everyone's very happy. Just in case you were worried or anything," he said.

"I wasn't."

"Well, good then. Keep not worrying."

The car ride home, she had a hard time not wishing things were different. With Alex. With Hal. She couldn't put her finger on it, but there was something about the guy...

Alex barely touched her these days. Not out of boredom or disgust or anything... their schedules conflicted just enough that sleep was the priority. They still talked and kissed and held each other. They said their I love yous.

Still. She missed being intimate. She missed the anticipation and the exhaustion behind it. She missed the hunger most of all.

Late one night, Carla got up to get some water. Alex, she knew, was in his office. He'd come home late, had some room-temperature dinner, talked with his son for a bit, and tucked him into bed. She went up to watch some late-night TV and fell asleep with the set on. She got up, went downstairs quietly, and saw the light under Alex's office door.

It had been like this for years. They'd gotten into a routine. Five nights out of the week, she slept alone.

She got the glass of water without turning any lights on. She walked over to his office and heard his voice.

Not him talking on the phone or talking to himself. She heard his voice as if it was recorded. Grunting, moaning, breathing heavily. She heard a woman, too, panting. She kept saying, "Fuck me, fuck me."

She heard him say, "I am, I am," and they both giggled.

She stood there for a few minutes, listening. Then she heard it repeat. The same thing. Same noises, same dialog.

Finally, she heard something she recognized. The shuddering breath of Alex coming, and the grunt of a collapse of energy. And then the audio shut off.

Carla moved away from the door then and walked upstairs to their bedroom.

Sleep proved to be impossible.

She said her goodbyes in the morning, to her husband and her son. She waited until she saw Alex's car drive off, waited until the bus picked up Jesse, and she went straight into the office.

She checked his computer. It was password protected, but she knew it. She'd been the one to set it up for him. She had no idea what she was looking for. She looked in random folders for audio or video files. Nothing.

She went over to a wall cabinet, where there was a television and DVD player. Nothing in the tray. Nothing out in the open. She went through the drawers. Nothing.

She looked over at the safe. It sat there, nestled between two filing cabinets.

She had no idea what the combination was.

She started with Alex's birthday. Nothing.

She tried Jesse's. Nothing.

She tried her own. Nothing.

She sat there for a long minute before trying a combination of their birthday months. First hers, then Jesse's, then his. Didn't work. She reversed Jesse's and Alex's. The same.

She tried Jesse's first, then hers, then Alex's. She felt the safe click.

She spun the wheel on the safe and opened it, praying he didn't have it rigged with an alarm.

Inside were two identical briefcases, a handgun, dozens of stacks of cash, files, and three DVD cases.

She popped one into the DVD player and hit play. It was a video of a hotel room. The camera was on a tripod and moved over to a young woman Carla recognized. She was naked and smiling and beckoning the cameraman over.

Carla saw her husband move into frame, get on top of the woman, and start with his mouth between her legs.

She turned it off.

She popped in the second and third DVDs. They were generally the same, and with the same woman. Same hotel room.

The goddamn Holiday Inn.

The woman was Rachel Johnson. She was a teller at the bank. Niece to Mrs. Swensen, who owned the B&B in town.

Rachel was 22, and had been a cheerleader. She couldn't remember why she knew that piece of information. Maybe a holiday party. Or Alex mentioning it like it was fascinating.

Carla felt an immediate impotent rage rise up in her.

She fucking hated cheerleaders.

She put the DVDs back into the safe, closed the door, spun the wheel, and then tugged on it to make sure it was closed.

Carla sat there in Alex's office for a long time before she picked up the phone and dialed.

"I need to see you."

They saw each other from their cars. Carla got out, walked over to the front desk of the Holiday Inn, and got a room. She walked back outside and walked over to Hal's car. He lowered the window. It was October. There was a bit of a chill in the air. It was two in the afternoon. He'd driven up directly after getting the phone call, like a bat out of hell.

"You sure you want to do this?" he asked her.

"Alex has been fucking one of the tellers at the bank. A twenty-two-year-old ex-cheerleader. Yeah. I'm sure I want to do this."

"Okie dokie," Hal said and got out of his Lexus.

"Did you just say 'okie dokie'?"

He looked at her, face blank. "I don't remember."

"Jesus."

They got to the room. Carla's hands were shaking. Hal grabbed the card key and opened the door. He let her go in first.

He shut the door and looked around the place. It was a typical room, two queen-sized beds. "So..." he said, and walked over to one of the beds. Carla was on the other, not looking at him. "How do you want to do this?"

She looked over. "What?"

"Well... I mean. Do you want to rationalize it? You want to just dive in? You want to take a shower first? Flip a coin? Get drunk? Maybe meditate—"

"Hal? Are we going to fuck, or what?"

They laid there exhausted, sweating, breathing heavily. The sheets were off the bed. Pillows were everywhere. Props for different positions. The room had a sweet tinge to it, and something like its own humidity.

"I don't know how I'm going to explain this to him," Hal said.

"Who, Alex?"

"No. John."

She looked at him to see if he was serious. He was. "Wait, what?"

"I keep making excuses, coming up here. My absence has been noted."

"Jesus, you sound like you're married."

"It *feels* like I'm married. The guy is impossible to live with."

She laughed.

Hal chuckled. "Thank God for separate bathrooms. I'd go insane. All he wants to eat is cereal. How do you take someone who wants cereal for every meal seriously?"

"I wish I could have cereal for every meal."

"Jesus, maybe I should introduce you two."

She looked at him strangely. "I've met John."

Hal made a face. "No you haven't."

"Of course I met him. At Woods Hole. Remember? Home schooled?"

"Jesus, that's right. I forgot." Hal laid back and closed his eyes.

"Did more than just meet him," she said. Hal looked over. Carla widened her eyes, then waggled her eyebrows.

"No."

"Yes."

"No way."

"Yes way."

"You... you dirty slut!"

Her mouth went wide and she slapped him in the face.

Hal was shocked for a second, then started laughing.

Carla pushed him off the bed, mock angry. "I'm not a slut. He just... we just..."

"You had sex with my best friend!"

"I didn't know—"

"It's *such* a betrayal."

"Oh, you're *so* dramatic."

"I feel like I'm in a Shakespeare play. Like I should check the room for poison or something."

"Oh my *God*."

"Who's a Shakespeare bad guy? Girl. Woman."

"You just called me a slut."

"In a totally endearing way."

"Keep on being endearing, I'll Lady Macbeth your ass."

"What did she do?"

"I have no idea."

"Just tell me this—"

"You're unbelievable—"

"Was it before or after me?"

"Before."

"Eww!" Hal stood up and started shaking, and wiping something invisible off of him. "Oh, God, I can't even look at you anymore!"

"Fuck you, Hal!"

He grabbed her, laughing. She tried to get away, half pissed, half joking. He kissed her. "No, you don't get to do that," she said, and tried to get away. He put her in a hug. "Stop it," she said, and got her hands in between them and pushed him away.

"Sweetheart—"

"*Sweetheart*?!"

"I was just kidding," he said, and sat on the bed.

"Didn't sound like you were 'just kidding.'"

"It's not like John and I haven't shared a woman before."

"EWW!" She threw a pillow at him. "That's disgusting."

"Why? Don't guys do that kind of thing?"

"No!"

"Really? It seemed so natural."

"I don't want to hear this."

"It's not like we... *we* didn't. I didn't see any... our, hey, look, these..." he pointed to his crotch, "... this... they were never near each other... I don't... I'm not... nu-uh."

"Uh huh. It's funny you think that *that's* the problem here."

They sat across from each other, staring, breathing heavily again.

Something dawned on Hal. "So... holy shit. You *really* don't know who the father is."

She shook her head. "*Alex* is the father. He'll always be Jesse's father. That'll never be in dispute, Hal. Not ever. OK?"

"Of course. Absolutely."

She lay on her side. "I'm hungry."

"I'll order something."

Hal went to the drawers under the television and found a Yellow Pages.

Carla stretched. He watched. Her body was something else.

"You think I'll ever see him again?" she asked.

"Who, John?"

"Yeah."

"I don't know. Maybe. I remember that night. He was fucked up, working on no sleep. One thing's for sure, he won't remember you."

"Now that's just insulting."

For the next four years, it became a regular thing. He fell in love with her about a month in. She did the same. They never talked about Alex.

Hal never suggested that she leave him.

Carla would have never considered it a real option.

CHAPTER FIFTY-SIX

Alex watched as the IRS guy, Miles Dobkins, walked out of the bank with all of the paperwork on Murray's Diner. "Fuck," Alex said. "Fuck, fuck." He made a mental calculation of the people in his life who knew what was going on.

His wife.

Bob Murcer, who'd come into the bank early one morning while Alex was transferring cash from his briefcase to one of Pamela Tully's safety deposit boxes. They had a long talk. In particular, about the bank's video cameras and placement. Bob was a self-taught video editor. Alex told him all he could without naming names, and Bob was strangely OK with it all.

And, last but not least, there was Hal.

That was it.

Alex got on the phone.

"Hello," Hal said, picking up after the fourth ring.

"It's me."

"Hi me."

"We have a problem."

"OK." Long pause. "Who is 'me'?"

"It's Alex, goddammit!"

"Oh. Hey, me. What's the problem?"

"You have to get up here."

"Sure. When?"

"Today."

"I can't do that."

"Tomorrow."

"I can't do that, either."

"Hal, goddammit—"

"What's the problem?"

"It's not something I should talk about on the phone."

"Give me a general idea of how big a problem—"

"The IRS just paid me a visit."

Silence.

"Give me a couple of hours."

"So? What did he say?" Hal asked.

They were at a rest stop just off of town on route 81.

"He wants records of taxes going back to 2000."

"OK."

"Yeah."

"So, what?"

"I don't *have* records for Murray going back that far. I didn't open the duplicate account until 2006. The guy's been in business since 1996. God knows if he has any of his tax documents before I started doing them."

"And this is the first time this has happened?"

"Of course. I got the ledgers mixed up. It was a stupid mistake, I'd been burning the candle at both ends."

"So? How bad can it be?"

"Well, the guy made about a hundred thousand more than he did previous years..."

"Shit."

"Yeah. Now, what I can do is, I can pre-date a loan from the bank for that amount for renovations..."

"OK."

"But the guy, the IRS guy has been to the diner. Murray hasn't touched the place since he opened it. In fact, the only thing that's changed is his waistline. He's still got the same fucking waitress working there, too." Alex didn't look happy.

Hal waited for the other shoe to drop. "What?" he asked.

"It means I have to talk to Murray."

"So? He gets a brand new diner—"

"No. About all of this."

"No you don't."

"Hal, Jesus fucking Christ, man. Would you just look at this from his perspective? He's being audited by the IRS, for money he doesn't know about. If the IRS guy catches on to the fake account, he's going to have the SEC or the OCC investigate the bank. And then we're fucked."

"You said we were protected."

"Fine. *I'm* fucked. Me. I've done everything I can to protect us, but if they come in with a fucking magnifying glass, there's not a single thing they won't find, because they have all the time in the world. I've kept us safe from prying eyes, but the pieces are there, and they're impossible to get rid of."

"What are they going to find?"

"Are you kidding me? They're going to find that this is the most successful small town in the country! Maybe even the world. That's what they're going to fucking find. If that IRS guy starts talking to the businesses around here, I'm fucked. We can't keep it a secret any longer. At least, not from Murray."

Hal leaned back. "So you fucked up."

"I fucked up."

"What's his name? The IRS guy?"

Alex brought out a business card, handed it over to Hal.

"Miles. OK. I'll be back."

"Back from where?"

"Just keep your shit together. Order a milkshake or something, and take your time with it."

Alex watched him leave.

Hal walked outside, went to his car, opened the trunk and pulled out a cell phone, in new packaging.

Alex went to McDonald's and ordered a chocolate shake.

Twenty minutes later, Hal came back with a smile on his face, and a shake of his own. "It's a wonder, you know? You buy coffee, you can't drink it for a while, it's too hot. You buy one of these fucking things, you can't drink it, cause it's too thick. I'd have a stroke if I tried to suck any more than a drop out of this thing right now." Hal took the top off and drank. Some slipped down the sides of his mouth and onto his jeans. "Shit. The perils of food."

Alex just stared at him. "Why the fuck are you smiling?"

Hal smiled. "Miles Dobkins. He works out of the Syracuse branch. Forty years old, two kids, fat wife. I'm not judging, I just saw a picture. And special informant to the D'Escopio family."

"You're fucking shitting me."

"I'm not. He was watching your accounts, flagged it when it triggered the whatever you call it, and came down. Gino knew all about it."

"He... Gino... but... why not just tell me this was happening? Why scare the fucking shit out of me?"

"Why do you think?"

Alex sighed. Color came back to his face. "Jesus, I think I aged about a decade."

"You look it."

"So we're OK."

"You have to amend the return. He'll switch them out. He needs it by tomorrow."

"Of course. Jesus. OK."

"So. Now you don't have to take care of this Murray guy."

"Yes, I do. Murray still got the audit notice. He's going to ask questions."

Hal shook his head, drank some more of the shake. "I don't like it. And I know Gino won't like it either."

"I'd say it's the price of doing business. If he's got a guy at the IRS, then he's definitely got a guy at the SEC and the OCC. The bank purchase would have been under *way* more scrutiny than one lousy tax return. And if we're that covered... one leak isn't going to hurt us. I'll compensate the guy out of my end. But I have to do this. I have relationships with all these people."

Hal tried to stir the shake. The straw was still able to stand straight up. "I'm going with you."

"Hal, Jesus—"

"If he tries to muscle you, you're useless to me, unless I take care of it. Get your shit. We're going. Now."

Murray barely fit into the booth. Hal and Alex sat next to each other.

"Who's this?" Murray asked.

"Business associate," Alex said. "Listen, first off, I'm sorry about the audit."

"You should be. More than twenty years I've been running this diner, not a single issue. Not ever."

"I made a mistake. A mistake that's being corrected. But..." Alex looked around. The place was empty, save the waitress, Betty, who was watching from the other side of the room.

Murray sighed. "You've been running money through my business."

Alex went to speak, closed his mouth. Hal looked at Murray with a half-smile. "Listen, Murray—" Alex started to say.

"Just say it."

"I've been running money through your business."

"Uh huh. And, so, what? Fake account, cash deposits? You tallied up the wrong number?"

"Something like that."

Murray nodded. "I figured you had to be up to something."

"Why's that?"

"Because you own too much. The buildings, the lots. Here? In this town? I mean, I get it. You think I give everything to the government? Fuck no. No one who runs a business that's cash heavy does. Well, maybe some do, but they're fucking idiots. And you've done some good here, so, OK. But... this isn't just you. You didn't buy the bank."

"Why do you say that?"

"Because you didn't do shit the first two years you were here, except work."

"No. I didn't buy the bank."

"Who did?"

Hal said, "None of your busi—"

"Shut the fuck up, business associate."

Hal gritted his teeth.

Alex sighed and put a hand on Hal's shoulder. "I can't tell you," he said.

"Is it cartel owned?"

Hal made a noise.

"No," Alex said.

"The mob?"

"No comment," Hal said, and regretted it.

Murray nodded. "You don't look Italian."

"I'm not." Hal leaned in. "I'm a German Irish mutt, and I work for terrible people."

Murray leaned in. "Are we in danger?"

"Who's we?"

"Me. Betty. Anyone else that this banker roped into this mess."

Hal said, "No. You're not in danger."

"You're certain of that?"

"One hundred percent. Because right now, you're the only one who knows. What you do with that information determines the answer to that question in the future."

Murray leaned back. "OK, then. So? What are you going to do for me?"

"Nothing," Hal said.

"Bull*shit.*"

"Hal, stay out of it," Alex said.

"Yeah, Hal. Stay out of it. This is a town issue, not a... whatever the fuck you are, issue. Errand boy? Muscle? Not much muscle on you..."

"Alex, don't do this," Hal said, getting angrier.

"I've got it, Hal. I'll call you later, OK?"

Hal shook his head and got out of the booth.

"Yeah, *Hal*. Why don't you let me talk to my banker..." Murray said.

Hal went to grab the front door.

"... you just go back to fucking Mrs. Holsfer."

The room stopped.

No one breathed. Hal heard the fans and noises from the kitchen. The popping of bubble gum from the waitress. The creaks in the old leather of the booth as Alex turned towards him. Hal turned and they caught each other's eyes. Both men's faces were stoic.

Hal pushed the door open and walked away.

Alex watched. When Hal was out of sight, he turned to Murray. "Seriously?"

"Yeah. Sorry. I thought you knew."

"Does everyone know?"

"Define everyone."

"Murray..."

"No. Not everyone. Betty's cousin works at the Holiday Inn. Made a big deal out of it until Betty told her to shut the fuck up. Said she saw *you* there too. With an employee."

"Jesus..."

"Hey, what people do in their spare time is no concern to me, and I'm not the blackmailing type. Not really."

Alex wiped his face.

Murray sighed, leaned back as far as he could. "You know... all this? It doesn't surprise me. This town is a joke. And when you came in here with your renovations and all... I still couldn't believe it. You, as a Square John. You acted more like a savior. I know the other businesses in this town. Intimately. They didn't care either. You see what I'm getting at? If things are good, they don't care. If things are only OK, they don't care. If things are shit... well, they start to care. But it takes them a while to build up steam. Mostly, they only care when things happen directly to them. That's not me. You started doing actual good around here. The other businesses, helping people. The loans. You finding a buyer for Farr's gas station. You didn't have to do that. So you get a pass from me. You'd get a pass from them, too, just in case you were wondering."

"Thank you. Not sure you would care about this, but I didn't have a choice."

"No shit. Who in their right mind would seek out that kind of life? Unless you're nuts." Murray jerked his thumb. "That guy nuts?"

"No."

"I guess that's good for you. And me. So maybe you're, what, trying to buy your soul back a bit? Here and there, where you can? What did you do? Kill a guy?"

"No."

"Kill a woman?"

"Jesus, no."

"You owe them money?"

Alex shook his head. "Doesn't matter. Look, I'll give you five percent of what I'm getting."

"Which is what?"

"Two percent per year."

"Fuck that."

"It's all I can give you."

"It's not enough."

"You don't even know how much it is."

"Still sounds light."

"Look, I've gotten you great end of the year returns—"

"Who gives a shit?"

"And... I'll give you a loan to renovate the place—"

"I don't want a fucking loan—"

"—that you won't have to pay back. Hundred grand. I'll make the payments. I'll even find you the contractors."

"I'm sure you will."

"Murray, do we have a deal?"

Murray nodded. "And what about the others?"

"What others?"

"Don't bullshit me."

Alex sighed. "Everyone gets the same."

"And do they know?"

"No."

"Well... I think you'd better tell them, and I'll tell you why. See, that guy might be on your side, to come up here and all... even though he's fucking your wife, he still stuck by you. But the people he works for? Bud... you're going to need all the friends you can get."

Alex got home that night, late. He'd taken Murray's advice and had face-to-faces with everyone whose business accounts he'd duplicated. Ten businesses including Murray's, who joined him. It gave him the courage he needed.

He threw up on the first one. Mrs. Swensen sat across from him, her eyes in shadow, mouth terse, listening, judging. He excused himself and went to the second-floor bathroom. He dry retched for what seemed like an eternity. When he came back down, she was all smiles. "You didn't say there was money in it for me!"

The others went about the same way.

It was around ten when he walked through the doors of the house the mob had bought him. It was furnished with mob money. The food in the pantry and the fridge. The car he drove. The car his wife drove. The trips they took. All of it. Tainted.

None of that compared to his wife sleeping with Hal.

"Hey, honey," Carla said. She was on the couch, reading a *People* magazine. He got a strong sense of déjà vu.

"Hey."

"How was your day?"

He smiled to himself as he threw his coat onto the far end of the couch, and put his briefcase down. "Illuminating."

"How so?"

"Long story. I'm exhausted. And starving."

"I made a plate for you."

"Thank you. How was your day?"

"Business as usual. No one died, so... I'm happy."

"Good."

He walked over to the row of bookshelves and found what he was looking for. He remembered picking it up a long time ago, looking through it, thinking about reading it, and finding the telephone number he used to call in case of an emergency.

He'd thought nothing of it. Two people meeting at a party, exchanging numbers. So much had happened since. She'd never given him a reason to think... well, anything like what they were doing. He picked up the copy of *Slaughterhouse-Five* and threw it onto the coffee table.

Carla looked at it, looked up at him.

"How long has this been going on?"

"How long has what been going on?"

Alex picked up the book and showed Carla Hal's number. "I have had a lot of... well, puzzle pieces come together today. *You* got Hal to give me the money to renovate."

"Yes," she said matter-of-factly.

"Every time there's been a problem... you talked to him."

"Yes."

"God*dammit*. I mean, it was driving me nuts! He knew things he couldn't possibly... I just... my own *wife*. I don't know what this feeling is. It's like, deep in my gut, like a ball of heat. Like a physical reaction to betrayal. That's what it is. You can't imagine what this has felt like, all day, just waiting to come home and confront—"

"I didn't betray you."

"No?"

"No. I'm in your fucking living room. Ten years after you completely fucked our lives up, I'm still here. That whatever you call it in your stomach? That isn't betrayal. It's guilt, you piece of shit."

"I'm the piece of shit? You've been fucking him this whole time."

"No, I haven't."

"Oh *bullshit*."

"I don't have a reason to lie, Alex."

"Well, since when then?"

"Few weeks. Not as long as you've been fucking Rachel."

Alex went to say something, decided against it.

She smiled. There was no humor in it. "Those were some DVDs, boy. You don't touch me anymore, but you masturbate to *them*. That filled me with a special kind of self-worth. Kind of like a hot ball in my stomach."

It hung there for a long time. He'd never felt so stalemated before in his life. "OK. OK. I deserve that." He sat down. "How long have you known?"

"Not long enough, but I should thank you. I never realized that infidelity could make me feel like a human being again."

Alex chuckled and leaned back, closed his eyes. "I'm sorry. I mean, I'm not sorry I did it. But I'm sorry I hurt you. I just..." She looked at him. "Boy, we're going to do this."

"Oh yeah." She sat there, rigid.

He sighed. "OK. Well... the long and the short of it is, I got bored. Bored at home. Bored at work. Things were working, like they've been working for years. The routine and the... I was on auto pilot... *she* was the aggressor, if that makes you feel any better."

"Well, I was the aggressor with Hal. And it felt good. So, I understand."

Fuck.

He looked over at her. "Are you going to leave?"

"No. Are you?"

"No. Why aren't you?"

She sighed. "Because Jesse needs his father. And as much as I hate you for doing this to us, you're good to him. For him." She looked at Alex. "You should know… he's now become the only important thing in my life."

Alex nodded. "Mine too."

They sat there together, on separate sides of the couch, for what seemed like forever.

Alex sat up, grabbed the book and fanned through it. "You know, I've never read this."

"It's good. I think they made a movie out of it."

Alex read the first page. "Cape Cod, huh? Funny. He give it to you?"

"No, I stole it from Brad's family library."

"No shit."

"No shit."

"OK. OK." He stood up. "What's for dinner?"

She stood up. "Lasagna."

CHAPTER FIFTY-SEVEN

"How do you feel?"

It was a year later.

Carla stretched on the hotel bed. Naked, the covers on her lower half, she scratched her stomach and grinned. "Good. This is the wrong word, but... content."

"Satisfied," Hal said.

"That's the word. *Good* word."

"Thanks."

Hal got up and went to the sink in the bathroom. They had plugged up the drain, filled it with ice, and put in a six pack of beer. Remnants of their pizza dinner were on the only table in the room. Hal popped open a beer and came back into the room.

"How do *you* feel?" she asked.

"It depends. Do you mean physically? Mentally? Physically, I feel fantastic. You're the reason I get out of bed and go to the gym. When I go, you know."

She smiled. "That's nice to hear. You've got a pretty good body there."

"Ugh. It's... what was the word you used?"

"Doughy."

"Do these arms look doughy to you?" He raised his arms and showed her his biceps.

"Honestly? You're so pale that—"

"Fuck you!"

"They look like lumps of dough! I can't help it." She laughed. He laughed. Hal sat down on the bed next to her. She traced circles on his back. "And mentally?"

Hal sighed deeply. "Mentally, I'm in a lot of trouble."

"Talk to me."

"I can't. Not about this."

She sighed. She'd heard this from him before. "Sounds serious."

"It is. And I think you'll look at me differently if I told you what happened."

Carla leaned up on an elbow. "You can tell me, if you need to. I know I don't know everything, but I know enough to be a threat to your people."

"You don't have to worry about them. Not now, anyway." Hal finished off the beer. "Let's just say, what happened... I've lost the taste for this."

"For us?"

"No. Jesus. No. What I do. What I'm doing. And I'm not going to be able to just walk away."

"Why not? You've been saving your money, haven't you?"

"Yeah, but it's not that. They won't let me. I'd have to disappear. Like, vanish. New passport, I.D., non-extradition country. Enough money to keep moving. And it wouldn't just be me."

"John?"

Hal made a noise, got himself another beer. "I don't know. Maybe. The guy's like a brother to me. It was a mistake, keeping him out of the loop on all this."

"Why didn't you tell him?"

"It wasn't my call to make. And... it might have created problems. Serious ones."

She held her hand out. He gave her the beer. She drank. "So, if not John, or not just John... who else?"

Hal looked at her. "The three of you."

"The *three* of us?"

"Well, I wouldn't leave Alex here, just holding the bag. I'm sorry all this got as fucked up as it did, but the guy doesn't deserve that, no matter what he did to you. And Gino wouldn't give a shit about the affair. He probably wouldn't even give a shit about Alex telling all those people..."

"You didn't tell him? About Alex talking to—"

"No. Alex has been doing great work, and like he said, it just seemed like the cost of business. I mean, Murray isn't stupid. I suspect the others took it about the same. As long as Alex kept Gino's name out of it—"

"He did."

"I know. I know he did. But Gino's not stupid, either. He would firebomb this town, if it meant wiping the slate clean." Hal leaned back. "So, yeah, the three of you."

"That's very nice of you, Hal."

"Well, it's nice, but it's not like I could afford it. Hopefully Alex has been smart with *his* money, and has a lot of it liquid. Does he?"

"I don't know. He tells me about... well, he used to tell me about general things. Not about money things. He has money in his home safe, but that's probably not his... I don't know. He owns real estate. He gets cuts of businesses... but after ten years. How much is enough?"

"Couple of million at least. Five."

"I don't know if he has that."

Hal nodded. "Well, let's put a cork in that, OK? We're not there yet, and when we do get there... we'll hash it out. You, me, and Alex."

"Won't that be fun. What's it going to take to get there?"

Hal looked at her. "I don't know. I guess a bell that can't be unrung."

CHAPTER FIFTY-EIGHT

Alex was a different person after that night of confessions. Things were out in the open, as much as they could be. He fell in love with Rachel. She reciprocated, as much as a young twenty-something could.

Over the next two years, Alex funneled payoff cash to the businesses in town out of his cut. He didn't miss it. He gave Murray the money to renovate the diner. Murray bought a new six-burner stove with a two-foot by six-foot skillet. New walk-in freezer. New fridge. New fire suppression system at Alex's request. The diner also got an interior and exterior paint job, the windows replaced, and a new sign outside the front door.

What should have cost fifty-two thousand and change came closer to a hundred and twenty thousand—on paper.

Murray was going to buy a new POS for the restaurant. Betty's exact words were, "You buy something I have to start from scratch with, I'll burn this place to the ground."

Betty had gotten a bit cynical after fifteen years of not following her dreams. She'd wanted to be able to speak at least three languages by the time she was thirty. She wanted to travel to every continent, eat exotic foods, make love to men from all the different countries, and study their cultures until she found a place she could call her adopted home. She would, every so often, look back on her life and wonder what she had to show for it. The answer was always nothing.

Alex and Carla worked out a schedule. She took night shifts so she wouldn't have to see him. He welcomed it, and started sleeping in their bed. He was finally getting a good night's sleep. In the morning, he would see Jesse off to school and, if it was a good day, he'd miss Carla completely. Every once in a while their paths would cross with barely a hello.

What brought it to a halt was Carla learning Jesse was having issues at school—with his homework, talking back to teachers, fighting, and generally not being social with the friends he had.

They had a long talk.

"You and dad hardly speak to each other anymore. What's going on?" Jesse had a hard time looking at her.

"Nothing. Just, our schedules are—"

"Mom, cut the shit." He was almost thirteen.

Carla smiled. "Language, all right?" He nodded. "You know, when you have kids, you don't think they'll pick up on things because you get them from scratch, and you teach them everything they know. Or, at least you think you do. But this..." she touched his forehead. "It does plenty of learning all on its own. I'm sorry I lied to you. We're supposed to be honest here. Especially here. Your father and I are just in a rough patch, and we both thought it would be better if we had some space."

"Are you getting a—"

"We're not getting a divorce. We're not."

"Mike's mom and dad are." Mike had been one of Jesse's best friends since the third grade.

"I know. The thing is Mike's dad is an alcoholic. You know what that is?"

He nodded.

"And he does some bad things to Mike's mom. And maybe to Mike. That kind of relationship doesn't last. It *shouldn't* last. What your dad and I are going through... moms and dads don't always get along. They fight, with words. They argue. But they still love each other. We still love each other. OK?"

"OK."

She stood up and grabbed her purse. "I have to go to work, sweetheart."

"Mom?"

"Yeah."

"I want things back the way they were."

She sighed, grabbed him, hugged him, kissed the top of his head. "Me too, baby. Me too."

She put in a request for shift change that night. She was back on day shifts the following week.

Alex and Carla kept their distance. He was back sleeping in his office (he bought a comfortable pull-out). She slept in their bedroom. They were both happy with their alone time.

Mornings, they were both chipper, for Jesse's sake. They got good at it. A switch flipped once he was out the door. It was another détente, this time with no end in sight.

The IRS guy, Miles Dobkins, visited a different business the next year. He audited Farr's gas station, which still had the fake business account. The "owner," Gloria Peligrino, was receiving a small percentage of the profits for doing absolutely nothing. The station was run by some local kids who got a good salary, kept the place clean, and Alex did the rest.

Nothing came of Dobkins' visit except for some sleepless nights. Alex figured it was another warning. Hal confirmed.

"Not really a warning, more like a reminder to not fuck up."

They were at the same rest stop where it all started.

"I'm not fucking up," Alex said.

"Not since, which is good. Think of it as an incentive, nothing more. Gino continues to be happy with your work."

"Fuck Gino. And fuck you, Hal."

Hal nodded.

"I don't need him scaring me like that. Scaring me like that is going to make me do something stupid," Alex said. Fake bravado. Not a bad performance, all things considered.

"No it isn't. You want to blow off some steam, OK. You're not talking to your wife, and all you have is a twenty-three-year-old—"

"Twenty-four."

"Twenty-four-year-old *biscuit*, who doesn't know any better, and thinks the sun rises and sets in your ass... or... how does that saying go?"

"What fucking saying?"

"Doesn't matter. Be angry. Be frustrated. You're pissed at me, I get it. But I never touched her after Woods Hole."

Alex slammed his hand on the table.

"You've got to be shitting me," Hal said. "She didn't tell you?"

"No. And I didn't... she probably just assumed I knew. Fuck. FUCK."

"It was before you were together, man."

"Yeah. Doesn't make me feel any better."

"It should."

"I don't deserve this. To be... *cuckolded* like this. From the guy who owns me."

Hal sighed. "Shit, man. I don't own you."

"Fuck you. You sure as hell do."

Hal thought for a second, nodded. "Maybe." He got up and threw money on the table. "But if you hadn't stuck your dick in the ex-cheerleader, we wouldn't be in this spot. All the way down the line... all of this is on you. So just accept it. Keep being angry, though. With Gino. With me. You'll need it to get by. But also, be scared. It'll keep you cautious. Don't let go of it, or you'll actually make a mistake that'll cost you everything. And that won't be on me, either. Not at all."

Hal left.

Alex watched him get into his car and drive away. He felt trapped. Angry. Scared, yeah.

Fuck you, Hal.

But he knew Hal was right. All of this was his fault.

He signaled a waitress and ordered an ice cream sundae. "Extra whipped cream, OK? I just got some bad news."

Alex kept his head down. He kept fucking Rachel. He kept sleeping in his office, and kept making life at the house a bubblegum kingdom so his son wouldn't be affected. He barely talked to Carla. Even when he was making an effort, it was perfunctory at best. He wished they could still be friends, but he knew he had hurt her deeply. Again.

Jesse was the glue. He always would be.

A year later, Hal would show up in town and change their lives forever.

CHAPTER FIFTY-NINE

Carla watched Hal throw up. She'd seen him shaky before. Nervous. Exhausted. She'd seen him with the flu one weekend where he decided he'd rather be miserable with her than without. She'd seen him bloody, bruised. Drunk, angry. Mostly, she'd seen him happy.

She'd never seen him upset.

He was crying between heaves, leaning his face against the toilet bowl. She gave him two minutes, then got him up on his feet.

She took his clothes off, turned the water on in the hotel room shower, took her own off, and got them both inside when it was warm enough.

She held him for a long time before her fingers started pruning. She got him out, dried him off, brought him over to the bed where their revolving order of junk food dinner was waiting. It was burgers and soggy fries this time, along with a bottle of Johnnie Walker Black. She'd picked them up on the way over, when she got his text.

NEED TO SEE YOU. BE UP ASAP.

"Breathe," she said. He wasn't. His eyes were wide and he was fidgeting.

"What?"

"You're not breathing."

"Of course I'm breathing." He took in some exaggerated breaths. "See?"

"Hal. Calm down."

"Calm down... yeah. Yeah. I, uhh... I'm starving. Even after what happened. Why is that?"

"Because you just threw up."

"That makes sense. Maybe I should eat something."

She poured him a drink. "Drink."

"On an empty stomach?"

"It'll settle your nerves. Then maybe you can stop scaring the shit out of me."

He looked over at her. He hadn't noticed the entire time he'd been there that her face was a mask of concern.

"Sorry. I'm sorry." He drank. "I just... I had to do something that I... I didn't want to do. But I didn't have a choice."

"OK. Whatever it was... I mean—"

"I shot someone."

She swallowed hard.

"A couple of people, actually. But not Maria. I made pretend... you know, like a firing squad, where you hope you've got the blank, you know? I just... I knew there wasn't a round in the... but I might as well have shot her. I didn't have a choice."

"Who's Maria?"

He shook his head, finished his drink. "There's video tape of it." He got up and walked to his bag, pulled out his laptop and opened it.

"I don't want to—"

"Yes, you do!" he said, too loud. He took a deep breath. "You do. You keep asking me what's happened, what's wrong. I'm going to show you. I'm going to show you and then, if you can still stomach looking at me in the face... we're going to get the fuck out of here. All of us."

Three days prior.

Hal stood in Gino's office. It was cool, dark. Gino was in a vest, dress shirt, tie, smoking a cigar.

"Want one? Arturo Fuente. Very nice. I'd offer you a Gurkha, but it's not that kind of occasion."

"No thanks."

"What is it? You're not a smoker?"

"I'm not, actually. Never appealed to me," Hal said.

"But it's not going to bother you if I smoke?"

"Of course not."

"Glad to hear it. Sit down."

Hal sat.

"I've got a problem, and I need your help."

"Shouldn't John be here for—"

"It's not that kind of problem. I don't need someone driven somewhere. Or a fake car planted. Or whatever the fuck else he does around here. No." He sighed. "What I need from you is... to convince me that when the time comes, you'll do what I need for you to do."

"With who?"

"Your friend Upstate."

"Alex?"

"Yes."

"'Friend' is stretching it..."

"Uh huh. Well... see, if this ever goes south, any of this? All of this? I need to know you're going to help clean it up."

"OK."

"So I need you to go to Jersey and help Sabbatini out with his daughter and her piece of shit boyfriend."

"For fuck's sake..."

"Listen. We did all we could. I got word it's going to happen again, and Genovia's had enough. You go out there, you follow his lead. But we're at the extreme-prejudice point of their relationship."

"You... you can't be serious."

"I am. This is how you prove your loyalty. I've never had a problem with you, Hal. Or John. But you know more than most. If I don't have you here..." he touched his vest pocket, by his heart, "then I don't have you at all. Not like I need you."

"Gino, listen—"

"This is non-negotiable. It has to happen. This is softball, if I'm being honest, but it'll do, for what I need it to do. Settle concerns. For all of us. After, you can tell or not tell John... he's had enough experience with this fucking bitch and that figlio di puttana. Everyone's sick of it, so, OK. Get it done."

Hal set up the video. He poured them both a drink. "Maria was the daughter of Genovia Sabbatini, an old-school mob boss who spends most of his time in Alpine, New Jersey. The Palisades. He's semi-retired, does the odd consulting. His daughter, who's always been his pride and joy, had consistently gotten into more and more trouble ever since high school. Genovia wanted to believe it was a combination of her knowing who her father was, and just being a teenager. The fact is he couldn't accept that she was a serious liability.

"Over the last two years or so, her boyfriend, Manuel, had gotten her to support his lifestyle. Heroin, meth, coke, strip clubs, some armed robbery. The guy was a walking cliché. She did it by basically guilt-tripping her father. John and I intervened a few times with the boyfriend. Beatings, threats, driving him out of town. In fact, that time I came up here, I told you I did something? I had to... well, I broke his arm. With a hammer. Like the one they used to kill cattle with."

"Jesus," Carla said, and put her drink down. "This is too much reality for—"

"Listen, he was a stupid kid. Useless, really. Still, it didn't sit with me at all. Genovia, this sweet guy... the soft spot he had for his little girl knew almost no bounds. He said very specifically 'hurt, but don't kill him.' We all thought he'd gotten the message."

Hal pressed play on the video.

"So, Manuel takes three of his friends to her house when he thinks the old man isn't home," Hal said.

The video was split into four screens, showing multiple camera angles. At first, they showed a van pulling through a gate, traveling down a five hundred foot driveway, and up to an enormous three-

403

level house. New angles showed a Gothic Revival style, built in the late 1800s. Floodlights lit the place up like a museum. Massive trees surrounded it on all sides. Palatial was the word.

The four videos disappeared. It was just one camera now.

The van pulled up towards the back of the house, stopped outside of a three-car garage. On the outskirts of the video was the shimmering of a pool.

The driver got out of the van.

"Oh, fuck," Carla said.

"Yeah. Like a robbery. Ski masks and everything."

"Guns?"

"Oh yeah."

She looked at him. "So it was them or you. Why do you feel so—"

"Just… just wait. So there were three waiting in the van. Manuel went into the house alone, right? Twenty minutes he's in there."

"Twenty? For what?"

"He raped her."

"Oh God."

"Yeah. Cameras in the house were… it was awful."

"Well, then fuck him," Carla said.

Hal nodded. He and John had seen surveillance tapes of her "getting kidnapped" by her boyfriend in the past. He'd drag her out of the house half-heartedly, his friends waiting by a car or a van, like they were lookouts. They'd leave and get high somewhere. She'd call and say some crackheads were holding them hostage, and her father would "pay" ransom money. It had become a biannual occurrence.

After the first time, Genovia installed the security cameras to make sure it never turned into a real kidnapping. He even put one in her bedroom, hidden.

One night, after John and Hal had delivered a ransom to some empty building in Jersey City, Genovia explained to Gino, "She's my daughter, for better or worse. What am I supposed to do?"

Gino told him what to do, in front of Hal and John. It was a particularly brutal suggestion.

Genovia shook his head and changed the subject. He didn't care the two were bleeding him dry.

"Watch," Hal said.

It was a high angle, above the van. Three guys were outside, pacing. All had guns.

"What the fuck is taking so long?" Man One.

"Probably fucking her." Man Two.

Muffled screams coming from somewhere. Manuel came into frame, carrying a woman over his shoulder.

"She's a good actress," Man Three said, who went and opened the sliding side door while Man One went to the passenger-side door.

"Never fought this much before." Man Two.

"Yeah, well she didn't know I was coming this time," Manuel said, and dumped her into the van.

Maria screamed. "Fucking asshole! I—"

Manuel punched her in the face.

"I can't watch this," Carla said.

"It's almost over," Hal said.

"The fuck are you doing?" Man Three.

Manuel grabbed Maria by the hair, said to her, "You know what I can do. I already did it once tonight. You don't shut the fuck up, I'll give each one of these guys a turn."

"Wait, what?" Man One.

"Dude, what are you talking about?" Man Two.

"Shit, we broke it off months ago." Manuel punched her again. "Doesn't mean she's not still my meal ticket." He shut the sliding door and walked around to the driver side. There was a flash of white off camera. Manuel's chest exploded. He was lifted off his feet, slammed into the van, and landed on the ground.

Blood glistened in the floodlights like rain.

Blasts rang out as the other men got shot to pieces.

The van rocked back and forth. Maria screamed from inside.

The guns stopped.

An old man came into frame holding a shotgun. Two large men walked behind him. One of them pointed a shotgun into the face of Man Two, fired.

The audio peaked, squelched.

Hal walked over to them, shotgun in hand. He wracked the slide on the shotgun, ejected a shell.

"Oh, Poppa!" Maria screamed as Genovia slid the door open. She rushed out and hugged him. "I didn't do it this time, Poppa, I swear it!" She buried her face into her father's chest and started crying.

Genovia said something. It was impossible to hear.

Hal said something. It was ignored.

Maria stood up straight and wiped her eyes.

Genovia backed off. She watched, eyes wide.

"Poppa!"

Genovia looked at Hal.

All four men raised their guns and shot her.

Carla noticed only three blasts.

Carla covered her mouth. "He killed his own daughter?"

"He fucking obliterated her!" Hal closed the laptop, hard.

Carla shook her head. She was sweating. She wiped her forehead. Her palms came away slick.

"Genovia's not even going to the have a funeral, and you know how they are about that kind of thing. Maybe you don't, but they're fucking serious about it." Hal walked to the bathroom, shaking his head. He washed his face. "And on top of it all, he was wrong to boot!"

"He didn't see the footage from inside the house, did he?"

"No, he didn't. Gino made sure of that."

"Oh my God..." Carla turned away, took in a deep breath, let it out, and finally heard what Hal had just said. "So how did you know he was wrong?"

Hal came back wiping his face. "One of Genovia's men, Fernando, went to see Gino the next day. He'd been working for him for about three months. Fresh off the boat. Friend of the family."

Dark in Gino's office. A tensor lamp was the only light in the room. Fernando was drinking a glass of something strong, for his nerves. Gino was sitting behind his desk. Paulie Grasso was behind Gino, as was Hal, who'd been given a 9mm with a silencer. It was pressed against his leg. His fuck-up with Maria hadn't gone unnoticed.

Fernando was sitting there crying his eyes out.

Hal related the story.

"This guy, he starts telling Gino how he was in love with Maria, that they were planning on getting married, and he thought she was pregnant and how he knew that the kidnapping wasn't planned because Maria had stopped seeing Manuel..."

"You did good, coming here," Gino said. "You told no one?"

Fernando was so upset that when he shook his head, his whole body convulsed. He looked at the glass he was holding. It became his whole world in that moment, as if he was coming to some profound realization.

He didn't see Hal bring the gun up.

The glass broke in Fernando's hand and it took him a second to realize that he'd been shot in the chest. It all happened in slow motion. His breathing became difficult. Pain spread out from the wound to the tips of his fingers, down his legs, his toes tingling. He looked up, his vision narrowing to the barrel of the gun just as the second shot hit him square in the forehead. His body was propelled to the other side of the room.

It made a considerable mess.

Hal lowered the handgun. He was pale. Sweating. His bottom lip was trembling slightly. He could see Paulie looking at him out of the corner of his eye.

To keep his mind off of what he'd just done, he unscrewed the silencer.

Gino shook his head. "What a waste." The chair was ruined. His wife was going to be pissed. "Next time, just the one shot, OK, Hal?" He didn't bother to look at him.

Hal asked, "What?"

Paulie patted him on the shoulder. "One shot, in the head. Maybe the neck, but that's a big fucking mess, unless you just sever the spine, but kid, you ain't that good a shot."

Hal nodded. "OK."

Gino looked at the body, looked at the spray of blood on the carpet. "Do what you can about that. If I have to fucking replace this carpet again..." he finished his drink. "And get rid of him," Gino said. "For good."

Hal sat there a long time. "I can't tell if I can feel you judging me... or if it's just me."

"I'm not sure," Carla said, and grabbed the bottle of scotch. She drank straight from it. "So, you had to kill someone, so that when the time comes, you'd come out here and you'd kill Alex. And presumably me."

He turned to her. "I did it to make sure that *I* was the one he *would* send. I did it to protect you. And him. And Jesse." Hal got up. "And John. That's the part that's going to be tricky."

"Hal, what are we going to do?"

He looked at her. "You're still with me?"

"Yes."

"You're sure?"

She stood up and grabbed one of his hands. "I am."

He nodded, kissed her. "Well, we have to go talk to Alex. I've got a plan."

They finished off half the bottle together and made love that night like they were making a pact. She kept her arms and legs wrapped around him as long as she could. He held her around her back, and stayed inside of her well after they were both finished.

They ate room-temperature food after, and watched some late night TV, both of them thinking instead of watching. They fell asleep with the set on, the sound off.

In the morning they had breakfast at Murray's diner, and, when they were ready, they went to talk to Alex at the bank.

Hal walked in first. Alex was nowhere to be seen. He turned to Carla. "You know, I never got to say it, but you did a great job with the place."

"Thanks. I couldn't have done it without—"

"Get the fuck out of here," Alex said from across the bank.

Everything stopped.

Hal walked over to him. "Alex, listen—"

"I said get the fuck out here." Alex snapped his fingers at the security guard. "Gerard, do your job." He pointed at Hal. "You. You don't come here, to my place, my bank, and—"

Hal grabbed Alex by the tie and lifted, choking him. He used his other hand, grabbed Alex's arm, twisted it around his back, and walked him to his office. "We've got this, Gerard. Have a seat."

Gerard looked at Carla, who nodded. He sat down.

"Everything's fine, everyone," Carla said. "Fine being relative..." she followed them into the office and closed the door.

Hal threw Alex against his desk. He landed and pushed most of what was on it onto the floor. "Who the fuck do you think you are? And coming here with her? That's an especially nice touch."

"Yeah? Which teller are you fucking?" Hal asked.

Silence in the room.

"It's the brunette," Carla said. "The really attractive one." She sighed and sat down. "I know it's a bit self-serving, but at least you have good taste in women."

Alex looked at her, smoothed out his clothing. Stood up and went toe-to-toe with Hal. "What the fuck do you want?"

409

"We need to talk, Alex... and you have to listen to me."

Alex got even closer. "Why the fuck would I ever listen to you?"

Noses almost touching.

Carla got between them. She put her hand on Alex's chest, jerked her thumb towards Hal and said, "Because *he's* the guy that Gino is going to send when he wants you dead. Now would you just listen to him? He's got a plan."

Alex looked at Hal a long moment, went around the desk and sat down.

Hal sat down in a chair across from him. Carla stood and refereed. Hal talked for half an hour.

Alex was incredulous at first. It all sounded ridiculous, when everything was going better than expected. Then he started asking questions. The more Hal talked, the more worried Alex became.

When Hal was done, the three of them sat there for a long while before Alex said, "OK. I'm in."

Hal was relieved.

Carla was relieved.

Alex was feeling threatened and cornered and guilty and angry. He didn't trust either of them, but knew he didn't have a choice. It was a good plan.

But none of it worked the way it was supposed to.

PART V

Last Piece of the Puzzle

CHAPTER SIXTY

By the time John got back to Brooklyn, after the Sherborn bank robbery, after the Nova at Dean's, after stealing the Cutlass and driving back home, it was evening, with barely any sun left in the sky. Traffic was a bear down the FDR, and then over the Brooklyn Bridge. He took the boulevard to Atlantic, made a left, took that to 4th Avenue, which was bumper to bumper, and finally made a left onto 25th street in Greenwood.

Theirs was a massive brick building sandwiched in the middle of the block, the D'Escopio family's old warehouse–distribution center. Gino had told them all about its history, from using it during prohibition, to storing and running rations, munitions and surplus to the Brooklyn Navy Yard throughout World War II.

It was a shipping and storage hub for imports throughout the late 40s and 50s. It then remained empty from the 60s until the early 70s. The building got an overhaul when Gino's Uncle Emilio, on his mother's side, decided to get into the porn industry in 1973. They'd used it for distribution and production. In the 80s it was also the central hub for the D'Escopios' cocaine trafficking. The business got shut down in the early 1990s, when the mayor and NYPD moved on the porn and sex industry in the city.

Again, it was left empty.

Emilio moved out to California, kept the business up for a few years, sold off his share once the internet became the bastion for porn, and retired in Santa Monica, spending the rest of his days on the pier, enjoying the sunshine.

Developers had tried to buy the building from Gino and Vincent for years. Vincent always vetoed it. "Why get rid of something we own free and clear, when we might need it in the future?"

How Hal and John came to use the building was, they spent a lot of time at the beginning of their partnership streamlining routes for pick-ups and drop-offs, both in the city or across state lines. Drugs, money, stolen goods. All of it. Gino had business interests in Miami that used the Gulf to funnel drugs from Mexico and all points south. Cash would flow from New York, back to Miami, to the Bahamas.

For years, Gino's contacts in Florida had been using different methods to try and outfox the DEA, local law enforcement, and the FBI. Mostly in trucks, up I-95.

Pre- 9/11, the trips had been easy. Or, at least, easier. Post-9/11, there were still people to buy off in the DEA, but it was getting dangerous, and expensive. Gino said they were losing twenty percent of their shipments. Most were just random stops anywhere along the super highway. Some were racial profiling. The majority of the drivers were Cuban. Even with clean I.D.s, one out of every five was getting picked off. Gino's partners in Miami simply had no gift for quality control when it came to their drivers.

"Solve it," Gino said to them. "Show me what you're good at."

Hal and John knew trucks weren't the answer. They started working the run from Miami to Queens without any contraband, in weighted-down, souped-up cars. They pushed speed limits. They found hole-in-the-wall motels they could stop for the night. They located every small gas station along the routes they tried, back and forth, over and over. They found parking garages that had no attendants. They found self-storage companies that had units that would fit cars. They did research online for speed traps, located every local police station, and found which municipalities were more corrupt than others. It took them three months to figure out the best possible routes back and forth up the east coast.

The trips were murder.

When they were confident to move forward, they interviewed and hired a few drivers from New York City. Six guys who were tangential to Gino's drug business.

They trained them. They gave them burner phones, along with contact numbers guaranteed to work. They insulated Gino from them completely and used false names whenever they were in the room. They gave them cars and had them transfer baby laxative or oregano the first few times, as tests.

They watched them from afar.

The drivers ended up not being half as cautious as Hal and John had hoped. Even with the full understanding of their cargo and its ramifications, some drove high or drunk. Some drove all-nighters, which made them erratic. Half of them had *Smokey and the Bandit* on the brain, and it cost them. Four were arrested fleeing police vehicles. Two of the four had drug charges stick due to lack of cooperation, even though they had no drugs in their cars. The other two were cut loose, but were so radioactive, John and Hal abandoned them.

Of the two that went to jail, one was killed in prison during a race riot. John and Hal picked up the other, Craig Gilroy (who liked to be called Gilly), when he got released. Craig said, "Just make sure you get me a faster car this time. Some more horse power and I woulda made it, boys."

Clearly there were no hard feelings.

With their first plan a bust, John and Hal regrouped. They figured they couldn't make all the runs themselves. Not with the weight Gino wanted to bring in. And not without going insane. So they sat down and figured out a new plan.

They kept on Gilly and found new drivers. Better drivers. Freelancers out of Miami. Hotrodders who loved the challenge of an open road, but who loved the sun and women more.

The freelancers were set up like relay racers up and down the East Coast. Whatever they were moving, they'd change cars and drivers every four hundred miles. Sometimes in a garage, sometimes out of a storage unit. Drivers were responsible for their cargo until the switch, and gave updates every two hours via text. Texts were also sent after a successful hand-off. With speed and routes a constant, John and Hal knew where everyone was, on any particular run, down to a few miles.

They were tested for drugs twice a month like clockwork. No one gave a shit if they smoked weed. Anything stronger, drivers were cut. They were given fake cargo every other week that was tracked, just to make sure there were no unnecessary stops or cutting of product. And they were all paid very well. Now, instead of losing twenty percent of their shipments, they were down to around eight percent. More than half of those losses were abandoned cargo, due to a funky feeling on the part of the driver.

John and Hal stressed caution above all else. Caution of Gino. Hal laid down the law. "You leave a car because of a feeling—OK. I get it. Make a habit of it, though, and no one will ever trust you again. We'd rather you get arrested and do your time than keep dumping your cars because you keep having a 'feeling.' That's the job. Get me? Just keep your head on straight, keep your mouth shut, and we'll take care of you."

Most of the time, the cargo was left alone and they were able to retrieve it. Every once in a while, someone got cute. Got rid of one GPS tracker, but not the backup. They'd steal the cargo and keep the car. It would get reported up the chain, and that person was never seen again.

When John saw the plan was taking off, he went to Gino one evening, had dinner, bullshitted him, and got ushered into his office to talk business. Gino poured them some drinks.

"We want to make your delivery guys safer, right? And so one of the things they're going to need is a collection of clean vehicles," John said.

416

"A collection? The fuck do you mean, a collection?"

"Well, I—"

"Jesus. I miss the old days when you could just steal a car, use it, wipe it, dump it. I'd even leave the keys in there, and someone else would take it for a ride. I knew guys who would share the same stolen car to get back and forth from *work*. Never got caught. Can you fucking believe that?" Gino asked, and sighed.

"If the average haul is worth five million wholesale, the cost of the car is inconsequential. But now we're using more cars, more drivers. We'd be using trucks, *but* they stick out—"

"I know—" Gino said and put his hands up.

"And they're easy to spot, easy to pull over—"

"You're giving me a headache here."

A week earlier, a truck got pulled over with $1.2 million in cash, headed for a yacht in Miami. The yacht was going to a bank in Nassau.

The truck was also filled with stolen appliances, headed to a discount store owned by Gino's partners in Flagami. Gino didn't mind his guys stealing whatever they could get their hands on, but he had a policy of not re-selling it in New York City. "Makes it too easy on the cops," he said.

John didn't mention the irony.

Every once in a while, Gino's guys sent down a truck filled with the stolen merch. His Miami partners loved it, and gave a good percentage. They'd been doing it for a few years and Gino had figured, why not kill two birds, and put a deposit in with the goods. John and Hal had tried to talk him out of it.

"What are the odds that this one truck gets pulled over? Come on guys, let's have just a little faith, huh?"

The truck got pulled over after it missed a weigh station. The driver just hadn't been paying attention. When the cops asked him to open the back, he panicked, and it showed.

Once he was brought in, once the police confiscated the truck, its contents, the cash... the driver, Kenny Something, rolled over and ratted out the buffer immediately. He'd been looking at twenty years for multiple counts of grand theft and said, "Fuck that noise."

He didn't even call the lawyer John and Hal provided to all the drivers.

The truck was traced back to a shell company with no connection to the store or Gino, who hadn't been worried about the ties, or the buffer, or the driver. He knew John and Hal had taken care of that side of things.

He was angry about the money, and the lack of loyalty. A month later, Kenny was murdered in prison by one of his fellow inmates.

"Don't these guys know one way or the other that we take care of our own people? Jesus." Gino downed his scotch.

"They know now." John had been there when his drivers were told. It went over as well as expected.

"Pssshhh," Gino said and poured himself another drink.

"The thing is... I've got an idea."

"You with the ideas."

"I want to start stealing twenty-year-old cars."

Gino sat there looking blank, like he hadn't heard John correctly. "You want to what now?"

"We change the plates, do a quick paint job... no GPS devices onboard, right? No electronics or software to track. We do our own upkeep, Hal and me... think of it as a series of fake I.D.s, OK? But for cars."

"Fake I.D.s for cars." Gino looked only half convinced. "The way your mind works..."

"If there's a problem, we have Dean, right? Need a decoy, or a drop car? Need a duplicate to confuse the cops—"

"All right, all right. I get it. So you need a what?"

"Well, money—"

Eye roll. "Uh huh..."

"—and I need a place to store the vehicles. A lot of them, so... a big place."

Gino gave him an address out in Greenwood, gave him a set of keys, too.

John took the R train out to 25th street in Brooklyn and found the place half a block away. It was a massive building, all brick, dirty, wire mesh windows, some of them boarded up. A big loading dock with an elevator that was more than forty feet long, twenty feet deep. He giggled when he saw it.

He unlocked the front door and saw a massive staircase that went up all four flights, with landings on each floor.

The ground-floor space was gigantic. He paced it, both directions. It was roughly a hundred feet wide and almost two hundred and fifty feet long. It had two-foot round concrete columns every twenty feet or so. Large oval-shaped industrial lamps dotted the ceiling. Not completely useless for what he had in mind.

The second floor was heaven. Half of it had columns supporting the upper floors. The rest was completely open. He could barely see out the windows. Concrete everything, and last stop for the elevator, which would fit two cars simultaneously. The entire ceiling was covered in banks of fluorescent lighting.

He started calculating costs for renovations.

The third floor was half the size of the first two, and full of abandoned distribution equipment. Shelving, conveyor systems, tables. He could dump a third of it and the space would still be bigger than his apartment.

He imagined an armory and a shooting range. Just in case.

The fourth floor was a massive loft, completely open and empty.

He wiped one of the windows with his hand. Most of it was salvageable. Put up some walls, add some plumbing, a kitchen.

Definitely big enough for two.

Hal saw it and swooned. It was an enterprising criminal's dream come true.

They spent a few weeks working out what the place should be for their needs, and then went to work.

A year later, it was up to code for a commercial space, with central air and heat on the top floor. They brought in contractors for water and sewage. They fixed up the bathrooms on the first, second, and third floors, and had two new bathrooms and showers built on the fourth, along with a full kitchen. They had sheetrock walls put up for two separate bedrooms. They had an electrician come in with all new wiring to make sure the place could take the juice of a full garage (first floor). They had half of the third floor soundproofed for a gun range.

The second floor was left as is.

They had an elevator guy come in to make sure it was in good working order, and had him check it twice a year.

Even though the two of them had their own places, their own lives, women, and other responsibilities... they spent most of their time at the garage.

Over the years, they made security improvements.

John drove up 25th Street and stopped outside the loading dock. He typed a code into a security system that was arm's length from the driver-side window, and waited as the garage door opened. He drove the car into the elevator and dialed for the second floor.

And then he heard it.

Piping through the speakers on the fourth floor and echoing through the open elevator shaft was Donna Summer's "Dim All the Lights."

"You've got to be fucking kidding me, man," John said. He was exhausted, he didn't want to deal with this disco shit, and how the fuck did Hal beat him home?

Scenic route my ass.

As the elevator crept upward, the music got louder.

Thirteen years since they got the place ready, the second floor had become almost a museum for every type of car they might ever need, ever.

In the back next to three wooden crates was his baby, Blue.

John drove the four-door just beyond the elevator, turned off the ignition and left it there. He'd do a prep on it in the morning. He grabbed the duffle bag with the money and the shotgun, walked up the two flights to the top floor and could hear Hal singing along to the music.

He didn't smell any food cooking. Fuck.

"Was that a four-door?" Hal asked, standing in the kitchen, eating a bowl of cereal, moving his hips back and forth.

"That better not be the last of the milk."

"It's not."

"It better not be."

"It's not."

John went to the fridge. The milk was gone. "Goddammit."

Hal smiled, started making like Travolta in *Saturday Night Fever*. "You want the leftovers?" Hal showed him what milk was left in the bowl.

"No I don't want the fucking... yes, it was a four-door."

"Great. Domestic?"

"Every time, you do this."

"A Cutlass?"

"Yes, goddammit! And what the fuck is it with this music?"

"I love this music," Hal said, mock offended.

"You're trying to kill me with it." He dropped the duffle.

Long pause. "That too."

Hal's mom, Cookie, was a regular on Soho GRAND, an NYC public access music and dance show that was trying to get some of those *American Bandstand* dollars, from 1976 to 1982. When she couldn't find a sitter, Hal would join her at the studio.

He'd watch her in the crowd or on stage and try and mimic her moves. Her best friend, Vespa, was a six foot two Black woman with an enormous afro and the world's most perfect skin. When Vespa wasn't on camera, she was taking care of Hal.

Hal had no idea who his father was. Cookie would, from time to time, delve deep into her memories for the names of men she knew around the time she'd gotten pregnant. She'd end the conversations with "Honestly, sweetheart, it could have been anybody."

She'd listen to music whenever she was home. He learned to live with it and, after a while, love it.

Cookie died when he was seventeen.

Vespa stayed in his life best she could, but Cookie's death hit her hard. It would take a decade for him to realize his mother and Vespa had been lovers.

Vespa would overdose a year and a half later in a motel in Secaucus. A month after that, Hal was drinking with his cousin Ben, who got to talking about his sister. She'd just gotten out of the hospital, a week after her boyfriend had broken her jaw.

On a whim, Hal called a friend asking to borrow his car. The two went to Prospect Heights, got the keys, got in, and drove out west to help her.

Hal moved over to the oven and opened up the door. He grabbed a bag and threw it to John, who caught it. The smell of hamburgers wafted up to him. His mouth began to salivate.

"You're lucky," John said, and ripped the bag open.

"Uh huh." Hal tilted the bowl into his mouth, drinking some of the milk.

"What's on the agenda for tomorrow?"

"Not sure."

"Well, good. I'm exhausted. Goodnight." John walked to his bedroom.

Hal pointed at the duffel bag. "Is that the money?"

"Yeah."

"I'll take care of it."

"Fine."

"You're eating in bed?"

"Absolutely." John shut the door.

Hal sat there and sighed. "Kids."

John opened the door again. "And lower the music!" He shut the door again.

Hal put the cereal bowl in the sink, smiled, went over to the stereo and raised the volume. He grabbed his cell phone and walked down the four flights to the street, closing the side door to the building behind him.

He pulled up Carla's number and texted her: *You OK?*

He waited for a minute. The return text indicator started moving.

She wrote back: *Not really. Alex didn't come home.*

Hal read it and sighed. "Shit." He started typing again, stopped. "Shit!" He sighed, wrote back: *Jesse OK?*

She wrote back: *He's OK. It looks like he got punched in the face.*

Hal shook his head. "Goddammit."

He wrote back: *I'm sorry that happened.*

She wrote back: *It's OK, he'll get over it. What are we going to do?*

Hal rubbed his face, texted back: *I'll take care of it.*

She wrote back: *Well, what should I do?*

He wrote back: *The usual. Go to work. Don't make people suspicious.*

She wrote back: *OK. What are you going to tell John?*

He wrote back: *The truth.*

She wrote back: *Really?*

He wrote back: *Well, the parts that matter. Goodnight. See you soon.*

She wrote back: *I love you.*

Hal smiled and texted: *I love you, too.*

He put the phone in his back pocket and walked over to the 24-hour deli, bought a half-gallon of skim milk and walked back home.

He looked at their building and sighed.

He was going to miss it.

CHAPTER SIXTY-ONE

"He *what*?" John looked like he barely slept. He stood there in his boxer shorts, scratching his chest.

"Yeah. The manager of the bank, the one we stopped the robbery of yesterday? Yeah, he went missing."

"Are you fucking kidding me?" John made a frustrated noise. "He just... I mean, was he kidnapped?"

"Don't know."

"Jesus fuck, Hal. Come *on*, man. It's a shitty bank in a shitty town and in no way shape or form does it have anything to do with—"

"Gino owns the bank."

John went to talk, closed his mouth. Went to talk again, decided against it, and walked to the fridge. He opened it, closed it without looking. "There's no fucking milk."

"There is. I bought some last night."

John opened the fridge, got the milk out, dumped out an enormous bowl of cereal, poured in the milk, put the milk on the counter, sat down and sulked while he ate.

Hal had spent the night concocting the story for John. He felt it had to be the perfect combination of truth and vagueness. As much as Hal was sure John cared about him, he wasn't sure how John would react to the real plan. Or how long he'd kept the truth from him.

Hal walked over and grabbed the milk, put it back into the fridge. "Listen, Gino called me, told me the details. He's got a guy on the inside at the bank, watching the manager—"

"Watching the manager what?"

"Jesus, man. It's a money laundering operation."

"Oh."

"Yeah. I helped Gino set it up a long time ago."

"Wait, what?"

"Yeah."

"You set it up without me?"

"Don't be offended, OK? That was all Gino. At the money level—"

John sighed. "He gets weird."

"He gets weird. Right. Gino had the new money coming in from Brooklyn—"

"Right."

"And Miami was stretched to the gills—"

"I got it."

Hal relaxed. "OK. So, Gino bought the bank up there and put this guy in charge. I guess some other outfit found out because... well, with the guy missing, I guess it wasn't just a regular bank robbery."

"No shit. Fuck. Well, I hope he is just missing and not kidnapped. I fucking hate kidnappings."

John and Hal's first kidnapping was with some guy who was kinda sorta tied to an associate of the Sabbatini family, the cousin of a guy who knew a guy, or some shit. A friend of a friend of a cousin of a roommate...

Gino got the call.

A father took his kids out of school without their mother knowing. They were in the middle of a nasty divorce and it looked like he was going to lose custody.

John and Hal tracked the guy down through an associate of Gino's at Citibank, via credit card purchases. Found them at a motel in Huntington, West Virginia. Been there two days. Hal and John figured the guy was on his way to his mother's, who lived in Oklahoma.

The kids were a boy, four, and girl, six. Gino said, "Don't hurt the guy if you can help it. At least, not in front of the kids. In fact, you find them, you let local law enforcement take care of it."

John said OK.

Hal nodded, didn't say anything.

They took a Ford Thunderbird out. John had found it on his way back from seeing a movie, sitting in a parking lot at the mall in Newport, New Jersey. His mother had owned one a long time ago, and he got nostalgic. It drove well enough, fit them both comfortably, and didn't stink of cigarette smoke, like a lot of the cars they'd stolen over the years.

"You've got that look in your eyes," John said, peeking over at Hal, who was just watching the road. It was getting late.

"I don't have a look in my eyes."

"Yeah, you've got that 'I have to save them' look."

Hal made a noise, like, *please*.

John shook his head. "I hate that look. Means you're going to do something stupid."

"I'm not."

John made a noise, like, *please*.

Hal looked out his window. "I'll stay in the car."

"You'll... what? You'll stay in the... the fuck are you even coming for if you're going to stay in the car?"

"Well, you seem to have this magical ability to see into the future..."

"Goddammit," John said.

It wasn't the first time they'd had this conversation.

"And all of a sudden, you know every single thing I'm going to do. I mean, my God, what a burden that must be for you."

John turned the rear-view mirror in the direction of Hal. "Look at your face!" John said. "You—you're gritting your teeth!"

"Because I want to punch you."

426

John rolled his eyes, moved the mirror back. They drove in silence for a while. They were in Rio Grande, Ohio, if you can believe it, and were about an hour out.

By the time they got there, they were talking again, and had figured it would be a no-brainer. Sure. The kids would be asleep. It was 10 p.m. The father would want it all to go down quietly.

They pulled into the Huntington Cottage Motel.

"You want to talk to the desk clerk, or should I?" John asked as he parked.

"I don't know. What do you see happening?" Hal put his fingers to his temples, like Kreskin. "Do I kill the guy? *How* do I kill him?"

"Jesus," John said. *It's like we're married.*

Hal shrugged. "I don't want to kill anyone tonight. Except maybe you."

"Fuck you," John said and got out. He grabbed a baseball hat from the back seat and shoved it down hard on his head, lowered the bill. He went to the desk and waited for a minute until the kid behind the counter finally paid attention to him. John didn't bother looking up at the ceiling. He knew there was a video camera.

"Yeah," the kid half-asked.

John tried on his best southern accent. It was a mixture of something you'd hear out of a bad Western and, for some reason, partly Jamaican. "Yeah, I'm a friend of Kyle Griffen." He inwardly groaned as he heard himself speaking. "Told me he was staying here, I just forgot the room number. And the phone number."

The clerk behind the counter didn't give a shit. He was watching wrestling on a small portable TV with the volume turned way up, three empty soda cans and a bunch of bags of chips lying around. He said, "Room 12," and pointed in the direction of the room in a very vague way.

John said thanks and left, discouraged by his accent abilities, but thankful Hal hadn't heard just how awful it had been.

Hal might not have killed the kid, but he would have definitely beaten the shit out of him.

427

He started walking towards the room. Hal got out with his own hat, fastening brass knuckles onto his hands.

"What the fuck?" John asked.

"What?"

"The fuck are you doing with those?"

"Just in case."

"In case of what? The guy works at a Radio Shack!"

"You never know."

John shook his head. "No, no. We're supposed to see if he's here. If he is, we call the cops. Gino said—"

"Gino's not here."

"Hal, come on man—"

Hal stopped and grabbed John by the arm. "God knows if this guy is on drugs, if he's got a gun, if he's drunk, if he's abusing those kids. Right? We don't know. You have to be a crazy motherfucker to steal your own kids. So, *these* are just in case. You get me?"

John was never sure if Hal had always been the White Knight type, or if he'd just gotten a taste for it after the subway incident. It wasn't that John didn't appreciate Hal's disposition, he knew his heart was in the right place. It was just that it had gotten them into trouble more than once. "OK, OK. But we're just looking, right?"

"Just looking."

"OK. You... you gonna hold my arm the whole time?"

Hal looked at his hand holding John's arm. He started moving the hand around. "Wow."

"Stop."

"You been working out?"

"Jesus," John said and pulled away from him.

"Those are some quads."

"Quads are in your leg you dumb fucker!"

"Well then your arms are as strong as your legs."

John rolled his eyes, tried to ignore him. He'd found that, whenever Hal knew he was wrong, he cracked jokes.

They got to room 12. The lights were on and the curtains were drawn.

John watched the parking lot, checked the other rooms to see if they had privacy. Not a soul was stirring. "How the fuck are we going to do this?" John whispered.

"I don't know," Hal whispered back, and went to one of the windows and tried to peek in. "Maybe we should—"

At that exact moment, that exact second, the curtain was pulled back by the little girl, who saw Hal and screamed.

Hal screamed, too.

John covered his face with his hands, shook his head. The noise was unbelievable.

The girl backed off and the curtain fell back in place.

Hal looked over at John and started laughing. "The fuck are the odds—?"

A gun went off. Once. Twice. Straight through the door of the room. Hal and John hit the deck and scrambled for cover.

"I told you he had a gun!" Hal said as they got behind a concrete pylon.

"Are you seriously telling me you told me so?"

"Yes!"

"We have to get out of here," John said and made a run for the Thunderbird.

Fifteen minutes later, the entire parking lot was swarmed by police officers. John and Hal watched from down the block. They sat in silence for a long time.

John leaned up against the steering wheel, peeking over it. "All we had to do was find him and call the cops. That's all we had to do."

"Well, we did that. Basically," Hal said. He was eating one of the leftover sandwiches they'd brought with them. He looked over at John. "Right? I mean, technically, they're... well, they're here." He pointed at the cops.

They left soon after. Dumped the Thunderbird, wiped it down, and stole a 1986 Buick Regal that was in decent shape.

The standoff lasted fourteen hours. It made national news the next morning. A reporter from CNN tied the Sabbatini family to the kidnapping.

Gino didn't speak to them for a week.

John shook off the memory. It was the second worst kidnapping job they'd been asked to help on. "Help me out here, Hal. You're giving me nothing. What are we walking into?"

Hal made with spooky hands. "The unknown…"

John just looked at him.

"Yeah, OK. Sorry. Look, the guy's family called Gino's inside guy and said he never came home… So Gino called and said we had to find him ASAP." Hal shook his head. He was trying to keep his lies straight.

"So, what? We're fucking detectives now?"

"If it makes you feel better to think of us as detectives… I guess."

"I don't like this."

"What's to like?"

"Well, we're going into something completely unprepared. A rival family, maybe? Bank robbers… and one of them is a kid, for chrissake. So does that mean guns? Half of the cars down there aren't retrofitted for a gun job. I'll need something with pick-up. The Nova's gone…"

Hal made a face, rocked his head slightly back and forth, thinking.

Fake thinking.

"Bring Blue," he said.

"What?"

"Yeah. Bring Blue. That'd make you sort of prepared…"

"Bring my baby Upstate? Ha! No. Hell no. Fuck no!"

Hal chuckled.

John stuffed his mouth with cereal. "There is no way I'm bringing her Upstate."

CHAPTER SIXTY-TWO

John drove Blue up I-88. He grumbled, cursed under his breath, kept a single hand on the wheel while he clenched and relaxed the other.

In the years since he first took Blue out, after the Irishman, John drove the car twice a year like clockwork. Once in the summer, and once in the winter. He'd take a few days off, pick a direction, and leave town with a cooler full of food, beer and some pocket cash. He'd find spots along the way and stop to marvel at the beauty of the countryside, whether it was natural or industrial or whatever. There was always something to appreciate.

The only other times he took Blue out was when the job required her.

Over the years, he'd turned the car from its original (rebuilt) condition into something more tactical. He replaced the original engine in 2005 with a 5.7 liter Hemi, and squeaked out 24m.p.g. up from 14 or so. He'd removed the back seat entirely and added a custom-made fuel reserve tank. Full up, the car held 48 gallons of gas, giving him a max distance of about 1,100 miles without stopping.

He'd been inspired to do so by all the traveling up and down I-95 and found that stops always presented problems. Even the necessary ones. He simply didn't trust everyday people.

The car had a police scanner. He kept a satellite phone in the glove compartment, along with a med kit in the trunk.

He added three antipersonnel measures that were controlled by a panel where the ashtray used to be. Tacks, oil slick, and fog. Real James Bond like. The fog never, ever worked, so he'd doubled up on the tacks.

The tires were self-healing, to a point, and reinforced with TAC Runflats. The windows were bullet resistant. The doors and sides of the car were reinforced with Kevlar panels, double thick around the extra fuel, which was encased in three-inch ballistic acrylic. The windows were tinted grey.

Under each seat were a 4-D Maglite flashlight and a collapsible baton. In the panels on both the driver and passenger doors were hidden compartments for handguns. They were rarely used.

He'd toyed with the idea of a nitrous system, but decided the extra weight in the car would've been too much, shredding the tires, pushing the TACs through asphalt. Not to mention the amount of liquid explosives in one vehicle.

The first time John and Hal took the newly re-enforced car out on a job, they went from Pittsburgh to Atlanta on a single tank, with room to spare. They drove through four states.

They had trouble in Kentucky.

John was managing a double cheeseburger from McDonald's, driving with one hand, as half a dozen patrol cars followed them down route 65 outside of Elizabethtown. "Don't eat all my fries," John said as they watched a deputy yelling at them from outside the passenger window of a white and tan.

"They're our fries," Hal said.

"You didn't want fries. Just because they're in the one bag doesn't mean they're 'our' fries."

"I paid for them."

"I said I'd pay you back," John said. Through the rear view mirror, he saw one of the patrol cars drop out.

"Where are we at?" Hal asked.

John looked at the dash. "Almost empty. You might want to—"

BOOM.

A car ahead of them fishtailed hard. John saw their tires were completely blown.

"You put them on?" Hal asked as he braced.

"Jesus, man, it's Sunday..."

"John!"

The car went over a strip of spikes, laid out by a deputy who'd gotten ahead of them. Blue went over them with only one pop. It took John a second to coax the car back into its lane. The TAC tire helped her stay true.

Behind them, two patrol cars hit the spikes and ended up on either side of the road. The remaining four braked, spread out, went around the spikes, and caught up after a minute.

"Please," John said, looking in the rear-view.

"OK, OK," Hal reached into the back seat. He turned a lever and spun a small wheel. Gas started siphoning into the tank. John watched as the gauge went from E to full. "Wow," Hal said.

"What?"

"No, nothing, man, just there's almost a third left out of tank two."

"No shit? We're going to have to see what it's like without the weight."

This had been going on for half an hour.

It all started outside of a McDonald's when Hal hit on a college girl who had big tits and pigtails. When she laughed in his face he asked her what her brother's dick tasted like.

"This fucking guy," John said and chuckled, bringing their food into the car.

The guy standing next to her was, in fact, her brother, who'd gotten a push in when Hal spun around and connected with his throat. The brother went wide-eyed and grabbed his neck hard, fell to his knees. Hal kneed him in the face and let him drop to the concrete, gasping, bleeding, his sister screaming and crying.

Hal turned around, pleased with himself, until he realized the brother and sister weren't alone. Half the restaurant emptied out as Hal got into the car, gave them all the finger, and John drove out of the parking lot.

"Happy?"

"Sort of," Hal said, and grabbed a Big Mac. He'd ordered two. "More starving than happy."

Ten minutes later and they were being asked to pull over. They kept tabs on the situation through the scanner. A deputy called for back-up and said they were going out of their jurisdiction. The sheriff said, "All of Kentucky is my jurisdiction today!"

It was one of those rare times, like a movie, were John and Hal turned to each other and smiled.

"I'm glad we stopped for food first," Hal said. The irony was not wasted on him.

"Yeah, well, the next thing I have to put in here is a catheter."

"Just use your cup, then dump it out the window like a fucking normal person—Jesus."

"And what, you're going to aim for me?"

Hal made a face, thinking about it.

"We're not that close, motherfucker..." John said and looked around.

Cop cars pulled up to them on both sides.

Sheriff Jack Fielding drove with his long-time friend, Deputy Sheriff Stoney. They'd come up together twenty years prior and prayed for days like this.

"Who the fuck *are* these guys?" Stoney asked. His window was down, looking at the Charger's tires. One had what looked like a metal ring. The Charger wasn't going very fast, around 45. It must have been weighted down with something because Holcomb had tried to PIT them. So did Deputy Cecil. Both times, the driver anticipated the maneuver and got out of it. That's when they'd called in the spikes.

"Grab that party pleaser out the back," Fielding said.

Stoney turned to Fielding wide-eyed. "What? You can't shoot at them, Fielding." Fielding looked back at him, not fucking around. Stoney shrugged. "Well, you can, but—"

"The wheels, you fucking dumb shit. Shoot the wheels. We'll just have to see what happens."

Stoney grabbed a Remington 870 shotgun out of the back and smiled.

From the radio: "Sheriff Fielding, you still on him?"

"From the beginning. What, those spikes get you, Manning?"

"Heh, no sir, I'm out of gas. I had half a tank... wasn't even looking. Been driving so long, I don't even know where I live."

Fielding looked at his gas gauge. Didn't like what he saw.

Stoney looked in his rear view. There was only one more patrol car following them. "Jack, you think maybe we should get some help from the locals? They might not appreciate—"

"No, we take care of this *now*. *I'll* deal with the locals," Fielding said as he glanced at the dash. He brought them up parallel to the Charger.

Stoney entered a shell into the chamber.

John saw the deputy come out from the window with a shotgun. "Seriously?" he asked.

"He *said* pull over," Hal said, and laughed, spraying food all over the dash, the windshield.

"That's disgusting, clean that up."

"I'm cleaning, I'm cleaning." Hal cleaned it.

John watched as the cop pointed the shotgun at the wheel. "Is it going to take that?"

"Hard to say," Hal said, mouth full of burger, smiling. "Depends on the slug. Probably should've tested it."

"Probably should've...?" John swerved a bit to throw the cop off balance. As he did, the cop car rocked away and Deputy Sheriff Stoney held on for dear life.

"Goddammit!" Stoney said as he grabbed the door. Fielding pulled the wheel and straightened the car.

"Get that sonofabitch," Fielding said as he positioned them again.

Stoney set himself, pointed the shotgun at the wheel, took a deep breath and adjusted his finger around the trigger... and saw the Charger pull ahead of them. First slowly, then very quickly.

"What the fuck are you doing?" he asked and turned to Fielding, who was clenching his jaw, clenching his hands around the steering wheel. His knuckles were so white Stoney thought he was going to snap it in half.

And he did.

Coughing sounds from the car. It stuttered a bit and coasted to a stop in the middle of the road.

"Oh fuck," Stoney said and sighed.

"Say one word. One word... you won't even be able to *walk* home," Fielding said. He stared straight ahead as he watched the Charger drive around a bend and out of sight.

It was a bright memory for John. He smiled, driving in the middle lane, as snow-covered trees flew past on either side of him.

When they would reminisce and share the story with others, they both told it with little variation, save one. As they drove away, one of them said "You know... one of these days, we have to try this in reverse."

They never agreed on who said it. They *both* agreed it would be a terrible idea. From there on out, whenever they got stuck in a jam, someone would always say "we should drive out of here backwards." It always got a laugh.

By the time he got into town he'd already had enough. It was like the place, the people, were stuck in a Norman Rockwell painting. The world had passed them by and they didn't even care.

The streets were basically clean. Rock salt kept smacking the undercarriage and dinging off the sides, the windows. "My baby," John said, whenever there was a particularly loud hit.

The cars that drove past him were ordinary. Nothing flashy or high-end. He stopped at a light and saw an abandoned strip mall that hadn't been renovated in twenty years, minimum. The signs, the exteriors. It felt like a regression, as if he'd passed through a barrier that took him back in time.

It depressed the hell out of him. He decided to watch the people instead.

An old man holding a door open for a woman with a stroller.

OK, that happens.

Two Boy Scouts helping an old lady across the street.

Uhh...

Two men drinking cocoa while looking under the hood of a 50s model Ford pick-up truck.

Come on.

Birds chirping. In the winter. Like he was in a goddamn Disney film.

A fire engine passed him on the left. There was a Dalmatian sitting in the cab.

"I fucking hate this place," he said, and drove Blue the speed limit through town. Stopped at another red light.

An old man walked across the street with a cane. Step. Step. Cane shaking. He turned to John, smiled, waved. John hunkered down a bit, embarrassed. Waved back, just over the dash.

How long have they been asleep? He wondered. *How long will they stay asleep? is the better question.*

He followed the guy with his eyes and noticed, across the street, a store that sold medieval clothing and weapons called *By The*

437

Sword... A fluorescent sign in the window screamed, "We also sell LARP gear!"

John shook his head. *OK, not completely asleep...*

He looked up and saw that the light had been green and was turning yellow, then red. "Fuck," he said and looked through the rear-view mirror. There were cars behind him. None of them had honked.

He opened the window and stuck his head out. "Sorry!" he said to the woman behind her. Two teenage kids with her, sitting patiently.

"Everything OK, young man?" she asked.

Oh God.

"Fine, thank you!" he said and closed the window.

He kept both eyes on the stoplight.

CHAPTER SIXTY-THREE

John felt fine until he reached Berman Street, and then suddenly he was very sleepy. He pulled into the large driveway of a two-story house. Swensen's Bed and Breakfast. He'd found it on Google. The price was reasonable, the rooms looked clean enough, and the woman who ran it had posted photos of food she cooked. He was sold.

John parked, got out of Blue, grabbed his go-bag from the passenger seat.

Before he'd left the Brooklyn garage with her, he put the kid's shotgun in the trunk, in a false panel on the left. God knew if he was going to run into him again, but he figured there was true sentimentality about only a few things in life. Family heirlooms, cars, women, and guns. It had been empty, like the kid said, which suggested a lot of strangeness about the whole thing.

Next to the spare was a small black box of audio and GPS transmitters he'd brought just in case, along with a med kit, a container of tacks and a bottle of engine oil for replacing the antipersonnel measures. Hal had suggested he bring them all.

"Seriously? It's Nowheresville man."

"Hey, you never know," Hal said as John was about to leave the garage. "Might be more than a kid with an empty shotgun up there."

John shut the trunk, walked around to the front of the B&B and went inside.

The owner greeted John with a quick introduction, and then proceeded to tell him her life story. She was Mrs. Swensen, widowed, lived in Sherborn all her life. Owned the place for over thirty years with her husband until he died in his favorite chair of a massive heart attack while she was asleep upstairs. She found him in the morning, where she normally found him, and didn't think anything was wrong until almost noon.

"Honestly, he'd sleep there all hours, I just assumed..." she looked off into the distance, motioned her hand with a flourish. "Well, anyway, I swapped out the chair, so..." she said to John as she gave him the tour. He nodded politely.

The place smelled like an enormous spice cabinet.

Mrs. Swensen was solidly built. A bit heavy, some grey in her reddish hair, which looked straight out of an Andrew Wyeth Helga painting. Large bosom trapped in a tight button-down shirt and covered with an apron that curved just right. She was in her late fifties, and he had a hard time not admiring her body.

Chest. He had a hard time not admiring her—

She had glasses on, plus a long, form-fitting skirt, brown shoes, and for some reason he was getting an erection without her giving him a second look.

"Dinner is at six. You let me know if you'll be here, I'll make sure there's a plate for you."

"I'll be here," he said, trying to adjust his pants.

"You a vegetarian?"

"No, ma'am."

She looked at him. "None of that ma'am nonsense. Mrs. Swensen will do."

Every word out of her mouth woke his cock up more and more.

"Yes, Mrs. Swensen." He felt like a schoolboy.

She nodded, turned and left.

He watched her go.

Mrs. Swensen hadn't always been John's type. In fact, she technically wasn't. She was his teenage self's dream come true.

His first girlfriend had been five foot one, an artsy smoker Goth type who drove a beat-up hand-me-down Ford Grenada. The car was too big for her, but she handled it like a pro.

They ended up never having sex.

It was their senior year in high school and she broke up with him just before the summer started. They were going to schools on opposite sides of the country, and she said pursuing the relationship wasn't worth it. He thought, at the time, that he was in love with her. It took years before he'd realized it was first-love, and not really real.

His second girlfriend, Trissa, she was older than he was by seven years. Smart, funny, a talented dancer, who just couldn't find any work. She spent most of her time doing odd jobs here and there, along with shifts at a dry cleaner's.

Their first date was him cooking dinner at her place and watching *A Clockwork Orange* on VHS. He stayed the night. No funny business until he woke up to her kissing him and then mounting him, and she took his virginity at the age of twenty.

They were together for a year. He broke up with her because he thought that he was missing out on not having been with other women. He came to regret the decision.

From there a string of women who were completely wrong, not so wrong, just OK, OK, pretty good for him, or almost perfect.

Until Caroline.

He'd met her at a bar that had been converted from a Turkish bath on the Lower East Side. He'd been playing pool and she was with a group of friends. A ladies night out. One of them, Rachel, had put quarters on the table to play, and they'd started talking.

He got invited back to their table, got introduced to them all, bought a round of drinks, and after a few minutes of trying to be entertaining, found he only had eyes for Caroline.

She was one of those women you knew where you stood with her at all times. Good or bad. She didn't have a filter. Not for bullshit, anyway. She kept a lot of her thoughts to herself, unless you were invited in. She was a realist from the get. "Don't confuse realism with pessimism," she said one night. "If the outlook of something is bleak, then it is what it is, no matter how you look at it. And, if it's negative in its nature, then how can that be pessimism?"

She suffered from depression most of the time. She was five foot seven, blonde hair, same age as John, in reasonable shape that was just a natural occurrence, and would look at him with eyes that were warm, inviting, and with a full understanding that she had his number, completely.

She was a chef who worked at a small restaurant down in the East Village. Partnered up with a friend of hers out of culinary school who couldn't hack the kitchen, but understood front of house very well. Megan. Caroline was her kid's godmother. They were close.

Caroline and John were together for four years. She knew what he did and didn't care. She loved his adopted brother, Hal. She met Gino twice. She told John that twice was enough. It didn't take long for John to have real excuses for her absence from Gino's social gatherings.

She had both breasts removed after two years together, something she'd always figured would happen. It ran in the family. She told him straight that if her having breasts was more important than what they had going, she'd leave, no problem.

It was the only time he ever got angry. It was the only time he ever called her stupid.

She'd look down at her chest and remember what had been, and wonder exactly what defined women. As a species. "Maybe I should just get rid of the rest. Then they'll have to come up with a new name for what I would become."

In the beginning, she'd stay up at night and worry about what it would feel like. Being eaten from the inside. It was hard to talk to her when she would bring things like that up. "Don't tell me to stop. It's what's happening to me!"

She would exhaust herself with her anxieties. He just had to ride it out.

442

Doctors were optimistic. Said they'd gotten most, and the chemo would take care of the rest. Three months of adjuvant treatment, with the throwing up and not eating and her hair gone (she'd shaved it before the chemo). And then into remission.

Things were back to normal for a long time. Just not long enough.

Hal and Gino gave him space when it came back.

She spent less time at the restaurant. Got there for rush, supervised mostly. Spent a lot of time reading and drinking tea and trying to sleep. After a week of insomnia, John got up, put his clothes on and said let's go for a drive. She owned a Volkswagen Phaeton. Caroline loved to shop for vegetables, spices, meats and fish and cheese outside of the city. The restaurant tried to do mostly farm-to-table. Mostly. Hence the car. He would take the West Side Highway all the way north, loop into Inwood, come back around on the FDR. By the time they'd passed Randall's Island, she'd be snoring. He did the loop two, three times, depending on how hard a day she'd had.

She'd ridden in Blue a couple of times. She loved that John loved her. But the sound, the rumbling... it didn't help her sleep.

For those last few months, she was too exhausted to do much of anything but be a spectator. The last trip to her oncologist, the scan showed it had metastasized to her lungs. They'd given her six weeks. She made it two months, and died in her sleep at home on a rainy day in March.

John had just given her a cup of tea he knew she wouldn't drink.

He'd been single ever since.

Sure, here and there he'd had a hanger-on of Gino's, or some woman he'd picked up from a bar or during a job, some crime groupie who thought danger was fun but really had no fucking idea at all.

He never felt dirty after. He knew Caroline would understand. But after a while it became exhausting to even try to meet women. She'd been the love of his life, and he didn't want that to change. Ever.

Now, Mrs. Swensen reminded John of Mrs. Bonner, who was his boss at the public library he worked at after class in high school.

Slightly thinner frame, same sized chest, the glasses, the hair, the air of authority, the mannerisms, her no-nonsense attitude. Hers was the first tit he'd ever felt.

By accident.

He'd been putting books away in the fiction section and she'd come up to give him some more returns. He hadn't been paying attention and turned to grab some books off the cart and... well, there you go.

Both were sufficiently embarrassed. John had masturbating material for... well, he still had masturbating material because of it. Word got around to the other library pages and he became something of a god.

After, he'd kept his distance, and she kept an extra eye on his hands at all times.

Dinner that first night was a full roasted chicken that had been placed in the center of the table with a reception of oohs and aahs. The dining room was full of guests. A couple from Ohio visiting friends in Manchester, New Hampshire, who decided to make a stop in their sleepy little town. A father and son from Rhode Island who were headed to Lake Erie for the fishing. A young guy who was on his way to Canada to see his girlfriend, driving up from Kentucky. Mrs. Swensen would later tell John that she thought "a girlfriend in Canada" was code for seeing whores up in Ottawa. "Or drugs. Could be drugs. Never can tell about people."

Mrs. Swensen cut the chicken up, doled out mashed potatoes, green beans, corn bread, gravy. John had two helpings, kept mostly to himself save for a polite nod here and there and left after the father and son called it a night.

He got into Blue, which was still parked near the back of the house, and decided to get the lay of the land. Pulled out of the garage, made a mental coin flip, took a left, made a phone call. "I need a nap. It's this place..."

"Yeah, yeah," Hal said. John had the car rigged for Bluetooth. He could hear the smile in Hal's voice. "It's not that bad."

"The Ingalls were bad. I mean, that was a farm, you know, with, with small pox or whatever. Here, they have running water, at least."

"See?"

"Probably still have small pox, though."

"That, or polio."

"I feel old here. That's what this place is doing to me. Making me feel old."

"You are old."

"I already *took* two naps today. Two!"

Hal chuckled.

"This Mrs. Swensen makes a mean chicken, though."

"Too bad she's a Mrs."

"I think it's more like an honorary title. The first thing she said was the story of her dead husband, as soon as I walked in the door. Remind me to tell you about it." John took a right and drove through a dead street. All the shops were closed except for a Chinese restaurant. The Long Wok.

"I'm sure it's a whopper," Hal said. He sounded bored.

"This doesn't end well for you, you know?"

"Do tell."

"Me doing the shitwork. I'm racking up favors."

"I'll take my chances."

"The fuck aren't you here, anyway?"

"Aww, it's nice to be missed. I'll probably be up by Friday, so don't worry."

"I wasn't worried."

"Well, you should have been at least a bit concerned."

"Not really," John said, and took a right. Another dead street.

Hal coughed. "Uh, Gino told me to have you look around the banker's house, talk to the family, that kind of thing. I sent you up a file. You get it?"

"No." John grabbed his phone and saw the email icon that was linked to their secure server. "Yeah. I mean, no. I mean, I see it, I haven't looked at it."

"You were too busy eating Mrs. Swanson."

"Swenson," John grated. But the thought remained.

"Swenson, OK. How's she taste?"

"Jesus." He pulled over and opened the file. One of the documents was an image of a man in his mid- to late forties. White, fake tan, fake smile. Alexander Holsfer. "Holsfer? Herr Holsfer. Germans in Upstate New York. That's great. It's the new Argentina."

"Yeah, well if you ever find him, make sure you click your heels or whatever the fuck you're supposed to do."

"Jawohl," John said, and scanned another document. "Who saw him last?"

"His son. Said he saw him about noon."

"So, before the robbery."

"Yeah."

"All right. And this guy is what, a friend of yours?"

"He's not a friend. He's just a guy. What's with all the questions?"

"Nothing, just... you know, it sounds like you don't know a lot about this case, do you? And it's starting to worry me."

"Well, don't worry. All *you* have to do is find the banker." He sounded frustrated. There was a click. Hal had disconnected.

"Seriously? What the fuck..." John asked as he scanned the landscape.

Still dead.

CHAPTER SIXTY-FOUR

John got back to the B&B, made a cup of tea in the kitchen (guests were allowed to do that), went to his room, opened the Holsfer file on his laptop, and read.

Alexander Holsfer was born in Philadelphia to a tax attorney and a stay-at-home mom, Charles and Helen. High School, Bachelor's from Temple University, got his CPA license no problem. He became an accountant, mostly corporate. In the early 2000s he moved to town and opened the bank, presumably with Gino's money.

Married, one kid, Jesse. His wife, Carla, worked as an RN. No pictures for either.

He drank some tea, leaned back, and felt exhaustion hit him. It was 11 p.m. He shook his head, let his eyes droop, and fell asleep.

He dreamed of engine noises and the shudder of exhaust.

John left early the following morning, skipped breakfast with Mrs. Swensen and the other guests. He drove past a five-and-dime and bought a local newspaper.

He found a diner nearby, newly renovated. Formica, round stools, checkered pattern on the floor and up the walls here and there. The waitress had her hair in a bun and a birthmark just above her lip on the right side of her face. The cook was the kind of guy who both lived for it and hated it.

Must own the place, John thought.

It was half empty, smelled like a combination of pancakes, rice pudding, cinnamon, hamburgers and coffee. Like every diner, ever.

Working-class types here and there. Locals. One family with well-behaved children.

He sat down and waited for the waitress, who was busy with a check. There was a ding from the pass. She went to the line, came around the counter with two plates of food, dropped them off and walked up to John. Her badge said Betty.

"What'll it be?"

"Well, a menu... to start?"

"Ever been in a diner?"

"Yeah."

"What'll it be?"

"Uh, French toast, home fries, coffee, and a large glass of milk."

She didn't bother to write it down. "Sure thing," she said and walked away. Got to the line, barked it. A grunt from the cook.

John opened the paper and took a look inside. The front page was a feel-good story about City Hall. Second page was about construction outside of town and how long it was taking. Big scandal.

Third page was an ad for a place that was kind of like Macy's, but not.

Fourth page, fifth page, sixth page.

No sign of Holsfer.

No sign of the bank robbery.

The waitress brought over his cup of coffee and a small metal pitcher of milk. He fixed up his coffee, went back to perusing.

By the time he got to the end of the paper, he knew who the mayor was. Donald Hayes. His family had been in town four generations. There'd been a Hayes in local politics for seventy-five years.

That was about it.

He skimmed the paper until he found what he was looking for. Their office address.

Another ding from the kitchen.

The waitress brought over steaming food on a plate that looked like every other plate he'd seen at a diner. Thick china, weird pattern around the edges, hot to the touch. The food looked good.

John spread some butter on his French toast. It melted instantly. He dumped syrup on it. He slammed the bottom of a ketchup bottle, poured it over his home fries, dusted it with pepper.

His first bite was French toast and some home fries and ketchup.

"Oh my God," he said, and chewed. And chewed. He finally swallowed and let the heat move down his throat, the flavor just sit in his mouth a bit.

After a while he chased it with some coffee.

John got the check, paid and left. He turned up the collar on his coat, which did almost nothing against the cold wind, got into Blue and turned the car over. He sat there for a few minutes until she warmed up.

He punched in the address for the paper's office into his phone, and followed the map until he was outside a three-story brick building he'd seen before.

He arched his neck and saw that it was about four hundred feet away from the bank.

"Well, that's disconcerting," he said, and parked. While the sky wasn't as clear as the day of the robbery, the people, the cars, the businesses, and the cold all seemed identical.

He got to the building and opened a glass door that lead straight to stairs. The door had a logo for *The Sherborn Caller*. Under it a sticker that read *Proudly Serving Chenango County since 1918*.

John walked up to the second floor where there was another glass door with the same logo and sticker. He went in.

Keyboard clacking noises was the first thing he heard. He smiled at what could only be described as the false nostalgia of a newsroom. His mind almost instantly harkened to *All the President's Men* for some reason.

Walls had blow-ups of articles and front-page headlines. Ceiling fans were moving at full speed, even though it was chilly in the office. Beige-colored woven shades were half pulled down, blocking some of the sunlight.

A woman with big glasses, grey hair in a bun, was working on her computer at the front desk, hunting and pecking at the keyboard. She noticed him, smiled, went back to the computer, like showing him she could do two things at once. "Can I help you?"

"Uh, hi, yeah. I was wondering if it would be possible to see back issues of your newspaper, say over the last three days."

"They're available for purchase," she said, and pointed towards a revolving stand near some empty chairs.

John walked over and skimmed dates. He found papers for the last three days, walked back over to her with them and dropped a twenty.

She looked completely put out. "I don't have change for that."

"Uh huh," he said, lost in thought. No mention of Holsfer on any of the covers.

"You might want to go to the pharmacy down the block, see if they can change it for you."

"Sure," he said, and kept reading. Page after page. The same ads in every paper. Same writers. Feel-good stories. The Wednesday issue had a larger classified section that seemed to draw ads from as far away as Buffalo.

Not a single mention of the disappearance. Or the robbery.

The woman was looking at him. "Sir?"

John looked up. "Yeah."

"I don't have change."

John nodded, grabbed the papers. "Keep it," he said and went to leave. He stopped, thought for a second, turned and walked back. "Just… I'm sorry. I'm just wondering why your paper hasn't written a story about the bank robbery? Or Alex Holsfer going missing."

Instantly, the place went quiet. People turned to look at him. They all looked spooked.

The old woman turned towards the other employees, as if looking for help. Then she started adjusting things around her desk, without looking at John. "P-pardon me?"

"Well, he's... I mean, he's a big deal here, right? Owns the bank...?"

A man came out of one of the offices to the right. White shirt with blue stripes, red tie, navy slacks and tan shoes. John inwardly groaned.

"Something I can do for you?" he asked. He was about fifty, with a belly and a hairpiece.

"Uh, not sure. Just wondering why your paper hasn't done a story on Alex Holsfer's disappearance."

"Are you a police officer?"

"No."

"A reporter?"

"No."

"A member of the Holsfer family?"

John rolled his eyes slightly. "No."

"Mind telling me what your business is with the Holsfers?"

"Yes, I do." John looked around the room. The people were definitely spooked. "A guy goes missing, his bank is robbed right down the block and..." he waved the papers around. "Kinda strange, right? Especially since they heard about it all the way down in New York City."

A woman gasped. John looked in the direction, but couldn't tell who it was. For some reason, he held his breath.

Spooked going on flat-out scared.

"We don't know anything about that, mister," the guy said. "Now, if you wouldn't mind, we're on a deadline." He looked into the bullpen. "Back to work, all of you." The guy waited until the clack, clack, clack of typing began again. He looked at John, nodded, and went back into his office.

John breathed out, took another look at the papers in his hand, opened the glass door and left.

CHAPTER SIXTY-FIVE

H al opened up the freezer and looked at the stiff body of the man Alex had killed. Miles Dobkins. Even dead, the man looked like he worked at the IRS.

The freezer was in a storage park outside of Poughkeepsie. Gino kept the place year round, just in case.

The sides of the freezer were covered in polyethylene sheets, so the body, or bodies, didn't stick. Hal put some gloves on, reached in and grabbed the guy's legs.

His phone started ringing.

"Are you shitting me?" he asked, and pulled the guy's legs so they were sticking out of the freezer. He grabbed his phone, saw it was John. "Yeah?"

"I stopped by the newspaper."

"The what?"

"The local newspaper."

"OK."

"They didn't run a story. Not on the robbery, not on the missing banker."

"Huh, that's strange."

"Are you fucking kidding me?"

"I'm just saying. You'd think they would have written a story about the town's only banker—"

"Goddammit!" John said, and paused dramatically. "Hal."

"Yes?"

"What the fuck is going on?"

"What do you mean?"

Hal could hear John was driving. "You know what? I don't have fucking time for this Mickey Mouse bullshit. I'm heading back into the city."

"What?"

"Yeah, fuck this job."

"John, Gino wants to know—"

"Oh, bullshit! The guy's not even fucking missing!"

Hal moved away from the body. "You don't know that."

"No, you're right. I don't, but I can use my fucking brain and make an educated guess, which I'd lay ten to one odds-on, for chrissake. No word from kidnappers. No ransom demands. He split because he works for a fucking *mob bank*. He's probably in Tunisia by now, goddammit!"

Hal looked back at the body. He cradled the phone between his ear and shoulder. "All the more reason to pick up his trail."

"Pick up his—"

"Did you talk to the family?"

"No."

"Maybe you should talk to the family." He grabbed the dead guy's feet and pulled.

"Why would I do that?"

"Well... I mean, I'm no expert, but they'd probably be the ones to tell you if the guy was missing or not. Right? Or maybe one of them knows where he is..."

John mumbled something under his breath.

Hal couldn't make it out. "How about the bank? Did you talk to anyone there?"

"No."

"What?"

"No, I didn't talk to anyone at the bank!"

"Well, Jesus, man. Is there a reason I have to think for you now?" He pulled hard, got the body more than halfway out.

Through the phone, Hal heard John slam on the brakes and yell unintelligibly.

They were both silent for a bit.

"Feel better?" Hal asked, panting.

"Who's the inside guy at the bank?"

Hal was silent for a long second. He held his breath, shook his head.

Fuck.

"I don't know."

"Hal. Seriously. Go fuck yourself."

CHAPTER SIXTY-SIX

John got the Holsfer address from the file, pulled up and parked outside the two-story house. White columns on the outside, brick exterior, shoveled driveway, completely dark inside.

He got out and headed over to the front door, his boots adjusting to the pebble walkway with each step, and rang the bell.

Nothing.

He looked around at the other houses. Mostly empty driveways at midday. People were probably at work. The two or three SUVs he saw sticking out of garages read housewives.

Strange, he thought. *Must be out looking for him.*

John walked over to the side of the house, ran the odds of someone seeing him, decided to chance it.

The path to the backyard was covered in snow. Every step seemed to make a lot of noise. Once he got behind the house, he saw that it was surrounded by a thick line of pine trees, the branches mostly barren.

Still, lots of privacy.

There were shrubs here and there, and a covered in-ground pool. It was nice, as backyards go. He could visualize what the place would look like in the summer.

Closer to the house, metal and wicker furniture surrounded a fire pit in the middle of a slate patio. He peeked inside the house—completely dark with no signs of life.

He made his way back around the house the same way he came. He got this crazy notion to follow his own footsteps back, just in case, then realized he would've still left footsteps in the snow. He shook his head and sighed, peered around the corner to see if anyone was paying attention.

John trotted back to Blue, got in, slammed the door, cursed that he did, and started the car.

He pulled out, headed towards the bank. He didn't need the GPS for directions. He remembered exactly where it was.

Frosted glass about chest-height across all of the bank's windows, and the double doors.

Two video cameras outside the place; one by the door, one above an exterior ATM. He knew where they were from scoping the place out before the robbery. The Nova had a deep enough curve on the roof that blocked his face from the cameras when he'd pulled up. And he'd had the mask on.

Still, he was nervous.

He pulled Blue into a spot on the street, walked over to the bank with his head down and went inside. He took the place in.

A few people lined up for the tellers. Some banker types helping customers at their desks. A guard, late forties, in shape, was standing there picking at his hand. There was a gun in his holster. They didn't make eye contact.

No one looked nervous. Conversations sounded casual, almost jovial. The place was clean, dated, but reasonable looking. There were additional security cameras pointed at the tellers, at an internal ATM, at the vault, which was in the back, and at a staircase towards the basement where, John figured, the safety deposit boxes were.

No one was acting like the place had just been robbed. Or, that their boss was missing.

The fuck is going on here?

"Can I help you?" a young woman asked. Glasses, grey pant suit, brown hair in a bun.

Jesus, another bun.

John looked over and caught the guard's eye for just a second. He turned to her and smiled. "I'm not sure. Maybe."

"Have a seat," she said and brought him over to a desk that was in an open-faced cubicle. Pictures in frames, office supplies, a Far Side calendar, keyboard, and a computer with a thick number keypad attached. "My name is Peggy Keesler."

"Keebler?"

"Keesler."

"That's fortunate."

"Are you looking to open a checking or savings account? We offer a competitive interest rate for new customers..."

"No, uh, listen. It's gonna sound strange—"

"OK."

"But I'm a friend of Alex Holsfer, and I was driving through town and I wanted to surprise him. I tried calling his house, but no one picked up. Not his cell, either."

She swallowed hard and looked around to catch someone, anyone's eye. Just like the newspaper office, except she acted more business-like than scared. Peggy smiled awkwardly and said, "Let me see if I can get Bob, our branch manager."

And she left.

John watched her leave and used it as an excuse to case the rest of the place. Both of the tellers were women in their mid-twenties. One of them looked vaguely familiar. Facial features he'd seen before. And hair.

None of the employees looked worn out or wary enough to work for Gino.

Peggy came back, two steps behind a guy who had a smile and the glad hand out to John before he stood up. "Hi, Mister, uhh..." he turned to the woman, who shrugged her shoulders.

"Bryant," John said, reaching for an alias. "Rick Bryant. Nice to meet you."

"Bob Murcer. Yup, before you say anything, just like the ball player. Never played, myself. Have a seat."

John sat. Bob sat. Peggy stood and watched.

"So, not here for a bank account," Bob said smiling. His teeth were too white.

John thought *Could this be the guy?* "No. Just a friend of Alex— wanted to surprise him for lunch."

Bob nodded. Waited. "Friend from where?"

"Temple. He went the CPA route, and I flunked out in my third year, decided to join the army." *Why the hell did you just say that—*

"No kidding. I went to Temple. You don't look familiar."

"I was there for, uh… Asian studies." *Holy fuck.*

"Really."

"Growth market. Couldn't hack the language. Or the food. Love the women, though…" *Jesus, stop already!*

"Ahh. Hah. Yeah. OK. Well… army, huh? I was in the navy. NROTC, then I signed up after graduation."

"Nice. Out of where?" John tried to sound genuine.

"Great Lakes, then I was out in San Francisco for a few years with the Pacific fleet. Got out after ten years and moved back to Jersey, and I couldn't find shit for work. Pardon my French. Alex hired me about a year later and, now, here's home."

Nope. Not him. Too easy to verify. "Nice," John said.

"You?"

"Me? Home?"

"Well, where were you stationed."

"Ah, well—" He tried to remember something, anything. Suddenly, he remembered Christopher Walken's face. "Biloxi."

Oh, God.

"Biloxi?"

"Yeah. In Mississ—"

"I know where Biloxi is. Now, isn't that an Air Force base?"

John froze for a second. Barely a second. His brain fired off any and every idea he could think of in that instant. He reached out with

458

both hands and grabbed one. "Yeah, they, uhh, they switch. You know. On and off. Every other... year. It's... tradition."

Bob nodded slowly. So did Peggy. "Well, I guess that's the South for you."

"Yeah."

"Where were you deployed?"

"Spent the rest of my time out of Miami."

"You spent your time in the army in Miami?"

What the fuck is wrong with you?! "Yeah, well... see, I caught my commanding officer in, let's say, a compromising position and—"

Bob started laughing. "No shit!"

Peggy was smiling, but very confused.

Bob slapped his knee. Literally. "You know if I'd found my C.O. in a compromising position... I'd probably had done the same. Too funny. Too funny."

John was trying to smile. His mouth had forgotten how.

"Well, Alex never mentioned you, Rick, but that doesn't mean much of anything. He's not a talker."

"No, he is not," John said, still trying to smile.

"He's out of town for a few days. With the family. I think he said—" Bob looked up at Peggy, who looked down at him "—where, Peggy?"

"Binghamton," she said quickly.

"Binghamton. Right," Bob said.

"For the shopping," she added.

"For the shopping. Great outlets in Binghamton, you know," Bob said, and smiled.

"Well. Sorry I missed him," John said. "And, you know, sorry to take you away from work."

"Not at all! They might be back tomorrow..."

"Yeah, I, uhh, won't be around. Heading back home."

"Too bad. Nice to finally meet a friend of Alex." Bob put his hand out again. John shook it.

459

"You too," John said, even though it didn't make sense. He let out a quick groan, nodded to Peggy, took one last look around the place, and headed for the door.

"Stop in any time," Bob said as John left.

When he got outside, the cold air crept into whatever nook or cranny it could find, through the gaps in his jacket, the sleeve holes, the collar. It froze the sweat around his body and made him shiver, like he was having a seizure.

CHAPTER SIXTY-SEVEN

J ohn sat in the car a long time before deciding to get something to eat. He went back to the diner. Same booth. The waitress came by without a menu.

"Cheeseburger, medium. Cheddar cheese—"

"Got American."

"That's fine. Fries and some water and coffee."

"You got it."

He got comfortable and let his eyes wander in no particular direction.

So.

No news story about Holsfer. The newspaper people got a little nutso when he mentioned him, but it was the bank people that got him thinking. They were *expecting* someone to come through and ask questions. The reaction of the news people when he said New York City, though... why would that bother them so much? Unless they knew Gino owned the bank, which was ridiculous.

The situation wasn't making much sense.

A car drove past. Early 90s Audi, white, in decent shape. Good pick-up. He'd stolen one of them before. He sank into the booth and started tallying cars he'd stolen, in order, just for something to do. He'd gotten through two years of working with Gino, and more than thirty cars when the food arrived. Same china. The burger looked like actual formed meat, not a frozen patty. The bun was toasted, came with lettuce, tomato, and a couple of slices of pickles. It was surrounded by steak fries. He built the hamburger, dumped ketchup in the empty spot, and started eating, dipping the hamburger with every bite.

He ate in silence, not knowing what to do, where to go, or who to talk to.

After he finished lunch he thought, *what would a detective do*? Like a private detective, like from a book. He got a refill on the coffee, drank it, and, after paying for the check, he did the only thing he could think of.

Stakeout.

He drove back to the Holsfer place and parked about a block away. He tried to recall every stakeout he'd ever seen in a film. None came to mind. He couldn't even remember the plot of the film *Stakeout*.

First, he parked facing away from the house, and looked at it through the driver-side and rear-view mirrors.

"Jesus, this is fucking stupid," he said out loud, after looking at the mirrors back and forth, over and over. He turned the car around and faced the house.

And waited.

Half an hour in, John decided stakeouts were the pits.

Half an hour after that, he had to take a piss.

He held it.

And held it.

"Fucking coffee," he said to no one, and shifted his seat. "And water. And what can only be a child-sized bladder, for chrissake..."

Nothing happening at the house. Not a goddamn thi—

He dialed Hal.

"Yeah?"

"How the fuck... I've been sitting here for an hour man, watching an empty fucking house! Explain to me how cops don't have a higher rate of suicide."

"They do, actually—"

"And I have to pee so bad my back teeth are floating."

"So piss in a cup."

"Who has a cup just lying around?"

"Detectives, P.I.s, rolling surveillance... they prepare for this kind of thing. You said you were going to put in that catheter—"

John cut the connection. He turned the car on, put it in gear and drove to the closest gas station, the *only* gas station, which was five minutes away.

By the time he got to there, his body was about to shut down his cognitive functions and just do what came naturally. He got into the men's room, ignored the smell, pulled the zipper on his jeans down, fought for the gap in his boxers, finally got his dick out and let go. The relief was palpable, and he laughed. He felt a shudder and the tremble of lightheadedness. He checked the tile wall in front of his face, just in case it was disgusting, and put one hand out, just in case he passed out.

Once he was finished, he washed up to his elbows, used his foot to get the door open and relished the fresh air.

He bought chips, a sandwich, two bottles of water, another cup of coffee, two chocolate bars, a six-month-old *Playboy* and a current *People* magazine.

He got back to the Holsfer house, decided that he hadn't missed shit, and settled in. Ms. June, Playmate of the Year. Not too shabby. Some articles and a short story by Chuck Palahniuk kept John entertained for a bit.

Around quitting time, people started driving up the street, heading home after a long day. He slinked down deep whenever he saw a car coming. Or heard a car. Or thought he heard a car. His ass was getting sore. He wondered what they did for a living, those people, and passed more time dreaming up job scenarios.

He came to a conclusion. The people in Sherborn all lived boring fucking lives.

Around six in the evening, a car drove up to the house, pulled into the driveway and stopped. A heavy-set woman walked up to the front door, used keys and went inside. Lights were turned on throughout.

Finally, John thought, and got out of the car. He walked over slowly, watching the other houses, again, just in case.

He went around the back, following his old footsteps, and peeked the corner. Lights were on in the kitchen and living room.

The woman had her back to him. She walked over to a radio that was mounted underneath some cabinets in the kitchen. Music started playing. Latin something something.

OK...

She moved over to the countertop and then bent over. When she righted herself, she made a motion with her hand...

The fuck is she doing?

A blaring noise came from inside the house, scaring the shit out of him. He ducked behind the patio furniture and, after realizing what the noise was, closed his eyes in frustration and embarrassment.

He peered over a chair and saw the woman walking back and forth through the dining room with a vacuum cleaner.

John put his hand up against his forehead, dragged it down the length of his face, shook his head lightly.

The woman finally faced his direction. She was clearly Spanish, about fifty-five, smiling, singing, moving around the dining room without a care in the world.

He was pretty sure that wasn't Carla Holsfer.

He left the backyard and walked straight back to his car, not giving a single fuck if anyone saw him or not.

CHAPTER SIXTY-EIGHT

John left the house and was on his way back to Brooklyn. "Fuck this place," were his exact words. He was pissed, but happy with his decision.

He was half an hour away when he remembered he still had all his stuff at the bed and breakfast.

He screamed in frustration and started going through the inventory of what he'd left and whether he could live without it.

He decided he couldn't.

He stopped at the diner on his way home. The waitress and the cook were still there.

"You got a steak special?"

She gave him that look.

"Medium. Baked potato and some vegetables, I don't care what."

"To drink?"

"A beer, anything that doesn't taste like watered down—"

He didn't get to finish.

The steak was decent, as was the rest. He slathered butter on the potato, added sour cream, and the vegetable of the day was broccoli.

The beer was domestic. He didn't bother finishing it.

Swensen's B&B was practically empty by the time he got back. She was in the living room, watching *Jeopardy!* with a mid-forties guy, a new guest.

John said goodnight.

"You here for breakfast tomorrow morning?" she asked.

"I don't know. What's for breakfast?"

"Oatmeal. Comes with brown sugar, dried cranberries, walnuts, bananas—"

"I'm sorry, Mrs. Swensen," John said. "I'm not an oatmeal fan."

"It sounds delicious," the guy in the room said.

"It is," she said. "Your loss, sonny boy. Goodnight."

"Night." John half-waved as he lumbered up the stairs, got into the room and called Hal, who picked up on the first ring.

"Yeah?"

"I'm giving it until tomorrow, then I'm coming back."

"Gino won't like it."

"There's nothing up here, man! The guy is gone. And you know what worries me the most? People are nervous about it, but it's like they don't want him found."

"Keep at it," Hal said. He seemed preoccupied.

"There's no one else to talk to!"

In the background, John could hear metal crunching.

"Talk to the cops," Hal said.

"Are you fucking kidding me? Where the fuck are you?"

"It's a missing person's case."

"I don't need the cops on our radar, man." He lowered his voice. "We fucking robbed the bank in this town."

"Well, technically we committed—"

"Fuck 'technically'!"

Hal sighed. "No one knows who you are. Would you grow some balls already?"

Wind was whipping through the phone. Hal was outside.

"Where are you? And why are you being such a dick about this case?"

Silence.

"Huh? You have a personal stake in this or something?" John was getting angrier. "It's a fucking banker! Who gives a shit?"

"Gino does."

"Explain it to me."

"I can't. He points us in the direction he wants us to go, we go. You want to ask Gino why he wants us to do something, be my guest. You think you're chummy enough with him that he'll just open up about his business practices? His *money*? Go ahead. Just stop asking me fucking questions about a simple goddamn job like finding a missing fucking person!"

Hal disconnected.

John breathed for a bit, sitting on the edge of the bed and said, "What the fuck." He hadn't said anything to get Hal *that* riled up. He leaned back on the headboard and tried to think it through.

Nothing. No further insights came.

He wanted to call him back, but decided against it. He never liked arguing with Hal. They were on the same side. They were both constantly frustrated with the parameters of the jobs Gino gave them. This job was no different.

Right?

CHAPTER SIXTY-NINE

John woke up the next morning, went to the bathroom, showered, got dressed, and headed out for the diner again. He passed Mrs. Swensen's kitchen and the smell wasn't as bad as he thought it would be. Ever since he was a kid, he had hated oatmeal. He was a notoriously picky eater when he was younger. Cereal was the go-to, and while his mother was the by-the-seat-of-her-pants mother type, she knew cereal was a bad idea for breakfast, lunch and dinner. He respected her enough, even at a young age, to realize that whatever she provided for meals, it was what she could afford. So, if it was something he normally hated, she let him drown his food in ketchup, which seemed to do the trick.

Except for oatmeal.

John got to the diner and just said, "Same as yesterday." The waitress cracked the tiniest of smiles and walked away.

It was a bit warmer that morning. Blue sky, sun shining. The place had a reasonable breakfast crowd.

Five minutes later, his food was in front of him. Exactly what he'd ordered the day before. The waitress was moving too fast to thank.

"They called her Iron Trap," he said under his breath. "No. Steel Trap. Steel."

Out of the corner of his eye, John saw a dark shape move towards him. Coffee cup lifted towards his lips, he couldn't believe it when he saw Gino D'Escopio come walking over. Three piece suit. Slicked back hair. Sunglasses. Knee-length wool coat.

Here. In Hicktown.

John put the coffee cup down, his mouth still open.

"What are you, drawing flies?" Gino asked as he sat down.

"Something like that," John said.

"Smells good."

"It is good. You want?"

"No, I ate already, thank you."

John looked outside. Goons by a late model Cadillac looking completely and utterly out of place.

"Get you anything?" the waitress asked, appearing out of nowhere.

"Cappuccino, please," Gino said.

She looked at him. "It's out of a machine. Can't say if it's good or not."

"I'll take my chances," Gino said, smiling. "Thank you."

She nodded and moved away. "You mind?" John asked Gino, motioning to his food.

Gino put his hands up. "I know better than to get in the way of you and food." He watched, amused. "I don't know where you put it," he said. "If you were Hal, I wouldn't be wondering."

John put butter on the French toast. "He'd say he was eating for two."

Gino just looked at him.

"You know, for both of us."

"Yeah, I get it."

John took his first bite and made a noise.

"Good?"

"Oh my God," John said, and savored the bite, a mixture of everything.

Gino smiled, put his hands together and rubbed them. They made a noise, like hard, dry skin does. "This is a delicate situation."

John speared some more food, nodded. "OK."

469

"I know you're an unreasonably patient person, John. I can't begin to tell you how much I appreciate that quality. But this is different."

"I'm trying, Gino. I just... it's difficult to understand what's happening when I don't know as much as Hal does."

"Yeah. I can see that. What did he tell you?"

"That the guy works for you. At the bank."

Gino studied John's face for a long moment, watched him eat. "OK... what else?"

"Nothing. Just to find the guy. I mean, it doesn't make any sense. Was the guy kidnapped? Did someone ask for a ransom?"

"I don't know. No one's asked for anything. And I get it. It's a conundrum."

"Yeah, that's a word for it," John said. The conversation was getting strange. "And since when do you own a bank? Is it new or—"

"Listen. I know this isn't the way you usually do things, and I can't get into it right now. Not now." He sighed, leaned back. "But when you find the banker, I need you to call me. Not Hal. Me. This situation... it's a real problem."

"Not Hal."

"No. Is that an issue?"

John shook his head no, and tried not to swallow hard. The flavor of the food had left his mouth.

No. It hadn't left. It had soured, instantly. Something was wrong. In all the years he'd worked with Hal, Gino had never asked John to keep something from him.

He wondered how Hal had gotten himself into such a position.

"I need you to trust me on this," Gino said, leaning in. He looked around to see if anyone was in earshot. "OK?"

Later that night, he would recall a lot about the meeting. The temperature of the diner, the smell of the food, of the coffee. He would recall hearing people talking, laughing, and the clink of silverware on china. Glasses moving out of the dishwasher. The sound of cooking. The cappuccino machine sputtering. The waitress filling up a glass with soda. How the light was streaming into the diner, and the dust particles that were floating in the beam.

As he looked at Gino with his fake sincerity, John's body and mind adjusted to new information. It was the first time he'd ever felt those hackles, deep within himself, shift against a person he trusted implicitly.

I need you to trust me on this was the backstabbing equivalent of *We'll take it from here.*

"Of course, Gino." John nodded as his mind pushed the search for the banker aside, pushed Gino's request aside, pushed all non-essential information out of reach, and left himself with a solitary question.

Where was Hal in all of this?

The question caused an instant sweat he could feel on his chest, down his back, and at his temples.

"This guy a friend of yours?" John said. He gave himself an internal pat on the back for keeping his voice steady.

"He's an associate."

"And all you want me to do is find him?"

"Nothing more." Gino leaned back, satisfied the way the conversation was going. "I know you talked to his employees. Stick with the family, see if you can find out what's been going on. You hear anything, you call me."

John nodded again, put on a face like he was thinking. He leaned in. Gino leaned in. "What does all this have to do with..." he lowered his voice "... the robbery?"

"The robbery..."

"Yeah."

Gino looked at John for a few seconds, trying to read his face. He took his phone out and started texting. "What about it?"

"Well, nothing. We stopped it, you know. You got the money, right?"

Gino looked up into John's eyes. "Of course."

471

John had a sneaking suspicion that the man was using up all of his will power to keep eye contact, and a straight face.

John did the same.

"Did you find out what family was responsible?"

Gino smiled, looked back to his phone. "Not yet, but I've got some ideas."

"Well, one of them was a kid. Hal told you, right?"

Gino nodded slowly. "The kid. Right. Listen, John, you find the banker for me. I'll take care of the people who robbed me."

Gino got up to leave, threw down $40, put his hand down on John's shoulder, patted it lightly like they'd signed a contract, and left... just as the waitress brought over his cappuccino. It was in a pristine white mug with a nice head of foam and some cinnamon sprinkled on top.

"He forgot his cappuccino," she said, disappointed.

"I'll take it," John said, watching Gino leave. He pushed his food away from him, his appetite gone. "To go."

CHAPTER SEVENTY

He dialed Hal right away. It went to voicemail. "Fuck!" he yelled, and slammed his fist into the passenger seat as hard as he could. His hand came back stinging.

It took Blue five minutes or so to heat up before John wasn't breathing steam. He put the car in drive, frustrated, and growled when he realized what he had to do.

Another fucking stakeout.

He drove, trying to wrap his mind around what just happened, and sipped the cappuccino. Wasn't bad, all things considered.

He felt he was in a unique situation. Could he trust Hal? He had, after all, sent him up here "on orders" from Gino.

Maybe. Maybe not.

There wasn't much out of the ordinary about the bank job. They got a tip, got there first, kept the money.

No. Gave the money back to Gino.

Right.

No red flags before, during, or after. They'd done it before. They'd stopped guys from ripping off poker games, dead drops, hand-offs. If the mafia was full of one thing, it was leaks.

Five minutes out from Holsfer's house.

Something inside was telling him Hal wasn't in on it. He knew more than he was letting on, yeah, but there was no way in hell Hal was going to double-cross Gino. *Or* him... if that's what was happening. Not over $10,000 and a banker no one gave a shit about.

He heard the kid say, *"Hell, I was about to take the quarters! It looks like enough, right?"*

Enough?

John shook his head, took his mind off things and listened to the car. Even in the cold, he could tell if she was running right or not.

He felt the hum through his forearm as it rested against the driver-side window. The seat shifted here and there, slightly. He hit the gas and heard the familiar uptick from the engine. The steadiness through the steering wheel.

There wasn't a thing wrong with her.

He pulled up and parked outside the Holsfers. Warm light flooded the inside of the house. There was a beige SUV parked next to the maid's two-door hatchback.

Fuck another stakeout.

He got out, walked to the front door and knocked. The maid opened the door. He got a closer look at her. Fifties, big eyebrows, not wearing a uniform, definitely had the air of help about her.

"Si?"

"Ahh, Mrs. Holsfer?"

"She's a sleeping."

"OK. Anyone here?"

"Who you?"

"Sorry, I'm sorry. A friend of Alex."

She looked at him, worried, trying to figure out if he was telling the truth. "One moment. I get Jesse."

The maid closed the door. John stamped his feet a bit, trying to stay warm.

He heard heavy footsteps inside. Put out, like a pissed-off teenager. The door opened and standing there was the shotgun kid from the bank robbery. He had a bandage on his nose and some black and blue under his eyes.

"Yeah? You a cop?"

Holy fucking shit.

John opened his mouth to speak and tried to process. It wouldn't come. He grabbed onto something. Anything. "No, I'm a friend of your father."

The kid got a little tense. A little nervous.

"From the city?" Like it meant something. Just like the news—

"Yes."

The kid slammed the door in John's face, locked a series of bolts. Then, like an afterthought, the chain.

John stood there a bit, looked around, waited for a face to peek out from curtains or something.

Nothing.

He backed off, kept his eyes on the house as he heard the familiar pebbles shifting under his feet. He got back into Blue and drove away.

Driving.

"Gino's in town?" Hal sounded confused.

"Yeah, man. What the fuck is Gino doing up—"

"He just sat down?"

"You ever see a fucking mob boss in a tiny little fucking..." he gestured to the air.

"Hamlet?"

"Scared the shit out of me! Sharing coffee with the Scorpion's brother out here is like waking up next to Jimmy Hoffa."

"I guess..." Hal sounded preoccupied.

"When are you getting your dumb ass up here?"

"I'm on my way, actually. And with company."

John arched an eyebrow. Company was their code word over open lines for guns. "You think that's necessary?"

"Well, if Gino's up there..."

"We're in the middle of fucking nowhere!"

"Yeah. Nothing bad has ever happened in the middle of nowhere."

"Doesn't make any sense. There's nothing doing here. No gangsters, no Aryans, no gangs... Gino said he's not sure who robbed the bank, but he's got some ideas..." Hal made a noise. John couldn't tell what it meant "... but, I found one—" he stopped. He was about to tell Hal about the kid. *Better to keep it under wraps*, he thought.

"One what?" Hal asked.

He reached for something. "Murder victim. Yeah. From 1945. It was a real whodunit."

"I bet."

"When will you be here? You staying at Mrs. Swensen's?"

"Why, you talk her into being double-teamed?"

John shook his head. *The heathen.*

"No," Hal said. "I'm staying at the Holiday Inn, off 95. Like, ten minutes away. Be there in a couple of hours."

"Well get here fast, OK, for chrissake? I'm freaking out."

"Take some Xanax."

"I didn't fucking bring any."

"So I'll give you some of mine," Hal said. "Say thank yo—"

John clicked off the phone, grabbed the cappuccino, finished it. It was cold.

He put the cup down and looked in the rear-view mirror, thinking.

Tick them off.

Hal didn't know Gino was coming up.

Gino never dealt with problems personally outside of the city.

Hal was coming up with guns to a shitty Upstate New York town that no one's ever heard of.

And now, the son of the banker helped rob the place.

Did Gino know that? Did Hal?

He pulled over and decided he only had one move.

476

CHAPTER SEVENTY-ONE

John sat in the car, again, down the block from the Holsfer house, thumbing through the local papers. Again. Glancing, not reading. He'd been sitting there all day, and it was finally dusk.

He hadn't eaten anything since breakfast, and he was starving. But he had a paper cup. That was something.

He stared at the house through the rear-view mirror every once in a while. Instead of waiting for someone to come home, now he was waiting for someone to leave. He figured its occupants wouldn't pay as much attention to his car, facing away from the house.

Maybe.

Shit, he didn't know.

He looked around at each of the houses. All of them had chimneys. A few were smoking.

He could hear Jesse ask: *From the city?*

Whatever was going on between Holsfer and Gino, this kid knew some of the story. He couldn't be older than fourteen, fifteen tops. Where was his father? Why was he robbing the family bank? And how did Gino and/or Hal know that the bank was going to be robbed in the first place?

Echoing around the neighborhood a halfway familiar sound. The engine from a muscle car got louder as it drove down the block and pulled into the Holsfer driveway.

1969 Camaro.

"You've got to be shitting me."

Jesse came out of the house, slammed the door, ran for the passenger side. He got in, slammed *that* door, and the car pulled out fast.

John threw the newspapers aside, put the car in reverse, pulled into an empty driveway, spun the car around and followed them.

No way it's this easy. No way.

They drove down streets that were becoming regrettably familiar to John. The guy drove the speed limit, stopped at a light. The two were talking. Jesse smacked the driver on the arm. The guy shook his head, hit the gas when the light turned green and drove for another five minutes until finally, they stopped in front of the diner.

Shit.

The driver got out and stretched. He was lanky, tall, maybe twenty, reddish-blondish hair, wearing a sweatshirt and jeans that barely covered his ass. Not an ounce of muscle on him.

John pulled over into a spot on the street, turned the car off and thought for a moment. *So, it's Little Big Man and the Getaway Driver, and neither of them are the brains of the operation.* He got out, opened the trunk, opened the fake panel, grabbed the shotgun and went to close the trunk.

To the right of the spare he saw the little black box. He opened it. Inside were the GPS devices and audio bugs. He grabbed a pair, shut the trunk.

He pressed the shotgun against his leg to hide it, walked over to the Camaro. The windows were half down. In the middle of winter. Jesus fucking Christ.

He made sure he was out of the line of sight of the two of them, threw the shotgun into the back seat. He put the bug behind the driver-side seat, the GPS under the back driver-side wheel well. Then he walked into the diner.

Jesse had his back to the door.

John shook his head with a smirk. The kid probably thought he was safe in town, or just didn't give a shit.

The driver didn't seem to care who was in the diner, or who walked in. There was a naïveté about his comfort level that didn't seem reasonable, rational, or anywhere close to the realm of being useful. "Yeah, but do you know how much a gas line costs?" he said to Jesse.

"Charlie, seriously, who gives a shit?" Jesse asked.

John sat at the counter. The waitress gave him the once over. "People are going to start talking."

"Let them talk," John said. "We're both adults. Or, at least, one of us is an adult. I'm referring to you, of course."

"Don't be so quick to judge."

The cook was working on a burger in the back.

"Coffee, please," John said. "And a blueberry muffin."

"I've got corn muffins. That's it."

"Corn was my second choice."

"Toasted? Butter?"

"Do your worst."

She smiled. Actually smiled, and put the order in verbally to the chef, who grunted. Maybe. It might have just been him breathing.

John noticed that the cook wasn't really paying attention to the burger. Not like he was on autopilot. He was looking at Jesse and Charlie. After a minute, he took the burger off the grill, wiped his hands on a greasy apron, walked over to a phone in the kitchen, dialed, and faced away from the dining room.

John did a slow turn on the swivel stool, willing it to stay quiet. He looked over at the two. Still oblivious.

He got up and walked over.

Charlie saw him, got a bad vibe, and kicked Jesse under the table in a very not subtle way.

"The hell are you kicking me for?" Jesse asked.

Charlie motioned with his eyes over to John, who couldn't help but smile. Jesse looked over his shoulder and shook his head.

"Now you're following me?"

"Just a nice place to eat, Jesse," John said and settled near their booth. "In fact, I've eaten here for practically every meal since I've been in town."

"He knows your name?" Charlie asked.

"He knows shit. Get the fuck out of here, City Man. I don't have to tell you anything."

John sat down next to Jesse, forcing himself into the booth. Close.

"The fuck—" Jesse said, getting uncomfortable quickly.

John leaned in. "You don't have your empty shotgun to threaten me with, kid. You keep your mouth shut, you tell your friend to go to the bathroom." John looked over at Charlie, whose eyes had gotten too big for his head. "Unless he wants trouble."

Charlie turned white. Whiter than John thought possible in such a short amount of time. His mouth bobbed open, closed, open. Charlie got up and walked backwards until he opened the door leading to the bathrooms. It swallowed him up.

"You fucking stole my money!" Jesse said low, but harshly.

"From what I've gathered, I stole your father's money which… well, *you* were stealing. I think. There're a lot of holes in this story, and I thought you and I would fill them in."

Jesse sighed. Acting tough. He grabbed his water as a prop.

"Where's your father?"

Jesse shook his head, unconvincingly.

"You don't know? Or you won't tell me?"

"Take your pick. Where's my shotgun?"

"In your car. His car. Whatever. It's still empty."

"Don't expect a thank you."

"OK."

"What did you do with the money? You put this town in a shit-ton of trouble, stealing that."

John clucked. "See, now you just gave me another question. What the hell does the town have to do with this?"

Jesse turned and looked out the window.

John looked around the diner. No one was paying them any attention. "I can't prove to you I'm the good guy, but I can tell you that if I were one of those guys from New York," Jesse turned to look at him. "You'd either be screaming or dead by now." John looked by the bathrooms. Charlie was peeking through one of the windows on the door. "Both of you."

Charlie moved away from the window.

Sirens in the distance.

John looked into the kitchen. The chef was peering through the kitchen door.

"Oh no," Jesse said under his breath.

John looked outside the windows of the diner. The sirens got louder. Less than a minute out.

"'Oh no,' huh? Looks like I'm the least of your problems." John got out of the booth and made his way to the counter. Next to his cup of coffee was a toasted corn muffin soaked in butter. "Jesus, lady," he said under his breath.

Charlie came back into the diner, his eyes on John just as a police car came to a screeching stop outside, boxing in the Camaro.

John took a bite of the corn muffin. Warm. Delicious. He chased it with some coffee, turned to see two officers get out of the patrol car, looking right at Jesse.

Wearing thick coats, standard navy uniforms, ties, badges, Glock 22's, handcuff cases, tasers, three or four zip-tie cuffs for some reason, flash lights, heavy boots... the works, in the middle of fucking nowhere.

"Surprised they didn't come in a BearCat," John said to himself.

Officer Gordon Briggs and Officer Harlan Cochrane walked into the diner like they owned the place. No pleasantries, no nods to waitress or cook, or the town's citizens. They walked over to Jesse and Charlie's table, ready to arrest them or shoot them or both.

CHAPTER SEVENTY-TWO

Briggs and Cochrane were townies, third generation. Briggs's father, Chester, used to be top cop in the area before he blew his heart out at the town fair three years prior. It was during a potato sack race, if you can believe it. Now he spends his time gardening, all year round. Treats composting like he invented it. Yeah.

Gordon Briggs was a football player in high school. Played mostly whenever someone was out sick or hurt. He went to a state college, worked on a Liberal Arts degree, spent most of his time at the frat house drinking, doing drugs, was smart enough not to rape anyone, and only *just* graduated, skirting by with a C-average.

Becoming a cop in town had always been the plan. His father figured college would grow him up a bit. It didn't.

Harlan Cochrane was a childhood friend of Briggs whose own father, Frank, was a truck driver, meth addict, and had two additional families in two other towns.

Chester knew how much of a piece of shit Frank Cochrane was. He took Harlan under his wing when he could, simply to keep him out of trouble. Mostly, it was out of pity.

Harlan went to a different state school than Gordon. He had no plan, no major in mind. College just seemed like the thing he was supposed to do. He took out a student loan and fucked around most days. After the first semester, he quit. "I'm not even paying attention in school," he told his mom one day. "And after four years, do you know how much money I would owe the government?" He told her. She said to come home, so he did. He got back to town, found work, and took care of his mom. She'd divorced his father after finding out he was being sued for child support and alimony.

Harlan got a job working at the Ace Hardware Store in town. Ben's Hardware, *since 1946*. Everyone in town went to Ben's. Not the Lowe's in Norwich or the Home Depot down in Binghamton.

When Gordon graduated and came back to town, the two were thick as thieves again. They'd hang out after their shifts, go to the bar, shoot pool, play the Galaga–Pac-Man machine all night. One night, Harlan said, "I can't stand this fucking job anymore, man. Ben's son Jim is a fucking moron. Once Ben's dead, I'll be working for the dumbest guy in town."

"And you'll be doing all the work," Gordon said.

"And I'll be doing all the fucking work!"

Gordon had been thinking about this very problem for a while now. He'd heard Harlan talk about the hardware store before. "I've got an idea."

"Kill Jim?"

"No, Jesus. Come work with me."

"What?"

"Yeah. Be a cop."

"Be a..." Harlan laughed. He laughed and then fell off the barstool.

Gordon wasn't laughing.

Harlan looked up at his friend and stopped laughing. "You're serious?"

"Absolutely."

They hashed out a plan. They would wait for Deputy Mike Janson to retire from the force. Mike was going on sixty-five and spent most of his day doing paperwork, fielding calls, and generally being a pain in everyone's ass. He complained constantly about his wife and her no-good brother, the state of his home, politics, local and national, and how he was going to run for governor one of these days, "Because I'm not a pussy like the one we've been stuck with."

Everyone wanted him gone.

When Janson died in his sleep one April morning, Gordon spoke with his father to hire Harlan for the office work. "You know, to replace Mike, may he rest in peace. Not that just anyone could replace Mike," Gordon said to him over beers, trying to sound magnanimous.

"A fucking monkey could replace Mike... rest in peace," Chester said, but, sure, he'd make a call.

Two months later, Harlan was hired as a full-time officer.

Harlan came around the booth and babysat Charlie, who was looking down at the Formica table, playing with his napkin, fork and knife, as if they were the most interesting things in the world.

Briggs came over and put his hand on the back of the booth behind Jesse. He took a deep breath, closed his eyes, tilted his head up to heaven, and let it out slow, like whatever he was going to say was going to be earth shattering.

"Where is it, Jesse?"

Earth. Shattering.

"How did you know I was here?" Jesse asked.

Briggs smiled. Cochrane did too. Briggs hooked a thumb over to the cook, who was watching events unfold. "I've got eyes and ears all over this town, Jesse. All of them are curious, and rightfully so, about what the hell is going on around here. Trust ain't so high on their list these days."

"Goddammit—"

"Watch your mouth," Briggs said.

"I had nothing to do with it, Briggs. Nothing. I swear it."

"Where's your father?"

"I don't know."

"Where is that son of a bitch?"

"I don't know!"

"The hell you don't," Cochrane said.

Charlie started shaking uncontrollably.

Briggs noticed and watched him, amused. "What in the hell is wrong with him?"

Charlie made a spastic motion to grab his water. His hand was shaking so hard, water sloshed out of the glass and onto the table. Jesse grabbed a straw from his Coke and put it into Charlie's water. Charlie smiled, grateful, started drinking.

"He's dehydrated," Jesse said.

"Dehydrated my ass—" Cochrane started.

"Or a vitamin deficiency—"

Briggs hit the table hard with his fist. The place went quiet. "You listen to me. That father of yours got the OK. What happened after, I don't fucking give a shit! Space aliens, fucking Russians came into town and cut his nuts off, I don't care. If he's not around, you answer for him."

"It wasn't my fault!" Jesse screamed.

Briggs grabbed Jesse out of the booth.

John watched the room, to see what would happen next. He turned on the stool towards them both, just in case.

The cook, having sensed that enough was enough, left the kitchen. He was massive. A huge belly that simply could not have just been fat. Or muscle. Or bones or organs. Something terrible was residing in there, silently waiting for the end of its host's life. He went over to Briggs and put a hand on his shoulder. "Gordon, come on now. Go easy."

"Go easy? Aren't you the least bit curious, Murray? We all have a stake in this, goddammit!"

"Yeah, but would he be here if he wasn't telling the truth?"

John watched as that idea seemed to make some sense to Briggs. He could see the wheels turning.

"Maybe." He turned to Jesse. "Maybe, you little shit. But I want answers. Tomorrow."

"OK, tomorrow. Great," Murray said, patting Briggs on the shoulder, trying to smile. He held out a hand for Cochrane, who took it, pumped twice, and went to get the door for Briggs.

"Tomorrow. My office. Don't make me come looking for you. Don't make this any harder than it already is," Briggs said, with an air of don't fuck with me.

Briggs straightened his shirt, reached around, tucked it deeper in back, and looked at John on his way out. The two got into the patrol car and drove away.

The room seemed to sigh with relief.

Jesse collapsed into the booth. Charlie, still shaking, made his way back to the bathroom on weak legs.

"Jesus, Jesse," Murray said and somehow slid into the booth across from him.

"Thanks for turning me in, and then getting me off the hook," Jesse said, and downed his coke too fast. Ice chips hit him in the face and fell to the ground.

"I didn't do much for you, believe me. I bought you some time is all." He looked at Jesse, looked at the waitress. John turned away, watched the scene in the reflection off the long, thin mirror above the pass.

"You don't know where he is?" Murray asked.

Jesse shook his head.

"And they just robbed you? Out of the blue?"

Jesse nodded, grabbed Charlie's half-glass of water and downed it. He turned towards John, said, "Out of the blue."

Murray sighed. "You two better get out of here. I don't know what's going to happen next, but I know it's best if you two weren't around for it."

"And go where?"

"I couldn't say. Who could, really? None of us are equipped to deal with this kind of thing. Except your father." He headed over to the bathroom and smacked on the door. "Out, Shaky!"

Jesse got up from the booth, threw some cash on the table as Charlie got out of the bathroom. They both headed for the door. Passing John, Jesse said, "Quit following me."

They left the diner, made their way to the Camaro.

John lowered his head and studied the remains of the corn muffin.

Murray came over to John and wiped at an imaginary spot on the counter. "You know him? Jesse?"

"Not really."

"Been following him?"

"Define 'following.'"

"They're good kids."

"If you say so."

"I do."

"OK."

"So leave them alone."

The Camaro drove away.

John noticed in the pass mirror a black Cadillac slowly following them. He got up to leave.

"Mister, I'm not their problem." John took some cash out, grabbed the rest of the muffin and stuffed his face.

"So they're in trouble?" Murray sighed. "You know something they don't?"

His mouth half full, John said "Shit, who doesn't?"

CHAPTER SEVENTY-THREE

John opened an app on his phone so he could listen to the bug he'd put in Charlie's car. "This is a mistake," Charlie's voice said. "We shouldn't be doing this. Why are we doing this?"

"Because we have to go see him," Jesse said.

"I think it's a mistake, man."

"Yeah, well, he didn't account for all of this bullshit. That dude at the diner... he's not who we should be worrying about."

"Briggs and Cochrane—"

"No, man, fuck them. But if that guy, whoever the hell he is... if that guy could find me, then the people we *do* have to worry about..." he sounded uneasy. "Just get us to the motel."

"OK, OK," Charlie said. Clearly, the tone in Jesse's voice was making him uneasy.

Charlie remembered when Jesse had approached him about this whole deal. They'd been friends for a while. Neighborhood friends. Charlie lived a few streets down from the Holsfers, and used to babysit Jesse every once in a while.

"It's going to be easy," Jesse said. They were in his living room, drinking chocolate milk and eating Entenmann's chocolate frosted donuts.

"Doesn't sound easy," Charlie said. He'd stayed out of trouble his whole life. His mom was a hard ass, but loved him. His father had been a drunk, but a quiet one. Depressed, too. He worked, he came home, he drank, watched TV or listened to music or tinkered in the garage. He'd basically been coasting through life, waiting to die, which he did when Charlie turned 12. Heart attack.

"It's all been arranged," Jesse said. "Dad made sure of it. We go in, we steal the money, we come out, we meet my dad, and then we leave town... it's going to take half an hour."

"What about your mom?"

"Dad's got to leave town. To protect her. I'm going with him."

"Does she know that?"

"No comment."

"She's going to be *pissed*!"

"She'll get over it."

Charlie tried to wrap his head around it. It wouldn't come. "I don't like this."

"They know we're coming, man."

"But you said we have to wear masks. If they know we're coming—"

"For the cameras, dude. It's got to look like a real robbery."

"OK."

"I even got one of these," Jesse said, got up, went to his bag, pulled something out, hid his face from Charlie, adjusted something and turned around.

Charlie almost spit out his chocolate milk.

Jesse had on a fake mustache that kinda sorta matched the color of his hair. Kinda.

"You look like you're about to drop the best gay porn video of all time," Charlie said, laughing.

"Fuck you, you dick! This thing cost me twenty dollars!"

"Twenty gay dollars."

"There's no such thing as gay dollars, you moron."

"I'm just saying. You look gay."

"Your face is gay."

"No it's not."

"Your mother's gay."

Charlie thought for a second. "Yeah, she might be."

That got Jesse. The two laughed out loud for a long time, talked logistics and agreed they would rob the bank on Monday.

Neither of them thought to think that the only 1969 black Camaro in town might stand out as a getaway car.

They got breakfast the morning of the robbery at the diner and didn't talk much. Murray came by, nodded to both of them solemnly, gave them eggs and toast and bacon and coffees and didn't charge them for it.

Betty the waitress gave Jesse a hug as he left. He'd had a crush on her since he was ten.

Charlie drove in silence. He was nervous and his hands were shaking. He kept dry swallowing and making a coughing sound that Jesse had never heard before. Like a tic. He realized he'd never seen Charlie nervous before.

Sunlight was streaming through the trees as they made their way to Main Street. Charlie pulled down the sun visor and grabbed a pair of sunglasses, put them on.

Once on Main he slowed down. Way slow, like he was trying to put off the inevitable.

"Come on, man," Jesse said in a quasi-comforting voice. Charlie nodded.

He parked the Camaro down the block from the bank, across from the newspaper offices. People were out on the street, the sidewalk, running errands or shopping or whatever.

Charlie put on his ski mask over his sunglasses. He had to take it off, take off the sunglasses, put the ski mask back on, *then* put the sunglasses on top.

The guy was a mess.

Jesse took a long, deep breath, put the fake mustache on, grabbed the shotgun from the back seat, and got out of the car. The shotgun made it all ridiculously awkward, since he was trying to hide it from sight. He pressed it against his chest, tried to wrap his jacket around it, hoping no one would see. The butt was still sticking out about six inches.

He made his way towards the bank. When he was close enough—close that he could see the video cameras—he grabbed the ski mask from his jacket pocket and, with one hand, tried putting it onto the top of his head. He couldn't get it on.

He tried to put the shotgun under his armpit so he could use his other hand, but it was too heavy and was slipping down, out of his coat. He tugged at the ski mask. First the left side, then the right, back and forth until it got down far enough he could grab the front of it and yank it down all the way. As he did, the mustache fell off his upper lip, onto the ground between his legs.

"Goddammit," he said under his breath.

"You know," Alex had said that morning, "you don't need to wear that ridiculous thing."

His mother was smiling into her hand. She was nervous about the whole thing, but this...

"Dad, I'm just trying to make it authentic."

"I know. And I appreciate it." He kissed his son on the top of his head. "Wear it."

"It makes you look older," Carla said.

"Really? How much older?"

"Twenty? I hate it."

Jesse smiled at her. He studied her face. He figured it was the last time he'd ever see her again.

Jesse tried to remember what the mustache looked like on, tried to approximate putting it in the exact same place. Satisfied, he walked to the bank, took a deep breath, and went inside.

The place was busy. Sort of.

Rachel and Ellen were the tellers, just like his dad had said. Peggy was there, looking straight ahead at her computer, eyes wide and unblinking. He wondered, for a split second, just how long she'd been frozen like that, waiting.

Bob was in his office. Gerard the guard (Jesse still couldn't believe that was really his name) was on a wooden stool, looking at Jesse as if he'd been waiting for him his whole life.

Two customers he recognized: Mr. Barber, from the newspaper, and Mrs. Heckler, who ran a flower shop in town.

Jesse didn't know all of the particulars about people's involvement in his father's business, but here were seven people keen on making sure their investments were sound.

The bank was full of friends.

Jesse pulled the shotgun out of his coat and yelled, "This is a robbery!" He pulled the trigger by accident, out of excitement, and it clicked dry.

Peggy made a nervous noise. Bob rolled his eyes. Gerard threw his gun on the ground *way* too early. Mr. Barber and Mrs. Heckler got down on the floor, face down. Ellen and Rachel put their hands up.

Jesse stopped. It all happened waaayyyy too fast, and he realized he was feeling disappointment. He'd had a whole speech planned and everything.

Don't give me a hard time, and don't be a hero, motherfuckers. Everyone just get on the ground and do what I say and no one will get hurt. You! Take me to the vault!

Bob was up and walking towards him with a set of keys, his arms tucked in, elbows bent, like he was doing half-hands up.

"Take me to the vault!" Jesse yelled as Bob passed.

Jesse grabbed Gerard's gun as they made their way to the back of the bank.

Outside, Charlie sat there, windows up, hyperventilating. He had to wipe away the condensation from the windshield every few minutes. Couldn't see shit out the back.

He was sweating profusely. The ski mask was bugging the fuck out of him, but he wanted to play it smart, just in case this came back to them.

He revved the Camaro's engine, ready for go time.

Bob opened the vault and showed Jesse the two duffle bags.

"You filled them already?" Jesse asked, incredulously.

"Yeah," Bob said, like, *of course I filled them*. Then his face kind of melted a bit, and he realized he'd made a mistake. There was a camera in the vault and they both looked at it.

"Bob..." Jesse said, not believing it.

"Shit," Bob said under his breath. "I'll fix it. Just... help me."

Bob grabbed one of the duffle bags and started emptying it onto a metal table. Singles mostly. Some fives, tens, twenties. Some in bundles. Jesse put the guard's gun on a table, grabbed the other duffle and started emptying it.

Outside of the vault, Gerard was still on the floor, as were Barber and Heckler. Peggy was staring at a blank screen. Her eyes were going batshit, but she was too nervous to do anything else.

Ellen and Rachel's arms were getting tired.

"So you're going to—"

"I'll just splice the video," Bob said as Jesse packed the duffle bags himself. Bob had his hands up and was standing against a wall. He angled his face away from the camera. "I make videos at home, like nature videos and stuff. I'm a wiz at editing."

"Isn't there a time code, and audio—?"

"It's fine, trust me. I'll make sure the date is for tomorrow. Just make the exit look real."

Jesse nodded. "There's still room in the bags..."

"You have to hit the tellers, too."

"Hit them?"

"Jesus, get the money from them, too," Bob said, gratingly.

Jesse closed the duffle bags, grabbed one of them and slung it over his shoulder. It shifted his body so much that he dropped the shotgun and fell against one of the walls.

"Edit that out, OK?" Jesse mumbled.

Bob lowered his hands. "We're going to go to prison."

Jesse steadied himself, grabbed the shotgun, grabbed the other duffle, left the guard's gun, balanced himself, pointed the shotgun at Bob and said, "Move it asshole!"

Bob put his hands back up and walked out of the vault.

"Everyone stay on the ground. I don't want to hurt you, but I will if I have to! Open the teller door," Jesse said.

Bob used his keys and opened the door. Jesse walked in, put one of the duffle bags on a chair. "Give me the cash."

Bob got down on his knees, put his hands on the ground and lay down. "Everyone just do as he says."

The tellers shoved cash into the open duffle bag by the fistful.

"That's right!" Jesse yelled. He'd thought of all the bank robbery movies he'd seen in the past week, and had what he thought was the best line to leave them with. "Your money is insured, so don't be a hero!"

Jesse checked a wall clock and saw that it was time. He went to the front of the bank and waited for Charlie to pull up.

And waited.

"You've got to be fucking kidding me." Charlie watched as a big white truck blocked his view of the bank. "No, no, no, no," he said as he honked and put the Camaro into gear. The truck was backing up, then moving forward, making an awful sound as it did.

"Get the fuck out of the—" he said to himself, then lowered his window. "Get the fuck out of the way!" he yelled. The guy in the truck put a hand up, waving.

Condensation fogged the windshield. He wiped it with his palm. The truck was finally moving past him as he saw Jesse get into a black car, right in front of him. Right there.

The car took off like a bat out of hell, down Main Street for parts unknown.

As the truck moved just enough to let Charlie's car go through, he hit the gas and turned into the street. The Camaro coughed once and shuddered. "What the..." It did it again, and died, right in the middle of the street.

"The hell?"

He looked at the battery light. He looked at the oil light. Water temperature gauge. Nothing. He looked at the fuel gauge, which was stupid because they filled it up...

The red line on the E pulsed as he looked at it. It got brighter and redder even though it was just a piece of plastic and he honestly thought he was having a heart attack.

And all of a sudden, from all around him, he smelled gas. His favorite smell in the world, and it was so strong...

Charlie took off the ski mask along with his sunglasses and just watched as the black car disappeared around a bend.

"This..." he said. "That..."

Mike Gentry, who worked at the auto shop up a few blocks, who was holding a paper grocery bag and a six pack of coke, walked up to the passenger side of the Camaro and knocked.

Charlie looked over slow and recognized the shape of Mike. Mike had been instrumental in helping him get the Camaro in working order.

Charlie reached over and lowered the window.

"Hey pal," Mike said.

"Mike."

"I think your fuel line ruptured, buddy. Yeah, there's gas all over the place here and right behind you. Here too. It's bad."

"Oh yeah...?"

"Yeah. You're gonna want to put some kitty litter or something down before the cops come by and give you a ticket. Plus, you know, it's dangerous. You want a push out of the road there?"

Charlie nodded, still dumbfounded.

Fuel line? Gas leak?

Jesse?

He put the car in neutral, got out, used the door jamb to help push. Two other townspeople came over and helped Charlie get the car by the curb.

"Damnedest thing," Mike said. "Must be the cold."

Charlie nodded. His whole body was numb.

"Don't forget now. Kitty litter. Look."

Charlie looked. Gallons of gas were all over the street. People were walking by holding their noses. "Yeah. OK, Mike, thanks."

"I can get a tow over here this afternoon—we'll take a look at her. I'm sure I've got something to fix her right up."

Charlie nodded and walked away. "Thanks, Mike."

Charlie went to the grocery store, bought a 24-pound box of kitty litter, went out, spread it on the gas, threw out the container, and walked home.

He got the angriest phone call of his life from Jesse about an hour later.

CHAPTER SEVENTY-FOUR

Dark out. A streetlight every hundred yards or so down a four-lane highway, just a bit outside of town. John looked at the GPS app on his phone and saw the Camaro was about three-quarters of a mile away.

He hit the gas and kept his eyes peeled until he saw, way up ahead, what he figured were the Camaro's brake lights, along with a shape following it, no lights on. He could tell it was the Cadillac, even in the dark.

"Don't park by the room," Jesse said. Charlie grunted. He pulled into the All Seasons Motel and drove up to a line of rooms. The place was two floors. Each room had a white door and a big window next to it. There was an electric lantern above each door, a concrete column on the path between every room, holding up second-floor balconies.

"Keep it running," Jesse said, and got out. Charlie nodded absentmindedly as the Caddy coasted into the parking lot behind them, and stopped.

Charlie took out a cigarette, lit it.

Two men got out of the Cadillac. Joey and Jimmy, cousins who worked for the D'Escopio family since they were small. Joey had a Remington sawed-off shotgun, loaded with No.12 rat shot. Jimmy had a DP-12, a double-barreled loaded with hollow points.

John was about four hundred yards from the turn.

Joey walked over to the Camaro, slow, while Jimmy followed Jesse.

Charlie saw Jimmy first and sat up straight. "Hey—" he started to say, when he heard the crunch of boots close, much closer to the car. He turned his head to see the barrels of the sawed off staring at him. "Oh no," he said.

Not much flashed through Charlie's mind at that moment. The only thing he saw was the face of his mother.

Joey fired. The shot from both barrels destroyed Charlie from his collarbones up. What didn't hit Charlie rocked the car he'd parked next to. The sound wave from the blast blew out the side windows in the Camaro.

Jesse heard the shot, turned around in time to see Jimmy point the sleek shotgun in his direction. Behind him, the door to room 11 opened. Alex Holsfer came out shooting. He hit Jimmy once in the leg, once in the stomach, and he went down grimacing in pain and fired into one of the rooms.

A woman started screaming.

Jesse turned to see his father's face.

Joey saw his cousin hit the ground.

Jimmy let the shotgun hit the ground, barrel first. He used it to lean against, as he assessed the damage.

Joey broke open the sawed-off, removed the two spent shells and went to load it with new ones.

"Jesse, get in here!" Alex yelled as he tried to get a clean shot on Joey.

A harsh engine sound got everyone's attention.

John drove Blue around the left side of the Camaro, smashing into Joey, and hit the brakes hard. The momentum sent Joey soaring towards room 8. His shotgun flew out of his hands and hit the pavement. His head hit the top of the window casing, breaking his neck.

The two shotgun shells went flying in opposite directions, one of them landing on the Camaro's hood.

John opened the driver-side door, got out and yelled, "Come on, goddammit!" to Jesse and Alex. His hands were shaking. His mouth went dry, instantly. It was the second time he'd ever run over someone. The second time he'd ever killed—

"Come on, Dad!" Jesse yelled, and made a run for it.

"OK, one second!" Alex yelled and went back into the motel room, grabbed a leather-bound planner, left the rest.

He'd never been so scared for someone else in his life.

CHAPTER SEVENTY-FIVE

For as far back as he could remember Alex had wanted to have kids. Even though his fuck-ups had damaged his relationship with his parents, things had been great when he was younger. He wanted that with his own. Better, even. A perfect kid or two, who would love him forever, no matter what.

The problem was, just out of college, he found that his independence, especially when he was single, was worth more to him than the joy of having a child. Not to mention, none of the women he dated wanted to have children. Plus, the idea of never getting sleep for those first two, three years... the stress, the crying, the worry... all of it. None of it appealed to him. Not that it appealed to his friends, either. Publicly, they found so much joy in their kids.

Privately, some of his friends admitted they'd made a mistake, and it started to change his mind about the whole thing.

"I love him," his friend Henry said one night over beers. "I do. You mold your kid into anything but a serial killer, and you did it right, you know? Or a child molester. Or a rapist. Or a plain ole garden variety murderer."

"What about a flat-earther?"

"Jesus. Yeah. Or one of those people who think the world is only 6,000 years old. But really, anything else. Even a white-collar criminal, or a drug dealer? I could live with that. At least they'd be enterprising."

"Would you do it again?"

"Fuck no, dude. Fuck. No. My life is over. People say it isn't, like I'll have my forties to enjoy while this fucking kid is in college without a care in the world. That's great. But my prime years are now at the behest of someone who shits himself on a daily basis."

"Then why did you do it?"

"Jennifer. She wouldn't fucking shut up about it. She was going to leave me if she didn't have a kid. Can you fucking believe it? I should have let her leave. Now, neither of us is sleeping. She's fucking AGED ten goddamn years. We get into an argument? She's a mother. You hear me?"

"Yeah."

"She's a *mother*. All the time now. Women change, dude, as soon as that happens. No one wins an argument against a mother. No one." He took a drink. "Sex is out of the question, too. We're either too exhausted or not in the mood. Or, you know, she isn't. I haven't jerked off this much since I was in middle school." Henry shook his head. "This kid is what's going to break up our marriage. Not cheating or money problems or just plain ole growing apart. The fucking kid. So then, I'm paying child support, alimony..."

"But you get to fuck who you want."

"But I get to fuck who I want, yes!" Henry slammed his drink down. "That's exactly fucking right. See? You just gave me a reason to live another five years, dude. Thank you."

"You're welcome."

"And you? What's new with you, you single dog motherfucker, I'm so goddamn jealous, shit!"

Alex chuckled. "Not much, man. About to go out to the Cape for Memorial Day with Carla. You remember Brad?"

"Yeah."

"You get an invite?"

"Yeah. Can't go. Fucking kid, man. I swear he's ruining my life."

"That's too bad. Should be a fun weekend."

501

Jesse had gotten Blue's passenger door opened when he heard the rack of the DP-12. He turned just in time to see Jimmy point the shotgun at Alex and fire.

Alex was lifted off his feet and slammed into a concrete column.

The planner flew out into the parking lot, a hole clear through it.

Alex landed in shock. With shaky hands he felt around the small hole in his stomach. He slowly moved a hand around to his back and realized he was able to fit his entire hand in the exit wound.

Alex died worrying about Jesse and wondering why the hole in his stomach wasn't bigger.

Jimmy smiled, mission accomplished. He leaned back and let his left arm drop.

John cursed, ran over to where Joey's sawed off shotgun had fallen, picked it up. He checked the chambers. Empty.

Jesse stared at his father, who was lying in an awkward position on the ground. One hand on his stomach, the other bent underneath him. He wasn't moving.

Jesse looked down, saw Charlie's remains in the Camaro. What he was looking at didn't register at all as his friend, let alone human. He turned his head to the right, saw that the guy who'd been following him had told the truth. The shotgun from the bank robbery was in the back seat. He reached in, grabbed it, checked to see if it was still empty. It was.

Things were moving in and out of focus. The guy who shot his father was laughing. The lights in the parking lot seemed to be getting brighter, and the shadows darker. He felt his heart beating in his ears. The darker parts of the parking lot seemed to vignette his vision, narrowing it, focusing it, until he saw a bright red shell on the hood of Charlie's pride and joy.

John looked around for the other shell. Instead of finding one, his eyes rested on the planner, just lying there in the middle of the parking lot.

He jogged over, watching Jimmy as he did, who was exhausted, in pain, and breathing heavily. He was also chuckling to himself.

As John bent down to pick up the planner, his finger reaching into the slug hole, a strong sense of déjà vu, he took his eyes off Jimmy for a second. Just one fucking second and he heard that distinct racking sound.

"Oh for fuck's sake..." John said and put his hands up without the planner. He threw the shotgun away and slowly turned around to see Jesse, pointing his shotgun into Jimmy's face, one handed.

"That's my dad," Jesse said, his voice trembling.

Jimmy laughed. "*Was* your dad. Get fucked, kid."

Jesse pulled the trigger.

A couple of things happened that John simply couldn't believe.

First, Jimmy's head caved in.

John had never seen a gun shot point-blank like that before. It was a very bizarre thing to witness, almost like an implosion. The entire skull caved in, and took the forehead, nose, lips, and teeth with it.

The only thing that didn't implode was the man's eyes, which bugged out in an almost cartoon-like fashion. Then he just fell over and blood poured out of his head like a hose.

The second thing that happened was the recoil from the blast was so violent that the shotgun swung up, hit Jesse in the face, and knocked him backwards, hard. He tripped over his own feet and slammed his head against the side of the Camaro, knocking him out.

His hand was still holding the shotgun.

Sirens in the distance. Guests looking out their windows. He saw at least one cell phone pointed in his direction. Maybe.

John grabbed the planner, put it in the inside pocket of his jacket, grabbed the sawed-off, went over to Jesse and dragged him to Blue's passenger-side door. He lifted him up and slid him into the seat, threw both shotguns into the back.

He took the audio device from the Camaro, got back into Blue, cursed out loud as he realized he forgot the GPS under the wheel well, and peeled out of the parking lot before the cops showed up.

CHAPTER SEVENTY-SIX

Fuzzy.

The amount of adrenalin pumping through his system, everything directly in front of John was bright and clear and moving at a ridiculous speed, like bad video footage. The edges were blurred, too. Almost like a tilt shift photograph.

The kid was unconscious. His arms were folded in his lap and he was breathing like he was experiencing a nightmare.

Not too far off.

The streets were empty and, after going through the mental gymnastics of where they could go to ground, he remembered the Holiday Inn. But he had no idea where it was located.

He hit the brakes and fishtailed for a hundred yards until he came to a stop. He took a deep breath and grabbed his phone, punched it into the GPS and saw they were only five minutes out. He called Hal, who picked up straight away.

"John—"

"Please tell me you're at the hotel."

"Yeah, I am."

"What room?"

"302. Just got room service—"

"I'm on my way," John said.

"Aww, come on, only for one, you dick!"

John cut him off, hit the gas.

Fuzzy.

Jesse could feel the vibrations of the car, could hear pockets of a phone conversation. He could see streetlights passing by the passenger window, pulsing, and the night-time landscape of suburbia. Trees, the abandoned strip mall, the Chinese restaurant.

His home town.

He moved his head to the left and saw the guy driving. The guy from New York. The guy following him.

He looked manic.

His name is John, he thought to himself. *Funny, the guy never introduced himself...*

Funny.

A lot of what had happened seemed quite funny.

Jesse moved a bit and knew he'd hurt himself. His arm hurt. His face hurt so badly, he was afraid it would look like a mashed-up sack of meat. In fact, everything hurt, more or less. He groaned and tried to sit up a bit more in the seat.

Then he remembered.

"He's dead, right?" It was hard to talk. His teeth felt weird.

John looked over at Jesse, looked back at the road.

"My dad's dead?" he asked again.

John nodded. "Yeah, he's dead. They all are."

Jesse shifted some more and brought his right hand up to feel his face. It took a second...

What the...

He had to look at it, look away, look at it again to really understand what it was he was seeing.

His wrist was bent at a completely wrong angle. Protruding from it were two white flat bones that reminded him of teeth for some reason. He chuckled, like, *you seeing this shit?*

"Ummm," Jesse said, turned to show the guy, and smiled.

John looked over and screamed.

Jesse didn't know how much time had passed since the scream. The car pulled into a parking lot. John got out, came around, dragged Jesse out of the car and over to a side door, down a corridor that was thankfully empty. The two got into an elevator. John pressed a button. Jesse's left arm was slung over his shoulder. The right one was leaking.

They got off on three.

The floor was quiet. The carpet, a repeated checkered pattern on the floor, looked like an American Indian design. Arrows pointing forward or backwards, depending on which direction you were walking. It was giving John a headache.

Still and stale air in the corridor, like all hotels.

John knocking on 302 hard, and a guy with a short comb-over opened the door with food sticking out of his mouth. Inside the room, the carpet was different.

The guy's mouth opened and food dropped out when he saw Jesse. John dragged him into the room and closed the door hard behind them.

Jesse could smell hamburger. French fries. Ketchup. Something sweet, maybe? He looked over to see the testicles of a man as he penetrated a woman on the television.

Having watched his fair share of porn, Jesse always hated that angle. He made a disgusted face.

"The fuck are you watching!?" John asked, incredulously.

"The fuck does it look like I'm watching?" Hal asked as he sat the kid down on one of the two double beds.

"You knew I was on my way."

"Hey, I paid good money for that—"

John grabbed what was left of the burger.

"Goddammit," Hal said, as he watched. "I'm fucking starving."

"So am I. How bad is it?"

Hal looked at the wound. "It's a compound fracture, it's fucking bad. Jesus." Hal got closer. "Clean, too." He turned to John. "It's always fucking weird, seeing bone, you know? It's so goddamn white."

"Fix it."

"Fix it? Are you shitting me?" Hal went into the bathroom and grabbed a towel.

"We can't take him to the city."

"He wouldn't make it to the city, and that's not something I can just suture up." Hal wrapped the towel around Jesse's hand. "He won't bleed out, but—"

"We just killed Joey and Jimmy."

"What?"

"Joey and Jimmy. They were here."

"You killed… wait—"

"They were here, following the kid. He went to his father, who was holed up in a motel about half a mile from here."

"Alex was—"

"They killed Alex. They were going to kill the kid, too, but—"

"Jesus Christ," Hal said and sat down on the other bed. "You… you shot someone?"

"I hit him with the car. *He* shot someone. So did Alex."

Jesse was sweating and in pain. He kept watching the television. This poor woman getting pounded, over and over. Finally, he fell back onto the bed, which felt like the most natural thing he could do. He heard the two men arguing. He felt the pain in his arm and his head. His mouth was drier than it had ever been before, but he croaked out, "Mom."

John and Hal stopped talking. John shook his head. "Jesus, your mom's not here, kid. She's fine, wherever she is."

"Is she?" Hal asked. He sounded worried.

John went to talk, closed his mouth. It was a good question.

Jesse tried to make sense of what they were saying. Yeah. She's not here. She's home. Of course she's home. Where else would she be? "She can help," he said and tried to sit up. His blood pressure dipped so low, he became nauseous. He looked at the towel and saw that it was soaked through with blood. He smiled again, looked at both men, and passed out.

CHAPTER SEVENTY-SEVEN

Carla paced the bedroom. No one was telling her anything. Hal wasn't picking up the phone. Bob from the bank called to say some guy stopped in, who said he was friends with Alex from college. That had to be the same guy who went by the newspaper. She got a call from Ken Barber, who said someone was asking about the robbery... and Alex. "Where is he?" Ken asked.

Carla hung up on him. She tried Hal again. It went straight to voicemail. "Goddammit!"

"She's going to be pissed," Jesse said, fading.

"Yeah, no shit," Hal said over Bluetooth.

John shook his head.

They took two cars. Hal insisted, since he had the guns. John had been so preoccupied he had no idea what Hal was driving, or where he was. "Just meet me there," he said.

"Jesus, OK."

"And don't park out front," Hal said.

"Why not?" John was beyond irritated.

"Because maybe Gino's there waiting for us. He'll recognize Blue. I'll check it out and let you know."

"Fine." John said, gritting his teeth. Hal being right, under the circumstances, was tough to swallow.

John parked down the block but kept her running. He grumbled under his breath. "So stupid... [mumble]... and the look on their faces... [mumble]... French toast... [mumble]... Biloxi! I mean, really, what the fuck was I thinking?"

Jesse looked at him like he was losing his mind.

"Coast is clear," Hal said through the speakers.

"OK," John said again. He turned the car off, got Jesse, limped him over to the house. Hal was standing there, parked out front, arms folded, waiting patiently next to the Cutlass John had stolen a few days prior. "This car stinks to high heaven. I mean, it's awful."

"Are you fucking kidding me?" John asked.

"What? No one will recognize it."

It took a lot of willpower not to drop Jesse, and then drop Hal.

Carla heard the front door getting pounded on from the upstairs bedroom. It was the type of noise you'd compare to getting a phone call at three in the morning, from a family member. She rushed down the stairs, got to the front door and saw a figure, no, two figures in the decorative glass around the front door.

Three figures.

"OK, OK, Jesus!" she said and she opened the door. There he was, the son of a— "Hal, what the fuck!?"

John noticed the *Hal* as he held on to Jesse.

Hal noticed John noticing it and ignored it. It would have to wait.

Carla noticed her son and the bloody towel and her entire body went into panicked mother mode. "Jesse!"

She grabbed him from John and brought him into the house.

"Dad's dead," Jesse slurred and tried to keep his legs under him. He threw up some bile, a line of it spilling out of his mouth as he was dragged to the living room.

Hal and John watched her get Jesse onto the couch, then run for her cell phone. "Make sure he doesn't fall asleep!" she yelled at them.

John went over to him and smacked Jesse lightly on the face. "Stay with us, kid."

Jesse smiled, leaked out some mucus bubbles and then threw up again.

Carla was on the phone. "I don't know." Pause. "I don't know! It's his wrist, and he's got a lump on the back of his head the size of a goddamn grapefruit. Yes, it's bleeding! B-positive." Pause. "Yeah, well, he means more to me than the money, goddammit!" Pause. "Alex? Alex is dead! Just get someone over here!"

She slammed her own cell phone onto the granite countertop in her own kitchen. There was something so unsettling about tragic things happening where so many normal, everyday things took place, and in such a safe space. It scared her even more. She turned, shaking, towards Hal. "You tell me what happened."

"I... I wasn't there," Hal said, turning to John for confirmation. John tilted his head up to look at him, but gave him nothing.

"You could have prevented this," she said.

"Alex left! How could I have—"

"You knew what was going to happen if they found out!"

"Carla, honey, I just got here a little while ago."

"'Carla, honey?'" John said to Hal and gave him a look.

"Just stop—" Hal said to John.

"Alex is dead, Hal!" she screamed. "Dead!"

"I know—"

"Are you fucking kidding me?" John asked. "And why does she look familiar?"

"Not now, John."

"It wasn't supposed to be like this..." Carla said, and started pacing.

"Who did you call?" Hal asked.

"I called the fucking doctor, you asshole!"

"Jesus, OK."

"It's more than you've done!"

Hal shook his head, turned to John. "Tell her what happened."

"Tell her...? Wait a fucking second. Who is this woman? And how do you know her? How does she know you?"

"See?" Hal said to Carla. "I told you he wouldn't remember you."

CHAPTER SEVENTY-EIGHT

A few minutes later, Doctor Bryan Lieber showed up. Tall, lanky, mid-fifties. He worked with Carla at the hospital just outside of town. He carried a leather case and a small cooler with him.

Carla went into a closet and came out with a mop and a hanger. She thrust it down in between two sections of the couch. The two then washed their hands, put on rubber gloves, and went about setting up a blood transfusion for Jesse. Carla took out an IV needle from Lieber's bag and found a vein. While she flushed it with saline, Lieber set up the y tubing and blood bag, jerry-rigged it with the hanger and mop, and held it as Carla braced the mop handle with pillows so it wouldn't fall over.

Lieber went into his bag, grabbed a syringe and a vial of liquid, drew some out and gave Jesse a shot. He pulled out some gauze, flopped Jesse's wrist back into place and began suturing.

"This is only temporary," he said. Carla nodded.

She came over to John and Hal who were sitting in the kitchen, watching.

"He'll be OK?" John asked.

"Define 'OK'," Carla said, pissed. "What happened?"

"Listen—" John started to say.

"Tell her," Hal said.

"Tell her... from where?"

"She already knows who we are and what we do and why we're in town."

"You've got to be fucking kidding..." John said, sounding more disappointed than anything else.

Hal wouldn't look at him.

"You went behind my back and did something stupid again, didn't you. You always do this, goddammit! Another White Knight situation from Hal Fucking Shipley..." John sighed, got up, started pacing and told Carla about coming into town, about the bank, the newspaper office, staking the house out, about Gino showing up, about following Charlie and Jesse to the diner, about the cops, the three-car tail, and about the shootout.

He didn't spare her the gory details.

"God," Carla said, tears rolling down her face. "Charlie." She sniffed.

"And your husband, lady—Jesus!" John said.

"Hey—" Hal started to defend her.

"How the fuck do you two know each other so well?" John asked.

Hal looked at Carla, who looked away.

"We've been seeing each other on and off for..."

Carla sobbed a little.

"For a long time now. She married Alex and... we tried to..."

"How the fuck did they get wrapped up in this shit, Hal?"

"Gino was looking for someone new to launder money with. He needed an out-of-the-way place, but close enough to the city. He didn't want to use the guys in Miami any more. He needed somewhere... isolated. I talked to some guys up at that party, that Woods Hole party that weekend, remember?"

"When? What party?"

"Jesus. The fucking party! Look, there were bankers there and I got some ideas. Gino had too much money coming in and one day I suggested he use Alex to launder it."

John looked at Hal strangely. "You brought him to Gino just like that?"

512

"No—"

"Jesus, you brought a *friend* to Gino just like—"

"Not just like that, for chrissake. Alex was... compromised."

Carla made coffee.

Lieber came over, handed her a pill bottle. "Listen, he's stable, but he lost a lot of blood. The transfusion helped, but I've done all I can for him here. I'm in tomorrow morning, you call me, we'll bring him through emergency. Off the books."

"Thank you, Bryan," Carla said, and hugged him.

Lieber nodded, went to the bathroom to clean up.

John watched the doctor leave the room, looked at Hal, his fingers covering half his face. "All of this was your idea?"

Hal made a face, shrugged his shoulders, like, *guilty*.

"Unbelievable. So, what was your big plan?" John asked.

"Well... the idea had been rolling around in my head for a while. Gino's got a lot of legit businesses, but not enough to help with the real money he had coming in. Not to mention he's got the Feds watching them like fucking hawks. So I thought... and this is going to sound crazy, but I thought 'why not a town?'"

"What?"

"Yeah, why not a depressed town, out in the middle of nowhere? Look it. Take over a small bank, right? Gino bought it through some shells and had Alex run it, so now he had a guy, an accountant with a clean record running his own fucking bank, a legitimate place to wash his cash. Alex runs it like normal. Has the town's people make their deposits, he offers businesses incentives to do their business there, and..."

"Offers to do their taxes," John said, putting the pieces together.

"That's right."

"Jesus. So... Gino was using the bank to launder money through Alex, and then Alex had his own kid rob the bank to steal from Gino...?"

513

"It's a little more complicated than that," Hal said, almost gloating.

"How much more complicated could—"

"We're all in on it," Carla said.

"What?"

"Yeah," Hal said. Carla sat down next to him. "Pretty much the whole town at this point. The businesses, I mean. Gino's wash percentage was down by almost a third, and he was thrilled. But there was a problem. Alex fucked up. The IRS sent a guy here, one of Gino's—"

"Gino has an IRS guy?"

"Yeah. Man, you don't even know. And so he squashed it before it became a problem, but not before people in town started figuring shit out on their own. And because Alex was doing all their taxes... he had to bring some of them in as partners." Hal rubbed his eyes.

"So, he was skimming."

"No. Alex just gave away his cut."

"So... wait. I don't understand the robbery."

"Originally, Jesse was supposed to rob the bank and head home, so we could all leave town together. Carla found out that Alex was going to leave town with Jesse, you know, without her... and she asked me to intercede."

"Which is where I came in," John said.

"Yeah. I thought what we did would change Alex's mind... but he was scared and..." he looked at Carla. "And pissed." He sighed. "See, those bags that you took from Jesse, they were there to *look* like a lot of cash. A lot. Not ten grand or whatever it was. The cameras would show him leaving with them... it's why they were filled with mostly singles. To make it seem like he stole more than he did."

"How much more?"

Hal took a second to answer. "Millions."

"Millions?" John laughed out loud. "No one's going to believe that a bank in this fucking shithole has that much cash lying around!"

514

"It wouldn't matter. By the time Bob at the bank called the cops and the Feds got up here and started investigating, we'd be long gone. Not to mention that anything tied to Gino would be more important than the missing money. And Alex made sure there was a legitimate connection between Gino and the bank."

Carla got up and walked over to Jesse.

John took it all in. Maybe it made sense. Didn't mean he was going to give Hal the satisfaction. Still. Something... "How long has this been going on behind my back?"

Hal sighed. "Twelve, thirteen years."

John looked physically wounded.

It made Hal sick. "It was Gino, John. And, honest, I was doing you a favor. If you got wrapped up in Gino's money..."

"And how long have you been planning this?"

Hal shook his head. "Couple of months."

John sat down, hard, stared at nothing.

"Look," Hal said and rubbed his face with his hands. "I'm tired, John. I've been doing this for too long, and... I was there when Maria got killed." John looked over at him. "And I... helped. Her and Fernando." Hal lowered his head. "It was Gino's way of, well, making sure he had me because, if he ever needed to get rid of Alex, I was the guy. I *was* the guy, and after that I wanted out." Hal shook his head, smiled at John. "This was fun at first, you know? And *you*..." the smile disappeared. "But I've seen too much, been a party to... too much. Alex called me up one day last week and said it was go-time. Gino had more than ten million in safety deposit boxes up here, and he wanted it back. Alex said that Gino was pulling out. That was definitely the sign, and chances were that Gino was going to ask me to kill Alex." He looked at Carla. "And maybe some other people. So, we staged the bank robbery. Alex's job was to take the cash out earlier that morning..."

"And then he never came home." Carla said. Jesse was lying down with his head in her lap.

"So, you're telling me... the town stole from the mob," John said.

515

Hal tilted his head. "Not the *whole* town... like, twenty..."

"Fuck..."

"... thirty people were involved—"

"Come *on*! So the people at the diner—"

"Yeah."

"The newspaper..."

"Yeah."

"And the people at the bank."

"Yeah."

"The doctor?" John jerked his thumb towards the bathroom.

"Yes," Carla said.

"Not that nut-job deputy—"

"A problem, I know," Hal said. He looked exhausted.

"Jesus fucking... this whole thing is nothing but problems, man! Why the hell did you wait to involve me in this thing until now?"

"Because I wanted you to come with us! I figured it was time for you and I to get out of this life. I didn't..." Hal shook his head. "I didn't think it was going to become the clusterfuck it did." Carla scoffed. "It wasn't supposed to, goddammit! Alex wasn't supposed to disappear like that."

"Then why did he?" John asked.

"I don't know."

"Where's the money?"

Jesse said something, groaned something. John thought he heard the words "tell her."

Hal shrugged.

"A shrug? Fantastic. So, now we have Gino in this tiny little—"

"Hamlet—"

"Fuck you, Hal! This isn't funny. Gino is here, two of his men are dead, ten million dollars of his money is missing..."

"It sounds worse than it is—"

"And you two were fucking behind Alex's back?"

Fresh tears from Carla. Hal hung his head.

"So, besides the money, you were going to get the girl, too? Did Alex fuck you over because of her? What's your real take in this, Hal?"

Hal looked at Carla, who shook her head. "It's kind of hard to explain," he said.

John hit him, hard, left side of his face. It sent Hal over the kitchen table, chairs scrambling.

It was only the second time he'd hit Hal since he'd met him.

John lifted him up by what hair he had left on his head. "Explain it to me outside," he growled, and pulled the patio door open.

"Oh, don't hurt him!" Carla yelled, but only half-heartedly.

CHAPTER SEVENTY-NINE

John threw Hal by the hair, by his head, over towards the patio set. He hit a chair and neatly fell into it, then it tipped over. John walked over, ready for another punch.

"Hey, man, take it easy! I have like only two hundred hairs left, goddammit!"

John stopped. He smirked. Hal smiled. John smiled. Hal laughed. John laughed. He put his hand out and Hal took it, righting the chair with him in it. Hal grabbed some snow from the patio table. He rubbed his face while John paced, collecting his thoughts, and sat down across from him.

"You've got to talk to me, man," John said.

"I just can't believe you don't remember her. I could have sworn once you saw her face you'd remember at least something."

"From where?"

"The party in Cape Cod. You did a runner from Miami to Boston for that lunatic... remember?"

John shook his head. "No. I don't remember much of anything. That was a long time ago..."

Hal watched him think it over. "She never told you her name, man."

He saw it dawn on John's face.

"Jesus, *that* was *her*?" John looked over at her. She was talking to Lieber who was looking at Jesse's bandaged wrist.

"Yeah, it was. Carla was there, and so was Alex… but I don't think you ever got to meet him, did you?"

John shook his head. No. Maybe. Some of it was coming back to him.

"They weren't together then. He was fucked up and trying to get with some twinkie. You and Carla were out on the beach and had sex all night."

"Come on. What the fuck…"

And suddenly he remembered cold water. And laughter. A woman after a 15-hour drive. He was exhausted. She said something about being able to help and handed him a pill. Some souped-up Ecstasy, cut with speed. They ate something near a fire… she had that sparkle in her eye that said love the one you're with.

"Anything?"

"Yeah. Some of it's coming back to me."

"Good, 'cause it's one of the reasons I brought you up here, man. Because I knew you had a stake in this."

"What? What stake could I possibly have in this bullshit, Hal? Just because I had sex with some lady, what…" he mentally calculated "… *sixteen* fucking years ago doesn't mean I have any responsibility…" He stopped. John looked into the living room where Carla still sat with Jesse. "Oh, come on. No, no, no. Don't even say it. That kid looks nothing like me. So, we both have blonde hair, so what?"

"Hey, I don't know if that kid is yours or not. She's not sure whose kid it is." Hal looked a bit sheepish, closed one eye, tilted his head and made this funny look, like he was about to confess something funny, stupid, embarrassing. "I had sex with her the next day."

"Oh, God!" John visibly shivered.

"Oh fuck you, Mr. Puritan."

"Puritan? We… we double-teamed a stripper!"

"Once!" Hal looked so serious.

John laughed.

519

"Look, I never told you about Jesse because you had your own thing going with Caroline... and after, you know... well, I didn't want to complicate things. Carla doesn't know whose kid that is... but she fell in love with Alex after we left that weekend, and she married Alex, and so he was the father." Hal sighed and leaned back. "Look, Alex got himself into trouble, and I got him out of it, and into this. He was on the hook in a really bad fucking way. And I swear—this? The bank, dealing with Gino? It was the better deal. All he had to do was keep his fucking head down and... and then the people in town, and the fucking IRS guy... he came back up here again, and he..."

"He what?"

"He tried to muscle Alex into giving him a cut."

"You're fucking kidding."

"So..." Hal said. "Alex... got a little stabby..."

"No."

"Yeah."

"You helped him kill a fucking IRS guy?"

"Me? No! No, Jesus. Alex did. Cut his throat and then stabbed him like a hundred times." Hal shook his head. "What a fucking mess."

"Where?"

"Same room Alex was staying in, at the All Seasons Motel. He booked the room for a month. He was paranoid, even after we cleaned the place up. Kept it on ice in Poughkeepsie, then got rid of the body over at Dean's."

"So, you and Alex got together to rob Gino of his money."

"Yeah."

"Alex got Jesse, his own son, to pose as the robber... and you told me Gino gave us the tip on the robbery."

"Yeah. Stupid, I know. I just thought the less you knew the better, until we got away with it."

"So, Gino's inside guy found out about the robbery."

"Well..."

"Well what?"

"There was no inside guy."

"What?"

"I made that part up."

"I don't understand."

"It was just to keep the whole Gino façade up..."

"Then how did Gino find out about what you were doing? Maybe there *was* an inside guy."

"There wasn't. Everyone at the bank was in on it."

"Then how?"

"I don't know. I'm wracking my brain... I'm just glad I kept you out of this—"

"Please. Don't act like you were doing me a favor."

"I was *trying* to do you a favor."

"Ten million doesn't split up *that* many times, Hal!"

Hal sighed. "I thought it would at least be a start. Plus, what I've got stashed and all... and I know Alex had money saved, he was making two percent. He was *supposed* to get three." Hal rubbed his face and smiled out of the side of his mouth. "I lied to him and traded the one back to Gino for the garage."

"What?"

"Yeah. I was making five percent since the beginning... my idea, right? I thought money would be the least of our problems with that much coming in, so, yeah, we own the garage."

"You mean the garage we can never go back to?"

Hal nodded. "Yeah, well, at the time I never thought I'd do something like this, and when things fell apart, what with Maria and the IRS guy, the time came... it's why I told you to bring Blue."

"Blue."

"Yeah. I knew you wouldn't leave her behind..."

John shook his head. This fucking unbelievable— "What the hell was Alex thinking, trying to pull a fast one on—"

"He was fucking one of the tellers. It's the reason Carla and I got together. Maybe it was too much for him. Maybe he was going to run out on everyone. Take Jesse... probably thought I could cover for Carla. I mean, could you blame him?"

"Hal. I mean, Jesus, who is *everyone*? Why would all of these people get involved? Didn't you warn them about what Gino was capable of?"

Hal sighed, shrugged his shoulders and looked away. "This is a nice place, John. The people are nice. But there's nothing here. They're all just stuck. Word got around, that's all. This money, it's like the lottery to them."

"OK, so, now you're all Musketeers?" John looked to see Lieber was leaving through the front door.

"Actually, I always thought of this place as Sherwood For—"

An explosion.

Lieber was blown off his feet, into the kitchen. Shrapnel or part of the slug shot through one of the patio's plate glass windows. Splinters flew everywhere.

John looked over at Lieber. There were too many holes.

Carla screamed.

"Please tell me you have a gun on you," John said.

"I left them in the car!" Hal yelled.

"You fucking left them in the... shit!" John hid beside a wall and peered inside. He could only see Jesse. His new bandage was leaking. "Left them in the... who the fuck does that?"

"Oh, who does that? Where are your guns, Mr. Pacifist?"

"Pacifist? I killed a guy with my car tonight!"

"So? That's not the point!"

"Oh, so you can leave yours in the car, but I—"

"Would you shut the fuck up?"

Hal reached into his jeans pocket and brought out a prescription bottle.

"The fuck are you doing?" John asked incredulously.

"Xanax," Hal said and took two.

"You remembered to bring fucking Xanax, but—" John looked inside again, looked down at Lieber's body. "Gimme," he said, holding his hand out. Hal gave him two.

John dry swallowed them, climbed into the house through the broken window. He couldn't see anything out the front door, which was wide open.

"I guess Gino brought more guys with him," John said as he crouched down. "Where is Carla?"

Hal peered in through the broken window. "I don't know. Look, I'll take care of the ones out front. You grab the kid and Carla, if she's still alive."

"Grab the...? You'll take care of the...? What the fuck are you talking about?"

Hal smiled.

It was the kind of smile that said, "*I know what I'm doing, even though there's a really good chance I'm going to die doing it.*"

John had seen that smile before. Too many times.

Hal took off and jumped over the neighbor's hedges. John heard a yell of pain as Hal hit the ground.

John shook his head, feeling kind of like Butch Cassidy for some reason. He duck-walked into the kitchen and grabbed the biggest knife he could find. It was stuck against one of those magnetic knife boards, a long, sharp butcher's knife. When he pulled on it, the whole block came down, making a racket. "Goddammit," he said under his breath.

From somewhere off to his left, Carla was sobbing. "I don't know where it is!"

"Bullshit, lady." He didn't recognize the voice. A distinctly Queens accent, low, no nonsense. There was a smack.

Carla fell into view and hit the ground. She didn't see John.

He could see her crawling, pawing away at the tiles on the floor.

Walking towards her, one of Gino's goons. Nick, maybe. Hard to say. The guy was big.

Somewhere in his mind, he was glad it wasn't Ivan.

Double-barreled shotgun in hand, the guy slowly walked towards Carla.

Everyone's got a fucking shotgun, John thought.

The guy pointed it at her. "Tell me where the fuck the money is!" Definitely Nick.

John stood up and got behind him. He poised the knife, ready to grab Nick by the shoulder, to stab him in the middle of his back.

No, John thought. *Won't work.*

He put the knife lower, to stab him in his side, near his kidney.

This won't work either, he thought. *Nick might still get a shot off.*

John raised the knife to where he'd grab Nick's hair and cut his throat, but the thought made John nauseous.

Finally, he held the knife way above his head and plunged it square into the back of Nick's neck. In the split second before he did it, John worried it would glance off a bone and barely penetrate.

The knife went clean through, came out through his throat.

Nick, unable to turn his head, twisted his entire body to see exactly what had happened. Blood gurgled up and into his mouth, bubbled at the sides, and poured out slowly. His eyes were full of recognition.

Carla took the shotgun out of his hands, like taking something from a sleeping child.

Nick looked at John. John looked back. Nick pawed at the blade and cut his hand, deep. He blinked a few times before his legs gave out and he collapsed on his side.

John took a deep breath, surveyed the room. "Give me that," he said to Carla, and held his hand out.

Carla checked the chambers to see if rounds were loaded. "I'm sure he has another one on him, John."

"Goddammit," John searched the guy, found a snub nose .38 in an ankle holster, loaded. Five shots. He felt for a speedloader. Nothing doing except for two more shotgun shells. He fucking hated snub nose .38s. They felt like tinker toys in his hand.

Carla walked backwards towards her son, grabbed him by the arm and got him up off the couch. "We're getting out of here, Jesse." She began moving him towards the back broken window, again walking backwards, the shotgun pointed out in front of her.

"Jesus, Carla, the fucking place is probably surrounded! Give me the shotgun so I can at least give us a chance!"

"Move out of the way, John."

"Carla, goddammit!"

"Move out of the way!"

"Move out... fine. You know what? You win, Carla, you wi—"

She fired at the front door. Both barrels. The shells must have been buckshot because the entire foyer was reduced to kindling. The guy who'd come through the front door was shredded.

Carla fell back, lost her balance and flew through an unbroken window at the back of the house. The pane broke into large pieces. They crashed to the ground with clanging noises.

She hit a piece of patio furniture and dropped the shotgun, which spun away from her.

John and Jesse ran out to her and lifted her off the ground.

"The recoil is a bitch, isn't it?" Jesse said weakly.

Carla steadied herself and said, "Watch. Your. Language." And then she collapsed, face forward. A large piece of plate glass was sticking out of her upper back. Right side, somewhere between her lung and her hip.

"Carla!" John yelled.

"Mom!" Jesse yelled.

Gunfire erupted on the front lawn. Shotgun blasts and the burp of an assault rifle. Sounded like Hal's ACR.

John felt a modicum of relief as he pocketed the snub nose, ran and grabbed the shotgun. He loaded it, came back, put Carla on her side. He checked her pulse, but his hand was slick with blood. It was welling up from a dozen wounds.

He lowered his ear next to her mouth and heard her breathing. It didn't sound great.

"We have to get the fuck out of here," John said.

"I'm not leaving her!"

"Blue is down the block."

"The fuck is a Blue?"

525

"We get there, we'll be OK."

Jesse shook his head. "I don't care. I don't care!"

"You'll care after we get out of this. Can you run?"

"I can walk fast, maybe," he said, looking down at his mother, who was looking up at him.

She mouthed the word "*go*." Jesse started crying.

John grabbed Jesse by the shoulder, walked him through the house. "You run, you understand me? I'm gonna go out first, you run like hell straight down the block, straight. You see the blue Charger, you take cover."

"Is it open?"

"No." John gave him the keys. "This is the key. You get there you open it up, turn on the ignition. It doesn't take much, she's got a hair trigger, understand? Don't flood it."

Jesse nodded.

"And don't forget to unlock my side!"

John got up, moved Jesse into position. At the front door, he peered out, carefully. Two Caddies out front, to the right of the Cutlass. Two dead guys on the front lawn, five other hit men taking cover behind the Caddies.

Hal had his ACR behind the sedan, resting on his haunches. He was reloading when he looked up and saw John and Jesse at the front door. He made a hand gesture, one John recognized that meant he'd cover them. John nodded.

Hal slapped in a new magazine and chambered a round. He took a deep breath, stood up, and let fly.

"Now!" John yelled.

He pushed Jesse out the door towards the street, brought the shotgun up and fired at the two Caddies. The five remaining hit men ducked for cover.

Jesse started a struggling run up the block.

John got over by the sedan. Hal ran out of bullets and hunkered down as the hit men opened fire.

John checked the shotgun. Empty. "You have anything else with you?"

"I've got a snub nose!" Hal yelled over the noise, pulled one out of a holster at his back.

"Goddammit!" John threw the shotgun off to the side and grabbed the snub nose in his pocket.

"Hey, look at that. Twins," Hal said, handing John the other gun. He smiled. "You know what I was thinking?"

"Don't say we should open a bar—"

"We should drive out of here backwards."

"You're making jokes now?!"

Hal smiled. "Yeah!"

"That's a terrible idea!"

"I know!"

"It was terrible the first time you suggested it!"

Hal looked at him, eyes wide. "Goddammit, I fucking *knew* you knew it was *my* idea!"

More gunfire. They both ducked lower.

"I have to get to Blue," John said, peering up to see where the hit men were.

"I'll cover you, OK? Just, you know, come back and get us," Hal said with that same smile. He reloaded.

Us.

John knew he couldn't say anything about Carla and have them all survive. He nodded, stood up firing.

The five hit men ducked, again.

It's a game, John thought as he pulled the triggers. *Who runs out of bullets first.*

Hal stood up and fired a long burst. One of the hit men screamed. Another didn't make a sound as he took a round to his forehead.

John took off running. The machine gun echoed through the neighborhood, a deeply violent noise that seemed even more frightening the further he got away from it.

Blue was running when he got there. John got into the driver's seat, threw the two empty snub noses onto the floor of the passenger side, closed the door, turned on the high beams and floored it.

"What the fuck are you doing, you're heading right towards them!" Jesse screamed.

"Got to get Hal."

CHAPTER EIGHTY

"Sorry, pal," Hal said to no one. "Didn't mean to lie to you. Again." From the trunk of the car he took out a Beretta ARX160 A3 assault rifle—thirty-round clip, laser sight— and an A1 grenade launcher. "*My* baby," he said as bullets shot through the sedan. Hal chambered a round, checked the tube, saw a 40mm High Explosive ready to launch.

In the distance he heard Blue.

That sound. That engine.

He waited until there were two, three seconds of silence before he stood up and shot the HE round into one of the Caddies. It hit the windshield, hit the front seat, hit the back seat, and sent the car up into the air about five feet. Flames shot out of the windows. The doors buckled and blew off, as did the trunk and the hood. It landed with a sound that he'd never heard before. Angry metal on fire.

One of the hit men screamed as he fell to the ground, a piece of the car stuck in his leg. The two others were behind the still intact Caddy.

"Get in the back!" John yelled.

"There is no back!" Jesse yelled back.

John grabbed him by the shirt, "Get the fuck back there!" and stuffed him on top of the gas container, watching the road the entire time. He could see one of the Cadillacs on fire. Hal was stuck behind the sedan. Lights were on in the house.

He could see a shadow moving through the firelight. Maybe.

John held the wheel with his left hand, extended himself just enough to reach the passenger door with his right, and skidded to a stop behind the on-fire Caddy. He opened the door for Hal.

"Get in here!"

Hal shook his head. "Wait! I've got to get Car—"

And stopped.

There was a *plink* sound, as if something hard had hit the car.

At first, John thought it was the crackle from the fire. Something.

The expression on Hal's face was... wrong. He dropped the assault rifle as if it was the heaviest thing in the world. He pawed at himself strangely. Opening his shirt, John saw a neat bullet hole in his chest, just right of center. Blood started flowing out of it.

"No, nonono, Hal!"

Hal dropped to his knees, reached out his hand to John, to Blue, and fell over.

Behind him, Gino was pointing a handgun.

John screamed as Gino pointed the gun at John.

The two remaining hit men started firing.

Bullets hit the windshield and bounced off. One ricocheted close to Gino. Too close. He ducked, his gun hand wavering. He got a shot off that went way wide.

John hit the gas. The passenger-side door hit the burning Caddy and slammed shut. Bullets continued to hit the car, making that same *plinking* noise.

Gino stepped forward and pushed Hal's body. No movement.

The two remaining hit men ran over to him.

"Call the others and get after them. Forget the kid. Kill 'em, whatever. But I need the guy alive."

They nodded, took off in the Caddy.

Gino sighed. He put the gun into his waistband, pushed his hair back with both hands and looked up into the night sky.

Even with the lights from the house, the fire from the car, he could see the stars more clearly than he ever could in the city. For a second there, he wondered what the simple life would have offered him, had he taken it all those years ago.

He got down, patted Hal, found his car keys, closed the trunk to the sedan, got in and started it up. *Even full of bullet holes. These boys sure do know how to pick them*, he thought.

He pulled out past the burning car and followed his men.

CHAPTER EIGHTY-ONE

John gripped the steering wheel tight. "Goddammit, fucking goddammit, FUCKING GODDAMMIT!"

Jesse was scrunched in the back, shaking. Scared. The adrenaline was making him feel nauseous. Or maybe it was the shooting. Or the pain. Or his mother. Or maybe it was the killing of that guy Hal.

"Jesse, get up here and put the seat belt on."

He did.

John looked in the rear-view mirror, saw the Caddy behind him.

"Fuckers." He slowed down.

"What are you *doing*?"

"Trust me."

John removed the panel that had the counter intrusions. "Swallow these, you fucking—" He flipped a switch.

Nothing happened.

He flipped another switch. Nothing happened. "Shit!" He flipped the third switch. "Goddammit, Hal!"

He smashed the panel.

Nothing.

He hit it again. His hand got cut up.

Again.

At the back of the car, a compartment opened up. Forty small, triangular tacks shot out and hit the road. A small nozzle sprayed the road with an oil slick.

The Caddy, too close to stop, hit the tacks and the oil slick. The two front tires blew out. The back tires lost their traction, spun to the right and hit a parked car, flipped and landed on its roof. John saw the driver fly out of the windshield and skid along the pavement.

"Ahahah!" John yelled triumphantly, looking through the rear-view mirror.

From a cross street behind them, two more Cadillac's made the turn and began following them.

"Oh, shit!" He hit the gas. "Jesse, check the shotgun."

Jesse pulled the shotgun from the back seat. It was empty.

"Shit, what else?"

Jesse opened up the cylinders of the two snub noses. Both were empty.

"Nothing," Jesse said, fear flooding in.

"Christ almighty, we need some weapons!"

Like a cartoon, like a cheesy comic book, Jesse could practically feel a light bulb over his head. "Go straight and turn left at the light! I have an idea."

"Right there," Jesse said, pointing. It was a store cloaked in darkness. John looked behind in the rear view. The two cars were gaining.

"Fuck it," he said, and plowed Blue through the front window of the store. A second compartment of triangular tacks opened up and fell out, just as John slammed on the brakes. The car fishtailed and stopped about twenty feet in.

They both got out.

It took a second for John's eyes to adjust. "What the fuck is this shit?"

Along one wall were suits of armor, knives, swords, shields, maces. Above the register was a weapon John had seen, but never knew the name of. It had a wooden handle about a foot and a half long, with a chain to match, and a large metal ball with spikes at the end. A sign under it said *Morning Star Flail.*

"Are you fucking kidding me?"

"You said weapons!"

"I meant a fucking sporting goods store!"

"Sorry…"

"You live in the bastion of the Second fucking Amendment, and we're going to fucking die at a Renaissance fair?!"

John looked and saw both Caddies stop outside of the shop. He grabbed Jesse and found some cover.

CHAPTER EIGHTY-TWO

Four men got out of the cars. Lenny, Max, Mike, and Benny.

"The fuck kind of place is this?" Mike asked. The sign outside looked like it was painted by a school kid, or someone's mom. Part of the front window that was still intact had a mannequin in medieval garb with a sign that said *LARP In Style!*

"This is... yeah, they have those weekends where they act like separatists or something," Max said.

"No, they act like Union soldiers and beat the shit out of the South," Benny said.

"With swords?" Mike asked.

Lenny took out an Uzi from the car. "Swords, shields, who gives a shit. And this is like the Renaissance fairs, you dumb fucks. Wizards and shit."

A collective "ohh."

The other three got their guns out.

John heard them, saw them, shook his head. "Are you fucking kidding me?"

"What?" Jesse asked.

"These are bad guys. Fucking hate these guys."

Jesse looked around him, spotted a hefty suit of armor. "You think this is bulletproof?"

Before John could answer, machine gun fire. Every-fucking-where.

John ducked, grabbed Jesse and pushed him to the floor. Bullets hit the cash register, windows, mirrors, glass cases, and the armor.

It took a while, but the gunfire finally stopped.

John lifted his head up a bit, blinking rapidly, a ringing in his ears. The noise had been deafening.

Behind them, a clinking noise, like something metal dropping down a drain.

John looked at the armor. It was Swiss cheese. "I don't think so."

Jesse nodded.

John made his way to one of the display cases.

Jesse couldn't take his eyes off the destroyed armor.

The store had two kinds of weapons. Real and fake. John grabbed a bunch of real knives from a case by the register, looked up and saw a broadsword displayed on the wall.

In the dark, fifty–fifty it was real.

He threw the knives towards their cover, making sure not to hit Jesse, carefully moved to the wall, grabbed the sword and hefted it. "Jesus fuck, this thing is heavy." He could see from the car light that edges were incredibly sharp.

Underneath the register, a series of monitors showing security camera footage here and there, and a digital recorder.

As he went to go back to Jesse, the flail on the wall grabbed his attention.

Staying out of sight, he put the broadsword under his arm, grabbed the flail off the wall. He was careful to hold both the handle and the ball, so it didn't make noise, didn't give away his position.

"What's the plan?" Jesse asked.

"Are... are you fucking kidding me?" John hissed. "I'm making this shit up as I go!" He showed the flail to Jesse. "Anyone but me, you understand?" Jesse nodded. "You hit them with this thing as hard as you can. Try and get them in the head." Jesse went to take it with his bandaged right hand. "No, use your good hand."

"I can't do shit with my left," he said.

"Doesn't matter, just start swinging."

Jesse held it in his left hand. It was heavier than he thought it would be. The spikes were at least three inches long.

John, staying out of the line of sight of the headlights, maneuvered himself to the front with the knives and the broadsword. As he got himself situated, he saw a shadow come walking in slowly.

"Who's going in first?"

It was a trick question.

Max loved being the point man. Most times, he got to blast the shit out of people, no matter who was in the room. He'd collected himself a hell of a body count.

He brought his gun up, waiting for any sign of movement. He was slow to move in because it was all harsh shadows. Dust, drywall, hay from a display, it was all suspended in the air.

Max got about ten feet into the store when he stepped on a bunch of the tacks. The tacks were long and sharp enough to rip through the sole of his right shoe. The pain was ridiculous. "Oww, Christ!" he yelled, and fell off balance.

"What did you do? Step on an elf?" Benny yelled. The others laughed.

John had waited for that exact thing to happen. He'd dumped all of the knives but one, and held onto the sword. He threw one of the knives into the corner as a diversion.

It worked.

Max, hopping in pain, righted himself, turned towards the noise and fired. It lit up the entire store.

John ran over fast, raised the sword and brought it down hard, chopping off both of Max's arms, somewhere between his elbows and his wrists.

The momentum brought John to his knees. He was genuinely surprised at how easy it had been, thinking there would be more resistance.

Max, in shock, started screaming. He watched as both arms started spray painting whatever he pointed them at.

He turned towards John, who was looking up from the ground, and showered him in blood. Max fell to his knees as the pumping slowed, slowed, slowed until he fell over, right on top of his hands.

Hands that were still holding the machine gun.

John was about to wrestle it out from under Max's body, when a fresh volley of gunfire erupted.

He grabbed the sword and ran back over to the knives, and to cover.

The barrage stopped. He figured they were reloading.

John put the sword down, hefted one of the knives and looked out towards the front of the store.

"Motherfucker," Lenny said. "I'm going to kill this fucking—"

"You think we hit Max?" Mike asked. They were having a hard time seeing anything inside the store.

"He was screaming before the shots," Lenny said, reloading. "Should have just brought some grenades."

"Gino said he needed him alive," Mike said.

"Who the fuck has grenades lying around?" Benny asked.

"I do," Lenny said.

Benny stopped reloading and started laughing at Lenny when a knife hit him in the chest.

Handle first.

It fell to the ground with a clink. "The fuck?" Benny picked it up and showed Lenny and Mike. "Jesus Christ, are you serious?"

Another knife came flying out of the store and bounced off the car windshield.

Mike looked at his friends. "Ummm..."

John didn't know what he was doing. He'd never thrown a knife before. He threw an ax one time at a tree that was ten feet away. He missed, and the ax went down a steep hill.

He wiped his hands again on his pants. He was covered in blood. He grabbed a tunic from the rack and wiped again. Better, but the copper smell...

No time to throw up.

He grabbed another knife, this time by the blade, and threw it out the window. The knife sliced his fingers as it left his hand. "Goddammit!" he said, and sucked on the wounds.

There was a clang as it bounced off the hood of a car.

Laughter from outside.

"Come on, we'll give you a few more chances!" Benny said.

Mike was having a hard time breathing from laughing. "Is this the dumbest fucking thing you've ever seen?"

Lenny was a bit more cautious. They were still knives. He pictured his friend Max's face. "I've seen dumber," he said under his breath. "Stupid fucking Polack, always had to be the first one in."

John's arm was starting to hurt.

The taunting wasn't helping.

He lined up the remaining knives in front of him, worked his right arm around a bit to get the kinks out, took a deep breath, and started throwing them as hard as he could. He picked points slightly higher than the headlights as targets.

By the time he was done, he was breathing heavily and sweating, and his right shoulder was burning.

Mike had never laughed so hard in his life. He'd positioned himself front and center of the Caddy, his shirt wide open, his Uzi on the hood. "Right here! I'm giving you a fucking target! You can't miss!" He laughed again. "Is this guy a fucking moron or what?" Mike turned around to his two friends and stopped.

Benny had a knife stuck in his throat. He was pawing at it like he didn't know what it was, or what to do.

Lenny had a knife in his stomach. He was down on the ground, his legs folded under him, slowly pulling it out with shaking hands. He dropped it to the ground and groaned in pain.

"Motherfucker," Mike yelled. "MOTHERFUCKER!" He grabbed his gun off the hood, ejected the magazine, slapped a new one in, racked it, and turned towards the store, when a sword whirled out of the darkness and pierced his chest.

The blade went clear through to the other side of his body, the force slamming him into the hood of the car. The blade went through that, and got stuck in the engine block.

Mike tried to get up. He wasn't in pain, but he was stuck, and it scared him.

He died looking up at the hilt, thinking of his father, both of them watching *The Sword and the Stone* at the old Avenue U Theatre when he was a boy.

"Didn't miss that time, did I?" John yelled, and sat down hard.

It was back to quiet. He could still smell the blood on him. His skin was sticky. He looked for Jesse. In the chaos, he couldn't remember where he last saw him. Which was fine. Better he hide while John made sure it was all—

CLICK.

John shut his eyes. "Come on..." *You let your guard down for one second...*

He tilted his head a bit, saw the gun pointed at his head, saw Gino standing there, backlit by the headlights.

"Jesus."

"Guess again," Gino said.

CHAPTER EIGHTY-THREE

"Gino, man. What the hell is going on?"

"I don't know, to be honest with you. I thought you could tell me." He walked around to face John, the gun still pointed at him. "Sonny boy, you look terrible. You get hit?"

"No, it's not my blood."

"Good. That's good. Not sure *why* it's good... you..." he sighed. "I'm not sure how all of this got started. It's a mess, that's for certain. I haven't lost this many guys in a long time. Honest, I didn't think either one of you had it in you. But, you throw in the money, and that cunt..." He looked out of the store. "Those were good boys. Expendable, don't get me wrong, but good. The ones at the house? Meh. But Joey and Jimmy... they're going to be a problem, being family, you know. But you..." He looked back at John. "You were one of my most prized possessions. You and Hal. He helped me make more money than any person that's ever worked for me."

"And you killed him."

"Well, come on. Of course I did. It's a hard lesson to learn, but once you get to a certain size, a certain amount of power, these things happen all the time. They have to happen. You kill the people you trust. Or the people you think you can trust. You definitely kill the ones you can't trust. It's inevitable, really. Most times, I just have someone else do it. But every once in a while, I have to remind people that I can still get my hands dirty. Even at my age. Makes things easier when you have to threaten people you can't just kill over the small stuff. Plus, it's cheaper. And fun."

"Well, you've been hanging around here long enough. Watching. Waiting. Why didn't you just kill me?"

Gino lowered the gun, but kept it pointed in John's general direction. "Because you're the only one who knows where my money is."

"I have no idea where your money is, Gino." John sank lower to the ground, exhausted. "I was being used by Hal, just like you."

"Bullshit. The two of you, hell, the three of you must have been planning this for months, maybe even years. I knew it was a mistake using Alex. A guy in those circumstances would do just about anything to save his own ass... but Hal really convinced me. And the idea was a good one. A fucking town? Who thinks of using an entire town to launder money? It was brilliant. Then Alex fucked up and I had to have my guy come up here and fix things. The same guy I sent up here last week, the IRS guy, the guy I miraculously can't find anymore... you know anything about that?"

John nodded. "Alex killed him."

"You don't say."

"Yeah. Hal got rid of the body. At Dean's."

"Do you know how hard it is to buy an IRS agent?" Gino sighed. "And now you're telling me *Alex* is the one who killed him, not Hal?"

"Yeah. Hal said the guy put the screws to him for a cut."

Gino chuckled. "No shit. Well, I didn't think Miles had it in him, either. Had I known it was Alex, I would have moved in sooner. He's caused me a significant amount of trouble. Him and Hal. Maybe you, too... I don't know." He studied John's face. "I'm on the fence about you now. You brought your baby out of storage." He pointed towards Blue.

"Hal's idea. So I'd leave with them."

Gino nodded. "Maybe. Still, I don't know how they thought I wouldn't miss forty million dollars."

The scene froze.

Gino stood there in the headlights of the Cadillacs, gun in hand, looking down at him. John could have sworn he heard groaning from one of the men outside. Dust swam through the air. John replayed it again. *Forty million...*

"F... what? Forty?"

Gino shook his head and smiled. "See? That looks like genuine surprise on your face. Now, you've either been practicing, or you honestly didn't know." Gino looked around the store. "What a strange place. The town, I mean, but this place, too. You know, I was paying Alex good money to do his job. Good money. He was getting two percent for doing almost nothing. This whole thing was practically running itself. I bought him the bank, I got him out of hock with the fucking..." he shook his head. "And all Hal had to do for *his* share was babysit him." Gino took a deep breath. "Greed's a killer, John. We all know it. You don't even have to be in this life to know it. We see people go down for greed all the time. Alex got greedy. And so did Hal." Gino sat on the front counter.

"Jesus, Hal didn't know there was forty million dollars."

"The hell he didn't."

"Alex said he was stealing ten, Gino."

"Just ten, huh?"

"Yeah." John thought it through. "In fact, that's how you found out, isn't it...? Why you're up here. Alex electronically transferred the forty million out of your account."

"That's right."

"Jesus, Hal didn't know that."

"So what? Ten, forty, what's the difference? Is that supposed to make all this better?"

"No. No of course not. Alex told Hal you were shutting down the operation, and the ten million was in safety deposit boxes."

"That's right." Gino rubbed his face with his free hand. "I was funneling up my Brooklyn interests here, and it was working, for a while. A long time. But I was going to lose Miami if I didn't start giving them more, and—"

"You can't lose Miami."

"No. I can't. *And*, I couldn't keep both, so... Alex had done *too* good a job. Made himself indispensable. He had access to everything. In the end, he simply had too much power over me." Gino stretched his legs.

John looked around for something—anything—to use against him.

Nothing.

"So," Gino said. "Alex doesn't tell Hal how much money there really was. Hal figures, what, Alex needs Hal to get him and his family away clean... which makes sense, the guy's been doing that for forever. They come up with a plan to stage the robbery, which, I have to admit, was pretty clever. Hal brings you in and, what? Makes it seem like it was a job from me?"

John nodded. "That's right."

"So he really kept you in the dark."

"Yeah."

"That must have hurt, when you found out."

John looked up at Gino. "It did."

"So they faked the robbery, even for *you*... Alex transferred the forty out of my personal account, *and* stole my cash." Gino chuckled. "You know, if Alex hadn't been so fucking greedy, it might've worked. A bank robbery would have brought the Feds, and it wouldn't have taken them long to find out about what we were doing here. But something went wrong."

"Yeah. Alex disappeared."

"That's right. You know why?"

"Hal was fucking his wife."

Gino chuckled. "Of course he was. You know, one of the things I've found wholly consistent in this line of work? How much of a pain in the ass women are. So, what, he was going to flee the country? Why didn't he?"

John shook his head.

"You know why, don't you?"

"Yeah. Because the people in town were allowing him to use their accounts to launder the money."

"Allowing? They didn't have a choice, pal."

"Your IRS guy interviewed one of them when Alex first fucked up. He couldn't keep it a secret anymore."

"Yeah? So?"

"So they got in on it."

"You're shitting me. So, first he uses all of these people, and then he got it into their heads that they were going to get a bit of my money for their troubles? Are you fucking telling me Alex grew a conscience? Jesus, that's the *other* thing that gets people into trouble."

"Whatever he was thinking, Alex still lied to Hal."

"So what? He was still stealing from me. You think it hurt, killing Hal? It didn't. You divorce those feelings from the people you love instantly once they hurt you. And he did. He broke my fucking heart." He pointed the gun at John. "Now where's the money?"

"I don't know."

"John, please. Do I have to shoot your knees out? Maybe one through your stomach? I can make all of this very painful. I don't want to, but..." he shrugged.

"Gino, I mean it. Maybe I can help you find it..." John said. He was resigned at this point. God only knew where the money was... everyone involved was dead.

"*Maybe* doesn't do shit for me. *Maybe*. Jesus. You gotta know, John, this isn't easy for me to do, but I gotta do this." He cocked the gun.

"What about the money?"

"It's not going to be too difficult to find out what happened to it. People in towns like this scare easy. *Someone* knows. I guess I'll have to start on Alex's cunt of a wife, if she's still ali—"

WHACK!

The sound was like a sledgehammer hitting a melon.

545

John thought he'd heard the chain before the swing but his eyes were fixed on the gun barrel, which went off, loud. The bullet grazed his shoulder.

Then Gino dropped the gun.

He backed off a bit and made a slow-motion turn of his head. Embedded in the top of his skull was the ball of the flail.

Gino saw a young boy, still holding the handle of the weapon, his bandaged hand covering his mouth. He was crying.

Gino's feet gave out and he landed hard, his knees under him. He slowly turned back to John. His eyes had gone red. Blood was slowly coming out of his mouth and nose and ears. "Who's the kid?" Gino's voice was slurred and weak.

John swallowed hard, leaned in close to Gino's ear, said under his breath, "He may or may not be my son."

Gino turned to him. Something registered in his eyes. He nodded slowly, smiled, and fell to the floor onto his face.

Jesse let go of the handle and fell back against the wall behind him. He was shaking. He toed Gino in the chest, once. Twice. No movement. "This guy..."

"Gino."

"He had my dad killed?"

John shook his head, whispered, "Maybe."

"What?"

"Yeah, kid. He had your dad killed."

"And my mom?" Jesse started crying heavier.

"Jesus, yeah, your mom, too."

Jesse buried his head in his hands.

John looked at the sphere sticking out of Gino's head. He turned his face towards the front window.

No sirens. Not even a store alarm.

Fucking small towns...

John walked over to Blue, got in, started her and backed out of the store.

He got out, saw Benny and Lenny dead on the ground. He saw Mike, skewered on the hood of one of the Caddies. John got into the other Caddy and drove it into the store. He got back out, went to the register, grabbed the digital recorder, tossed it on the ground and stepped on it, hard. Again. It broke. He picked it up, threw it into the Caddy, and went over to Jesse. "We have to go, Jesse." Jesse shook his head, crying. "We can't stay here," John said, and held his hand out.

"And where are we going to go, huh? Where?"

John knelt down so they were closer to eye to eye. "We'll figure it out. But we have to leave. Now. God knows when the cops are going to get here, but they will, and there's no explanation in the world for all this..." John grabbed Jesse's good hand, pulled him up on his feet and out of the store.

He opened Blue's passenger door and sat Jesse inside, grabbed his shirt and ripped off a piece of it. "What the hell are you doing?"

John looked at the piece of fabric. "Well, I didn't want to ruin mine." John walked over to the Caddy inside the store. He grabbed an arrow from a quiver mounted on a wall, and a lighter in the shape of a dragon's head.

Jesse watched as John speared the cloth, pushed open the Caddy's gas tank and stuck the fabric in.

John dipped it in and out a few times to make sure it soaked up some gas. He left half the fabric outside of the gas tank, lit the piece of fabric and tore ass out of the store. He skidded across Blue's hood, got into the car and hit reverse, hard.

He stopped about fifty feet away and waited.

And waited.

"Are you sure you lit it?" Jesse asked.

"Of course I lit it."

Jesse looked at him.

"It was fucking lit, I saw it take with the stupid—" he showed Jesse the dragon lighter. "Whatever the fuck kind of lizard this is."

Jesse grabbed the lighter and got out of the car.

"Hey!" John yelled, and watched the kid run towards the store. "Are you fucking kidding me?"

Jesse disappeared inside.

"That's all this night needs, is the kid blown to bits," John said, waiting for an explosion. He was holding his breath when he saw Jesse come running out of the store.

"It was just charred!" Jesse yelled as he hit the street—

BOOM!

Jesse hit the pavement, using his good hand to break his fall, and turned around to watch.

Flames shot out of the store. The entire place caught fire quickly.

John shook his head as Jesse ran for the car and got in. Jesse was smiling. "Proud of yourself?"

Jesse watched the store burn, still smiling. For a moment, he'd forgotten everything that happened to him.

John hit the gas, the car still in reverse.

CHAPTER EIGHTY-FOUR

The bed and breakfast was dark. John pulled into the back, and the two of them went into the house in a daze. They hadn't spoken the entire car ride.

As they were making their way to John's room, a light went on in the living room.

"Jesus!" John yelled. His nerves were shot.

Mrs. Swensen was sitting in her favorite chair, a rifle in her lap.

"You scared the hell out of me," John said.

"Hello, Mrs. Swensen," Jesse said, raising his good hand.

"Don't hello me, young man!" She got up, pointed the gun between the two of them. She looked at John's clothes. "My God, what happened to you?"

"It's not his blood," Jesse said.

"Yeah, not my—"

"Forget the blood. I want some answers! Where's my money?"

John looked at Jesse. "Are you fucking kidding me?" Jesse shrugged. John put his hand up and walked slowly over to her. "Mrs. Swensen..."

"You should mind your own business, John," she said, pointing the rifle in his general direction. John put his hand on the barrel and lowered it towards the ground. He led her back to her chair, sat next to her on the couch. "His father—" she started.

"Is dead."

"What?"

"His father is dead, Mrs. Swensen," John said.

"And my mother," Jesse said, leaning against the wall.

"Right, kid, and your mother. I didn't forget."

"Alex... Carla? They're dead?"

John nodded.

"Oh, oh my God. Jesse!" She put the rifle down and went over to him. "I'm so sorry, I didn't know!" She hugged him. He hugged her with his good hand. "Oh, my God, what happened to you?"

"Shotgun."

"What!?"

"No, I just... the recoil."

"Everyone just take it easy," John said, and leaned back. Now that he was sitting, he realized how exhausted he was. "You were in on this deal, Mrs. Swensen?"

"Of course! I'm sixty-two years old and I hate this place. I don't want to die here. Alex used my name to open an account to... well, do whatever he had to do. He used my social security number, did my taxes..."

"And you were going to get a cut."

"Yes. One night, a few years ago, Alex got us all together and told us what was happening with our accounts without our knowledge. He told us what he was going to do for us, and we all gave Alex what he needed to make it work." She looked at Jesse. "He was very smart."

"Not Hal, too?"

"No. Who's Hal?"

"Forget it. And, so, after he told you, you were all just OK with it?"

"Of course not! He used us, our businesses, our livelihoods, our friendship! It was a wonder they didn't cut him into tiny pieces and send him up to Lake Erie!"

"So what happened?"

"He told us the plan, and after he'd got the money, we'd get deposits into our business accounts that would appear as loans from the bank. Loans we wouldn't ever have to pay back. He said we'd be safe, too, from the men he was working for because, while it was a lot of money, they'd prefer losing it to going to jail."

"So, what was your cut?"

"Five percent."

"Five… percent? Mrs. Swensen, weren't there like thirty people involved?"

"Well, yes."

"Five percent… thirty people…"

"Oh, sorry. Thirty people, but only ten businesses. Each business got a percentage—"

"Oh—"

"Of the ten million dollars."

John stopped. "Of the *ten* million."

"Yes."

"I see." John wiped his face, looked at Jesse, whose eyes were wide. John coughed. Jesse looked over. John shook his head, almost imperceptibly. "And so, uhh, he told you about the robbery?" he asked.

"He did." He turned to Jesse. "He was so proud of you for volunteering to help."

"Volunteering, huh?" John asked, looking at Jesse.

Jesse smiled, shrugged.

"The master criminal here. And did Alex tell you who he gave the ten million to?"

"I told you, he gave it to the tellers," Jesse said. He sat on the stairs.

"Which tellers?" John and Mrs. Swensen asked at the same time.

"Rachel and Ellen."

"Oh!" Mrs. Swensen said, nodding.

"He told me that they could be trusted," Jesse said.

"Not the skip town type?" John asked.

"I would hope not," Mrs. Swensen said. "Rachel is my niece, and Ellen Harding… well, she's about as honest as a person can get."

"Except when she's stealing from the mob."

"Well, yes. Except then."

John stood up from the couch. "Goodnight, Mrs. Swensen. We'll work this out in the morning."

"What about the cops?" Jesse asked.

"What about them?" John asked, heading for the stairs.

"They'll be looking for me, that's what?"

"You mean the cops that are in on this? Those cops? Yeah. I wouldn't worry about those cops." John patted him on the shoulder, led him up the stairs.

"Goodnight, you two," Mrs. Swensen said. She put the rifle on the couch, sat down and watched them walk up the stairs.

It didn't take long for Jesse to fall dead asleep.

John watched him for a while. *Have to do something about that wrist*, he thought, and did a mental calculation of how safe the city would be.

It didn't look great.

Hard to say what would filter down there, and how fast. Paulie Grasso would be in charge now. He wasn't sure how he would react, or how John could spin it so it looked better for him. All that was probably wishful thinking. He'd have to think about it, but not now.

John took his jacket off, took off his shoes and socks, and made his way out into the hallway, shuffling more than stepping so he wasn't making too much noise. In the short time he'd been there, he found the house had a way of not caring where you stepped. It would crack and settle in new places, no matter what.

John got into the bathroom. The tile floor was chilly, even though there was radiator heat that made the room a furnace.

He sat down on the toilet and let the day wash over him. Not much of it mattered except for Hal. He didn't care about the money or the townspeople or the hit men, Carla, Jesse, or Gino...

In his mind, he saw Gino shoot Hal. Again. The look on his face. The *plink* against the car, even amidst the fire from the explosion. The sound was crystal clear.

It hurt to remember that, but he pushed it aside and, as he sat there, he focused on good memories. Fun memories. Even times when the guy was a severe pain in the ass.

"You left him there," he said under his breath. That's when he started crying. He knew he didn't have a choice. Didn't matter. A hard lump formed in his throat, and he knew it wasn't going to go away until he got it all out.

It took a long time.

John splashed some water on his face and took a long look at himself in the mirror. He thought he saw new wrinkles. There were heavy bags under his eyes. There had always been bags. It came with the stress of the job. These were wearier. The kind you would find on a man who would never be safe again.

He splashed more water, dried his face with one of the guest towels and made his way back to his room. Jesse was where he left him, but awake now.

"John?"

"Yeah, kid."

"What's going to happen to me?" Jesse asked.

"What do you mean?"

"Everyone's dead. I don't have anywhere to go."

John sat down on the bed and nodded, even though the kid was looking away. "Well, you can come with me if you want."

"What?"

"Yeah."

He turned to look at John. "I... I don't even know you."

"Well—"

"You're just some guy who stole the money that I stole."

"That's true. And, you know, saved your life."

"I saved *your* life."

"Yeah, but I saved yours first," John said.

Jesse frowned a bit, nodded. "Yeah. That's right."

"And I knew Hal. And Hal knew your dad. They were friends, sort of. And Hal was my friend. In fact, he was my best friend." Fresh tears started. He blinked them away. "And we both knew your mother, too. From a long time ago."

"You did?"

"Yeah. We did. I promise, kid, if she cared about Hal as much as I think she did... she'd tell you that you could trust me."

Jesse looked at him for a long time before saying "OK."

"Get some rest. Tomorrow we'll go get the money and we'll get out of here, all right?"

"OK." He thought about it for a second. "Maybe we should go see my grandparents."

John smiled, made a noise, like, *why didn't I think of that?* "Good idea, kid. We'll do that. Go back to sleep."

Jesse nodded, got comfortable again and in a few minutes was breathing heavily, out like a light.

John grabbed his coat and started to fold it when he felt something hard in the inside pocket. He took it out and looked at it, trying to remember what it was.

It was Alex's planner.

He was too exhausted to care. He tossed it aside, put his coat on the floor, used it as a pillow and fell asleep instantly.

CHAPTER EIGHTY-FIVE

Early morning. The sun was out, it was cold, and John was standing in the kitchen with Mrs. Swensen, a cup of coffee in his hand.

"You're fucking kidding me."

"I'm not fucking kidding you," she said. She was smiling. More like beaming.

"Well, that complicates things."

"What? I thought you'd be happy."

"I didn't say I was upset… it's good news. Really good. I just… now we have to go see her. *And* Rachel. It's a just a lot of stops." He took a sip of coffee. "How the hell are we going to get to the hospital without the cops seeing us?"

"I don't know. Maybe a diversion?"

Diversion brought back a good memory. *Do you know how to build a bomb?* John smiled, turned when he heard Jesse come down the stairs.

"Jesse, I packed you some breakfast, sweetheart," Mrs. Swensen said, in full mother-mode.

"Thanks, Mrs. Swensen." He took the brown bag from her. She kissed him on the cheek.

"You ready?" John asked.

"Ready," Jesse said.

Jesse ran his hand across Blue's trunk. "This is a nice car."

"Yeah, she is. She's seen better days, but thanks. Maybe you can help me fix her up."

Jesse smiled, nodded. He looked tired, and in pain. John could see the weariness and the look of loss behind his eyes. *He knows we're still in the shit*, John thought.

They got in, drove out of the B&B's driveway. John hit the horn lightly, twice. Mrs. Swensen waved from the front porch.

"Make a left," Jesse said. He was co-pilot to Rachel's house, five minutes away. A modest single story with blue aluminum siding and a battered Ford Escape in the driveway. They got out and knocked on the door.

A woman in her late twenties answered. Dark, curly hair, wearing a robe, towel over her shoulders, getting ready for the day. She'd been crying.

She saw John and had a questioning look on her face. Then she saw Jesse.

"Oh, lord! Jesse, I just heard, I'm so sorry!" She grabbed him and hugged him.

"Who'd you hear it from?" John asked. News was traveling too fast.

Rachel looked at him. "Who's this?"

"John. Uhh... Uncle John." Jesse looked up at him, shrugged. John nodded. "He's here for the money."

Rachel broke off the hug with Jesse, turned to John. "My aunt called. And it's on the news. They didn't release any names, but..." She turned to Jesse. "There was no 'Uncle John' in the deal, Jesse."

"Yeah, well, there's no Alex in the deal anymore either," John said.

Rachel looked at him like he'd said the most insensitive thing in the world. Then she worked it over in her mind. "Let's talk inside."

The house was warm. Coffee had been brewed, they could smell it, but the pot was practically empty. Morning sun was coming in through the kitchen windows. No other lights were on.

John and Jesse sat on the couch. Floral pattern with a clear plastic covering. Very uncomfortable. Rachel sat across from them on a comfy looking chair, drinking the last of the coffee.

"I'd offer you some, but I just ran out."

"It's OK," John said and adjusted himself. The plastic made a loud plastic noise. "You look like your aunt."

"Yeah. Sometimes I think she's my real mom. I don't look anything like my actual mother."

"There's a lot of that going around," John said, and sighed.

"What?"

"Nothing. Listen, how much of the money do you have?"

Rachel got uncomfortable. "I don't—"

"You can tell him Rachel, it's OK," Jesse said.

"Five hundred thousand."

"Really? So... Ellen has the rest of it?" John asked.

Rachel nodded, sipped her coffee. "She has the other five hundred thousand."

"The other... wait. What?"

"Alex only gave us five hundred thousand. Each. 'Only', I mean... it was the deal. For helping. Not that I'd need it where we were going."

"But there's supposed to be ten million in cash."

"Yeah, that's right. There was."

Alex paced Rachel's living room. "Who the fuck does Carla think she is?"

Rachel rolled her eyes. "Who cares? And I told you, I don't want you talking about her here!"

Alex made a frustrated noise. He wanted to punch his legs. Punch his fist into his open hand. He wanted to lay waste to something. To someone. "I don't deserve this," he said.

Rachel made a noise, somewhere between *oh honey* and *oh for God's sake*. "Alex? Alex, look at me."

He did. Rachel was a stunner. He never thought women as beautiful as she was could possibly be born anywhere outside of major cities. Cities where they'd get noticed immediately by those who knew how to take advantage of that beauty. Seemed like such a waste here in Sherborn. He was going to take her someplace. Someplace special, so others could appreciate—

"We're getting out of here," she said soothingly. "With enough money so that we never have to worry about anything ever again. Right?"

He nodded. "Right."

She caressed his face. "Then we're getting what we deserve." She kissed him. "Right?"

Alex nodded again. "Yeah." He smiled. "Yeah." He moved away from her, thinking.

She watched him pace. "Alex? What is it?"

He turned to her slowly. "I'm going to change the plan."

"What? Why? How?"

"If she wants Hal—"

"Oh, *Alex*..."

"She can have him. But *I'm* taking Jesse. I'm not going to let that fucking asshole near my son." He walked up to her and held her shoulders. "And they're not getting a dime of this money."

Rachel looked between John and Jesse. "That night, he told me the new plan. 'Forget the cash,' he said. He was going to transfer money out of the accounts he'd been putting the laundered money into, and once he was out of the country with Jesse, he'd send for me. He went to the bank the morning of the robbery, like usual. Everyone was on edge. He gave a good pep talk. Promised us it was all going to work out. He kissed me goodbye in front of everybody... and that was the last time I saw him." She started tearing up.

John shook his head. What a clusterfuck. "Rachel? Where's the forty million dollars?"

She sniffed. "It's in the account. In New York."

With both hands, John smacked himself in the cheeks. "Are you fucking kidding me?"

"No, he set that up years ago—"

"In New York? What the fuck is wrong with these... what about the people in town? Their money?"

"It was supposed to come out of the forty. Alex was going to send them cash through the bank in the form of loans—"

John held his hand up. "I get it. I get it. Do you have the account info?"

"No, only Alex had it. Wouldn't even put the info on his computer, he kept it in—"

"His planner," John said, and smacked himself upside the head. "Fuck! Jesse, we have to go back to—"

Jesse lifted out the planner from his jacket, his finger sticking out of the slug hole. "I saw it in the room. It's my dad's."

"It's got a hole clean through it," Rachel said, wide eyed as John grabbed it.

"Yeah, you can only guess where that came from. Whose name is the account under?" John started thumbing through the planner.

"Both of theirs."

"Whose?"

"Alex and Jesse's."

John stopped thumbing.

"Mine?" Jesse asked.

"Yeah, your dad believed that if something happened to him, you'd figure out a way to get the money. For *some* reason, he didn't trust his wife."

"Do you know which account number?"

Rachel took the planner and went through it, finally stopping on a page. She highlighted the number with her finger. "This one."

"You're sure?" He let out a deep breath, thankful the bullet didn't damage the number.

"Positive. I remember when he wrote it in there. We'd just gotten back from a long weekend in the city..." Rachel swallowed, looked over at Jesse.

He looked down, embarrassed.

"Anyway, he had you sign some paperwork a couple of years ago, made you a co-signer on the account," Rachel said.

"I don't remember that at all."

"What are they saying on the news?" John asked.

"Just that there was a shootout at the All Seasons Motel and the Medieval Times store, which is weird, right?"

"Nothing else?"

"I mean, a sword fight I could see, but a shootout?"

John sighed. "No suspects?"

"They were looking for two men in a dark Cadillac. No description."

"OK. How long before this comes back to bite us?"

"Well, no one at the bank is going to say anything. No one reported the burglary yet because Jesse had the money stolen from him."

"Yeah, that was me."

Rachel looked at Jesse questioningly. He nodded. "Really? Why?"

John had given it thought the night before. Hal knew him better than anyone. Anyone alive, anyway. He figured Hal would have brought him in if John had complained more. About Gino, about the jobs they worked on.

In the end, Hal had put him in a position where he would either have to go with them on the run, or die.

"Why don't you take Blue?" he heard Hal say. John shook his head.

What a fucker.

"It's hard to say," he said to Rachel, and got up to leave.

Rachel hugged Jesse, shook John's hand and showed them out.

They made their way to Blue and got in. "Forty million dollars," John said.

"Yeah."

"That's a lot of money."

"Yeah."

John looked at him. The kid had aged over the last twenty-four hours. "What do you want to do with it?"

Jesse bit his lip, thinking. "I think we should give the people my dad used their fair share." He looked at John.

John smiled, put the keys in the ignition. "Sounds good to me." He turned Blue over. She sounded good, all things considered. "One more stop."

"Where?"

"To see your mom at the hospital."

"What!?"

"Yeah."

"She's alive?" Jesse started crying.

"Yeah, kid."

Jesse hit John in the face with an open hand. "Why didn't you fucking tell me!?" He hit him again, a punch this time, glancing off his chin. John grabbed his hands, careful of the bad wrist.

"Hey, hey! I just, I'm sorry man—I just thought it would be a great surprise!"

"I spent the last day thinking my mom's dead you dick!"

"Come *on*," John said, smirking. "It hasn't been a whole day."

"Asshole!" Jesse tried to break free from John's grip.

"Hey, calm down, OK? I'm sorry. I just found out this morning..."

Jesse struggled free and sat there, pissed.

"... *and* I had to figure out how we could get there without the cops seeing us. We couldn't get caught without the money, kid. Going to see her would be like a fucking suicide mission—"

"I get it!" Still pissed.

John sat down, rubbed his chin, rubbed his face. "You've got a pretty good left. Glad you didn't really connect."

Jesse shook his head. *Fuck your compliment.*

"Hal was a boxer, once. He would've shown you some things..."

561

"How are we going to get to the hospital without them seeing us?"

John grabbed his phone and dialed and put it on speaker. Mrs. Swensen picked up.

"Swensen's B&B."

"Mrs. Swensen, it's John and Jesse."

"Oh my. Alex's death made the news!"

"They said his name?" John asked. *Shit.*

"Well, no, but—"

John sighed, relieved. "OK, Mrs. Swensen—"

"And something about a Renaissance war?"

"Christ," John said under his breath. "We know, Mrs. Swensen. You can make the call now."

"What call?" Jesse asked. John shushed him.

"I will," she said. "You two be careful."

John nodded. "We will. I'll be in touch once we get things sorted."

"Sounds good to me. Bye sweethearts!"

She hung up.

Mrs. Swensen dialed 911. The house was quiet. Most of her guests were out. One was using the shower.

"911, what's your emergency?"

"I need to speak with Sheriff Briggs, it's an emergency!"

"Mrs. Swensen?" the dispatcher asked.

"Yes!"

"Hold, please," the dispatcher said. "I'm patching you through to his car, Mrs. Swensen."

The connection took a few seconds. Unfamiliar noises came through the telephone. Ticks, squelches, a high keening noise for a second.

"This is Briggs."

"Gordon, it's Mrs. Swensen. I know where they're going."

"Who?"

"Who? Who do you think! Jesse and—"

"Goddammit, woman. You're telling me this on an open line?"

"*Woman*?"

"I mean—"

"*Excuse* me? I was your mother's best friend!"

"Mrs. Swensen, I—"

"I watched you as a baby!"

"If I could just—"

"I was there for you when Alice Bertrand dumped you two days before prom, you remember that? Two boxes of Kleenex you went through!" Her indignation almost got the better of her and she focused on the task at hand... even though it was also fun.

There was a long silence and a sigh that simply had the weight of the world attached to it. The entire Sherborn police force had been listening in. "Mrs. Swensen. I'm sorry. Thank you, for all of it. Please tell me which way they're headed."

"They said they were stopping by Rachel's place."

"Goddammit! I mean... when did they leave?"

"Just a few minutes ago. I was so scared, I didn't know—"

"OK, we'll take it from here," Briggs said and cut the connection.

She looked at the phone with a smile, sighed, then dialed Rachel who picked up right away.

"Rachel, honey? I need you to do something for me."

CHAPTER EIGHTY-SIX

B riggs got into his car and turned the ignition. And stopped. Cochrane was sitting there, chomping at the bit. "What?"

"Something ain't right. They're still in town."

"Yeah, so let's get those fuckers!"

"Yeah." He grabbed the radio. "Dispatch?"

"Go ahead."

"I want a road block on both 54 leading out of town, and I-17."

"I'll have to call in Davis and Montgomery."

"Do it."

"They're gonna want to get paid for it—"

"Just fucking do it. And keep Stanley at the hospital, guarding the room."

"Copy."

Briggs put the patrol car in gear and headed to Rachel's.

The hospital was two levels. Clean. Brick all along the outside, windows with the reinforced metal wire in them, white vertical blinds pulled on some of the rooms. Not a bad place to go, if you had to.

No patrol car out front. John drove up and parked in the visitor parking lot. Jesse watched him back in. He was going to ask why, then smiled when he figured it out.

They got out of the car and headed towards the emergency room entrance.

When the doors opened, John had a real sense of déjà vu. It looked like every other hospital he'd ever been in. The white tile with the flecks in it. Off-white paint job on the walls. Hand sanitizer dispensers, wood chairs with a patterned fabric. Benches along the walls. Fluorescent lights on, even in the daytime. The smell of sterilized air. They could have been anywhere in the country.

Five people in the emergency waiting room. Two were asleep. One had his arm in a cast, stuck up in the air by a thin piece of rod that went down to his chest. Two were drinking water from paper cups, talking amongst themselves.

Gerard the guard was pacing back and forth near the front desk. A woman was standing there, blue scrubs, going over a chart. Another woman, wearing jeans and a sweater, was sitting at a computer, trying to work something out.

Jesse walked up. "I'm here to see Carla Holsfer."

"Are you related?" the woman at the computer asked. She didn't look at him.

"She's my mom."

"I need to see I.D."

"He's fifteen," John said.

She looked up.

"So? It's policy. Something. Anything. Library card?"

Gerard walked over, bent down and whispered into her ear. He looked at Jesse, winked, nodded.

"You can go ahead, room 216," the woman at the computer said. "Just you."

"He's family, too," Jesse said.

She rolled her eyes, shook her head, motioned with her hand.

They made their way down the hall.

"Let me guess. The security guy—"

"Yeah, he works at the bank, too."

"Of course he does." John looked around as Jesse hit the up button on the wall. He noticed an emergency stairwell off to the left. *This might be tight*, he thought.

"You're not going to believe this. His name is *Gerard*. Gerard the *guard*," Jesse said.

"Get the fuck out of here."

They got into the elevator, hit two. It took forever.

Once the doors opened, John saw directly across from them was a room directory. To the left was 216. They got out and started walking.

Playing low through the hallway, John could hear music. It was loud enough to recognize. "Tuesday Afternoon" by the Moody Blues. At first, he thought it might be getting pumped in through the PA system.

They passed the nurses' station. There were three of them. Elizabeth, Kelly, and Satomi. Townie best friends who came up together from elementary to nursing school.

"I like it," Kelly said.

"I don't like his voice. The music is fine..." Elizabeth said.

John noticed the music wasn't coming from the nurses' station.

Satomi saw Jesse. "Oh my God, Jesse!" She came around the station and hugged him. "You're here to see your mom? Come on. What happened to your *hand*?"

She grabbed him by the good arm and rushed him to the room. John slowly followed, drifting down the hall. It was clean and quiet.

Printed PSAs on diabetes, HIV, high blood pressure dotted the walls. Kids' drawings on a long corkboard. Doors here and there were open, mostly old people sitting up, lying down, looking bored, watching TV, or sleeping.

John turned and saw an officer, way down the hallway in the opposite direction. He was sitting on a chair, looking at his phone. It's where the music was coming.

John turned and peered into room 216. The reunion was as one would expect.

Carla was attached to machines and an IV. The nurse was wiping tears from her eyes as Jesse was hugging his mom. Another woman was there, watching. Black, older than Carla.

Carla looked over Jesse's shoulder, saw John and became instantly grateful. She mouthed the words *"thank you"* to him. He nodded.

"Abigail, that's John," Carla said. "John, Abigail."

"Hi," John said.

"Nice to meet you."

Jesse stood up, hugged Abigail.

"Jesse honey, just stand over here for a…"

She looked back and forth between John and Jesse.

"Uh huh…" Abigail looked at Carla, who looked away.

The nurse left the room and went back to the station as "Tuesday Afternoon" finished.

John walked out of the room, knowing Jesse was telling her the plan they'd come up with.

It might work if they were lucky and there were no more hiccups. Get to New York before the I.D.s of the bodies hit the city, before Paulie Grasso was able to mobilize the troops and come after them. Get access to the funds, disperse them and hightail it to Philly, then south somewhere, and wait for Carla. Change their names, lay low, etcetera, etcetera.

It might work.

He walked up to the nurses' station to ask about Carla's condition.

The one who had hugged Jesse said, "I hope he plays some Bee Gees next," as she got back behind the counter.

"Or the Pointer Sisters," another said.

"Aretha Franklin!" said the third.

A new track started. It was "Fernando" by ABBA.

"Oh my God, this is one of my favorites!"

"Oh, mine too!"

John smiled to himself. Fucking ABBA.

He looked up and saw the cop was now on the phone, talking.

Strange. He can't be on the phone when…

That…

Wait...

John slowly started walking towards the music. The cop got up, covered his free ear, and moved away from the room he was outside of.

The nurses, happy for the break in the monotony, started singing along.

John slowly walked over, got to the room where the music was loudest. Room 203. He slowly peered in.

It was empty.

The bed was messed up. On one of those movable tables with a half-finished lunch on a plastic tray, was a cell phone propped up on a book. The source of the music.

The cop came back and grabbed John's arm. "Hey, you can't be here, mister."

"No, I... I just... sorry." John went to turn away, when he heard a toilet flushing.

It was like slow motion.

The cop still had his hand on John's arm, who turned slowly as the bathroom door opened.

Limping, his ass sticking out of a gown, his hand cuffed to an IV stand, was Hal.

"Oh my God," John said, his eyes wide, smiling.

"I said..." the cop started, and put it together. "Wait, shit!" The officer went for his gun. John spun and hit him in the jaw with his elbow. He pulled the back of the cop's shirt collar down, brought his knee up into his stomach, and let him drop to the floor slowly. John grabbed him by the hair and slammed his head into the wall.

The cop was out cold.

John looked to see if the nurses had heard. They hadn't.

He turned to see Hal, who was looking at him, slowly shaking his head. "The hell did you do that for?" he said in a low, coarse voice. He motioned with his hands at the unconscious cop. "That's Stanley."

"You're alive!" John whispered loudly.

"Of course I'm alive. He only shot me the once…" Hal pulled his gown down. There was a bandage on his chest, right side, just above his nipple. Seeping. "Not that I didn't die. I did. But they got me going again. Did you get shot?"

"No." John grabbed the cop's legs and began to drag him into Hal's room.

"Well, you're an asshole."

"No, wait! I did." He dropped the cop. "Right here," John said, pulled down his shirt and showed Hal his shoulder, where Gino hit him at the end.

"That… that's barely a flesh wound."

John picked up the cop's legs again, dragged him into the room. "Hal, I gotta—we have to get out of here."

"Forget it." Hal waved him off and got back into bed, slowly, deliberately.

"Forget it?" He dropped the cop again.

"I can't go anywhere. See this?" He held up one of the tubes going into him. "Drainage. It punctured my lung, and I… well, I'm not leaving."

"Then why didn't you call me to let me know you made it?"

"Why? Because I didn't know if you were alive or not. Or what the situation was. Or where you were. *Or* who you were with. Maybe Gino had you, or someone else. Too many unknowns."

He sounded terrible. And weak. And finished.

"Jesus, Hal."

"You find the money?"

"Yeah. It's in the city. We've got the account numbers."

"So you have the kid?"

"Yeah."

"And my girl is safe." Hal sighed. "You did good. Really good." He turned to John. "I'm sorry I got you mixed up in this mess."

"Stop. Just stop."

"Gino?"

"He's gone."

"Gone? Back to the city?"

"No. Dead."

Hal nodded again. "You gotta get out of here."

"I'm not just leaving you."

"No, you're not just leaving me." He smiled, beckoned John closer, told him the new plan.

John listened for a long while as Hal told him the back-up plan he'd put into motion all those years ago. The guy was full of surprises, and after he was finished, John saw the angles. He nodded, straightened up when Hal leaned back into his pillow. He looked over at the unconscious cop. John had uncuffed Hal and put them on the guy's wrists, behind his back. "That's not going to help things any. Like getting out of town," Hal said.

"Yeah, well, I was surprised."

"Uh huh. Get going. I'll see you in New Orleans. Take care of the kid."

John nodded. Then, in a rush, his feelings caught up with him. He started tearing up and sobbed just the once. "I'm glad you're OK, Hal."

Hal looked like a person who could finally relax. "Me too, pal." He held out his hand. John took it. "Me too. See you soon."

John went back to Carla's room to get Jesse, who was in the middle of getting his arm casted. He'd gotten the stitches removed and re-done too, and the nurse told them he had to get the wrist checked in a week. John nodded, told Carla they had to go. She nodded, kissed her son goodbye, grabbed John's hand and squeezed it. "See you soon," she said. Weak, but on the mend.

They took the stairs.

CHAPTER EIGHTY-SEVEN

John got into Blue with a renewed spirit. He couldn't believe it had only been forty-eight hours since this mess took shape. Took shape for *him*. He put the car in drive and slowly pulled her out of the spot, through the parking lot, and onto the street.

It was a crystal-clear day.

"These are the kinds of days you see at Coney Island," he said to Jesse. "Blue like this."

"Where's Coney Island?"

"It's in Brooklyn. It's a huge beach, and an amusement park. There's a ride there called the Cyclone."

"What kind of ride?"

"It's a rollercoaster. It's ninety years old."

"Jeez, and people still ride it?"

"They ride it. They love it." He made a turn. "They've got a Nathan's Hot Dog stand there, right on the boardwalk, and an aquarium." He chuckled. "And the Russian mob."

"Can we go?"

"Maybe. Yeah. One day."

John pulled into Farr's gas station, drove up to number 3, and had Jesse fill it up. "Just keep pumping, don't worry about the money."

"OK," Jesse said.

"And get the good stuff."

Jesse grabbed the premium nozzle, unscrewed the tank cap and started pumping gas.

John went into the station, started grabbing food. Pretzels, potato chips, beef jerky. He grabbed some hot dogs, a bottle of Coke, two big bottles of water, some protein bars and a bag of corn nuts, which he hadn't eaten since he was a kid. On his way to the register, he grabbed a can of motor oil.

The guy ringing him up didn't have much of a chin. Not really. Hair sprouted on it as if by mistake, and some patches were on his upper lip. John figured he'd been trying to grow it for some time. The guy was thin, and really upbeat. "You going cross country or something, mister?" he said with a chuckle.

"Something like that. I'm on number 3."

"OK," he said and hit 3 on the cash register. "Uhh..." he said. "That..." he looked out to see the Charger. "This says..."

"Yeah," John said.

"It says—"

"Yeah."

"Mister, I don't mean nothing by it, but did you *drink* that gas?"

"No comment," John said, and put his credit card in the machine. The total came to $232.14. "Oh, hey, I need a coffee and a slushie, too."

The guy behind the counter bowed, actually bowed and said, "Help yourself. They're on me."

John threw the bags of food at Jesse while he balanced both cups and slid into the car. He handed one to over to him.

"What's this?"

"Slushie."

"I don't drink slushies."

"Who doesn't drink slushies?"

"I just hate the taste," he said.

"You'll get used to it. Open the trunk."

Jesse took the keys and went to the back of the car.

John opened the lid on his coffee and took a sip. For gas station coffee, it wasn't bad.

Jesse pulled the trunk open. John got down on his haunches and inspected the antipersonnel compartments. They seemed in good shape.

He grabbed a handful of the metal tacks from their container, pushed them into both compartments and pushed the flaps shut until their latches were secure. He pulled open a rubber stopper in the trunk, grabbed the bottle of motor oil and poured it in until the mini-tank was full. He replaced the stopper, threw out the mostly empty container, closed the trunk and they got into the car.

Jesse took a sip of his slushie, made a face. "Oh, God. I don't want this."

"It's kiwi-something. Look, and I got hot dogs and chips and beef jerky. It'll be fun. Then we'll get the money and go to New Orleans." He turned on the ignition.

"What?"

"What."

"New Orleans?"

"What?"

"You just said New Orleans."

"No I didn't."

"Just now—"

"Nope."

"I heard you."

"No." John shook his head. "I said New... Yorkies. Which is what I call New York."

"That's not what you said."

"I'm pretty sure I know what I said."

"So do I!"

"Just relax, would you? It's a long drive to New York... ies."

Jesse leaned back, unsatisfied. "I'm not drinking this."

"I'll drink it, you pain in the ass."

Jesse looked out the window, looked back at John. "Are we really going to New Orleans?"

"Yes! OK? Just... shut up." John said, and put the car in gear. He pulled out of the gas station and made his way towards 54.

"I can't believe it. We're going to New Orleans. I've seen videos, you know... of women and..." he was blushing.

"Women and...?"

"Nothing. You know."

"Uh huh."

"So, why there? What's in New Orleans?"

John smiled. "Supposedly, all kinds of things..."

Not much in the way of traffic. John had tried to leave town enough over the past few days that he knew the way. Still, he had Jesse point them in the right direction.

As they made their way up the hill leading out of town, Jesse took his seat belt off, turned back and looked out the rear-view window. He'd drunk half his slushie.

"She'll be fine, kid."

"I know."

"And you'll see her again."

"I know that too," he said, and sat down.

"Come on. Seat belt," John said. Jesse sat back down, put it on and took a swallow of his drink just as John slammed on the brakes.

Jesse choked hard and started coughing. "What the hell, man?" Slushie splashed onto his chest. "Jeez!"

"You OK?" John asked.

Jesse nodded and looked ahead. With his good hand, a shaky finger pointed out the windshield and he started stammering.

"Yeah, kid, I see them." He looked behind him. Nothing doing. "Glad we stopped for food."

Three hundred yards ahead, five police cars were blocking the road. Eight officers, most of them with guns drawn.

Standing out in front of them was Sheriff Gordon Briggs, hands on his belt, looking triumphant.

By the time Gordon had gotten to Rachel's, and she'd given him the song and dance about them going to Ellen's next, he knew it was all bullshit. Then he got the call from Stanley that they'd been at the hospital, and that last one, the last guy had sucker punched him and cuffed him. A nurse had set him free.

Briggs knew there was no fucking way they were getting out of town in one piece. Not with his money.

He and Cochrane had torn ass to 54, which was where he figured they'd go—17 took them too far west, and while the loop would make sense for someone who wanted to stay off their radar, he figured they would be in a hurry, 'cause of all those dead mobsters and all.

Well, fuck that.

He saw the Charger fishtail to a stop at the top of the hill and smiled. Something had finally worked out. "Harlan, tell them to close in off I-17. Not block it. Close it."

Harlan got on the radio and called it in.

Briggs unclipped his holster, pulled out his service piece and chambered a round. "This son of a bitch is going... to..." His voice died as he saw the Charger hit the gas. In reverse. Fast. "Holy fucking SHIT!" Briggs raised his hand and twirled it in the air for the other officers. "Get after them!"

Officers rushed to their cars and gave pursuit.

John started out looking through the rear-view mirror. Practically no traffic. He was in the center lane and, what cars there were, they moved for him.

"John, they—" Jesse said.

"I know," he said.

Take care of the kid.

OK.

"But they're—" Jesse was pointing, aghast.

"I know, just a second," John said smiling. He looked over at Jesse. "Grab my phone. Inside jacket pocket."

Jesse grabbed it. John took it with his free hand and dialed a number, hit speaker. It connected. A gravelly sound followed by a cough. "Jesus, what the hell are you calling me for?" Hal said, hushed.

John smiled, happy to hear his best friend's voice. Memories, relief, the stress of the last eighteen years of his life, and an incredible feeling of freedom washed over him. "Hal," he said looking through the rear windshield, his left hand on the steering wheel, his right behind the passenger seat. His voice broke a bit, but pure joy won out and he smiled as he hit the gas. Blue growled down the highway in reverse. "You're not going to believe this…"

First and foremost, my thanks to Cat Skinner, beta reader extraordinaire, who took a look at the book in its early stages and said, "Carla should be a main character."

Jim Brennan and Sally Aboelela both took time out of their schedules to talk to me about the world of money laundering and nursing, respectively. Their help was invaluable.

My thanks to Michael Gaydos for taking on the challenge of the cover art (it's perfect), and to Al Rotches for getting the title font just right. I couldn't do it. I'm glad he could.

Thank you to Jayne Lewis for her patience in teaching me the English language.

To N.T. Anderson and Jon Ford, thank you for helping me navigate the world of self-publishing. I would have killed someone otherwise.

Marc Palmieri read the book just before publishing and gave me some advice that was also invaluable. I met Marc at an interesting point in my life. I can't begin to tell you how different my life would be had I not met him and the wonderful friends he introduced me to along the way.

While there is no town of Sherborn, NY, there is a Sherburne, NY. I visited that town for a week when I was sixteen. My Uncle Mike and Aunt Carol had a home and a business there, and I have fond memories of it all. While the real Sherburne did not fit the type of town I needed for the book, I wanted to honor it all the same.

Thank you for giving my book a chance. I hope you enjoyed it.

• • •

John Painz is an award-winning writer-director in New York City. His first feature film, *Stuck*, screened at a number of film festivals in the U.S., was nominated for best script, best film, best director, and best actor at the Soho International Film Festival, and won the Programmers Award at the Hell's Half Mile Film Festival in 2015. *Stuck* is currently being taught in screenplay classes at two colleges in New York. His second feature film, *Four Bottles*, won the Audience Award at the Art of Brooklyn Film Festival in 2017.

Blue, Upstate is his first novel.